The Collected Supernatural and Weird Fiction of Rosa Mulholland

The Collected Supernatural and Weird Fiction of Rosa Mulholland

Thirteen Short Stories of the Strange and Unusual Including 'A Strange Love Story', 'The Ghost at Wildwood Chase', 'The Fit of Ailsie's Shoe', 'The Mystery of Ora' and 'Not to be Taken at Bedtime'

Rosa Mulholland

LEONAUR

The Collected
Supernatural and Weird
Fiction of
Rosa Mulholland
Thirteen Short Stories of the Strange and Unusual Including 'A Strange Love Story',
'The Ghost at Wildwood Chase', 'The Fit of Ailsie's Shoe', 'The Mystery of Ora' and
'Not to be Taken at Bedtime'
by Rosa Mulholland

FIRST EDITION

Leonaur is an imprint of Oakpast Ltd

Copyright in this form © 2025 Oakpast Ltd

ISBN: 978-1-971666-42-8 (hardcover)
ISBN: 978-1-971666-43-5 (softcover)

http://www.leonaur.com

Publisher's Notes

Contents

A Strange Love Story

At the foot of a certain street in Innsbruck, right above the famous gold-roofed house, rise the purple walls of the Alps, mountain walls so apparently straight and perpendicular that they seem, according to the mood of the spectator, either to block the way to heaven, or to lead to it by difficult ascent. On a summer day a young girl, who knew all the accessible paths of yonder great stepping-stones to the skies, walked down this street in Innsbruck with her back to the golden roof, and all the purple glory of the Alps behind and above her.

She wore a high-crowned Alpine hat with a silver tassel, and a costume of hunting-green cloth. Her face was round and fair, and her crystal-clear eyes had a look of unusually vivid intelligence. The hair which curled softly and crisply round her temples, and was plaited in thick masses at the back of her head, was of that fairness which is almost white, and is seldom seen except on very young children. Her features were small and softly moulded, and something very like the light of genius was shining from her countenance.

She walked on with a bright pre-occupied look, as if something beautiful which other people could not see had caught her eye and fixed her attention; and then suddenly turned in at the open door of that curious church, where a strange company of bronze men and women occupy for ever the centre of the nave.

The only living creatures in the church were a few old women in furry head-dresses, at prayer, and a very young man who was standing with folded arms studying the bronze statues. The girl made no noise crossing the threshold of the door, but the moment she entered, the young man started electrically and turned to see her coming towards him, a glow of delight on his face as if the sun had suddenly shone out upon it. She came quietly and stood by his side.

"Have you gazed enough for today?" she asked with a twinkle of glee in her eyes. "Come, Max, it is your work I want to see, not these."

Max shook his head, but caught the little hand she placed imperatively on his, and followed her out of the shadows of the church into the dazzling summer street, where the sun was glittering on the eaves of the gold-roofed house, and making the huge Alpine walls behind it take a richer purple than before.

Max was a tall youth, with a square-browed dreamy face, full of a kind of rugged beauty. His eyes had not the vivid light that glanced from the eyes of the girl, but they were full of dreams of glories to come, burning with a latent fire destined yet to give its share towards the warming and lighting up of the world. He led the way into a small house at the corner of the street, and up a staircase into a bare room littered with clay, with half-formed images and casts, and where an unfinished statue in clay stood near the window. From the face of this statue, he withdrew the cloth, and gazed discontentedly at the face of the creature he had made, a nymph graceful and lovely, with the features of the girl at his side.

"It is you, Hilda," he said, "but without your soul in the eyes. When you are not here it is like you, but when I see your face beside it—"

"Nonsense! you do not want a likeness of me," said Hilda; "you want an ideal being! It only wants a little tenderness, dear Max. May I touch it?"

Max nodded, and Hilda's little fingers passed over the clay with a few delicate touches, while a curious look of intellectual power grew on her face and changed its character for a moment. After a few minutes she withdrew behind Max, and peeped over his shoulder to see the effect of what she had done.

Max drew a deep breath and stared in amazement at the change which had been wrought. The statue which had been coldly perfect seemed to breathe.

"Your power is supernatural," he murmured; "the work is now divine."

"You are dreaming," said Hilda, laughing. "All the divinity in it is your own; I but drew forth what you had left slightly veiled."

Max shook his head. "I am too much the artist," he said, "not to recognise your gift. But I am not jealous of you, Hilda. With you by my side what may I not hope to accomplish?"

Hilda laid a hand on his arm and looked into his face with joyful eyes.

"Do not make me vain," she said; "but if cooking your dinner and keeping your house in order, doing all that woman can do to make your home happy, and your difficult upward path a little easier; if all that helps you to accomplish great things, then, indeed, I shall feel you are the better for me."

Max took both her hands in his, and looked down into her eyes with a wondering, worshipping gaze, which troubled almost as much as it delighted her. As if she feared what might be his next change of mood she turned away her head, and said gaily,—

"Come with me now at once. You promised to take holiday today. Let us be off to the mountains, and leave this nymph to her solitary thoughts."

He put on his hat mechanically, and again followed her whither she would lead him. They went out of the town, and took the road to the mountains. The world was exquisite, and Max shook himself out of his dreams to enjoy it. Hilda prattled to him between bursts of laughter about all that had occurred at home, up yonder in the blue, since his last visit there; what droll things the children had said; what a pleasant dance there had been at a neighbour's wedding; how Lisbeth had burned a hole in her new dress, and all the trouble there had been to get it nicely mended. People going down to the town passed them, and said, "That is Max Edelstein and his betrothed, Hilda."

"What a pity they cannot get married at once," said one.

"They could if they liked, for Hilda has a nice little penny which her father left her."

"It is a pity when people are too clever, you see. Nothing will suit them but going to Rome."

"They will be a long time saving to go to Rome. Who is there to buy his sculptures in Innsbruck? Better if he had been content with wood-carving like so many of his friends."

The lovers reached the nook of the mountains in which their village nestled. Lisbeth, Hilda's sister-in-law, was expecting them, and had made a little feast. A table was spread under a tree at her door, and a troop of little sun-burnt children came dashing out to meet Hilda and her Max.

Lisbeth, a good-humoured, brown-eyed woman, with a flame-coloured handkerchief twisted round her head, and wearing her holiday jacket of black, embroidered with threads of gold, came out of the house with a baby on one arm, and placed some fruit upon the table. The wooden chalet was set deep in a cool green cave of boughs, on a platform of rock, and under it, and opposite to it, lay a dazzling landscape of purple crag, teeming golden valley, and woods of all the richest hues of green. Up a pathway, seemingly made for goats, our lovers climbed, and were welcomed by the motherly Lisbeth. The master of the little home, Lisbeth's husband, Hilda's brother, wood-carver, hunter, and tiller of the earth, now appeared, and the elders partook of Lisbeth's feast in the shade, while the little sun-burnt children capered and danced in the sun.

Max cast off the cloud of dreaminess that often wrapped him up, and talked to Fritz about the crops and the hunts, and all that was interesting in the mountaineer's life. The artist disappeared for the time, and Max was merely a stalwart youth of the mountains, with an unusually picturesque and intellectual face. Hilda took the baby in her arms, and laughter and prattle made the time fly fast, till Lisbeth said,—

"Ah, Max, have you seen the present that Hilda has given me? She has modelled my little dead Lisa, so that I think I have her back."

"Will not you show it to me, Hilda?"

"Yes, if you please; but it is only interesting to Lisbeth, dear Max."

The day passed and evening came. Songs were sung, and Hilda accompanied them on the zither. Throwing away her silver-tasselled hat she put on an apron, prepared the supper, and carried it out under the trees. Her fair head gleamed in the sunset as she went and came, and as a wave of warm light suddenly fell across her face and hands, Max thought she looked like a ministering angel descended to wait upon them. After supper some young friends came from a little distance, and Fritz strummed the zither while a dance was held on a bit of green close by. Hilda danced with as much glee as any of the children. The moon shone out, the children pulled Hilda's hair about, till it flowed around her like a gold and silver mantle, and Max would not have it put up again, and danced with her while it streamed about her shoulders.

"Hilda looks beautiful tonight, does she not?" said one of her friends. "What a pity she will marry that melancholy Max!"

"He is not melancholy now when he is dancing."

"He is always strange, and full of fancies. I would rather marry a man who could make a joke."

The dancing was over, the neighbours had gone home, and Max was asking again to see Hilda's model of Lisbeth's little angel Lisa. Hilda led him up the narrow stairs, and into her own small chamber, where one of the ruddy little dancers of an hour ago was asleep in her bed. It was a tiny brown room, where almost the only decoration was the oblong moonlit picture of pine and crag framed by the open window. Hilda struck a light and lit a hand-lamp, and discovered on a bench the model of the child who was dead.

Max folded his arms, and gazed at it long and critically.

"Hilda!" he said, "I wonder if you know what a genius you possess!"

"Through my love for you I have learned to dabble in clay; that is all," said Hilda. "I have no genius, and I do not want it."

"About this going to Rome. It is you who ought to go, not I."

"Max! where are your wits? I wish there was money enough for two, then we could go together. But as there is not, why I must wait till you can afford to send for me."

"What I mean is this, Hilda," said Max, with the sadness in his eyes deepening to gloom: "you have a distinct genius of your own, and I ought not to be so selfish as to absorb you into my own life and work. You have money to take yourself to Rome, and there you ought to go. Marriage for you will be the ruin of an artist."

"Not the ruin of you, I hope."

"No, of yourself."

"Then let me be ruined, dear Max, and let the world lose what it will never have possessed. I belong to you, and not either to art or to the world."

"I am a traitor to art to listen to you."

"Then be a traitor. I love you better as a traitor."

Max shook his head, and gloomily withdrew the hand which Hilda had touched with her own.

Hilda uttered a sudden cry, and snatching a hammer which lay near, raised it in her hands as if she would strike the model of the child, and destroy it.

"Hilda!" cried Max, seizing her wrists and struggling with her.

"It shall not part us!" she cried passionately.

"Hush! here is Lisbeth," whispered Max.

"Is it not lovely?" said Lisbeth, coming in on tiptoe, and speaking softly as if in a sacred place. "See, dear Max, how Hilda loves my children. One of them sleeps alive in her arms"—pointing to the bed—"another sleeps here in death always before our eyes, by the magic of her hands. Ah, what a tender mother our clever Hilda will be!"

Hilda burst into tears, dropped the hammer, and turning abruptly to the window, leaned her arms on the sash, and wept with sobs into the night.

11

"She has never quite got over the death of that child," murmured Lisbeth. "Come away, Max, and let her have her cry in peace."

An hour later still, Lisbeth was sitting spinning at her door in the moonlight, and singing to herself simple songs about little child-angels who sometimes come down for a time, and live in good men's houses, and lie in fond mothers' arms, but after a time have to go back to heaven.

At a little distance Max and Hilda were walking up and down, their faces now gleaming in the shade under the trees, their figures now casting shadows in the light of the moon. Round them lay a great circling abyss of gloomy darkness, fringed with black pine-tops and crowned by frowning crags; and a silver veil was hanging over all.

"What I mean is this," Hilda was saying; "you forget that I am a woman, and judge me by yourself. You think because you have taught me to model in clay a little, that I must want to be an artist and conquer the world. But you are my world, and I will conquer no other!"

Max's clasp tightened on her hand.

"You must not deny your own power."

"But I am jealous of it, and I hate it. Whenever it comes before you as today, as tonight, a cloud covers your face, and a shadow rises up between us. Though you love the woman, you would banish the artist from your heart; and therefore, Max, because I love you, I will kill that power that disturbs you in me. Never while I live will I touch clay again."

"Then you will make me a murderer, a destroyer of one of Heaven's best gifts."

"Rather I will save you from being the murderer of my heart. Why, oh! why will you not let me be happy? I would rather bake your bread and sweep your floor than be owner of the best studio in Rome."

"Would we were there side by side, Hilda. Without you my inspiration will be gone; my works will be dull and dead."

"Because your coffee will not be as good as some, I could make for you?"

"Because I shall be without your suggestions, your criticism, your touch that calls life into a face. What would I not give to possess that magic touch!"

"Me, perhaps," said Hilda sadly. "I would die to give it to you—that is, if it has any existence."

Max shuddered.

"Do not talk of dying," he said. "If you were to die there is no kind

12

of death so hateful as my life would become."

"Hush!" said Hilda, putting her fingers across his lips; "only the good God knows anything about death."

Summer deepened, and as the time approached for Max's departure for Rome he found it more and more difficult to think of tearing himself away from Hilda.

"You are my inspiration, my soul," he said. "Without you I shall fail, and be only half a sculptor."

"Dear Max, I will come to you whenever you can send for me. Do you think the mountains will not be dreary, and the very children's voices sad in my ears till I can stand by your side again?"

"Hilda, would you dare—would you venture to come with me?"

"With you?" Hilda's pale face coloured to the hue of a rose for a moment, and turned paler than before. She trembled and drew her breath hard; and then she spoke with the gladness of a bird's song in her voice: "If you will dare it, Max, why so will I."

All the shadows disappeared at once from the young man's face, and his eyes shone.

"You may have hardships to endure, my darling," he said, kissing her hands rapturously.

"They will be welcome," laughed Hilda, "if only to prove how strong I am. You mean to walk across the mountains, Max, and so will I, if you will take me. What an autumn walk it will be! And once in Rome, why, Max, I will save your money by my economy."

"Your money, Hilda!"'

"Ah, Max, you forget that the cast of your nymph has gone on before us, and that before we get there she may be sold."

"Heaven grant it!" cried Max, while a lightning flash crossed his face. "If I were ambitious before, my Hilda, I am ten times more ambitious now."

Hilda was one of those women to whom no personal sacrifice is too great to add, be it never so little, to the happiness of the beloved. She was well aware that in accompanying Max hardships and difficulties were awaiting her, but she also knew that with her by his side Max would have better courage to cope with and conquer the world. She said to herself that she would eat little, labour hard, patch and mend her clothes and his, do all that lay within her to cover the extra expense of her presence in his home.

They were married in a little church in their mountains, with a band of children smiling round them, and Lisbeth weeping behind their backs. Oh, why had not Max been satisfied to remain a carver of wood at home? Then Hilda need not have left her kindred, and might have flourished among them through long and happy days. Why, indeed, good Lisbeth? Yours is one of those questions which can never be answered.

The day after their marriage they set out to cross the mountains on foot. A wallet on Max's shoulder held all their luggage, a purse sewn into Hilda's dress contained their wealth. Glorious autumn weather reigned over the mountain world. The hollows under the pines had never looked so purple, the peaks and crags so roseate, the clouds so gold, the firmament so blue as when Max, the sculptor, with his wife by the hand, went trudging along the narrow paths that led the way from Innsbruck up to Trent.

In this memorable journey they spent their honeymoon. In the morning travelling bravely over the rough roads, climbing rude heights, the while hardly daring to expend their breath in speech; at noon cooling their tired feet in some running water, and eating their frugal dinner under the deep broad shadow of the pines. At evening saying a prayer at some simple shrine, and afterwards stepping on gaily through the cooler atmosphere, seeing the sunset colours fade along the mountains, and the moonshine come forth to light them upon yet another mile of the way. Nights spent in the rudest chalets, a day stolen here and there to explore some town through which they passed; endless happy conversations about their love, their art, their future, the heaven of united life that lay on before them; so was accomplished the passage of the mountains, not the greatest of the difficulties that lay in their path, by Edelstein and Hilda his wife.

Through the queer old streets of Verona, they walked, and under its lofty arches; and then away across the Italian plains, dropping like a pair of swallows into art-galleries and churches, but hurrying ever with eager steps towards Rome. And there they stood at last one day, weary, dusty, poor, and friendless, but glad at heart and full of hope.

A studio and two rooms were hired at once, and Max went to work upon marble and clay.

The nymph was not sold, but what of that? It would do to furnish the studio till other works were created by the sculptor's hand. Hilda's ingenuity was exerted to make the vast, almost empty rooms which were their dwelling look homelike and gay. A curtain here, a spray of flowers there, a rude vase of fine form and striking colour in a corner; trifles like these made a home out of a wilderness. Singing, sewing, tripping in and out on household errands, or standing behind her husband's shoulder discussing his work with him, Hilda's days were as happy as a queen's.

They were in Rome, they were together; Max had lost his melancholy, and he had forgotten his strange fancy about that genius of hers which surely never could have existed. If he remembered it at all he but glanced at it pleasantly, and the thought of it passed easily away. If in moments of depression he called her to him and asked her to touch his work, she would answer reproachfully that her hands were full of flour, and that his dinner must spoil were she to soil them with his clay!

Winter and spring passed over, the little store of money had diminished sadly, and no work of Max's had been sold to replenish the household purse. Hilda held the said purse, and always spoke cheerfully of its contents to Max, who, rapt in his dreams, scarcely realized how the passing days were running away with silver and gold. Neither did he notice that Hilda's always pale face was growing paler and paler. Accustomed to gazing on faces of marble, he was not so struck with her pallor as another might have been, and the look of care always disappeared from her eyes when his were turned upon her. Max in Rome, conscious of growing power, with a brain full of beautiful things as yet uncreated, had all he wanted, and noticed nothing wrong. His home was bright and pleasant, and the food he needed was regularly placed before him. The long summer in Rome did not tell upon his strength as it told upon hers, but, as she did not complain, he was not aware that she had become less healthy than of old.

It was when winter came round again that Hilda took fear to her heart in earnest, and counted the money that was left with paling lips. How could she tell Max that the funds were so low? She would not tell him. And yet, where could she find money to go on with?

Then it was that she broke her resolution never to touch clay again.

On the chill winter mornings when Max was sleeping soundly, having got to rest late at night, Hilda would creep into the studio and go to work. What she produced there, Max little dreamed of; but from time to time sundry small, graceful, and original figures found their way into shops where such things are sold. They were quickly disposed of, and the money they fetched replenished Hilda's exhausted purse. She jealously guarded her secret, and Max toiled on, dreaming of glorious works he was to do in the future, and only occasionally waking up to observe that Hilda was a wonderful manager of their slender means.

15

He never guessed that she was giving her health, her talents, her life for the pittance that supported them both from one week on to another.

It was by means of these little figures of Hilda's that the nymph came to be sold after all. She was in the habit of going in, on her way to market in the mornings, to speak to the dealer who had her works in charge, and to learn if any orders had been left for her.

One day an English gentleman was standing in conversation with the dealer when she appeared, and as she entered the shop she heard the words,—

"Here, sir, is the lady herself!"

The gentleman was young and of fair complexion, and had a shrewd, sensible, and withal refined and sympathetic face. He bowed to Hilda, and made known his business at once. He wanted two other original figures besides those of hers he had already bought.

Hilda took the order; and then, with a sudden impulse, said,—

"If you would kindly come to see me at my home, my husband could show you something more worthy of your attention."

The stranger was interested, and promised to call as she desired. Then she said with a little embarrassment,—

"Please do not speak to my husband of these figures of mine. I do not wish him to know of their existence. He would think I fatigued myself."

The stranger took in the situation at once, bowed, and assured her he would remember her wishes. He thought she looked thoroughly fatigued, indeed, and wondered for a moment how long she would have the power so to exhaust herself. And this was the beginning of the friendship between Max Edelstein and Donald Stewart, which lasted through so many after years.

That very day Donald paid his first visit to the studio, and bought the nymph with Hilda's features, paying for it with a noble sum.

The patronage of the wealthy Englishman, or rather Scotchman, was all that was needed to bring Edelstein's genius into notice. Money and orders for work flowed upon him, and the crisis of his fortune was past.

Many new comforts appeared in his home, and Hilda no longer rose in the chill hours to do secret work with her hands in the clay. Her figures were seen no more in the shops, her artistic efforts were all in the past, and on the sweet spring days she lay on a couch at her window, with her eyes fixed steadfastly on the everlasting hills.

Still Max did not see that she was dying. Donald Stewart did, and to him she spoke of her approaching death.

"Do not disturb Max," she said to this good friend, when he would come from the studio into her little sitting-room to visit her. "He thinks I shall be strong soon, and his thoughts are with his work. One day, I know, he will astonish the world, and in that day, he will not so much need me. Nay, I do not mean to doubt his heart. I know he loves me well, and, perhaps, will never love another. But he has passed the point up to which he needed a woman's devoted love and care."

"When does a man cease to need that?" said Donald Stewart.

Hilda was gazing wistfully at the purple hills.

"During the next twenty years," she said, "Max will live in his art alone. His own creations will be his idols, sweetened to him by my memory, which will cling around them. His life will pass in the happy throes of work such as his, and he will hardly miss me from his home. After twenty years have passed—"

She paused, and a look of intense pity and longing settled in her eyes.

"Who can look so far ahead as twenty years?" said Stewart, guessing her thought.

"At the end of that time he will begin to need me again," said Hilda. "The first harvest of life will be won, the desire for a little rest will have begun to awake in him. He will look around and want me at his fireside. Oh, God! that I then could come back to him!"

Stewart's eyes filled with tears.

"A strange idea!" he said softly. "But I have no doubt or fear but that you will really be near him. Your spirit will never lose sight of him."

Hilda smiled.

"Never!" she said. "Never, as God is good! But oh, I meant more than that. If the Creator would but grant me my heaven in letting me return, even years hence, to this world to Max!"

Donald's heart was shaken by the pathetic cry in her voice; but he knew not what to answer to so startling a speech.

"Do not be shocked at me, Mr. Stewart," she said, turning to him with one of her old smiles; "but this is an idea that at times charms away my pain. And if I come," she added playfully, laying her little palms together like a child at prayer, "I will come without the talent which I believe was the only flaw that Max could ever see in me. Anything of genius I may have I hereby solemnly bequeath to my

17

husband. If I come again from heaven, I come without it."

In the flush of the Roman spring, she slipped away from them almost unawares one morning; and covered with Italian wild flowers she was laid in her grave.

Max took her death in a way that surprised even Donald Stewart. He appeared stunned, and unable to realize what had happened. So happy had he been in their late good fortune that this sudden and unforeseen ending of all their joy seemed to unhinge his mind. He became dull, absent, almost stupid, absorbed in the memory of Hilda, whose presence was still around him, and whom he could not let go into the past. He did not hear when spoken to, took no part in the life around him, neglected his work, and forgot to enter his studio. Orders remained unfinished, and people began to say that the promising young sculptor had got softening of the brain. He would not stir from Rome that summer, nor leave the rooms where Hilda's dresses and little ornaments and possessions still held their place as if they might be needed at any moment. Through all the dangers of that hot season in Rome Donald stuck fast by his side; and when at last Max fell ill of a terrible fever, Donald took the place of a nurse by his bed.

Thanks to his friend's unwearied efforts, Max arose out of this sickness, but pale and cadaverous like the living skeleton of himself. His mind seemed clearer now, and, on the first occasion when, sitting in Hilda's chair at the window, he spoke to Stewart of his wife, he wept like a child over his vanished happiness. He blamed himself bitterly for his conduct to her in many ways. Having learned from the dealer who had sold her wonderful little figures how hard she had worked to produce and dispose of them unknown to him, he made a misery of this proof of her unselfish devotion to him.

"I knew she had distinct genius," he said, "and if I had insisted on her developing it, she might have been alive today. She denied herself sleep, and suffered cold and weariness to provide the money which I was stupid enough not to perceive she must have earned."

"Her love was indeed limitless," said Stewart consolingly, "but you need not blame yourself. She had no wish to develop a separate genius from yours. She said to me——"

"What?" said Edelstein. "Anything that she said I must hear."

"That if she could come back to you, she would come without that talent which she thought you magnified, and which she did not love in herself."

"Come back?"

18

"Yes; it was an odd thing to say, but another proof of her devotion to you. It grew out of a conversation I had with her one day."

"When I was wrapped up in my selfish work. When you saw what was coming and I would not."

"That was her comfort. She dreaded a lingering trial for you."

"If she could come back! Did she say that, Donald?"

"She said—I think there is no harm in my repeating to you her tender and fantastic thought—she said she could wish that God would give her, her heaven, by allowing her to come back to you twenty years hence."

"Twenty years hence?"

"She thought for twenty years you could live absorbed in the splendid labours that are around and before you. After that——"

"Ay?"

"After that you would want her more. I understood her to mean that if she could return to you then, as young and sweet as she was a year ago, then, when your genius had slaked its thirst for work, and, a little tired, you might look round for companionship and human love, that so to come would be the desire of her soul."

A strange light came on Edelstein's face, brightening steadily into a glow of exultation.

"Do you think she will come, Donald?"

Stewart started and stared. He felt a qualm of fear that he had been unwise in speaking as he had done, while his friend's brain might be still in a delicate state.

"I think, dear old fellow," he said gently, "that such a fancy of hers only assures you that she will watch and wait for you in eternity. Who can count on living twenty years? And two like you will be sure to clasp hands when you at last have passed the verge of the grave."

"But that was not what she meant," said Max almost querulously. "Since I have survived her death, I may live to be a hundred. And she spoke of twenty years. Mark me, Donald, she will come!

I must get on with my work, and be ready to receive her."

Stewart was pained and puzzled by the strange manner in which Max fastened on this fanciful idea. He said no more then, but could not fail to notice how this conversation formed a sort of turning-point in his friend's convalescence. Max began to recover in earnest, and now worried himself because his weakness prevented his returning to work at once. A little more alarmed for his friend's mind than for his bodily health, Stewart determined to leave no effort unmade to restore the poor fellow to his normal state of health and strength; and, being himself a rich man, he saw his way to providing the necessary care and change for the invalid who interested him so much. He ordered his yacht to come to meet them in the Mediterranean; and packing up Max, he carried him away for a summer's cruise across the world.

The voyage was a great success, and Edelstein was, or appeared to be, completely restored to health of body and mind. He no longer talked despondingly, and ceased altogether to speak of his dead wife. Donald was almost inclined to blame him for this, and said to himself that, after all, those who sorrow most wildly for bereavement are apt to be those who forget the soonest. Edelstein did not return to Rome, but set up a studio in Paris. After that the star of his fortunes rose higher and higher. Stewart had married and settled down on his Scottish estate, and only occasionally saw or heard of his friend during a few days spent from time to time in the French capital, or by a short but affectionate letter penned in moments of weariness by the great sculptor to his friend. And so, the years went over; and the name of Max Edelstein was of European fame.

Twenty years passed away. Edelstein had been established long in London, and many of his most beautiful works had been created for, and prized by Englishmen. Unbounded success was his, and admiration and adulation had been poured out upon him. Nevertheless, he lived in his work alone, had few friends, took long walks with his pipe for sole companion, and was never to be seen in large social gatherings. His only society was that of one or two friends who sometimes dined with him in his perfectly appointed house. In women he felt no interest whatever, and would not have their company, no matter how flatteringly it might be offered to him. Invitations from great ladies dropped into his hands, but they failed to bring him captive into even the most charming drawing-rooms. People said it was affectation, moroseness, conceit which made him live the life of a recluse in the heyday of his fame. But Edelstein did not hear, or did not heed what they had to say.

PART 2

On a certain hot night in the end of June, Max Edelstein sat at his lonely dinner-table with wine before him which he did not drink. His eyes were fixed on the opposite wall with a strange look of intense expectation mingled with longing. From time to time a slight frown of impatience contracted his brows, his fingers moved restlessly, lifted the glass of wine, but set it down again untasted; and then again, the nerves of his face relaxed, and, as if obedient to a familiar self-control, the whole man dropped back into a quiescent state of thought.

Twenty years had made a great change in the youthful sculptor of Innsbruck. His dark locks had changed to silver-white, but, waving and plentiful as they were, this peculiarity only enhanced the beauty of a singularly vigorous and noble countenance. His dark eyes burned under a brow on which intellectual power sat enthroned. The dreamy sadness which lurked in some of the lines of the face had no weakening effect on its general expression, but just tempered the overwhelming force that was visible in every feature and every movement of the head. After sitting for an hour wrapped in his reverie he got up, and leaving the room, walked down a long passage to his studio, which was at the back of the house.

Here a lamp burned low, and he did not turn the flame to a fuller height, but paced up and down the large room, till by degrees the white figures around him became quite visible to his eyes in the semi-darkness. With folded arms and head sunk on his breast, he continued thus to give himself up to his thoughts or dreams, and at last paused before a statue at the feet of which burned the lamp which gave its dim light to the place. It was the marble statue of the nymph which bore Hilda's features, and which had been touched to greater tenderness of expression by her fingers in the days of their betrothal and in the spring of their lives. This first work of his, sold to Donald Stewart, had been returned to him by that faithful friend after Hilda's death, and for it he had substituted a work of equal beauty which held a high place of honour in the Scotchman's home.

As Edelstein stood gazing at the features, dimly seen, but kissed to warmth by the red light of the lamp, a knock came on the door, and before the owner of the studio had time to express impatience at being interrupted, the door opened, and somebody came in.

"Max!"

Edelstein uttered a kind of cry, strange to hear from the lips of such a man.

"You, Donald?" he said, after a moment's struggle with some violent emotion. "I thought—it was someone else."

"Are you not going to welcome me, old fellow?" said Stewart, struck by something strange in his friend. "And why are you mooning here alone in the dark?"

"We artists have ways of our own of going on," said Edelstein, with a short laugh. "But you are welcome, indeed, my friend." And he seized Donald's hand in both his own, and almost crushed it with the energy of his grip. "When were you not welcome?"

"All right, old fellow! Get some more light, that I may see how you are thriving."

Edelstein struck a match, and applied it to a large lamp on a bracket.

"I never let servants in here if I can help it," he said; offered a box of cigars to his friend, lit his own pipe, and the two smoked for a few minutes in silence.

Stewart watched his friend's face as it settled back into its habitual lines, and something that he saw there and did not like, something indescribable which he had seen there before on occasions, but never so plainly as now, disturbed him.

He scarcely knew how to begin a conversation, so full was his mind of something he did not venture to mention; but Max saved him the trouble of starting a subject.

"Donald," he said suddenly, "do you remember what night this is?"

"Ah!" said Stewart.

"This night twenty years I held Hilda dead in my arms."

"My dear friend——" began Stewart.

"And some months later you told me of something she said."

"Said?"

"About coming back."

"Max!"

"Stewart, I am expecting her. That is why I started when you came in at the door. I thought it was she."

"Good Heaven, Edelstein! are you in earnest?"

"Earnest?" said Edelstein, laying down his pipe. "Am I a man to jest, and on such a subject?"

"Are those we love allowed to come back?" Stewart said gently, trying to control his uneasiness and to speak naturally.

"Of that I know nothing. She never broke a promise, and her love was perfect. That is all I know."

"I do not believe in ghosts," said Stewart gravely.

"Ghosts! Nor I; she will not come as a ghost, Donald. She will come as my wife, real as herself, to live with me and comfort me for the rest of my life."

Stewart was silent. The words fell heavily on his heart. Max had overworked himself, and his friend remembered painfully how, many long years ago, certain fears for his friend had troubled his mind.

"Max, old fellow," he said, "if Providence should alter the usual order of Nature's laws to comfort a heart so noble as yours, I, for one, will rejoice, as I think you know. In the meantime, come out of this place for a while. You work too hard, and live too much alone."

"Where shall I go?"

"Take my advice for once, and let me take you, not for a solitary ramble, but into a crowd. Believe me, old friend, you have been doing yourself harm. Strange ideas are getting into your brain. There can be nothing like a complete change for putting you straight."

Max passed his hand over his head.

"I believe you are right, Stewart. I want a change. I will do anything you bid me."

"First of all, then, before we make further plans, come off with me now to Lady B——'s. I am intimate with her, and she will only be too proud to receive you."

Edelstein winced.

"I cannot bear a ballroom," he said. "The sight of dancing has a curious effect upon me. I think of whirling dervishes. Now our dancing in the mountains——" He stopped, as a vision, clear and vivid as if only seen yesterday, arose before his eye, of Hilda and himself dancing among the children and neighbours, in the light of the sinking sun, under the shadow of the purple hills.

"There will be no dancing. It is only a solemn reception. There will be a brilliant crowd, and we will just walk through. You need not speak unless you like, and we will come away any moment you please."

"It is sorely against the grain," said Max; "but I will go to please you." He rose, and made a weary movement of hand to head. "You will wait a few minutes while I dress. Stewart," he added, suddenly turning his hand on the door, and making a step towards his friend, "forgive me if I seem ungracious. I am going not only to please you, but to escape from myself. These rooms have begun to seem haunted to me. Something has been going wrong. I will shake off a weakness."

"All right," said Stewart. "Blues from over-work, and over-concentration of thought in one spot. I know all about it, though I am not a worker."

Half an hour afterwards they entered a brilliantly lighted house in St. James's, and were soon moving through a crowd composed of many of the most distinguished men and women in London. The hostess, who had seen Edelstein's noble face before, in his own studio, was gratified at his appearance in her rooms, and received him with flattering kindness. At a whispered word from Stewart, however, she allowed him to pass on into the crowd where few knew him by sight, owing to the extremely retired life which he had hitherto led.

"He is not very well," Donald said to Lady B——, "and I have coaxed him out for once. But we must not frighten him. If a fuss is made about him, he will go back to his shell."

And tact being one of Lady B——'s virtues, she took no further notice of the famous sculptor.

Out of one magnificent room into another the friends sauntered, keeping together, till at last Stewart paused to talk to some friends who greeted him warmly and held him fast, and Edelstein, straying on alone, found his way into a drawing-room smaller than the others, with walls panelled in faint gold-coloured silk, upon which a few rare deep-toned pictures were shown to the fullest advantage. There he took up his position at a corner of the tall carven mantelpiece, and looked abstractedly round the place, with the air and with the feeling of a man who has no part in the lives of the people by whom he finds himself surrounded. Suddenly his eye became fixed, and an extraordinary change passed over his countenance.

A shifting of the groups of people who occupied the centre of the room took place, and an opening in the crowd showed him the figure of a woman dressed in white, sitting against the corner of an antique cabinet, and looking like a picture of St. Barbara with her tower rising straight behind her. She was a girl about twenty, exceedingly fair and pale, with a quantity of that faint-gold hair which belongs to babes, and which near the delicate yellow in the silken panels looked strangely approaching to silver.

Although womanly in figure there was a certain snowily ethereal look about her, the only deep touch of colour lying in the depths of her blue and crystal-clear eyes. She had a lonely look, and the air of awaiting someone whom she expected to come for her, and she seemed as little belonging to the crowd as Edelstein himself. She was gazing through the doorway near, yet as if seeing nothing, utter unconsciousness of self in her face and attitude.

It is said that if one human being looks long and intently at another, the person so observed will soon feel the effect of the unseen gaze, and be constrained to meet it. However that may be, the fair-haired girl turned her graceful head after some time, and looked straight across the room at Edelstein, who was gazing at her with Heaven knows what expression of recognition and rapture in his eyes. A shock of surprise passed over her, and then a puzzled look crossed her face, as if she thought she ought to know the distinguished-looking person who thus seemed to claim her acquaintance, and was embarrassed at not remembering his identity.

At this moment Stewart reached the room and stood by his friend's side, who did not see him, but started at hearing the Scotchman's voice at his ear.

"Look, Donald, there she is," said Edelstein, in a low voice thrilling with emotion, and without removing his eager gaze from the white-clad girl at the other side of the room.

"She! Who?" asked Donald, startled by his tone and manner.

"Hilda—my wife," murmured Max, in a voice in which, low as was the utterance, an agony of joy and amazement spoke.

"Max, are you aware of how oddly you are looking at that lady, who is a perfect stranger to you?" said Stewart, and passed his hand through his friend's arm, trying to draw him away.

"Stranger!" said Edelstein, with a little laugh of joy. "Do you mean to say, man, that you do not recognise her?"

"I do indeed see a curious likeness, Edelstein, but surely I need hardly say to you, be yourself, and do not give way to hallucination."

Max did not appear to hear him.

"See how she looks at me!" he muttered, as the girl once more turned her fascinated eyes, half frightened, half attracted, on his. "Donald, do not hold me back. I must go and claim her. Oh, Heaven! how strange to meet in such a place as this!"

Stewart was shocked and agitated at this unexpected result of his attempt to cure his friend of a monomania. Amazed himself at the extraordinary resemblance in the girl before him to the long-lost Hilda, who slept in her Italian grave, he could only think of one way of cutting short so painful a moment as this, and strove to induce Edelstein to quit the room with him.

But another glance at Max told him he must humour the great sculptor as he would humour a madman.

"Listen to me, Edelstein," he said. "Even if it be she, there are certain rules of etiquette to be observed. We must ask our hostess to introduce you to her."

"What, to my own wife?"

"Yes. No one here knows that she is your wife, except yourself, and you would not appear to be rude to a lady?"

"You are right, Donald—always right."

"Come, then, and let us lose no time."

Stewart had hoped to make his friend forget this craze, and tried to lead him into other rooms, to interest him in the sculptures of an old and richly decorated mansion; but he found that such a hope was vain, for Edelstein dragged him straight to Lady B——'s presence, and obliged him to ask for the desired introduction.

"Lady B——, my friend Mr. Edelstein wishes to be introduced to a certain young lady in white in the yellow drawing-room. Can you kindly gratify his wish?"

"I can guess who she is," said Lady B——, pleased at the interest shown by the great artist, usually so indifferent, in a favourite of her own. "She is Miss Trevelyan, a peculiarly beautiful and striking girl."

Max smiled a strange smile at Stewart, as if to say: "We will humour this amiable woman, and keep our own secret for the present," and then both men followed their hostess as she moved towards the yellow drawing-room.

The introduction was made, Lady B—— returned to the friends who required her presence elsewhere, and Edelstein stood by the girl in white, trying to frame a sentence with his trembling lips.

Stewart also stood by, having been introduced to the lady, and endeavoured, by his matter-of-fact remarks, to restore equanimity to two evidently embarrassed people. An acquaintance coming up claimed his attention for a few minutes; he was obliged to stand aside to let some ladies pass; in the crowd he drifted to some distance. When he was once more disengaged, he turned to look for his friend, but Edelstein and the lady were gone.

With a misgiving which he could not smother, Donald Stewart set out to search the rooms for his friend. After an interval of half an hour, and when he was almost thinking of returning to Edelstein's house, to seek him there, he at last discovered the sculptor and the white lady sitting in a retired nook half behind a curtain, and at an open window, beyond which the lighted tower of Westminster was seen to loom and burn in the purple-dark midnight sky.

The sculptor's fine head was in relief against the sky, and he was gazing in his companion's face with an intensity of love and joy which no words could express. What he was saying Donald could not hear, but he was pouring forth rapid words in a low impassioned voice. The girl was pale as death, and sat listening like a person who strives to remember, her eyes fixed on Edelstein's face. A look of awe was on her broad white brow, and with a strange, almost supernatural feeling which he could not account for, Stewart felt shocked at her amazing likeness to the long dead and buried Hilda.

"Edelstein," said Stewart, "excuse me, but I think you said you were anxious to leave this place early, and it is now about half-past twelve."

Max looked up at him with a smile. Without noticing his words, he turned to the lady, and taking her hand, laid it in Stewart's, saying,—

"Hilda, this is our dear good friend Donald. You remember Donald, my Hilda?"

The girl suffered her hand to rest in Stewart's, and murmured dreamily,—

"Yes, I remember; he seems quite familiar to me."

"Good Heavens!" thought Stewart, "has my madman met with a madwoman to complete his ruin? or has she found out that he is mad, and is she humouring his whim through fear?"

"Miss Trevelyan," he said, relinquishing her hand, "I must beg you to excuse the peculiarity of my friend's conduct in addressing you so, and by a name that is not yours. He has not been well, and I see that he is hardly himself."

"They call me Hilda," said the girl, looking strangely and reproachfully at Stewart. "Why should he address me by another name?"

Then she turned her face again towards Max, who seemed at once to forget Donald's presence; and they continued their low-voiced communing as though he had not been there.

Amazed and pained Stewart turned away, and uncertain how to act, found himself in the room with Lady B——, his hostess.

"Lady B——," he said, "my friend Edelstein is greatly taken with your friend, Miss Trevelyan. By the way, what is her Christian name?"

"Hilda. Why do you ask?"

"I have a fancy in ladies' names."

"'Tis a pretty name. And, by the way, a story is told of a curious dream her mother had which was the cause of her being so called. They are Cornish people, and the girl is full of romance. So was the mother, who is dead."

"You interest me greatly," said Donald. "My friend seems wonderfully taken with her."

"Don't let him put his heart into the matter," said Lady B——, laughing, "for the child is already engaged. It is a long story, and she has been very troublesome. Were I to tell you the whole you would understand why I call her romantic."

Lady B—— turned away to answer a question asked from another side, and Stewart stood musing perplexedly over the information he had received.

"Already engaged! And Max calls her his wife!" he reflected. "The girl is full of romance; and to me she seemed quite ready to obey his thought. There is a storm of trouble in the air, if I cannot get Max out of England by tomorrow night. And yet he may forget all this tomorrow morning, if he be the madman I fear I must take him to be."

After some time spent very uneasily, Stewart went back to the window where he had left his friend with the lady he had called his wife. Both were gone.

Five minutes afterwards he met Edelstein coming through the crowd to meet him with a beaming countenance.

"They took her away," he said, with a slight laugh, "the people who are her friends. I could not object, of course, and we are parted for the present. But think of it, Stewart, letting my own wife go away with strangers! But I shall see her tomorrow, and explain everything to her father."

Donald felt sick at heart. He was too much perplexed and troubled to try to reason with his friend, and besides, he feared to quarrel with a madman. He accompanied Edelstein home, and went with him into his studio.

As they stood before the statue whose face had been modelled from Hilda's, Max raised the lamp till the red light fell full on the marble features.

"Look, Donald, look! she has not changed one atom!"

The likeness was indeed marvellous. Even Stewart acknowledged that the two Hildas were, outwardly at least, the same.

"My dear fellow," he said, "I acknowledge that there is a startling resemblance; but go to sleep on this, and tomorrow your thoughts will be more clear. You must not make people talk about Miss Trevelyan."

Max smiled a peculiar smile.

"You think I am mad, Stewart," he said; "I know you think I am mad. But can she be mad too? That would be too singular a coincidence."

"Do you mean to tell me that the young lady you met for the first time tonight has declared that she knows herself to be your dead wife, returned to this world to be with you?"

"You have put it into excellent words, good Donald. Knowing your sceptical mind, I almost shrank from stating the facts to you so plainly."

"My poor Max!"

"Tush, Donald! don't put me in a passion. Did you yourself not solemnly convey to me her promise?"

"She made no promise, Max. It was the fond and futile wish of a dying woman that I unfortunately repeated to you. Your wife was too sensible, too religious a woman to believe that such return from the dead could ever be."

"There is nothing in religion to forbid such belief," said Max doggedly. "She has returned out of her heaven by the force of her all-powerful love. She was re-born into this world the very year after she quitted it."

"I wish you would go to bed, Edelstein, and sleep upon it."

Max smiled.

"After twenty years of silence I have talked with my wife tonight," said he, "and I have much to think over before I can sleep. But, dear old friend, I would not keep you here wrangling with me. When I have a little recovered from the shock of this wonderful happiness, I shall be able to thank you for being the bearer, a second time, of a blessing into my life. Meantime take your rest. When you have a little got over your natural surprise you will wake up and recognise my Hilda."

Donald left his friend, feeling half-stunned with amazement at the occurrences of the night. That Max, whom he believed to be mad, should reason with him pityingly, as if his were the weaker mind, seemed to finish the extreme oddity of the whole situation. His only hope for Edelstein lay now in the likelihood that the girl might lead the way out of the confusion of this hour. If indeed she had been subject to some spell while in Edelstein's presence, perhaps when no longer under his personal influence she might be roused to see the folly of the position in which she placed him as well as herself. Before laying his head on his pillow that night Stewart resolved to go in the morning, as early as might be, and to ask an interview with the woman whom Edelstein claimed as his wife.

The next morning, however, Donald remembered that he must go to Lady B—— for Miss Trevelyan's address, and on his way to that lady he decided on opening his mind to her at once as Miss Trevelyan's friend; at least in as far as he dared. He was fortunate in finding Lady B—— at home.

"I have come to you on a curious errand," he said; "I want you to give me some account of Miss Trevelyan's character, disposition, and circumstances. I am prompted by no idle curiosity."

"You come in the interest of your friend the sculptor," said the lady, "who evidently fell in love with her last night. If her father had been here, he would hardly have been pleased, for I think I mentioned to you he has already promised her to another man."

"He has promised her?"

"Well, that is the way to put it. The girl is, as I told you, full of romance. She has been brought up in a gloomy old house on a wild Cornish coast, without a mother and without youthful friends and companions. She is dreamy and sentimental, and has fancies about herself."

"Every woman has a right to a little of that kind of thing," said Stewart, who had married his own wife for love; "Heaven knows there are enough women of a different type. I suppose the man her father has chosen is rich?"

"Enormously wealthy, and very much in love with her. 'Tis true he is neither young nor interesting. He is a City banker; and Mr. Trevelyan is a needy, almost a ruined man."

"You mean that there is not a glimpse of hope for my friend Edelstein?"

"I think there is none."

"But if she herself should prefer him? He is not poor, and he is a distinguished man. And he is probably younger than the person of her father's choice."

"Considerably so, I should say, and a thousand times more fascinating, I am sure. In every way more desirable, I believe. Nevertheless, his suit is hopeless."

"Lady B——, I will confide in you wholly. My friend is no common man. Early in life he married a wife whom he tenderly loved, and whose untimely death almost unhinged his brain. Miss Trevelyan bears an extraordinary resemblance to the dead Hilda."

"Hilda! How odd!"

"Yes; the case is full of peculiarities. Now I greatly fear that if Edelstein should continue to see Miss Trevelyan, and afterwards lose her, the total wreck of his mind may be the consequence. Believe me, I am not over-stating the truth. I appeal to you to ascertain immediately whether there is hope for him or not, and, if not, to remove Miss Trevelyan out of his path."

"You make a strange demand, my friend. Why should not Mr. Edelstein be able to take care of himself; or his friends be able to take care of him? Why should the girl's movements be interfered with? She is enjoying her first season in London, and it is only half over. Her father is in Parliament, and it does not suit him to move about just now. How can I ask him to take his daughter out of Mr. Edelstein's way?"

"Dear Lady B——, for the sake of our old friendship I ask you to see what can be done. I myself will do my best to get Max out of London. For the present I will only ask you to see Miss Trevelyan and learn her mind, and appeal to her not to encourage Edelstein."

"There I am all with you. I will see the child at once. Though I cannot but think, friend Donald, that you take an exaggerated view of the situation, and allow your own turn for romance to run away with your judgment."

Late that afternoon Lady B—— took her way to the lodging in St. James's where Mr. Trevelyan and his daughter had taken up their abode for the season. The house and its appointments bore out Lady B——'s assertion that Mr. Trevelyan was a needy if not a ruined gentleman.

She was shown into a rather dingy drawing-room, and in a few minutes the pale girl of the night before, the second Hilda, came into the room with a radiant countenance. She was dressed in a soft white woollen gown with crimson roses at her throat. Her clear blue eyes were dilated with joy, her face was paler than ever, her fair hair, which shone like mixed gold and silver, glittered softly on her temples, and fell back in a heavy plait on her shoulders. She extended her hands to her friend with a happy, eager movement.

"Why, Hilda, how glorified you look! I am glad to see you looking so happy, my dear."

"Yes, I am happy," said Hilda quietly, and stole her arms round her friend's neck.

"Yet you were rather naughty last night, Hilda, talking so much to that Mr. Edelstein in the absence of your *fiancé*."

The girl withdrew from her friend's embrace, and sat down by her side.

"You do not understand," she said, "and how can I tell you? Mr. Edelstein and I are no new friends."

"Indeed! You surprise me extremely."

"I am sure I do. And I fear I shall also surprise others who love me. But Max has the first and highest claim."

"My dear Hilda, can anything be the matter with my ears?"

"You seem to hear me pretty well."

31

"Hilda, I am angry with you. You mean to tell me that you have thrown over your betrothed, set your father's will at naught, and all for a stranger?"

"Not for a stranger, Lady B——. I am Max Edelstein's wife."

Lady B—— uttered a cry, and then sat still, gazing at the girl before her.

"You are either quite mad," she said at last, "or you are a double-dealing and unworthy woman."

Hilda smiled mysteriously, and putting her hands on her friend's shoulders kissed her tenderly.

"Do not be angry," she said, "till you hear my story;" and then she sat down at Lady B——'s feet, and began to speak at length, while her friend listened patiently to her tale. The burthen of what she had to say was the same as that reiterated by Edelstein to Stewart. She was the Hilda of Innsbruck. She had died, and had promised to return. They had recognised each other on the instant they had met. They were husband and wife, and no strangers of a day. Nobody should dare to part them.

Looking at her innocent, ingenuous face, Lady B—— seized her hands and sighed heavily. Here was a mind gone astray. How sad, how incomprehensible! A lonely unnatural bringing-up had induced eccentricity, a romantic incident had inflamed her imagination, and reason was overturned at a blow. What could be done for this unfortunate girl?

"My friend Stewart knew something of this," she reflected, "and that is why he so urgently desired that they should not meet again. Now, which is the lunatic here? And is lunacy catching, like the measles?"

When Lady B—— reached home again she found Stewart awaiting her return. As she entered her own drawing-room with a scared pale face, Donald came to meet her. She sank into a chair, and Stewart waited impatiently till she was able to speak.

"Your friend is a madman," she said at last.

"That is what I dread," said Stewart sadly. "My only hope for him rested upon the lady. From your manner I conclude that my worst fears are realised."

"What are your worst fears?"

"That she shares his delusion."

"What is his delusion?"

"That his dead wife has fulfilled a promise he fancies she made, and has returned to this world to be near him."

"He has communicated his mania to her."

"What does she say about herself?"

"That she has always been followed by indistinct memories of a former life. That the moment she saw him she recognised him. That everything he told her of the past she instantly recollected. That Heaven has granted them both the boon of her return. That she belongs, and will belong, to no one else but him; and that nothing shall part them but death."

"It seems too strange a coincidence. Yet an imaginative girl might be influenced by a mind like Edelstein's."

"My friend, what shall we do with them?"

"If they could marry, they might possibly be happy."

"It can never be, I believe. I, for one, do not like to open the matter to her father. Yet I think he ought to be told."

The next day Lady B—— wrote a carefully worded letter to Mr. Trevelyan, and by night had a short note from him in answer. It said:—

"That madman Edelstein has been here, and Hilda and he have told me their ridiculous story. I have given him my mind; and tomorrow Hilda goes away to friends. Even to you I will not tell where I have sent her. Let her be lost to the world till she has returned to her senses."

The next day Lady B—— handed this note to Mr. Stewart, and Donald at once went off to Edelstein, whom he found lost in grief, having just returned from the Trevelyans' lodgings, where he had learned that the young lady was gone.

Stewart tried to rouse him up.

"Come, come," he said, "be a man and shake this madness off! Think of your wife in heaven, and leave this girl to the disposal of her father. She is already pledged to another man."

"Against her will," said Edelstein calmly. "She herself had given no pledge. How could she, being already my wife? But do not torture me, Donald. She is gone, it is true; but I shall find her again."

"Be it so, old friend. All that I can do to help you I will do. In the meantime, while we are all at fault, come with me to my Scotch mountain side. There you can get up your strength, and consider what further steps to take."

After much persuasion Edelstein consented to accompany his friend. All his attempts to hear further tidings of Hilda had proved vain, and, as no letter came from her to him, he concluded that she was closely watched. Donald hoped, on the contrary, that she had only returned to her senses.

On a lovely June evening the two friends arrived at the gate leading into Stewart's private grounds in a lovely part of Scotland, and leaving their carriage with the servants, walked up a winding by-path which tacked along a garden-wreathed mountain-side. At their feet lay the sea, guarded by cliffs which were low here and high there, and at one part formed themselves into a sort of lofty bridge leading from Stewart's charming dwelling on the upper heights to the sand-strewn and rock-bound shore beneath.

At one point they stood still to admire the magnificent view, their gaze resting on the violet-tipped peaks in the clouds, and then falling and following the golden light that ran "along the smooth wave towards the golden west;" and Edelstein raised his hat with a gesture of reverent delight.

"Colour is hardly a sculptor's province," he said with a smile; "but I could almost wish at this moment to be a painter."

Donald was delighted.

"I think I can make you happy here," he said, "for a week at least. You can go when you are tired of us."

Edelstein smiled his answer. His thoughts had been carried away to the Alps—to the Roman hills. That delicate violet on these lovely mountains had coloured his imagination with their own suggestions. His soul was away with Hilda on the Alps.

They continued their walk, still climbing, and presently here and there, between bush and scaur, glimpses of Donald's home came into view. One steep path of a few yards remained to be travelled, and at the top of it a figure in white appeared with one arm thrown round a young ash-tree, a figure leaning forward as if watching for their approach. A few more steps, and they were face to face with Hilda.

"Good Heavens!" cried Donald. "Miss Trevelyan—how have you come here?"

She had slipped her hand through Edelstein's arm, and, looking at Stewart frankly, said,—

"Ah, Mr. Stewart, what an unkind welcome! How often in the old days have you hoped I should come here!"

Donald turned to his friend.

"What does this mean, Max?" he said. "Has it been a preconcerted plan?"

"If a plan at all, a plan of Providence," said Edelstein, whose face

34

was shining with satisfaction. "The same Power that has sent Hilda back into the world has been able to place her feet upon your hills. That is all I have to say. Hilda will tell us the rest. As for me, I have felt that, turn where I might, I should meet her again."

"My father sent me here," said Hilda. "Indirectly he sent me here. He placed me with his friends a mile away, and Mrs. Stewart met me with them, and invited me to spend a few days with her. I have felt, like Max, that our parting would not be for long. This morning Mrs. Stewart said to me, 'My husband arrives this evening, and he brings with him his old friend, the sculptor, Edelstein.' And I was not the least surprised to hear it."

Then they turned away, hand in hand, just as Hilda and Max used to saunter together on the Alps long ago, and Donald, amazed and troubled, went in at his own door and retired to take counsel with his wife.

Mrs. Stewart was greatly astonished at the tale her husband had to tell.

"I took a fancy to the girl," she said. "There is something so uncommon about her. It was but natural to ask her to come here. The people she was with are stiff and hard in their way, and she seemed so pleased to get away from them."

"It was very natural, Jeanie," said her husband. "And it was also natural in me to bring poor Edelstein here. The coincidence is the part of it that takes away my breath."

"I think we can hardly be to blame," said Mrs. Stewart.

"If Trevelyan had been acquainted with me it could not have happened," said Donald. "But he knows nothing of me and I know little of him. The only thing for me to do now is to write to him stating the case as it stands; and meantime, if possible, to get Edelstein away with me on an excursion somewhere."

The evening passed quietly away. The host and hostess, secretly ill at ease, exerted themselves to appear as if nothing was wrong. At dinner-time Edelstein talked brilliantly, and was so transformed that Donald, his friend of years, scarcely knew him. Hilda appeared in the rich dress of pure white in which he had met her in London, and her face was shining with tranquil happiness. There were no other guests.

As the hours passed by, Mrs. Stewart, who could not detect symptoms of madness in either of her guests, reflected that it was a thousand pities that these two must be parted. Later in the evening Hilda sang Scotch and German ballads—sang the songs that the other Hilda had sung twenty years ago before the door of her Alpine home. Edelstein sat by her side, gazing at her with looks of worship.

After the ladies had retired to rest Stewart put his arm through that of his friend, and drew him out on the terrace overlooking the sea.

"My dear fellow," he said, "fortune has been playing curiously into your hands, I admit; but, you see, I cannot allow this sort of thing to go on. Miss Trevelyan is here by a strange accident. Now, until her father comes or sends to remove her, you must take yourself away. I will go with you on an excursion round the coast—anywhere you like, so that you get out of this house for a time."

Edelstein smiled.

"Donald," he said, "you are the soul of honour, and always were. You would sacrifice even the happiness of your old friend to your idea of honour. I respect you. I feel with you where any other matter than this is concerned. But when you speak of Miss Trevelyan, you forget that you speak of Max Edelstein's wife. That is the one point which I cannot keep before you."

"Man, man!" cried Donald, out of all patience, "will you not give up this unholy craze? Does Providence work miracles for you alone? Come, come, old friend, do not exasperate me!"

"The world is full of miracles, Donald, only we do not perceive them. I will not believe that you do not recognise Hilda."

"I see a startling likeness, but that does not overturn my reason. I see a likeness in person, but many differences in character. The first Hilda had a noble mind, strong clear common sense—nay, she had genius, which is not always allied with the other quality. Miss Trevelyan is weak, imaginative, and without any strength of character."

"I have thought of some differences, and they only strengthen my belief—if, indeed, it needed strengthening. In the first place, you wrong the lady you are pleased to call Miss Trevelyan (and Miss Trevelyan I am willing you should call her till our marriage can be solemnised again). She is not weak in character, as you believe. She is feminine, believing—— In short, she knows what you will not admit. As for the genius that once distinguished her—ah, Donald, do you forget what you told me she said when promising to return to me, if she could? 'If I come,' she said, 'I will come without the talent which I believe was the only flaw that Max could ever see in me.'

"She was wrong there. I saw no flaw in her, and by her talent and devotion she carried me over the worst, the hardest bit of my career; but she thought it. 'Anything of genius I may possess,' she continued,

'I hereby solemnly bequeath to Max.' And herein lies the secret of my later complete success. 'If I come again,' she said, 'I will come without it.'"

He drew a little pocket-book out of his breast, and read over again the words in Stewart's writing.

"Do you forget jotting this down," he said, "and afterwards giving it, at my request, to me? I have never parted with it for a moment since you put it in my hands."

"And so have driven yourself mad on one point," said Stewart, aghast at this result of his own well-meant action.

"I am not mad, Donald," said Max quietly, putting the book back in its resting-place; "but these are among the things that are beyond our ken."

"There is no use in battling with a madman," said Stewart to his wife that night. "I cannot bring him to reason, and the girl seems as much astray as he. I have communicated with her father already; in the morning I will write him a fuller account of the unexpected meeting here; and this is all I can do."

"I cannot see that either is mad," said Mrs. Stewart, "and to me it seems like sin to meddle between them. Why can they not marry and be happy in their touching delusion, if delusion it be?"

"'If delusion it be'!" said Stewart. "My dear, are you losing your senses too?"

"I hope not, Donald. I have always been called matter-of-fact; but I would rather not dwell on this point. I take my stand simply on this—that I would like to see so interesting a pair married and happy."

"There I heartily agree with you; but I am not her father, nor are you her mother; and her father must have his voice in the matter,"

Nothing more was said, but early in the morning Stewart rose and went to his study to write his letter to Hilda's father. This written and despatched, he went out to the garden to wait for the summons to breakfast. Returning to the house, he met his wife coming down the path.

"Neither Mr. Edelstein nor Hilda is to be found," she said hurriedly.

"Good Heavens!" said Stewart, "has no one seen them?"

"The gardener saw them about six o'clock this morning."

"Where?"

"Here in the garden. When he arrived to begin his work, he met Mr. Edelstein walking about, and looking as if he had not slept all night. Presently Miss Trevelyan appeared, fresh and bright after her sleep, and walked among the roses, gathering them as she went, and splashing herself with dew. She seemed surprised to see Mr. Edelstein. They spoke together for some time, never seeming to notice the presence of the gardener. At last, Mr. Edelstein said, 'Come then!' and took her by the hand, and they walked away together hand-in-hand; and then the sun rose high, suddenly, and he could not see where they went for the blaze of light. He thinks they went down towards the cliffs."

"Perhaps they have only gone for a walk," said Stewart, but with a face of anxiety.

Mrs. Stewart shook her head.

"I think," she said, "that you will never see them again till they are indeed man and wife. Hasty marriages are easily made in this country, remember."

"And all your sympathies are with the crazy pair," said Stewart, almost angrily. "You do not think of the trouble that I shall get into with her friends."

Even while the husband and wife talked in the garden, the sky darkened, and great drops of rain began to fall. The wind rose, and there was every sign of a storm.

Stewart, nothing daunted by the weather, set off post-haste in a carriage with a pair of horses to follow in the track of his friend. He felt a conviction that his wife's words were true—that Edelstein had taken the matter into his own hands, and would make Hilda his wife before friends or enemies could interfere.

The route he followed ran along by the sea, and after an hour's driving through the storm he arrived at a small fishing seaport, where he made inquiries among the people. He soon learned that his fears were realized. A lady and gentleman had presented themselves that morning to the clergyman of the place, and had been married. Immediately afterwards they had hired a *hooker* to carry them, some said to France, some said to Ireland. Half an hour after they left the pier the storm began to rise; many had watched the *hooker* through a glass with some anxiety, but it had seemed to hold on its way steadily enough, and was now out of sight.

"Ireland or France!" said Mr. Stewart impatiently. "Surely someone knows where they are gone. Who would take them in a *hooker* from here to France?"

"Our *hookers* will do better work than ye think," said a brawny fisherman. "But I heard them talk about Ireland."

Mr. Stewart was in despair. It did not matter, after all, towards what country the husband and wife had set their faces. He thought bitterly of Lady B—— and her friend, Mr. Trevelyan, and wished impatiently that this extraordinary elopement had taken place from under any roof rather than his own. Of Edelstein's happiness he could not then even think, so vexatious were the circumstances in which he found himself unexpectedly placed.

Stamping up and down the pier while he made his reflections, he scarcely noticed that the storm was becoming wilder every moment, till suddenly a furious gust, almost sweeping him from his foothold, startled him out of his musing, and changed his feeling of anger against the runaway pair into anxious fears for their safety.

Gazing round him after a long look at the now raging sea, he was aware of a group of solemn weatherbeaten faces scanning his features with sympathy, and he immediately questioned the men as to the amount of danger to be apprehended from the storm.

"It's a bad day, and it'll be a waur night," said one who made himself spokesman for the rest. "A wad rather yer friens had ta'en their flight by land."

Sick at heart now, Stewart pressed the seafaring men with questions. Their fear was that the *hooker* would be run upon some of the rocks along the coast. Donald took his way to the inn of the village, where his horses were put up, and decided on sending a message to his wife, and remaining in this place for the night. It did not appear to him that he could effect much good by doing so, yet he felt more within reach of news on this spot than he should have felt in his drawing-room at home.

Towards evening the tempest swelled into a hurricane. One or two houses were flung down in the little town, slates and chimneys from all sides clattered into the street, and the bells from the various points of danger on the rocky coast clanged and tolled the black night through. Stewart walked his room hour after hour, and tried to check his gloomy thoughts by recurring to the suggestion of one of the sailors, that after all the *hooker* might have put in somewhere along the coast, before the storm became so furious.

This was the only hope that presented itself in the midst of horror, and he clung to it with all his might. Nevertheless, as he left his room in the wild scared light of the morning, and went out to look about, he felt a dread at heart that some unforeseen catastrophe had ended the curious drama in which he had been obliged, unwillingly, to take a part.

About twelve o'clock the storm went down, but the weather remained bleak and sullen. Stewart ordered his carriage, and set off by the coast road, stopping at all the dwellings and villages as he went along, asking if a *hooker* had been harboured or wrecked in the neighbourhood. His search was vain, the answer to questions as to harbour generally was, "No *hooker* could live in such a hurricane as that of last night."

When it was quite evening, he at last met a man upon the road who had some little news to give him, having heard of people who had been washed in that morning near a village some miles further on by the shore. Yes, there was a man, and there was a woman. The woman was a lady; and had been taken into somebody's house.

Stewart now drove as fast as his horses could carry him, and arrived at the place where the sea had given up its prey. "Oh, ay!" said the folks he met; a sailor-boy and a lady had been washed in alive; a gentleman and one or two others had been drowned.

Then a revulsion of feeling swept over Donald Stewart, and his heart cried out for the faithful friend of so many bygone years. If one must be taken, why could it not have been the woman who had lent her weakness to help a great mind to its ruin? He forgot the father who would hold him, Donald Stewart, accountable for the fate of a child; and thought only of his own irreparable loss.

He was taken into a humble fisherman's house, and there, by the fire, sat the sailor-lad who had survived the wreck.

In a few strong words he told the story of the night's catastrophe. The gentleman was as brave as a lion, he said. He lashed the lady to the mast, and that was how she was saved. For himself the gentleman counted surely on his swimming. He was a powerful swimmer, and must have been dashed upon the rocks and stunned. He (the lad saved) could not swim a stroke. These things were well known to be all chance or fate. The waves which had killed the skilful swimmer had but tossed the helpless boy roughly in their embrace, and hurled him safe upon the sand.

In an inner room Hilda was lying upon a bed. She did not speak, but fixed one long, strange look upon Donald Stewart, and then turned away her face to the wall. Stewart sent for his wife immediately, and that kind woman nursed the girl through what proved to be a dangerous illness. When she was sufficiently restored, they carried her home to their house, where her father had arrived to meet her.

A rather narrow-minded, unsympathetic man, Mr. Trevelyan was unable to take any lenient view of his daughter's conduct. While she lay in peril of death his grief was extreme, but once she was out of danger his anger rose high again, and he resolved that, as soon as she was able to bear them, his reproaches should be equal to her deserts.

However, when he saw her sit listening to his hard words with an absent, unmoved expression of face, as if she hardly heard him, or did not understand him, his eloquence failed, and he felt more fear than wrath stirring within him.

"What do you think of her?" he asked timorously of Mrs. Stewart.

"I know what you mean," she said, "but I do not find any flaw in her brain; she is simply overwhelmed by a depth of agony which you and I cannot fathom."

"But how can she feel such grief for a man of whom she knew so little? You surely do not believe her story that she lived a former existence and was Edelstein's wife?"

"I cannot tell you exactly what I believe," said Mrs. Stewart with a troubled look. "Perhaps I am a little over-tired myself with anxiety and nursing, but I have been powerfully impressed by the strength and vividness of her own conviction on this subject. Her ravings were most strange. She does not speak about the matter now."

"Try to get her to speak," said the father, who was softening every moment towards his child.

Mrs. Stewart tried to lead her to open her mind on the strange subject which engrossed it. Hilda sat at the window, her fair, almost silvery head set in a framework of roses, her face deadly pale, her eyes darkened with their habitual shadow of grief. Stewart, looking at her, was startled afresh by her extraordinary resemblance to the dying Hilda, who, sitting thus at a window looking out at the Roman hills, had spoken to him those fatal words which he had too faithfully recorded and repeated to her husband. Overwhelmed by an almost supernatural feeling that forced him against his will to share momentarily the delusion of his lamented friend, and to imagine that he saw the Hilda of Rome in the flesh before him, he arose hastily and went out of the room.

"My dear," said Mrs. Stewart, struck with something in the girl's eyes which had suddenly turned on her, "will you not speak to me a little, if only to ease your poor heart?"

"What can I say?" said Hilda, with a wan smile. "There is one thought ever in my mind; and who can share it with me? I rashly asked to have my heaven in returning to the earth to him. My prayer was granted—not for my heaven, but for my purgatory."

"Dear child!"

"And my punishment I shall have to endure. I am not going to die, as you all seem to fear. I shall live many years in my purgatory; and I shall not be allowed to be idle in my pain. Work will be found for me to do."

As soon as she was sufficiently restored to health her father took her away to her old home in Cornwall, where she lived with him as a dutiful and tender daughter till his death, which occurred a few years after these events. But there was always something in her face which seemed to mark her as different from other girls; and no man dared ask her to be his wife.

After her father's death she went abroad, and joined the devoted ranks of the Sisters of Charity. Further we cannot follow her; but she is living still.

The Country Cousin

CHAPTER 1

Old Tony Spence kept a second-hand book shop at the corner of a back street in the busy town of Smokeford; a brown dingy little place with dusty windows, through which the light came feebly. From the door one could peer down the narrow interior, with its book-lined walls and strip of counter, to the twinkling fire at the far end, where the old fellow sat in his armchair, poring over ancient editions, and making acquaintance with the latest acquisitions to his stock. He was a dreamy-looking old man, with a parchment-like face and a snuff-coloured coat, and seemed made of the same stuff as the books among which he lived, with their dusty-brown covers and pages yellowed by time.

He had been a schoolmaster in his youth, and had wandered a good deal about the world, and picked up odds and ends of a queer kind of knowledge. Of late years he had developed a literary turn, and now and again gave forth to his generation a book full of quaint conceits, a sort of mosaic fragment of some of the scraps of knowledge and observation stored up in his brain, which was as full of incongruous images as a curiosity shop. In the morning, he used to turn out of his shuttered dwelling about six, when there was light, and go roving from the town to the downs beyond it, where he would stroll along with his hands behind his back and his head thrown upward, musing over many things he found puzzling, and some that he found delightful in a bewildering world.

His house consisted of four chambers, and a kitchen above a ladder-like stair, which led up out of the bookshelves; and his family of an ancient housekeeper, a large cat, and his daughter Hetty, soon to be increased by the addition of a young girl, the child of his dead sister, to whom he had promised to give a shelter for a time. Hetty was often both hands and eyes to him, and wrote down oddities at his dictation when the evening candles burned too faintly, or his spectacles had got dim—oddities whose flavour was not seldom sharpened or sweetened by the sentiment or wit of the amanuensis.

"That's not mine, Hetty; that's your own!" the old man would cry.

"Only to try how it would go, father."

"'Tis good, my little girl; go on."

And thus, in scribbling on rusty foolscap, and poring into musty volumes, tending a small roof-garden, and sketching fancies in the chimney corner, Hetty had grown to be a woman almost without knowing it.

She possessed her father's good sense, with more imagination than was ever owned by the bookseller. She saw pictures with closed eyes, and wove her thoughts in a sort of poetry which never got written down, giving audience to strange assemblages in her dingy chamber, where a faded curtain of tawny damask did duty for arras, and some rich dark woodcuts pasted on the brown walls stood for gems of the old masters in her eyes. Lying on her bed with hands folded and eyes wide open, she first decorated then peopled her room, while the moonshine glimmered across the shadows that hung from roof and beam. Sleep always surprised her in fantastic company, and with gorgeous surroundings, but waking found her contented with her realities. She was out of her window early, tending the flowers which flourished wonderfully between sloping roofs, in a nook where the chimneys luckily stood aside, as if to let the sun in across many obstacles upon the garden.

One summer morning she was admiring the crimson and yellow of a fine tulip which had just opened, when a young man appeared, threading his way out of a distance of house-tops, stepping carefully along the leads as he approached Hetty's flower-beds, and smiling to see her kneeling on the tiles of a sloping roof and clinging to a chimney for support. He carried in his hand a piece of half-sculptured wood and an instrument for carving. Hetty, looking up, greeted him with a happy smile, and he sat on the roof beside her, and praised the tulips and chipped his wood, while the sun rose right above the chimneys, and gilded the red-tiled roofs, and flamed through the wreaths of smoke that went silently curling up to heaven above their heads, like the incense of morning prayer out of the dwellings.

"I have got a pretty idea for your carving," said Hetty, still gazing into the flower as if she saw her fancy there. "I dreamed last night of a beautiful face, half wrapped up in lilies, like a vision of Undine. I shall sketch it for you this evening, and you will see what you can make of it."

"What a useful wife you will be!" said the young man. "If I do not become a skilful artist, it need not be for want of help. Even your dreams you turn to account for me."

"They are not dreams," said Hetty merrily. "They are adventures. A broomstick arrives for me at the window here at night, and I am travelling round the world on it when you are asleep. I visit very queer places, and see things that I could not describe to you. But I take care to pick up anything that seems likely to be of use."

Hetty stood up and leaned back laughing against the red-brick chimney, with the morning sunshine around her. She was not very handsome, but looked now quite beautiful, with her smiling grey eyes and spiritual forehead, and the dimples all a-quiver in her soft pale cheeks. She had not yet bound up her dark hair for the day, and it lay like a rich mantle over her head and shoulders.

"I want to talk to you about something, Hetty. I have made up my mind to go abroad, and see the carvings in the churches; and we might live awhile in the Tyrol, and learn something there."

"Oh, Anthony!" the girl clasped her hands softly together, and gazed at her lover. "Is it possible we could have been born for such good fortune?"

Anthony was a young man who had come to the town without friends, to learn furniture-making, and, developing a taste for carving in wood, had turned his attention to that, instead of to the coarser part of the business. His love of reading had led him to make acquaintance with the old book-man and his daughter. Evening after evening he had passed, poring over Tony Spence's stores, and growing to look on the book-lined chimney-corner as his home. He and Hetty had been plighted since Christmas, and it was now June.

That evening, when the evening meal was spread in the sitting-room above the steps, Anthony came up the ladder out of the book-shelves just as Hetty appeared at another door carrying a dish of pancakes. The old man was in his chair by the fire, his spectacles off duty thrust up into his hair, gazing between the bars, ruminating over something that Hetty had told him.

"So," he said, looking up from under his shaggy brows, as Anthony sat down before him at the fire, "So you want to be off to travel! It's coming true what I told you the day you asked me for Hetty. I said you were a rover, didn't I?"

"Yes," said Anthony, smiling and tossing back his hair, "but you meant a different kind of a rover. I have not moved from Hetty. I shall not move a mile without Hetty. And you too, sir, you must come with us."

Old Spence lay back in his chair, and peered through half-closed eyes at the speaker. Anthony had a bright keen face, with rapidly changing expressions, spoke quickly and decidedly, with a charm in his pleasant voice, and had a general look of skilfulness and cleverness about him. There was not to be seen in his eyes that patient dreamy light which is shed from the soul of the artist; but that was in Hetty's eyes, and would be supplied to him now and evermore to make him really a poet in his craft. Hetty's fancies were to be woven into his carvings that he might be famous.

"I don't know about breaking up and going abroad," said the old bookworm. "I'm too old for it, I'm afraid. Leaving the chimney corner, and floating away off into the Nibelungen Land! You two must go without me, if go you must."

"I will not leave you alone, father," said Hetty.

"And I will not go without Hetty," said Anthony. "In the meantime, just for play, let us look over the maps and guide-books."

These were brought down, and after some poring the old man fell asleep, and the young people pursued their way from town to town and from village to village, across mountains and rivers, till they finally settled themselves in the Bavarian Tyrol. From a pretty home they could see pine-covered peaks and distant glaciers, and within doors they possessed many curious things to which they were unaccustomed.

"And I wonder if the mountains are so blue and the lakes of that wonderful jasper colour which we see in pictures," said Hetty. How beautiful life must be in the midst of it all!"

"Yes," said Anthony; "and, Hetty, you shall wear a round-peaked hat with silver tassels on the brim, and your hair in two long plaits coming down your back. 'Tis well you have such splendid hair," he said, touching her heavy braids with loving pride in his eyes and finger-ends.

Hetty blushed with delight and looked all round the familiar room, seeing blue mountains, and dizzy villages perched on heights, people in strange costumes, brass-capped steeples, and strange wooden shrines, all lying before her under a glittering sun. Twilight was falling, the homely objects in the room were getting dim, the dream-world was round her, and with her hand in Anthony's she could imagine that they two were already roaming through its labyrinths together. It was not that in reality she could have quitted the old home without regret; but the home was still there, and the visions of the future had only floated in to beautify it. They had not pushed away the old walls, but only covered them with bloom.

The love of Anthony and Hetty was singularly fitting. He had gradually and deliberately chosen to draw her to him for the happiness and comfort of his life; his character was all restlessness, and hers was full of repose. She refreshed him, and the sight of her face and sound of her voice were as necessary to him as his daily bread. Hetty's was that spiritual love which spins a halo of light round the creature that leans upon it, and garners everything sweet to feed a holy fire that is to burn through all eternity. In the hush of her nature a bird of joy was perpetually singing, and its music was heard by all who came in contact with her. No small clouds of selfishness came between her and the sun. She knew her meetness for Anthony and her usefulness to his welfare, and this knowledge lay at the root of her content.

It was quite dusk, and the scrubby lines on the maps which marked the mountains of Hetty's dreamland were no longer discernible to peering eyes, when a faint ting-ting was heard from the shop-bell below. The lovers did not mind it. It might be a note from the little brazen belfry up among the pines against the Tyrolese sky, or from the chiming necklace of a mule plodding along the edge of the precipice, or from the tossing head of the leader of a herd on a neighbouring Alp; or it might be the little pot-boy bringing the beer for Sib's supper. Sib, the old serving-woman, had come to the latter conclusion, for she was heard descending by a back way to open the door.

After an interval of some minutes there was a sound of feet ascending the ladder, and the door of the sitting-room was thrown open. The light figure of a girl appeared in the doorway, and behind followed Sib, holding a lamp above her head.

"Who is it?" cried Hetty, springing forward. "Ah! it must be Primula, my cousin from the country. Come in, dear; you are welcome;" and she threw an arm round the glimmering figure and drew it into the room. "Sib, put down the lamp and get some supper for her. Father, wake up! here is your niece at last. Tell us about your journey, cousin, and let me take your bonnet."

Hetty took the girl's hat off, and stood wondering at the beauty of her visitor.

Primula's father had brought her up in a country village, where he had died and left her. She had come to her uncle, who had offered to place her with a dressmaker in Smokeford. The fashions of Smokeford would be eagerly sought at Moor-Edge, and it was expected that Primula would make a good livelihood on her return, with her thimble in her pocket and her trade at her finger-ends.

She had been named by a hedgerow-loving mother, who died eighteen years ago in the spring-time, and left her newly-born infant behind her in the budding world. The motherless girl had, as if by an instinct of nature, grown up to womanhood modelled on her mother's fancy for the delicate flower whose name she bore. She had glistening yellow hair, lying in smooth uneven-edged folds across her low fair forehead. A liquid light lay under the rims of her heavy white eyelids, and over all her features there was a mellow and exquisite paleness, warmed only by the faintest rose-blush on her cheeks and lips. She wore a very straight and faded calico gown, her shawl was darned, and her straw hat was burned by the sun.

"She is very lovely—prettier far than I," thought Hetty, with that slight pang which even a generous young girl may feel for a moment when she sees another by her side who must make her look homely in the eyes of her lover. "But I will not envy her, I will love her instead," was the next thought; and she threw her arms round the stranger and kissed her.

Primula seemed surprised at the embrace.

"I did not think you would be so glad to see me," she said. "People said you would find me a deal of trouble."

Old Spence was now awake and taking his share in the scene.

"Bless me! bless me!" he cried, "you are like your mother—a sweet woman, but with no brains at all, nor strength of mind. Nay, don't cry, child! I did not mean to hurt you. I have a way of my own of speaking out my thoughts. Hetty does not mind it, nor must you."

Primula was trembling, and had begun to cry; and Hetty and Anthony drew nearer and comforted her.

CHAPTER 2

"This is a dull place, after all," said Primula next day, when Hetty, having shown her everything in the house, took her a walk through the best streets to see the shops. "I thought that in a town one would see gay ladies walking about, and soldiers in red coats, and a great deal of amusement going on about us. Moor-Edge is as good nearly, and there isn't so much smoke."

"You thought it was a city," said Hetty, laughing. "I never thought about it being dull, but perhaps it is. We have gay ladies in Smokeford,

48

but they do not walk about in the streets. You may meet them sometimes in their carriages. It is a manufacturing town, and that makes the smoke. I don't wonder at all that Moor-Edge should be prettier."

"Oh, there is a lady! Look at her hat! and there is certainly embroidery on her dress. I should like a dress like that, only I've got no money. Do you never see any company in your house, cousin Hetty?"

"Anthony comes often," said Hetty happily, "and others come in and out, but we have nothing you could call company. You will see more of life when you go to the milliner's. There will be other young girls, and you will find it pleasant."

"I ought to have a better dress to go in," said Primula. "All the girls in the shops are nicely dressed. Have you got any money, cousin Hetty?" she added hesitatingly.

Hetty blushed, and was embarrassed for a moment. She had indeed a pound, the savings of years, about the expending of which she had made many a scheme—a present for her father or for Anthony, she had not quite decided. Well, here was her cousin who wanted clothing. She could not refuse her.

"I have a pound," said Hetty faintly, "and you can buy what you please with it."

"Oh, thank you," said her cousin. "Let us go in and buy the dress at once!" And they went into the finest shop, where the counter was soon covered with materials for their choice.

"This lilac is charming," said Primula longingly. "What a pity it is so dear!"

"The grey is almost as nice," said Hetty; "and I assure you it will wear much better."

"Do you think you have not got five shillings more?" pleaded Primula. "The lilac is so much prettier!"

"No," said Hetty, in distress; "indeed I have not a penny more."

"The young lady can pay me at some other time," said the shopman, seeing the grieved look on Primula's face.

"Oh, thank you!" murmured Primula, gazing at him gratefully.

"No, no, cousin; you must not indeed think of going into debt," said Hetty. "Come home and let us talk about it."

"Ah, I shall never get it!" said Primula, with a heavy sigh, and the tears rushed into her eyes.

"I will take off the five shillings," said the fascinated shopman. "You may have the lilac for the same price as the grey."

Primula blushed scarlet, and murmured some tremulous enraptured thanks; and the shopman bowed her out of the shop with the parcel in her arms.

Though Primula was going to be a dressmaker, Hetty had to make this particular dress. "I don't know how to do it yet, cousin," said Primula; "at least not the cutting out." When the cutting out was done, the owner of the dress was not at all inclined for the trouble of sewing it. Hetty had turned her room into a work-room, and stitched with good will, while the new inmate of the chamber sat on the little bed which had been set up for her own accommodation in the corner, and entertained Hetty with her prattle about the life at Moor-Edge, the number of the neighbours' cows, and the flavour of their butter; the dances on the green in summer-time, the pleasure of being elected Queen of the May.

When the dress was finished and put on, Primula willingly took her steps to a house in a prominent street, with "Miss Betty Flounce" on a brass plate on the door, and was stared at on her first appearance by all the new apprentices, who never had had so pretty a creature among them before.

Summer was past, and the dark evenings had begun.

"Anthony," said Hetty one day, "your work-place is near to Primula's. Could you call for her every evening and bring her home?"

Anthony changed colour, and looked at Hetty in surprise.

"Not if it annoys you," said Hetty quickly; "but I don't think you would find it much trouble. She is greatly remarked in the streets, and someone who calls himself a gentleman has been following her about lately."

Anthony frowned. "I should not wonder," he said angrily; "she is a thoughtless creature."

"You need not be so hard on her," said Hetty. "She is soft and childlike, and does not know how to speak to people and frighten them off."

"Well, I will be her knight, only to please you," said Anthony. "And see, here is the carving of the design out of your dream. Don't you remember?"

"The face among the lilies!" cried Hetty, examining it. "And it has turned out quite beautiful. Why, Anthony, I declare it looks like Primula!"

"So it does, indeed," said Anthony, turning away.

"I suppose her face must have come in my dreams," said Hetty, "for I never had seen her when this was designed. I have heard of dreams foreshadowing things, but I never believed it. However, you could not have a lovelier model, I am sure."

"No," said Anthony; and thenceforth he called for Primula every evening and brought her home. Sometimes Hetty came to meet them; more often she remained at home to have the tea ready. At first Primula did not like being so escorted, for she had made many acquaintances, and had been accustomed to stop and say good-evening to various friends whom she met on her way from Miss Flounce's door. And Anthony walked by her side like a policeman, and kept everybody at a distance. But she had to submit.

"Hetty," said Anthony, one day, when things had gone on like this for some time, "don't you think it is time she was going home?"

"What! Primula?" cried Hetty, surprised. "Why, no; she does not think of it: nor we, neither!"

"She is sometimes in the way," said Anthony moodily.

"I never saw you so unkind," said Hetty. "Poor little Primula, whom everybody loves!"

"You and I are not the same to each other since she came."

"Oh, Anthony!"

"We never have any private talks together now. You never speak as you used, because Primula is present, and she does not understand you."

"I have noticed that," said Hetty; "but I thought you did not. I believed it was not my fault. You often talk to Primula about the things that please her. I thought it seemed to amuse you, and so I was content."

Anthony lifted Hetty's little brown hand off the table, and kissed it; then he turned away without another word, and went out of the house.

The kitchen was a pleasant enough place that evening, with firelight twinkling on the lattice-windows; coppers glinting on the walls; Hetty making cakes at a long table; Anthony smoking in the chimney-corner; while Primula moved about with a sort of frolicsome grace of her own, teasing Hetty and prattling to Anthony, playing tricks on the cat, and provoking old Sib, by taking liberties with her bellows to make sparks fly up the chimney. She stole some dough from Hetty, and kneaded it into a grotesque-looking face, glancing roguishly at Anthony while she shaped eyes and nose and mouth.

"What are you doing, you foolish kitten?" said Anthony, taking the pipe from his lips.

"Making a model for your carving, sir," and Primula displayed her handiwork.

"Bake it," said Anthony, "and let me eat it; and who knows but it may fill me with inspiration?"

Primula laughed gaily, and proceeded to obey; and Hetty looked over her shoulder to enjoy the scene which followed.

"It was a sweet face certainly," said Anthony. And Primula clapped her hands with glee at the joke.

Anthony put away his pipe and seemed ready for more play. It was no wonder Hetty had said that he seemed to like Primula's nonsense.

By this time Primula had learned to find Smokeford a pleasant place. Her beautiful face became well known as she passed through the streets to and from her work. Young artisans and shopkeepers began to look out of their open doors at the hour for her passing, and idle gentlemen riding about the town did not fail to take note of her. Her companions were jealous, her mistress was dissatisfied with the progress of her work, and the head of the little apprentice was nearly turned with vanity.

One night, Hetty, going into her bedroom, found Primula at the glass fastening a handsome pair of gold earrings in her ears.

"Oh, Prim!" cried Hetty, in amazement. "Where did you get anything so costly?"

"From a friend," said Primula, smiling, and shaking her head so that the earrings flashed in her ears. "From someone who likes me very much."

"Oh, Primula!"

"How cross you are, Hetty; you needn't envy me," said Primula, rubbing one of her treasures caressingly against her sleeve. "I'll lend them to you any time you like."

"You know I am not envious, cousin. You know I mean that it was wrong of you to take them."

"Why?" pouted Primula; "they were not stolen. The person who gave them is a gentleman, and has plenty of money to buy what he likes."

"Oh, you silly child! You are a baby! Don't you know that you ought not to take jewellery from any gentleman?"

"You are unkind, unkind!" sobbed Primula, with the tears rolling down the creamy satin-smooth cheeks that Hetty liked to kiss and pinch. "Why do you get so angry and call me names? I will go home to Moor-Edge and not annoy you anymore."

"Nonsense, Prim! I won't call you baby unless you deserve it. Do you know the address of the gentleman who gave these to you? You must send them back at once."

Primula knew the address, but vowed she would keep her property. He bought them, he gave them to her, and there was nothing wrong about it. Hetty gave up talking to her and went to bed, and Primula cried herself to sleep with the treasures under her pillow.

The next day, Hetty, in some distress, consulted Anthony about Primula's earrings. Anthony was greatly disturbed.

"I will talk to her," he said; "leave her to me, and I will make her give them back." And he spent an hour alone with her, breaking down her stubborn childish will. At the end of that time he returned to Hetty, flushed and triumphant—looking as if he had been routing an army, and bearing in his hand a little box containing the earrings and a piece of paper on which Primula had scrawled some words. The present went back to its donor, and Primula was sulky for a week.

One evening, when the spring was coming round again, Anthony called as usual for Primula, but found that she had left the work-room early, as if for home. Arrived at the old book-shop he learned that she had not returned there since leaving, as usual, in the morning for her work.

"She has gone for a walk with some of her companions," suggested Hetty.

"She went alone," replied Anthony; and he thought of the earrings. "I must go and look for her."

Outside the town of Smokeford there were some pleasant downs, where, in fine weather, the townspeople loved to turn out for an evening walk. It was too early in the season as yet for such strollers; and yet Anthony, when he had gone a little way on the grass, could descry two figures moving slowly along in the twilight. These were Primula and the gentleman who had given her the earrings; a person whom Anthony had been watching very closely for some time past, whom he had often perceived following upon Primula's steps, and whom, for his own part, he detested and despised.

"Primula!" he said, walking up to the young girl and ignoring her companion, "come home! It is too late for you to be here unprotected."

Primula pouted and hung her head.

"The young lady is not unprotected," said the gentleman, smiling. "And pray, sir, who are you?"

"I am her nearest masculine friend," said Anthony wrathfully; "I stand here at present in her father's place."

The gentleman laughed. "You are too young to be her father," he said. "Go away, young man, and I will bring her safely to her home when she wishes to go."

"Primula," said Anthony, white with anger, "go yonder directly to the tree, and wait there till I join you." The girl, terrified out of her senses, turned and fled as she was bidden; the gentleman raised his stick to strike this insolent tradesman who had dared to defy him; but, before it could descend, Anthony had grappled with him. There was a struggle, and Primula's admirer lay stretched on the green.

Anthony brought home the truant in silence, and for many days he came in and out of the house and did not speak to her. Primula sulked and fretted and was miserable because Anthony looked so crossly at her. Anthony was moody and dull, and Hetty, with a vague sense of coming trouble, wondered what it all could mean.

CHAPTER 3

Old Tony Spence was taken ill that spring, and Hetty was a good deal occupied in attending on him. Anthony came as usual in the evenings, but he did not expect to see Hetty much, and Primula and he amused themselves together. Hetty's face got paler during this time, and she fell into a habit of indulging in reveries, which were not happy ones, if one might judge by the knotted clasp of her hands, and the deep line of pain between her brows. Her housekeeping duties were hurried over, she fetched the wrong book from the bookshelves for customers, her sewing was thrown aside, her only wish seemed to be to sit behind her father's bed-curtain, with her head leaned against the wall, and her eyes closed to the world. Sorrow was coming to seek for her, and she hid from it as long as she could.

One night, old Spence asked to have a particular volume brought him from the shop, and Hetty took her lamp in hand and went down to fetch it for him. There was a faint light already burning in the place, which Hetty did not at first perceive, as she opened the door at the top of the staircase, and put her foot on the first step to descend. She went down a little way, but was stopped by the sound of voices. Anthony and Primula were there.

"Yes," Primula was saying, in her soft, cooing voice, "I love you better than anyone. You fought for me, and I love you."

"Hetty——" murmured Anthony.

"Hetty won't mind," whispered Primula. "She gives me her money and her ribbons. She won't refuse to give me you too—I'm sure of that."

They moved a little from behind the screen of a projecting stand of books, and saw Hetty standing on the stairs, gazing straight before her, and looking like a sleepwalker. Primula gave a little cry, and covered her face. Hetty started, turned, and fled up into the sitting-room, shutting the door behind her.

She sat down at the table and leaned her head heavily upon her hands. The blow she had been half dreading, half believing to be an impossibility, had fallen and crushed her; Anthony loved her no more. He had taken away his love from her, and given it to Primula; who, with pleading eyes and craving hands, had robbed and cheated her. The greediness which she had tried to satisfy with ribbons and shillings had not scrupled to grasp the only thing she would have kept, and held till death as her very own. Hetty's thoughts spun round and round in the whirl of new and uncomprehended agony. She had no thought of doing or saying anything, no wish to take revenge nor to give reproach. She was stunned, bruised, benighted, and willing to die.

Primula came creeping up the staircase, after crying for an hour all alone among the old books. Life was very troublesome, thought Primula; everybody was selfish and cross, and everything was either wrong or disagreeable. People petted and loved her one moment, and were angry with her the next. Anthony had rushed away from her in a fit of grief, although she had told him she loved him, and had given up a fine gentleman for his sake. Hetty, who used to be so tender with her, and so ready to give her everything, had looked so dreadfully there on that step of the stairs, that she, Primula, was afraid to go up, though she was tired, and longing to be in bed.

Sobbing and fretting, she crept up the staircase, and, her desire to be comfortable overcoming her fear, she opened the door of the sitting-room, and came in. Hetty was sitting quietly at the table, with her head leaned on her hands, and she did not look up. "That is a good thing," thought Primula. "How dreadful if she were to scold me! 'Tis well it is not her way to make a talk about things." And she stole across the floor and shut herself up in the bedroom.

It was quite late at night when Hetty followed her into the bedroom, and then Primula was fast asleep, with the sheet pulled over her head and face, as if she would hide herself from the glance of Hetty's anger, even while she was happily unconscious of it. Hetty's lamp burned itself out, and she kneeled down in the dark to say her prayers. Her knees bent themselves mechanically in a certain corner of the room, but no words would come to Hetty's lips, and no clear thoughts to her mind. She only remembered that she ought to pray, and stretched out her arms, dumbly hoping vaguely that God would know what she meant. Nothing would come into her mind but pictures of the happy hours that Anthony and she had spent together in their love.

She fell asleep stupidly dwelling on these memories, and unable to realise that Anthony had given her up; then she dreamed that she had awakened out of a terrible dream, in which Anthony had seemed to have forgotten her for Primula. How joyful she was in that dream! How she laughed and sang for ecstasy, and chattered about the foolish fancies that will come into people's minds when they are asleep! And then she wakened, and saw the dawn-light shining on Primula's golden head and sweetly tinted face, and she knew and remembered that Primula was the beloved one, and that she, Hetty, was an exile and an outcast from her paradise for evermore.

Then, in that moment of exquisite anguish, in the leisure of the quiet dawn, a terrible passion of anger and hatred broke out in her breast. Everything that the light revealed had something to tell of her lost happiness, every moment that sped was bringing her nearer to the hour when she must rise up and give Anthony to Primula, and stand aside and behold their bliss, and accept their thanks. She dare not let that moment come—she would not have it, she could not confront it. She should do them some mischief if she were to see them together again before her as she had seen them last night.

What, then, was she to do with herself? She dared not kill them, she could not wish them dead. It would not comfort her at all that they should suffer or be swept out of the world to atone for their sin. They had murdered her heart, and they could not by any suffering of theirs bring back the dead to life. What, then, must she do with herself? The only thing that remained for her was to get away, far out of their sight and out of their reach, never to behold them, nor to hear of them again, between this and the coming of her death.

She sprang out of bed and dressed herself hastily, keeping her back turned upon the sleeping Primula, and, creeping down the stairs, she got out of the house. She felt no pang at leaving her home, and never once remembered her father; her only thought was to get away, away, where Anthony could never find her more. She hurried along the deserted streets and got out on the downs, and then she slackened her speed a little, quite out of breath. She knew that the path across the downs led to a little town, about ten miles away, in the direction of London. She had been too long accustomed to the practical management of her father's affairs not to feel conscious, from mere habit and without reflection, that she must work when she got to London, in order to keep herself unknown. She would help in a shop somewhere, or get sewing at a dressmaker's. In the meantime, her only difficulty was to get there.

The whirl of her passion had carried her five miles away from Smokeford, when she came to a little roadside inn. She was faint with exhaustion, feeling the waste caused by excitement, want of sleep and food, and by extraordinary exertion. She bought some bread and sat on a stone at the gate of a field to eat it. She saw the ploughman come into the field at a distant opening, and watched him coming towards her; a grey head and stooping figure, an old man meekly submitting his feebleness to the yoke of the day's labour, though knowing that time had deprived him of his fitness for it.

Hetty watched him, her eyes followed him as if fascinated; the look in his face had drawn her out of herself somehow, and made her forget her trouble. She wanted to go and help him to hold the plough, to ask if he had had his breakfast; to put her hand on his shoulder and be kind to him. She did not know what it was about him that bewitched her. He turned his plough beside her, and as he did so he noticed the pale girl sitting by the gate, and a smile lit up his rugged face.

Then it was that Hetty knew why she had watched him. He looked like her father. Her father! He was ill, and she had deserted him; had left him among those who would vex and neglect him! The untasted bread fell from Hetty's hands; the tears overflowed her eyes; she fell prone on the grass, and sobbed for her own wickedness, and for the grief and desolation of the sick old man at home.

"What is the matter, lass?" asked the old ploughman, kindly bending over her.

Hetty rose up ashamed.

"Sir," she said humbly, "I was running away from my father, who is ill; but I am going back to him."

"That is right, lass. Stick by the poor old father. Maybe, he was hard on you."

"No, no, no; he never was hard on me. I have a sorrow of my own, sir, that made me mad. I forgot all about him until I saw his look in your face. I shall run back now, sir, and be in time to get him his breakfast."

The clock of the roadside inn struck six, and Hetty set off running back to Smokeford.

She ran so fast that she had not time to think of how she should act when she got home. When arrived there, she found she could have a long day to think of it, for Primula had gone to her work-room, and there was nobody about the house but Sib, and her father, and herself.

The old man had never missed her; but Sib met her on the threshold, and looked at her dusty garments with a wondering face.

"Well, Hetty!" she said, "you did take an early start out of us this morning."

"I wanted a walk," said Hetty, throwing off her cloak, and making a change in her forlorn appearance. "Is my father's breakfast ready? I'm afraid I am late."

Old Tony Spence did not even remark that his daughter was unusually pale, nor that her dress was less neat than usual, as she carried in his tea and toast. She was there, and that was everything for him. That she had been this morning flying like a hunted thing from Smokeford, sobbing in the grass five miles away from her home; that he had lost her for ever, only for a strange old man following a plough in a distant field; of these things he never could know. Hetty was one of the people who do not complain of the rigour of the struggle that is past.

All day she sat by her father's side, in the old place behind the bed-curtain. He was getting better, and showed more lively interest in the world than she had seen in him since he first fell ill. Through the window he could see, as he lay, the little roof-garden which had been accustomed to look gay every summer for years. It was colourless now and untrimmed.

"Hetty, dear," he said, "how is it that you have been neglecting your flowers? Perhaps you think it isn't worthwhile to keep up the little garden any longer? You will be going off with Anthony. Is any day settled for the wedding?"

"No, father," said Hetty, keeping her white, drawn face well behind the curtain. "We could not think of that until you are on your feet again."

In spite of her effort to save him the pain of an unhappy thought just now, something in her voice struck upon the old man strangely. He was silent for a while, and lay ruminating.

"Hetty, let me see your face."

Hetty looked forth from her hiding-place unwillingly, but kept her face as much as possible from the light.

"What do you want with it, daddy? You have seen it before."

"'Tis a comely face, Hetty; and others have thought so besides me. I don't like the look on it now, my girl. Child! what's the matter with you? Out with it this minute! If he's going to fail you, it will be a black day for the man. I'll murder him!"

"Hush! hush! I have told you nothing of the kind."

"Deny it, then, this moment; and tell me no lie."

Hetty sat silent and scared.

"Is it that doll from Moor-Edge that has taken his fancy?"

"He has not told me so."

"My lass! why do you play hide-and-seek with your old father? I know it is as I have said. Let me rise! Do not hold me; for I will horse-whip him to death!"

Hetty held him fast by the wrists.

"I will turn her out-of-doors without a character; and, though I am a weak, old man, I will punish him before the eyes of the town."

For a moment Hetty's angry heart declared in silence that they would deserve such punishment; and that she could bear to see it. But she said—

"Father, you know you will do neither of those cruel things. Listen to me, father. I am tired of Anthony! Let him go with—Primula. You and I will be happy here together when they are gone."

The old man fell back on his pillow exhausted. After a time, he drew his daughter towards him, took her face between his hands, and looked at it.

"Let it be as you say," he said, "only don't let me see them. You're a brave girl; and I'll never scold you again. We'll be happy when they're gone. We'll finish that little book of mine, and—and—and——"

His voice became indistinct, and he dropped suddenly asleep. Hetty sat on in her corner, thinking over her future, and thanking Heaven that she had at least this loving father left to her. After an hour or two had passed, she looked up and noticed a change in the old man's face. He was dead.

CHAPTER 4

It was new and awful to Hetty to have neither father nor lover to turn to in her desolation. She got over one terrible week, and then when the old man was fairly under the clay she broke down and fell ill, and Sib nursed her. Primula hung about the house, feeling guilty and uncomfortable, and Anthony came sometimes to ask how Hetty fared. He brought fruit and ice for her, offering them timidly, and Sib accepted them gladly and poured out her anxiety to him, all unconscious that there was anything wrong between the lovers. Primula sulked at Anthony, who seemed to be thinking much more of Hetty than of her. The old book-shop was closed for good, and the Spences' happy little home was already a thing of the past.

Hetty thought she would be glad to die; but people cannot die through mere wishing, and so she got better. When she was able to rise Sib carried her into the little sitting-room and placed her in her father's old armchair; and seated here, one warm summer evening, she sent to beg Anthony to come and speak with her.

Anthony's heart turned sick within him as he looked on the wreck of his once-adored Hetty. Her wasted cheeks and hollow eyes made a striking contrast to Primula's fair smooth beauty. Yet in her spiritual gaze and on her delicate lips there still sat a charm which Anthony knew of old, and still felt; a charm which Primula never could possess.

"We are not going to talk about the past," said Hetty, when the first difficult moments were over. "I only want to tell you that Primula and you are not to look on me as an enemy. I am her only living friend, and this is her only home. She shall be married from here; and then we will separate and meet no more."

"You are too good," he stammered, "too thoughtful for us both. Hetty," he added, hesitatingly, "I dare not apologise for my conduct, nor ask your forgiveness. I can only say I did not intend it. I know not how it came about—she bewitched me."

Hetty bowed her head with a cold, stately little gesture, and Anthony backed out of the room, feeling himself rebuked, dismissed, forgiven. He went to Primula; and Hetty sat alone in the soft summer evening, just where they two had sat a year ago planning their future life.

"She is too good for me," thought Anthony, as he walked up the street. "Primula will vex me more, but she will suit me better."

Still, he felt a bitter pang as he told himself that Hetty's love for him was completely gone. Of course, it was better that it should be so, but still—he knew well that Primula could never be to him the sweet enduring wife that Hetty would have been. He knew also that his love for Primula was not of the kind that would last; whereas Hetty would have made his peace for all time. Well, the mischief was done now, and could not be helped. He hardly knew himself how he had slipped into his present position.

When Hetty found that she had indeed got to go on with her life, she at once set about marking out her future. She had a cousin living on an American prairie with her husband and little children, who had often wished that Hetty would come out to her. And Hetty determined to go. She sold off the contents of the old book-shop, only keeping one or two volumes, which, with her father's unfinished manuscript, she stowed away carefully in her trunk. Primula had given up her work at the dressmaker's, and was busy making her clothing for her wedding. Hetty was engaged in getting ready for her journey. The two girls sat all day together sewing. They spoke little, and there was no pretence of cordiality between them. Hetty had strained herself to do her utmost for this friendless creature, who had wronged her, but she could find no smiles nor pleasant words to lighten the task.

Pale and silent, she did her work with trembling fingers and a frozen heart. Primula, on her side, sulked at Hetty, as if Hetty had been the aggressor, and sighed and shed little tears between the fitting on and the trimming of her pretty garments. In the evenings, Primula was wont to fold up her sewing, and go out to walk; with Anthony, supposed Hetty, who sometimes allowed herself to weep in the twilight, and sometimes walked about the darkening room, chafing for the hour to come which would carry her far away from these old walls, with their intolerable memories.

So Hetty endured the purgatory to which she had voluntarily condemned herself. Anthony came into the house no more; Primula had her walks with him, and sometimes it was very late when she came home. But Hetty never chid her now. Primula was her own mistress, and could come and go as she liked, from under this roof, which her cousin's generosity was upholding over her head.

One evening, a gossip of the neighbourhood, one who had known Hetty in her cradle, came in with a long piece of knitting in her hands, to sit an hour with Hetty, and keep her company.

"And so they do say you are going to America," she said, "all alone, that long journey, and everybody thinking this many a day that it was you that was to marry Anthony Frost. And now it is that Primula. People did say, my dear, that they have treated you badly between them, but I couldn't believe that, and you behaving so beautifully to them. Of course, it shuts people's mouths to see the girl stopping here with you and preparing for her wedding."

Said Hetty, "I cannot take the trouble to contradict idle stories. Anthony Frost is a very old friend, and Primula is my cousin. It would be strange if I did not try to be of use to them."

"Of course, of course, when there's no reason for your being angry with them; but all the same, my dear, you'd have been a far better wife for him than that flighty little fool that he has chosen. He has changed his mind about many a thing it seems, for he has taken a house in Smokeford, and is setting up as a cabinet-maker, instead of turning out a sculptor, no less, as some people said he had a mind to do. Well, well! it's none of my business to be sure, and I do hope they'll be as happy as if they had both been a bit wiser."

"I see no reason why they should not be happy," said Hetty, determined to act her part to the end. And the gossip went away protesting to her neighbours that there never could have been anything but friendship between Anthony and Hetty.

"There's no girl that had been cheated could behave as she's doing," said the gossip, "and she's as brave as a lion about the journey to America." And after this people found Hetty not so interesting as they had thought her some time ago.

The time for the wedding approached. Primula's pretty dresses and knick-knacks of ornaments were finished and folded in a trunk, and she arranged them and re-arranged them; took them out and tried them on, and put them back again. She went out for her evening walks, and Hetty waited up for her return, and let her into the house in the fine starlight of the summer nights, and the two girls went to bed in silence, and neither sought to know anything of the thoughts of the other. And so, it went on till the night that was the eve of Primula's wedding. On that night Primula went out as usual and did not come back.

The arrangement for the next day had been that Anthony and Primula should be married early in the morning, and go from church to their home. Hetty intended starting on her own journey a few hours later, but she said nothing about her intention, wishing to slip away quietly out of her old life at the moment when the minds of her acquaintance were occupied, and their eyes fully filled with the wedding.

She did not wonder that Primula should stay out late on that particular evening. It was a beautiful night, the sky a dark blue, the moonlight soft and clear. Hetty wandered restlessly in and out the few narrow chambers of her old home, once so delightful and beloved, now grown so dreary and haunted, and saw the silver light shining on the roofs and chimneys, and on the dead flowers and melancholy evergreens of her little roof-garden. Only a year ago she had cherished those withered stalks, with Anthony by her side, and they had smiled together over their future in the glory of the sunrise. Now all that fresh morning light was gone, the blossoms were withered away, and her heart was withered also. Faith and hope were dead, and life remained with its burden to be carried. She shut her eyes from sight of the deserted walls, with their memories, and thought of the great world-wide sea, which she had never beheld, but must now reach and cross; and she longed to be on its bosom with her burden.

The hours passed and Primula did not return. Hetty thought this strange, but it did not concern her. Primula and her lover and their affairs seemed to have already passed out of her life and left her alone. She did not go to bed all night, and she knew she was waiting for Primula, but her mind was so lost in its own loneliness that it could not dwell upon the conduct of the girl. The daylight broke, and found her sitting pale and astonished in the empty house, and then her eyes fell on a letter which the night-shadows had hidden from her where it lay on the table. It was written in Primula's scratchy writing, and was addressed to Hetty.

Primula wrote:

I am going away to be married. Anthony and you were very good to me once, but you are too cold and stern for me lately. The person I am going with is kinder and pleasanter. I am to be married in London, and after that I am to be taken to travel. When I come back, I shall be a grand lady, and I shall come to Smokeford; and I shall order some dresses from Miss Flounce, I can tell you. I am very glad that Anthony and you can be married after all. He was always thinking of you more than me; I could see that this long while back. I hope you will be happy, and that you will be glad to see me on my return.

Your affectionate Primula.

Hetty sat a long time motionless, quite stupefied, with the letter in her hand.

"Poor little ungrateful mortal," thought she; "Heaven shield her, and keep her from harm!" And then she thought of her own little cup of life-happiness spilled on the earth for this.

"Oh, what waste! what waste!" moaned poor Hetty, twisting the note in her fingers. And then she straightened it and folded it again, and put it in an envelope addressed to Anthony, and she hastened to send it to him, lest the hour should arrive for the wedding, and the bridegroom should come into her presence seeking his bride.

When this had been despatched, she set about cording her trunks, and taking her last farewell of Sib, who was too old to follow her to America, and was nigh heartbroken at staying behind. When the last moment came, she ran out of the house without looking right or left. And she was soon in the coach, and the coach was on its way to the seaport from whence her vessel was to sail.

When Anthony received the note, he felt much anger and amazement, but very little grief. Primula's audacity electrified him; and then he remembered that she was not treating him worse than he had treated Hetty. Let her go! she was a light creature, and would have brought him misery if she had married him. Her soft foolish beauty and bewitching ways faded from his mind after half-an-hour's meditation; and Anthony declared himself free. And there was Hetty still in her nest behind the old book-shop; as sweet and as precious as when they were lovers a year ago. The last few months were only a dream, and this was the satisfactory awaking.

Hetty's pale cheeks would become round and rosy once more. She must forgive him for the past, so urgently would he plead with her. How exceedingly badly he had behaved!

Anthony put on his hat and went out to take a walk along a road little frequented, eager to escape from the gaze of his acquaintance in the town, anxious to think things thoroughly over, and to consider how soon he could dare to present himself to Hetty. Not for a long time, he was afraid. He remembered her stern pale look when he had last seen her, and how sure he had felt when turning away from her that her love was dead. A chill came over him, and he hung his head as he walked. Hetty was never quite like other girls, and it might be—it might be that her heart would be frozen to him for evermore.

Just at this moment a cloud of dust enveloped Anthony, and the mail coach passed him, whirling along at rapid speed. Hetty was in the coach, and she saw him, walking dejectedly on the road alone with his trouble. She turned her face away lest he should see her; and then her heart gave one throb that made her lean from the window, and wave her hand to him in farewell. He saw her; he rushed forward; the coach whirled round a bend of the road.

Hetty was gone.

The Fit of Ailsie's Shoe

CHAPTER 1

On a certain mellow August afternoon an old woman was travelling along the sea-girt road between Portrush and Dunluce. She wore a long grey cloak, and a scarlet neckerchief thrown over her white cap. Her face was unusually sallow and wrinkled, with small, shrewd, furtive eyes. She carried a stick, and halted now and then from fatigue.

She looked often from right to left, and from left to right, over the sea, heaving helplessly under its load of blazing brooding glory, and inland, over the stretches of green and golden, where cattle browsed and corn ripened. She seemed like one not assured of her way, and looking for landmarks. Presently she stopped beside some boys who were playing marbles under a hedge to ask whereabouts might stand the house of one James MacQuillan.

"Is it Jamie's you want?" said the eldest lad; "there it's up the hill yonder, with its shoulder agin the haystack. But if you're goin' there, I'll tell you that Ailsie's out at the fair. Mother saw her pass our door at sunrise this mornin'."

From the way he gave his information, the urchin evidently thought that, Ailsie being from home, it was worth no one's while to climb the hill to Jamie's. No way staggered in her purpose by the news, however, the old woman proceeded on her travels, and took her way towards the haystack.

She plodded up a green-hedged lonan, and emerged from it on a causeway of round stones bedded in clay. Here stood "Jamie's," a white cottage smothered in fuchsia-trees. There was a sweet scent of musk and sitherwood hanging about, and a wild rose was nailed against the gable. A purple pigeon was cooing on the russet thatch, and a lazy cloud of smoke was reluctantly mingling its blue vapour with the yellow evening air. Overtopping the chimney there rose a golden cock of new-made hay. The old woman snuffed the fragrant breath of the place, poked at the fuchsia-bushes with her stick, and peered all about

65

her with her shrewd bright eyes. At last, she approached the open door, and looked across the threshold.

There was a small room with a clay floor, a fire winking on the hearth almost blinded out by the sun, a spinning-wheel in the corner, an elderly woman knitting beside the window, and a check-curtained bed standing in the corner, in which a sickly man sat up with a newspaper spread on his knees.

"God save all here!" said the visitor, pushing in her head at the door. "An' is this Jamie MacQuillan's?"

"As sure as my name's Jamie," said the weakly man, taking off his spectacles. "Take a seat, ma'am. You'd be a thraveller maybe, comin' home from the fair?"

The old woman had dropped into a chair, panting with fatigue.

"It's no shame for ye," she gasped, "that ye don't know me, seein' that ye never set eyes on me before; but I'm wan o' the McCambridges, from beyont Lough Neagh, an' I've walked every foot o' the road to see you an' yours."

"Why, you don't mane to say that?" cried Jamie, his pale face lighting up. "You don't mane to say you're Shaun McCambridge's sisther, Penny, own cousin to my father's second wife, that was to have stood for our Ailsie at her christenin', only she took a pain in her heel and couldn't stir from home? Faith, an' I might have knowed you by the fine hook o' your nose, always an' ever the sign o' the rale ould blood. Throth that same blood's thicker nor wather. Mary machree, it's Penny McCambridge, from Lough Neagh side!"

Mary, the wife, now lifted her voice in welcome.

"Good luck to you, Cousin Penny," she said. "The sight o' wan o' your folks is the cure for sore eyes. Come over an' give us the shake o' your han', for not a stir can I stir this year past with the pains, no more nor Jamie there that's down on his back since May. Och, it's the poor do-less pair we'd be only for our Ailsie, that's han's an' feet to us both, an' keeps things together out an' in."

A great hand-shaking followed this speech, and then the visitor began to inquire for Ailsie, her god-daughter, that was to have been, only for the unfortunate pain in the heel.

"Wait a bit, wait a bit," said the father; "she'll be in from the fair by-an'-by, an' then if ye don't give her the degree for the han'somest girl and the best manager that ever stepped about a house, I'll give ye lave to go back to Lough Neagh an' spend the rest o' your days sarchin' for her aiquals."

"Whisht, Jamie," said the mother; "self-praise is no praise, no more is praise o' yer own flesh an' blood. All the same, I wisht Ailsie was in to make Cousin Penny the cup o' tay afther her thravels. She was to bring a grain o' the best green from Misther McShane's, in Portrush, as well as all the news from Castle Craigie, an' of the doin's of ould Lady Betty MacQuillan, more power to her!"

"Is that the ould lady that's come home from Ingia?" asked she who was called Penny McCambridge.

"Ay, ay," said the wife of Jamie eagerly. "Ye've passed through Portrush, an' ye'll maybe have the foreway of Ailsie with the news. What are they saying in the town?"

"Well, ye see," said Penny, "bein' a sthranger, and spakin' to few, I heard but little. But they do say that her husband was the last of the MacQuillans of Castle Craigie, an' that as she has ne'er a child of her own, all the MacQuillans in the counthry are claimin' kin with her, an' fightin' among them about which'll be her heir."

"An' is that all ye know, Penny dear?" said Mary. "Why, I have more nor that mysel'. Sure she's written round an' round to every MacQuillan o' them all, biddin' them to a grand house-warmin' on Wensday come eight days, when she'll settle it all, an' name who's to come afther her. An' though she's in London now, she'll be at Castle Craigie afore then to resave them. An' sich a resavin' as that'll be! Sich fixin' an' furbishin' as there is at the ould castle. They say there never was the likes o' it seen since the day Sir Archie MacQuillan brought home his fairy bride, an' then it wasn't painters an' bricklayers, but the good people themselves that laid han's on the rooms."

"She must be a queer sort of a body," said Penny. "But I hope, Jamie, that you, as honest a man, an' as good a MacQuillan as ever a wan among them, I hope you haven't been shy of sendin' in your claim."

"Och, Penny, if you'd only put that much spunk into him!" cried Mary, with energy, "it's what I'm sayin' to him mornin', noon, an' night, an' it's no more to him than the crickets chirpin'."

"Stop your grumblin', Mary," said the husband; "there's richer nor us, and there's poorer, but we're not so mane yet as to go cravin' for what we're not likely to get. It's not to MacQuillans like us that Lady Betty has sent her invite."

"An' more shame for her!" cried Mary, waxing wroth. "Listen to me, Cousin Penny. When Lady Betty's husband, Sir Dinis MacQuillan that's dead an' gone, was nothing but plain Dinis, an' the youngest of seven sons, he went off an' married wan or'nary-faced, low-born lass, called Betty O'Flanigan, an' brought her all the way from County Wexford to Castle Craigie here, thinkin' he had nothin' to do in the world but ring the gate bell, an' walk in with his wife. It was Christmas-time, an' hard weather, an' sich feastin' an' visitin' goin' on at the castle, when all at wanst the news o' the marriage come down like a clap on the family.

"It took six men to hold ould Sir Patrick, he was in that mad a rage, an' you may guess it was little welcome poor Betty got when Dinis brought her to the door. The two o' them had just to turn back the way they come, an' it beginnin' to snow, when Jamie there, that was then a lad of fifteen, he was standin' out by his mother's door, an' he spied them comin' down the road. Betty had on a fine gown, but she looked very lonesome, poor body, an' Jamie knowin' what had happened, he up an' he says:

"'Mrs. MacQuillan,' says he, 'it's comin' on a storrm, an' it'll be hard on you goin' further the night,' says he. 'And if you'll be so. good as to step inside,' says he, 'it's my mother'll be glad to see you.'

"Poor Betty was glad to hear the word, an' in she went, an' stay there she did for two weeks, till her husband got their passage taken out to Ingia. An' when she was goin' away, an' biddin' goodbye, she says to Jamie, she says, 'Jamie, my boy, if ever Betty MacQuillan comes home from Ingia a rich woman, she'll find out you an' yours, if you're above the arth, an' mind you, she'll pay you back your good turn!'

"Many's the time I hard the story from Jamie's mother, rest her sowl!" Mary went on. "An' it's the fine fortune Dinis an' Betty made in Ingia. Two years back, when the last of the brothers died without childer, we hard that Sir Dinis was comin' back to end his days in Castle Craigie. But that news wasn't stale till we hard o' his death, poor man! An' now Betty's comin' back her lone, a rich woman, an' a fine lady. An' I'll just ax you, Cousin Penny, if it wouldn't fit her betther to be lookin' afther Jamie there, that offered her the shelter o' the roof when she was in need o't, than to be huntin' up a pack o' highfliers, the very set that sneered an' sniggered over her disgrace in the dhrawn-room at the castle, the day she was turned from the gates?"

Cousin Penny had given attentive ear to the wife, and now she turned to the husband.

"What do you say to that now, Jamie?" she asked, with a knowing twinkle of her shrewd bright eyes.

"I say this," cried Jamie, crackling and folding at his paper with energy. "I say that the man or boy, it's all wan, that does a good turn expectin' to be paid for it, desarves no more thanks than a man that sells a cow and dhrives a good bargain. An' I say that Mary ought to be ashamed to sit there talking of sich a thing that happened forty year ago, an' if Ailsie was here she wouldn't—but good luck to her! there she is hersel', gone past the window."

All the three pairs of eyes were now turned to the doorway, whose sunny space was obscured for a moment by as pretty a figure as any lover of fresh and pleasant sights could wish to see. This was a ripe-faced, dark-haired country girl, with her coarse straw bonnet tipped over her forehead, to save her eyes from the sun, and her neat print gown tucked tidily up over her white petticoat.

"Come in, Ailsie!" cried Jamie, "come in an' see your cousin, Penny McCambridge, from Lough Neagh side, that was to have been your godmother, an' has come every fut o' the road from that to this, to see what sort o' lass you've turned out."

"Make haste an' make us the cup o' tay," said her mother. "I hope you didn't forget to bring us a grain o' the best green from Misther McShane's? Good girl! An' how did yer eggs an' butter sell? I'll lay you a shillin' you haven't the sign o' either wan or the other to set before the sthranger this day!"

"Maybe I haven't though!" said Ailsie, laughing. "It's by the fine good luck I put by two nice little pats undher a dish, afore I went off this mornin'. An' as for eggs, if Mehaffy hasn't laid wan afore this time o' day, I'll put her in the pot for a lazy big hen, an' Cousin Penny 'll stay an' help to ate her."

A nice little meal was set, and Ailsie flung herself on a bench to rest.

"An' now you'll have breath to tell us the news, Ailsie," said Mary, the mother, sipping her tea complacently. "What's doin' an' sayin' in Portrush about Lady Betty?"

"Oh troth, mother!" said Ailsie, tossing her head, "troth I'm sick, sore, an' tired, hearin' o' the quare old house she's pulled down on her back, poor body! Sich gregin' an' comparin' you never hard since the day you were born. The frien's o' wan MacQuillan, an' the frien's o' another, at it hard an' fast for which'll have the best chance of comin' in for the ould lady's favour. An' sich preparations! Mrs. Quinn, the housekeeper, took me all through the castle to see the new grandeur; an' sich curtains, an' pictures, an' marble images, an' sich lookin'-glass-es! feth, when I went to the dhrawn-room door, I thought I'd gone crazy, for half-a-dozen other Ailsies started up in the corners an' all

69

over the walls, an' come to meet me with their baskets on their arms.

"An' then there's the ballroom where the dancin's to be, all hung round with green things, an' the floor as slippy an' as shiny as the duck-pond was last Christmas in the long frost. An' I went into Miss O'Trimmins', the dressmaker, to see if her toothache was better, an' I do declare she could hardly reach me her little finger across the heaps of silks an' muzlins that she had piled about her there in her room. An' while I was there, a carriage dashed up to the door, an' out stepped the five Miss MacQuillans from Bally Scuffling, an' in they all came to have their dresses tried on.

"An' Miss O'Trimmins kept me to hold the pins while she was fittin' them, for all her girls were that busy they could hardly stop to thread their needles. An' sich pinchin' an' screwin'! When they went away, I said to Miss O'Trimmins, 'I'm thankful,' says I, 'that none o' these gowns is for me.' An' she laughed, and says she, 'I wouldn't put it past you, Ailsie, to be right glad to go to the same ball if you got the chance.'

"'I'm not so sure o' that,' says I, 'but, as for chance, my name's Mac-Quillan as well as it's theirs that were here this minute lookin' at me as if I was the dirt undher their feet. An' put it to pride or not,' says I, 'but I do think, if I was done up grand, I could manage to cut as good a figure in a ball-room as e'er a wan o' them red-nosed things that are goin' to dress themsel's up in all this fine grass-coloured satin!' It was very impident an' ill done o' me to make such a speech," said Ailsie, blushing at her confession, which had sent Cousin Penny into fits of laughter, "but my blood was up, somehow, with the looks o' them old things from Bally Scuffling, an' I couldn't hold my tongue!"

"Go on, go on, Ailsie dear!" said Penny, wiping her eyes.

"Oh, then," said Ailsie, "she began talkin' the same kind o' stuff that they were botherin' me with the day through, axin' me why my father hadn't sent word to Lady Betty like the rest o' the MacQuillans, tellin' me we were the only wans o' the name that hadn't spoken. It's just the wan word in all their mouths. Mrs. Maginty, that buys my eggs, she was at it; an' ould Dan Carr, that takes my butter from me, I thought I'd never get him talked down, an' Nancy McDonnell that was sellin' sweeties in the fair, an' Katty O'Neil that was goin' about with me all day, an' Mrs. McShane that I bought the tea from. Och! I couldn't remember the wan half o' them!"

"An' what did you say to them, Ailsie dear?" asked Mary, the mother, insinuatingly.

"Why," said Ailsie, "I tould them first, that all the rest o' the Mac-Quillans about were ladies an' gentlemen, an' would be creditable to Lady Betty when she made her choice, but that my father was a poor man that had nothin' to do with the comin's an' goin's o' genthry. But when that wouldn't do, I up an' told them that he had too much feelin' for a lonely old woman comin' home without a friend in her ould age, to think of beginnin' to worry her about what would be to divide afther her death, afore ever she set foot in the counthry. 'It's an ill welcome for all their fine talking,' said I, 'an' if they hadn't put her an' pesthered her to it, she would never be for doin' the quare thing she's goin' to do on Wensday week night.' An' what do you think she is goin' to do, father?" said Ailsie, turning to Jamie, "but she's to have a big cake made, an' a ring in it, an' every MacQuillan at the feast gets a piece o' the cake, an' whoever finds the ring, as sure as he's there he's the wan to share Lady Betty's fortune, an' come afther her in Castle Craigie!"

Here Mary the mother began to groan and rock herself, and complain of the obstinacy of people who would not stretch out their hands for a piece of that lucky cake, when it might be theirs for the asking. Jamie was getting very red in the face, and crumpling his paper very fiercely, when Penny, who had been laughing again, once more wiped her eyes, and taking her stick from the corner, prepared to depart.

"It's getting far in the day," she said, "an' I have a good bit further to go afore night, to see my old friend Madgey Mucklehern, that lives in the Windy Gap; good luck is hers she hasn't been blown out o't house an' all afore this! But I'll be back this way," she added; "don't you think ye've seen the last o' Penny McCambridge, Cousin Jamie, for feth ye'll know more o' me shortly, if the Lord spares me my breath for a wheen more o' weeks."

And Penny McCambridge shook hands with her kinsfolk, and trotted away down the lonan, as she had come.

CHAPTER 2

It was only a few evenings after this that Ailsie was sitting on the end of the kitchen-table, reading the newspaper to her father.

" Na—na," said Ailsie, stumbling at a word, "vi—vi, ga—ga Och, my blessin' to the word, I can't make head or tail o't. Ye'll read it betther yersel', father; an' it's time I was goin' feedin' my hens, anyhow!"

"Ailsie," said Jamie, rubbing his spectacles, "I'm feared you're

71

turnin' out a bad dark afther all the throuble Misther Devnish has taken wi' you. Ye'r' gettin' a big woman, Ailsie, an' there's not a thing ye'r' bad at but the clarkin'. Go off to school, now, this very evenin', and give my respects to Hughie Devnish, an' tell him to tache you how to spell navigation afore you come back."

Ailsie coloured, and her thick black lashes rested on her russet cheeks while she tucked up her gown and kneaded the wet meal for the hens with her gipsy hands. But as she left the house she looked back with a wicked little toss of her head.

"Then you an' Hughie Devnish may put it out o' yer heads that ye'll ever make a dark o' Ailsie," she said; "for if ye wer to boil down all the larnin'-books that ever cracked a school-masther's skull, an' feed her on nothin' but that for the next ten years, ye wouldn't have her wan bit the larnder in the hinder end!"

So saying, she stepped out into the sun, and was busy feeding her hens under the shelter of the golden haycock, when she saw a servant in a showy livery coming riding up the lonan.

"Can you tell me where Miss MacQuillan lives about here, my good girl?" he asked, with a supercilious glance at Ailsie's wooden dish.

"No," said Ailsie, looking at him with her head thrown back. "That's Jamie MacQuillan's house"—pointing to the gable—"an' I'm his daughter Ailsie, but there's no Miss MacQuillan here; none nearer by this road nor Bally Scuffling."

"I beg your pardon, miss," said the man, with an altered manner, "but I believe this must be for you."

And then he rode off, leaving her standing staring at a dainty pink note which she held by one corner between two mealy fingers. "Miss Ailsie MacQuillan," said the ink on the back of the narrow satin envelope.

"That's me!" said Ailsie, with a gasp. "The rest o' them's all Lizabeths, an' Isabellas, an' Aramintys. An', as thrue as I'm a livin' girl, it's the Castle Craigie liveries yon fine fellow was dressed up so grand in, an' here's the Castle Craigie crest on this purty little seal."

It was a note of invitation to Lady Betty's ball, and, in spite of her bad "clarkin'," Ailsie was able to read it, spelling it out word after word, turning it back and forward and upside-down, and feeling sure all the time that somebody had played a trick on her by writing to Lady Betty in her name. She sat on a stone and made her reflections, with the sun all the while burning her cheeks, and making them more and more unfit to appear in a ballroom.

"An' she thinks I'm some fine young lady in a low neck an' satin shoes, waitin' all ready to step into her ballroom an' make her a curtsey. Good luck to her! What'd she say if she heard Ailsie's brogues hammerin' away on yon fine slippy floor o' hers?" And Ailsie, as she spoke, extended one little roughshod foot and looked at it critically. "Then thank you, Lady Betty; but I'm not goin' to make mysel' a laughin' stock for the counthry yet!"

"Who came ridin' up the lonan a bit ago, Ailsie ?" said the mother, when she went in with the note safely hidden in her pocket.

"Ridin' up the lonan is it?" said Ailsie.

"Ay, ay," said Mary, "I thought I hard a horse's fut on the road, but it be to been yer father snorin'."

"Me snorin'!" cried Jamie, starting and rubbing his eyes. "Ye'r dhramin' yersel', Mary. Ailsie, ye witch, are ye not gone to school yet?"

"Well, I'll go now, father," said Ailsie. "Maybe," she thought, "Hughie 'll tell me what to do with that letter afore I come back."

A thatched house, with a row of small latticed windows blinking down at the sea in the strong sunset, with a grotesque thorn looking over the more distant gable, and an army of fierce hollyhocks mustering about the little entry-door. This was the school, and Mr. Hugh Devnish was at this moment standing at his desk, writing "head-line" in the copy-books of his pupils; a young man with a grave busy face, and one hand concealed in the breast of his coat.

That hand was deformed, and so Hugh Devnish had been brought up to teach school, instead of to follow the plough. That such breeding had not been wasted, his face announced. Even the country people around held him in unusual respect, though he did not give them half as many long words, nor talk Latin to them, like his predecessor, Larry O'Mullan, who had died of hard study, poor boy! at the age of eighty-five.

Hughie glanced through the window before him, got suddenly red in the face, and cried, "Attention!" in a voice which made all the lads and lasses look up from their copy-books. The next moment a gipsy-faced girl walked in, hung up her bonnet, and sat down on a form.

"What's your word, Ailsie MacQuillan?" asked the schoolmaster, taking her book with a severe and business-like air.

"Invitation, sir—navigation, I mane," said Ailsie, demurely, studying her folded hands.

The master looked at her sharply, and afterwards frowned severely when, on going the rounds of the desks, he found "Lady Betty Mac-

Quillan," "Castle Craigie," and other foolish and meaningless words, scrawled profanely over the page which was to have been sacred to navigation alone. Ailsie was "kept in" for bad conduct, and locked up alone in the school after the other pupils had gone home. And there, when the schoolmaster came to release her, she was found plucking the roses that hung in at the window, and sticking them in the holes for the ink-bottles along the desks. A crumpled note lay open before her.

We should hardly have said the schoolmaster came in, for, though it was Hughie Devnish, he appeared in a new character. This punished girl was his wildest and least creditable pupil, and yet, when he walked up to her in her disgrace, he was trembling and blushing like his own youngest "scholar" coming up for a whipping. His eye caught the crumpled note, and he picked it up and read it.

"I guessed how 'twas," he said, "but you're surely not thinkin' of goin'?"

Now Ailsie had intended to ask his advice, but the mischief that was in her would come out.

"Why should I not go as well as another?" she asked pettishly.

"Aroon, you know I would not like it," he said.

"An' that's a reason, feth!" said Ailsie, tossing her head, and beginning to pick a rose to pieces.

"Ailsie," said the young man vehemently, "it was only the other day you told me here that you could like me better than all the world, better than Ned Mucklehern, for all his fine land and his presents o' butther an' crame; better than Mehaffy the miller, that gave you the fine speckled hen; better than MacQuillan o' the Reek——"

"Bad manners to him!" struck in Ailsie angrily, flinging a shower of rose-leaves from her hand over the desks.

"You promised to be my wife, Ailsie."

"It all come o' keepin' me in for bad conduct," said Ailsie, swinging one foot with provoking unconcern.

"No matter what it came of," said Hughie, "you promised me. And you promised me as well that you wouldn't go thrustin' yourself among these people, that would only laugh at you for your pains."

"I don't know why you should think I'd be laughed at," said Ailsie, "barrin' you're ashamed o' me!"

The schoolmaster's face blazed up, and with all his heart in his eyes he gazed at her where she sat with her ripe face half turned from the sun coming through the lattice, and her dark head framed in the roses.

"Ashamed o' you, mavoureen?" he said tenderly, "No; but there might be some there that I wouldn't like you to come across, an' you alone an' unprotected. MacQuillan o' the Reek———"

"I slapped his face wanst!" cried Ailsie, firing up again, "an' it's not likely he'll come axin' me to do't again."

"And there'll be others there," he went on, "that'd fall in love wi' you maybe, an' snatch you up from Hughie before he has enough earned to marry you out o' hand."

"An' what if they did?" said Ailsie, with wicked coolness.

"What if they did?" repeated Devnish slowly, looking at her with a pained appealing look, as if expecting her to retract the cruel words. "I tell you what it is, Ailsie," he broke out passionately, drawing his left hand from its concealment, "I believe it's this that's workin' at the bottom o' all your coldness. You're tired already of a deformed lover. Go to Lady Betty's ball then, an' find a husband for yourself that you'll not be ashamed of. Go———"

Just as Ailsie was getting pale, and the tears were coming into her eyes, a little door opened, and a good-humoured-looking country-woman came into the schoolroom.

"Come in to your supper, Hughie," she said. "Och, is it Ailsie Mac-Quillan in penance the night again? Girl alive! is it a love-letther you're showin' the masther?"

"No, indeed, Mrs. Devnish," said Ailsie, erecting her head; "it's a note of invitation from Lady Betty MacQuillan, axin' me to do her the honour of dancin' at her ball at Castle Craigie on Wensday come eight days."

"Oh, then, then! but you're the lucky girl," cried the Widow Devnish, clapping her hands over the note, while Hughie stalked away silently to a window by himself. "I declare it's as grand an' as beautyful as if it was written to the Queen. Asthore! an' has your mother any sense left at all, with the dint o' the joy?"

"She didn't see it yet," stammered Ailsie, seeing now the scrape into which she had got herself through yielding to her reckless whim of tormenting her lover. "I got it just as I left home, an' she didn't see it yet."

"An' you're stan'in' up there as if nothin' had happened you, you ongrateful colleen," said the Widow Devnish, pocketing the note. "Wait a minute, then, till I get the cloak, an' it's mysel' 'll go home wi' you, an' help to tell the news."

It was speedily settled between Mary MacQuillan and the Widow Devnish that Ailsie should go the ball.

"I have a fine piece of yellow Chaney silk," said the Widow Devnish, "that Sailor Johnny sent me from beyont the says. It would make her a skirt, barrin' it wasn't too long, an' a hem o' somethin' else lined on behind."

"An' I've a ducky bit o' cherry tabinet," said Mary, the mother, "that brother Pat, the weaver, sent me from Dublin to make a bonnet o'. It'll cut into a beautyful jockey for her, barrin' we don't make the sleeves too wide."

So, on the eventful night Ailsie was dressed out in the yellow silk skirt and cherry-coloured bodice, with a fine pair of stockings of Mary's own knitting, with magnificent clocks up the sides. Her little bog-trotting brogues were polished till you could see yourself in the toes, and a pair of elegant black silk mittens covered her hands up to her little brown knuckles, stretching up past her wrists to make amends for the scantiness of her sleeves. Then, she had a grand pair of clanking earrings as long as your little finger, which the Widow Devnish had worn as a bride; and the two mothers, taking each a side of the victim's head, plaited her thick black hair into endless numbers of fanciful braids, which they rolled round the crown of her head, and into which they planted a tortoiseshell comb, curved like the back of an armchair, which Jamie's mother had worn at his christening, and which towered over Ailsie's head like Minerva's helmet put on the wrong way.

Ned Mucklehern of the Windy Gap was to take her to Castle Craigie in his new spring cart; and two good hours before dark Ailsie was standing at the door, looking longingly for a glimpse of Hughie coming over the hill, to see how handsome she looked in her strange finery. But Hughie did not appear, and vowing vengeance on him for his "sulks," Ailsie submitted to be packed up in the cart.

"But it's no use takin' the rue now," she said. "I be to go through with it!" And 'with desperate bravery she said "goodnight" to Ned Mucklehern, who, at her command, set her down at a little distance from the entrance gates, out and in of which the carriages were rolling at such a rate as made poor Ailsie's heart thump against her side, till it was like to burst through Pat-the-weaver's tabinet.

She crept in through a little side-gate, and up the avenue, keeping as much as possible in shelter of the trees; but it was not quite dark yet, and the coachmen coming and going stared at her, taking her, maybe, for some masquerading gipsy or strolling actress, whom Lady Betty had engaged to amuse the company. She arrived at the hall door just in time to see a flock of young ladies in white robes float gracefully over the threshold, and the absurdity of her own costume came before her in its terrible reality. Covered with confusion, she looked about to see if she could escape among the trees, and hide there till morning; but one of the grand servants had espied her, and under his eyes Ailsie scorned to beat a retreat.

"What is your business here, young woman?" asked this awful person, as she stepped into the glare of the hall lights.

"I am one of Lady Betty's guests," said Ailsie, lifting her head. But a horrible tittering greeted this announcement from a crowd of other servants, who were all eyeing her curiously from head to foot. Ailsie was ready to sink into the earth with shame and mortification, when, happily, the arrival of a fresh carriageful of guests diverted the general attention from herself, and she heard someone saying, "This way, miss." Glad to escape anywhere, she followed a servant whose face she could not see, but whose voice was wonderfully familiar. Passing through an inner hall, her hand was grasped by this person, and she was swiftly drawn into a pantry and the door shut.

"Oh, Hughie, Hughie!" cried Ailsie, bursting into tears, and clinging to his arm. "Then where did you dhrop from, anyways?"

"Whisht, avourneen!" said Hughie, "we haven't a minute to stay, for yon chaps'll be runnin' in an' out here all night. But do you think Hughie could rest aisy at home an' you unprotected in this place? Wan o' the fellows was knocked up with all the wine that's goin', an' they were glad to give me his place, an' his clothes. Ye won't feel so lonesome."

"Oh, Hughie, I wisht I'd stayed at home as you bid me. An' your han', Hughie?"

"Och, never mind it, asthore. I'll only carry small thrays, and the wan hand'll do beautiful. Come now, aroon." So, resuming his character of servant, Hughie squired his trembling lady-love up Lady Betty's gilded staircase.

The ball was held in an old-fashioned hall whose roof was crossed with dark rafters, from which gloomy old banners were swinging. The door was partly open and Ailsie peeped in.

"Oh, Hughie, Hughie!" she whispered, "take me back to the panthry! I'll lie close in a cupboard, an' never stir a stir till morning."

77

"It couldn't be done, darlin'," whispered Hughie. "Ye must put a bold face on it, an' take your chance."

He opened the door wide, and Ailsie felt herself swallowed up in a blaze of light and colour, with a hum in her ears as of a thousand bees all buzzing round her head at once. When she recovered from her first stunned sensation, and regained consciousness of her own identity, she found herself seated side by side with the five Miss MacQuillans from Bally Scuffling, all dressed in their grass-coloured satin, all with their noses redder than ever, all eyeing her askance from her comb to her brogues, and tittering just as the servants had done in the hall.

A band was playing, and a crowd of people were dancing, but it seemed to Ailsie, whenever she looked up, that nobody had got anything to do but to stare at her. When she saw the elegant slippers of the dancers she was afraid to stir lest the "hammerin'" of her feet should be heard all over the room; and when MacQuillan of the Reek came up to her, and, making a low bow, begged the honour of dancing with her, Ailsie's ears began to sing with confusion, and her teeth to chatter with fright.

But as she did not know how to refuse, she got up and accompanied him to where there was an empty space on the floor. The band was playing a lively tune as a quadrille, and Ailsie, thinking anything better than standing still, fell to dancing her familiar jig with energy. She had once slapped this gentleman's face for his impertinence, and she believed that he had now led her out to avenge himself by her confusion. So Ailsie danced her jig, and finding that the clatter of her brogues was drowned by the music, she gained courage and danced it with spirit, round and round her astonished partner, till the lookers-on cried "*Brava!*" and the laugh was turned against MacQuillan of the Reek, who was, after all, very glad when she made him her curtsey, and allowed him to take her back again to the Bally Scuffling maidens, who had not been dancing at all, and who held up their five fans before their five faces in disgust at Ailsie's performance.

A magic word, *supper* acted like a charm on all. The crowd thinned and disappeared, and nobody noticed Ailsie. Every gentleman had his own partner to attend to, and no one came near the little peasant girl. Ailsie was very glad, for she would rather endure hunger than be laughed at, and she was just beginning to nod asleep in her seat, when in came Hughie.

"I'm goin' to fetch you somethin' to ate, darlin'," he said, and hurried away again. And Ailsie was just beginning to nod asleep once more, when MacQuillan of the Reek came in, saying that Lady Betty had sent him to conduct her (Ailsie) to the supper-room.

Lady Betty was sitting at the head of the most distant table, with a knife in her hand and a huge cake before her. The more substantial eatables seemed to have been already discussed, for every guest had a slice of this cake on a plate before him or her. They were nibbling it, and mincing it up with knives. All were silent, and all looked anxious and dissatisfied. Ailsie thought the silence and the dissatisfaction were all on account of her audacious entrance.

"This way!" said Lady Betty MacQuillan, in a voice that made Ailsie start, and the august hostess cleared a place at her side for our blushing heroine. The wax-lights blazed on Lady Betty's golden turban, and Ailsie did not dare to look at her face. She sat down, and Lady Betty with her own hand helped her to a small cut of the wonderful cake. Ailsie was very hungry, and the cake was very good. She devoured a few morsels eagerly; then she ceased eating.

"Why don't you eat, child?" said Lady Betty, in a voice that again made Ailsie start; and this time she ventured to look up.

She looked up, and stared as if the clouds had opened above her head. There was a little withered yellow face, with twinkling black eyes, looking down on her—a face that she had seen before. It was Penny McCambridge, from Lough Neagh side, who was to have been her godmother only for the unfortunate pain in her heel, who was sitting there, dressed up in purple velvet and a cloth-of-gold turban. Oh, murther! What would be the end of this? Penny McCambridge befooling all the gentry folks of the country round, pretending to be the lady of Castle Craigie! Or, stay! Whether was Penny McCambridge acting Lady Betty MacQuillan, or had Lady Betty MacQuillan been acting Penny McCambridge?

"Why don't you eat, child?" repeated Lady Betty, as Ailsie sat turning her piece of cake about on her plate.

"I'm hungry enough," said Ailsie, "but I cannot ate this, my lady, barrin' you want me to choke mysel'!"

And Ailsie held up her bit of cake, in which was wedged the ring that declared her the heiress of Castle Craigie.

Well, I need not tell how, after supper, some of the guests who were spiteful ordered their carriages and whirled away in disgust; how others, who were not spiteful, stayed and danced the morning in; how some, who were good-natured, congratulated Ailsie on her good luck; how others, who were quite the reverse, yet fawned on the bewildered heroine of the evening. How Ailsie was kept close by the wonderful Lady Betty all the rest of the time; how she watched in vain for another glimpse of Hughie; how, in the end, she was conducted to a splendid bedchamber, where she was frightened out of her senses at the grandeur of the furniture, and could not get a wink of sleep for the softness of the stately bed.

The news was not long in travelling over the country, and next day, when a carriage dashed up to the foot of the lonan, Jamie and his wife thought they were prepared to receive their fortunate daughter with dignity. But when Ailsie walked in to them in a white pelisse and sandalled slippers, her bonnie dark eyes looking out at them from under a shade of a pink satin hat and feathers, this delusion of theirs was dispelled.

Mary's exultation knew no bounds, and Jamie said, "Can this fine lady be my daughter?" nervously, and with tears in his eyes. And Ailsie sat on a chair in the middle of the floor she had swept so often, and cried, and pulled off her fine hat, and threw it to the furthest corner of the kitchen, vowing she would never leave her father and mother to go and live with Lady Betty. And Lady Betty, who was present, was not a bit angry, although the beautiful hat was spoiled; but began telling how she would educate Ailsie, and take her to see the distant world, and how she would dress her like a princess, and marry her to some grand gentleman, who should bear the name of MacQuillan, or adopt it.

But Ailsie only crying worse at this than before, she threw a purse of gold into Mary's lap, and began describing all the good things she would do for Jamie and his wife if Ailsie would only come with her; how she would build them a pretty house; how they should have servants to attend them, and horses and cows, and money at command. And Ailsie, listening to this, cried more violently than ever, with her swollen eyes staring through the door, out to the hill that led across to Hughie's. Then, when Lady Betty had done, Mary the mother began.

Ailsie took her eyes from the open door, and looked at the father. But Jamie, afraid to mar his child's brilliant prospects, only hung his head, and said never a word at all.

Then Ailsie's heart seemed to break with one loud sob. "I'll go, feth!" cried she, "an' may God forgive ye all!" and rushed out of the cottage and down the lonan, bareheaded and weeping. Midway she stopped on the road, and, pulling off one of her pretty shoes, she flung it from her with all her might, till it struck the trunk of a far tree growing on the hill that led to Hughie's.

"That's the slipper to you, for good luck, Hughie Devnish!" she said; "an' if ever I forget you to marry a fine gentleman, may the Lord turn my gran' gowns into rags again, an' the bit that I ate into sand in my mouth!"

So Ailsie said goodbye to home. The next day Lady Betty and Miss MacQuillan departed from Castle Craigie for the Continent.

Four years passed away, and Jamie and Mary had grown accustomed to their improved circumstances, Lady Betty having proved as good as her word in bestowing on them all those benefits which she had enumerated when coaxing Ailsie away with her. Whether they were quite satisfied with the freak that fortune had played with them, they themselves knew best. When a neighbour went in to see them, Mary had always some grand talk about "my daughter, Miss MacQuillan;" but the Widow Devnish often shook her head, saying that they were dull enough when nobody was by, and feared Ailsie had forgotten them.

Ned Mucklehern and Mehaffy the miller had each consoled himself with a wife long ago. Hughie Devnish still taught his school, and his mother still called him in to his supper of evenings; but he was not the same Hughie, the widow vowed, never since the night of Lady Betty's ball, when he had taken the strange whim of going serving at the castle. That someone had put a charm on him that night, from the effects of which he had never recovered, was the Widow Devnish's firm belief. He was "as grave as a judge," she said, from morning till night, all wrapped up in the improvement of his school, never would go to a dance or a fair like other young men, and, say what she might to him, would admit no thought of taking a wife, though his means would allow of it now, since he had got some tuitions among the gentry folks of the neighbourhood.

The Widow Devnish was very proud of her son, but she was sorely afraid there was "something on him." For, strangest of all, once, when she came into his schoolroom at dusk unnoticed, she saw him looking at a little kid shoe, with long silken sandals hanging from it. "She'll forget," he was saying, as he turned it about, and wound the sandals round it, "of course, *of course* she'll forget."

All this time, while things had been going on so with these vulgar and insignificant folks at home, neither Ailsie nor Lady Betty had been seen at Castle Craigie. Lady Betty surrounded her *protégée* with French, Italian, drawing, and music masters. But with these had Ailsie concerned herself but little. "Hughie Devnish could never tache me," she would say, coolly, when they were ready to wring their hands with vexation, "an' I don't think it's likely ye're any cleverer than him." However, there were some things that Ailsie did learn in time. Being observant and imitative, she acquired a habit of speaking tolerable French, and when talking English, she modified, though she did not by any means give up, her brogue.

She very soon learnt to flirt a fan, to carry her handsome gowns with ease, and to develop certain original graces of manner, which were considered by many to be very charming in the pretty heiress to Lady Betty's Indian thousands. Altogether, the patroness found herself obliged to be content, though the young lady could read neither French nor Italian, nor yet could she play on the spinet or guitar.

Ailsie's education being thus finished, Lady Betty set her heart on an ambitious marriage for her favourite. She introduced her to society in Paris, and saw her making conquests right and left at the most fashionable watering-places on the Continent. Ailsie's sparkling eyes were enchantingly foiled by her diamonds, and proposals in plenty were laid at her feet. But Ailsie, though enjoying right merrily the homage so freely paid her, only laughed at the offers of marriage, as though it were quite impossible to regard them as anything but so many very capital jokes. Lady Betty did not join in this view of the matter, but she had patience with her heiress for a considerable time, as Ailsie always mollified her displeasure by saying, on her refusal of each "good match," "I will marry a better man still, Lady Betty."

After four years, Lady Betty, who was a wilful old lady, and whose patience was exhausted, quarrelled with her about it, and before she recovered her temper she took ill and died, and Ailsie found herself one day sad and solitary in Paris, without the protection of her kind indulgent friend.

Tears would not mend the matter now, nor would they alter the will which Lady Betty had left behind her, the conditions of which were fair enough, said Ailsie's suitors, when the contents of the important document became known. One year had the impatient old lady given her chosen heiress, in the space of which time to become a wife. And if at the end of that year she was still found to be a spinster, not a penny had she, but might go back to the cottage at the top of the lonan, and take with her her father and mother to work for them as before, to milk her cows, and feed her hens, and persuade herself, if she liked, that her wit, and her diamonds, and her beauty, and her lovers, had all had their existence in a tantalizing dream, which had visited her between roosting-time in the evening and cock-crow of a churning morning.

But, should she marry before the year was out, bestowing on her husband the name of MacQuillan, then would the shade of Lady Betty be appeased, and the Indian thousands and the Irish rentals, together with the old ancestral halls of Castle Craigie, would all belong to Ailsie and the fortunate possessor of her wealthy little hand.

Very fair conditions, said the suitors, and proposals poured in on Ailsie. But lo and behold! the flinty-hearted damsel proved as obstinate as ever; and, in the midst of wonderment and disappointment, having attained the age of twenty-one, and being altogether her own mistress, she wrote to her retainers at Castle Craigie to announce her arrival there upon a certain summer day. Great was the glory of Mary MacQuillan when she received a letter from her daughter, desiring that her father and mother should at once take up their abode at the castle, being there to receive her on her arrival. Great, indeed, was her triumph when Miss O'Trimmins sat making her a gown of brown velvet, and a lace cap with lappets, in which to meet her child, and when Jamie's blue coat with the bright gold buttons came home.

Ailsie brought a whole horde of foreigners with her, brilliant ladies of rank, who called her pet and darling in broken English—and needy marquises—and counts with slender means, who were nevertheless very magnificent persons, and still hoped to win the Irish charmer. Balls, plays, and sports of all kinds went on at; the castle, and those of the gentry-folks who, from curiosity or a better feeling, came to visit Ailsie, found her in the midst of a roomful of glittering company, dressed in a blue satin sacque and pearl earrings, with her hair dipping into her eyes in very bewitching little curls, and seated between Mary in the brown velvet and lappets and Jamie in the new coat with the buttons.

They went away saying she was wonderful indeed, considering, delightfully odd and pretty, and they wondered which of those flaunting foreigners she was going to marry in the end. Meantime the year was flying away, and old neighbours of her mother's began to shake their heads over the fire of nights, and to say that if Ailsie did not take care she might be a penniless lass yet.

Things were in this position when, one fine morning, Miss Mac-

Quillan, driving out with some of her grand friends, thought proper to stop at the door of Hughie Devnish's schoolhouse. The schoolmaster turned red and then pale as he saw Ailsie's feathers coming nodding in to him through the doorway, followed by a brilliant party of *grandees*, and two footmen dragging a huge parcel of presents for his girls and boys. Ailsie coolly set her ladies and gentlemen unpacking the parcel and distributing its contents, whilst she questioned the schoolmaster upon many subjects with the air of a little duchess, whose humour it was to make inquiries, and who never, certainly, had seen that place, much less conversed with that person, before.

Hughie endured her whim with proud patience, till, just before she left him, on opening his desk to restore a book to its place, she demanded to see a certain little dark thing which was peeping out from under some papers. Then, with evident annoyance, he produced a little black kid shoe. So, the story runs.

"Why, it's only a slipper!" said Ailsie, turning it about and looking at it, just as the Widow Devnish had detected Hughie in doing. "What an odd thing to keep a shoe in a desk! But it looked like the cover of a book. Good-morning."

As the party drove off, it is said that one of the gentlemen re-marked that the schoolmaster was a fine-looking intelligent fellow, fit for a better station than that which he filled. And it is further said that next day Ailsie made a present to this gentleman of a snuffbox worth a hundred guineas.

When Ailsie went to her room on her return home on this August afternoon, she walked over to a handsome gold casket which stood upon her table, unlocked it, and took out a little kid slipper which looked as if she must have stolen it out of Hughie's desk. In the sole of it was pinned a slip of paper, on which were scrawled, in a crude hand, the words:—

"If ever I forget you, Hughie Devnish, to marry a fine gentleman, may the Lord turn my gran' gowns into Rags agen, and the bit that I ate into Sand in my mouth."

"And the Lord's goin' to do it very fast," said Ailsie, falling back into her old way of talking, as she looked at this specimen of her old way of writing, "if I do not look to't very soon, an' be keepin' my word! An' God knows, Hughie Devnish," she added, as she locked her box again with a sharp snap, "you're more of a gentleman any day the sun rises on you, than ever poor Ailsie'll be a lady!"

And I am given to understand that shortly after this the lady of the castle sent a message to her guests to say she was indisposed (Ailsie had picked up a few pretty words) from the heat, and must beg them to excuse her absence from amongst them for the rest of the day.

It was on this very evening that Hughie Devnish was walking up and down his schoolroom floor, musing, I am told, on the impossibility of his enduring in the future to have Ailsie coming into his school at any hour she pleased, to play the mischief with his feelings, and the lady patroness amongst his boys and girls. He had just come to the point of resolving to give up his labours here, and to go off to seek his fortune in America, when click! went the latch of the door, and (of course, thinks he, it must be a dream) in walked Ailsie. Not the Lady Bountiful of the morning, in satin gown and nodding feathers, but the veritable old Ailsie of four years ago, in the same old garb, cotton dress, brogues, straw bonnet tipped over her nose, and all (where on earth did she get them?) in which she had tripped in to him on that other August evening, of which this was the anniversary, when she had shown him her invitation to Lady Betty's ball.

Now, the gloaming was just putting out the glare of the sunset behind the latticed windows, and when Hughie had pinched himself and found that he was not dreaming at all, he next became very sure that he had gone out of his senses with trouble, and that he was looking at an object conjured up before his eyes by his own diseased imagination. However, the apparition looked very substantial as it approached, and sitting down on the end of one of the forms, it displayed a paper which it unfolded in its hands—hands that were white instead of brown, making the only difference between this and the old Ailsie.

"I've got a letther here, Misther Devnish," said Ailsie's old voice, speaking with Ailsie's old brogue, and in the sly, mischievous tone that Hughie remembered well: "an' if ye plase, I want ye to answer it for me. I'm a bad dark mysel', ye know."

Not knowing what to say to her, he took the letter out of her hand and glanced over it. It was a proposal of marriage from Ailsie's old tormentor, MacQuillan of the Reek.

The schoolmaster was trembling, you may believe, with many confused ideas and sensations when he folded the letter and returned it; but he inked his pen manfully, and produced a sheet of paper, then sat waiting with much patience for his visitor's dictation. But Ailsie sat quiet, with her eyes upon the floor, and so there was a cruel pause.

"Well?" says Hughie, at last, with a bewitched feeling, as if he were addressing only his pupil of old days, "what am I to say in the answer?"

"Feth, I don't know," says Ailsie.

"But what reply do you mean to give?" asked Hughie, striving, we are assured, to command himself. "Am I to say yes or no in the letter?"

"I tell ye I don't know, Hughie Devnish," said Ailsie, crossly. "I gave a promise to another, an' he never has freed me from it yet. I b'lieve ye'll know best what to put in the letther yersel'."

"Ailsie!" cried Hughie, rising to his feet, "did you come here for nothing but to dhrive me mad? Or, avourneen, is it possible you would marry me yet?"

"Feth it is, Hughie," said Ailsie.

And after the letter was written they went in and had tea with the Widow Devnish.

The next morning Miss MacQuillan appeared amongst her guests as if nothing had happened, but before night a whisper flew from ear to ear that the heiress was engaged; while the lady herself did not contradict the report. Every man looked darkly at his neighbour, and "Who is he?" was the question on every lip. At last, "It is not I," said one noble drone, and flew off to seek honey elsewhere; and "It is not I," said the others, one by one, and followed his example; and by-and-by Ailsie was left peacefully in possession of her castle; whereupon there was a quiet wedding, at which Mary, Jamie, and the Widow Devnish were the only guests.

A nine days' wonder expires on the tenth, and after a few years Hugh Devnish MacQuillan, Esq., was looked upon as no despicable person by many who thought it their duty to sneer on his wedding-day.

The Ghost at the Rath

Many may disbelieve this story, yet there are some still living who can remember hearing, when children, of the events which it details, and of the strange sensation which their publicity excited. The tale, in its present form, is copied, by permission, from a *memoir* written by the chief actor in the romance, and preserved as a sort of heirloom in the family whom it concerns.

In the year —— I, John Thunder, Captain in the —— Regiment, having passed many years abroad following my profession, received notice that I had become owner of certain properties which I had never thought to inherit. I set off for my native land, arrived in Dublin, found that my good fortune was real, and at once began to look about me for old friends. The first I met with, quite by accident, was curly-headed Frank O'Brien, who had been at school with me, though I was ten years his senior. He was curly-headed still, and handsome, as he had promised to be, but careworn and poor. During an evening spent at his chambers I drew all his history from him. He was a briefless barrister.

As a man he was not more talented than he had been as a boy. Hard work and anxiety had not brought him success, only broken his health and soured his mind. He was in love, and he could not marry. I soon knew all about Mary Leonard, his *fiancée*, whom he had met at a house in the country somewhere, in which she was governess. They had now been engaged for two years—she active and hopeful, he sick and despondent. From the letters of hers which he showed me, I thought she was worth all the devotion he felt for her. I considered a good deal about what could be done for Frank, but I could not easily hit upon a plan to assist him. For ten chances you have of helping a sharp man, you have not two for a dull one.

In the meantime, my friend must regain his health, and a change of air and scene was necessary. I urged him to make a voyage of discovery to the Rath, an old house and park which had come into my possession as portion of my recently acquired estates. I had never been to the place myself; but it had once been the residence of Sir Luke Thunder, of generous memory, and I knew that it was furnished, and provided with a caretaker. I pressed him to leave Dublin at once, and promised to follow him as soon as I found it possible to do so.

So, Frank went down to the Rath. The place was two hundred miles away; he was a stranger there, and far from well. When the first week came to an end, and I had heard nothing from him, I did not like the silence; when a fortnight had passed, and still not a word to say he was alive, I felt decidedly uncomfortable; and when the third week of his absence arrived at Saturday without bringing me news, I found myself whizzing through a part of the country I had never travelled before, in the same train in which I had seen Frank seated at our parting.

I reached D——, and, shouldering my knapsack, walked right into the heart of a lovely woody country. Following the directions I had received, I made my way to a lonely road, on which I met not a soul, and which seemed cut out of the heart of a forest, so closely were the trees ranked on either side, and so dense was the twilight made by the meeting and intertwining of the thick branches overhead. In these shades I came upon a gate, like a gate run to seed, with tall, thin, brick pillars, brandishing long grasses from their heads, and spotted with a melancholy crust of creeping moss. I jangled a cracked bell, and an old man appeared from the thickets within, stared at me, then admitted me with a rusty key. I breathed freely on hearing that my friend was well and to be seen. I presented a letter to the old man, having a fancy not to avow myself.

I found my friend walking up and down the alleys of a neglected orchard, with the lichened branches tangled above his head, and ripe apples rotting about his feet. His hands were locked behind his back, and his head was set on one side, listening to the singing of a bird. I never had seen him look so well; yet there was a vacancy about his whole air which I did not like. He did not seem at all surprised to see me, asked had he really not written to me; thought he had; was so comfortable that he had forgotten everything else. He fancied he had only been there about three days; could not imagine how the time had passed. He seemed to talk wildly, and this, coupled with the unusual happy placidity of his manner, confounded me. The place knew him, he told me confidentially; the place belonged to him, or should; the birds sang him this, the very trees bent before him as he passed, the air whispered him that he had been long expected, and should be poor no more. Wrestling with my judgment ere it might pronounce him mad, I followed him indoors.

The Rath was no ordinary old country-house. The acres around it were so wildly overgrown that it was hard to decide which had been pleasure-ground and where the thickets had begun. The plan of the house was fine, with mullioned windows, and here and there a fleck of stained glass flinging back the challenge of an angry sunset. The vast rooms were full of a dusky glare from the sky as I strolled through them in the twilight. The antique furniture had many a blood-red stain on the abrupt notches of its dark carvings; the dusty mirrors flared back at the windows, while the faded curtains produced streaks of uncertain colour from the depths of their sullen foldings.

Dinner was laid for us in the library, a long, wainscoted room, with an enormous fire roaring up the chimney, sending a dancing light over the dingy titles of long unopened books. The old man who had un-locked the gate for me served us at table, and, after drawing the dusty curtains, and furnishing us with a plentiful supply of fuel and wine, left us. His clanking hobnailed shoes went echoing away in the distance over the unmatted tiles of the vacant hall till a door closed with a resounding clang very far away, letting us know that we were shut up together for the night in this vast, mouldy, oppressive old house.

I felt as if I could scarcely breathe in it. I could not eat with my usual appetite. The air of the place seemed heavy and tainted. I grew sick and restless. The very wine tasted badly, as if it had been drugged. I had a strange feeling that I had been in the house before, and that something evil had happened to me in it. Yet such could not be the case. What puzzled me most was, that I should feel dissatisfied at see-ing Frank looking so well, and eating so heartily. A little time before I should have been glad to suffer something to see him as he looked now; and yet not quite as he looked now. There was a drowsy content-ment about him which I could not understand. He did not talk of his work, or of any wish to return to it. He seemed to have no thought of anything but the delight of hanging about that old house, which had certainly cast a spell over him.

About midnight he seized a light, and proposed retiring to our rooms. "I have such delightful dreams in this place," he said. He vol-unteered, as we issued into the hall, to take me upstairs and show me the upper regions of his paradise.

I said, "Not tonight." I felt a strange creeping sensation as I looked up the vast black staircase, wide enough for a coach to drive down, and at the heavy darkness bending over it like a curse, while our lamps made drips of light down the first two or three gloomy steps. Our bedrooms were on the ground floor, and stood opposite one another off a passage which led to a garden. Into mine Frank conducted me, and left me for his own.

The uneasy feeling which I have described did not go from me with him, and I felt a restlessness amounting to pain when left alone in my chamber. Efforts had evidently been made to render the room habitable, but there was a something antagonistic to sleep in every angle of its many crooked corners. I kicked chairs out of their prim order along the wall, and banged things about here and there; finally, thinking that a good night's rest was the best cure for an inexplicably disturbed frame of mind, I undressed as quickly as possible, and laid my head on my pillow under a canopy, like the wings of a gigantic bird of prey wheeling above me ready to pounce.

But I could not sleep. The wind grumbled in the chimney, and the boughs swished in the garden outside; and between these noises I thought I heard sounds coming from the interior of the old house, where all should have been still as the dead down in their vaults. I could not make out what these sounds were. Sometimes I thought I heard feet running about, sometimes I could have sworn there were double knocks, tremendous tantarararas at the great hall door. Sometimes I heard the clashing of dishes, the echo of voices calling, and the dragging about of furniture. Whilst I sat up in bed trying to account for these noises, my door suddenly flew open, a bright light streamed in from the passage without, and a powdered servant in an elaborate livery of antique pattern stood holding the handle of the door in his hand, and bowing low to me in the bed.

"Her ladyship, my mistress, desires your presence in the drawing-room, sir."

This was announced in the measured tone of a well-trained domestic. Then with another bow he retired, the door closed, and I was left in the dark to determine whether I had not suddenly awakened from a tantalising dream. In spite of my very wakeful sensations, I believe I should have endeavoured to convince myself that I had been sleeping, but that I perceived light shining under my door, and through the keyhole, from the passage. I got up, lit my lamp, and dressed myself as hastily as I was able.

I opened my door, and the passage down which a short time before I had almost groped my way, with my lamp blinking in the dense foggy darkness, was now illuminated with a light as bright as gas. I walked along it quickly, looking right and left to see whence the glare proceeded. Arriving at the hall, I found it also blazing with light, and filled with perfume. Groups of choice plants, heavy with blossoms, made it look like a garden. The mosaic floor was strewn with costly mats. Soft colours and gilding shone from the walls, and canvases that had been black gave forth faces of men and women looking brightly from their burnished frames.

Servants were running about, the dining-room and drawing-room doors were opening and shutting, and as I looked through each, I saw *vistas* of light and colour, the moving of brilliant crowds, the waving of feathers, and glancing of brilliant dresses and uniforms. A festive hum reached me with a drowsy subdued sound, as if I were listening with stuffed ears. Standing aside by an orange tree, I gave up speculating on what this might be, and concentrated all my powers on observation.

Wheels were heard suddenly, and a resounding knock banged at the door till it seemed that the very rooks in the chimneys must be startled out of their nests. The door flew open, a flaming of lanterns was seen outside, and a dazzling lady came up the steps and swept into the hall. When she held up her cloth of silver train, I could see the diamonds that twinkled on her feet. Her bosom was covered with roses, and there was a red light in her eyes like the reflection from a hundred glowing fires. Her black hair went coiling about her head, and couched among the braids lay a jewel not unlike the head of a snake. She was flashing and glowing with gems and flowers. Her beauty and brilliance made me dizzy. Then came a faintness in the air, as if her breath had poisoned it. A whirl of storm came in with her, and rushed up the staircase like a moan. The plants shuddered and shed their blossoms, and all the lights grew dim a moment, then flared up again.

Now the drawing-room door opened, and a gentleman came out with a young girl leaning on his arm. He was a fine-looking, middle-aged gentleman, with a mild countenance.

The girl was a slender creature, with golden hair and a pale face. She was dressed in pure white, with a large ruby like a drop of blood at her throat. They advanced together to receive the lady who had arrived. The gentleman offered his arm to the stranger, and the girl who was displaced for her fell back, and walked behind them with a downcast air. I felt irresistibly impelled to follow them, and passed with them into the drawing-room. Never had I mixed in a finer, gay-er crowd. The costumes were rich and of an old-fashioned pattern. Dancing was going forward with spirit—minuets and country dances. The stately gentleman was evidently the host, and moved among the company, introducing the magnificent lady right and left. He led her to the head of the room presently, and they mixed in the dance. The arrogance of her manner and the fascination of her beauty were wonderful.

I cannot attempt to describe the strange manner in which I was in this company, and yet not of it. I seemed to view all I beheld through some fine and subtle medium. I saw clearly, yet I felt that it was not with my ordinary naked eyesight. I can compare it to nothing but looking at a scene through a piece of smoked or coloured glass. And just in the same way (as I have said before) all sounds seemed to reach me as if I were listening with ears imperfectly stuffed. No one present took any notice of me. I spoke to several, and they made no reply—did not even turn their eyes upon me, nor show in any way that they heard me. I planted myself straight in the way of a fine fellow in a general's uniform, but he, swerving neither to right nor left by an inch, kept on his way, as though I were a streak of mist, and left me behind him.

Everyone I touched eluded me somehow. Substantial as they all looked, I could not contrive to lay my hand on anything that felt like solid flesh. Two or three times I felt a momentary relief from the oppressive sensations which distracted me, when I firmly believed I saw Frank's head at some distance among the crowd, now in one room and now in another, and again in the conservatory, which was hung with lamps, and filled with people walking about among the flowers. But, whenever I approached, he had vanished. At last, I came upon him, sitting by himself on a couch behind a curtain watching the dancers. I laid my hand upon his shoulder. Here was something substantial at last. He did not look up; he seemed aware neither of my touch nor my speech. I looked in his staring eyes, and found that he was sound asleep. I could not wake him.

Curiosity would not let me remain by his side. I again mixed with the crowd, and found the stately host still leading about the magnificent lady. No one seemed to notice that the golden-haired girl was sitting weeping in a corner; no one but the beauty in the silver train, who sometimes glanced at her contemptuously. Whilst I watched her distress a group came between me and her, and I wandered into another room, where, as though I had turned from one picture of her to look at another, I beheld her dancing gaily, in the full glee of Sir Roger de Coverley, with a fine-looking youth, who was more plainly dressed than any other person in the room.

Never was a better-matched pair to look at. Down the middle they danced, hand in hand, his face full of tenderness, hers beaming with joy, right and left bowing and curtseying, parted and meeting again, smiling and whispering; but over the heads of smaller women there were the fierce eyes of the magnificent beauty scowling at them. Then again, the crowd shifted around me, and this scene was lost.

For some time, I could see no trace of the golden-haired girl in any of the rooms. I looked for her in vain, till at last I caught a glimpse of her standing smiling in a doorway with her finger lifted, beckoning. At whom? Could it be at me? Her eyes were fixed on mine. I hastened into the hall, and caught sight of her white dress passing up the wide black staircase from which I had shrunk some hours earlier. I followed her, she keeping some steps in advance. It was intensely dark, but by the gleaming of her gown I was able to trace her flying figure. Where we went, I knew not, up how many stairs, down how many passages, till we arrived at a low-roofed large room with sloping roof and queer windows where there was a dim light, like the sanctuary light in a deserted church.

Here, when I entered, the golden head was glimmering over something which I presently discerned to be a cradle wrapped round with white curtains, and with a few fresh flowers fastened up on the hood of it, as if to catch a baby's eye. The fair sweet face looked up at me with a glow of pride on it, smiling with happy dimples. The white hands unfolded the curtains, and stripped back the coverlet. Then, suddenly there went a rushing moan all round the weird room, that seemed like a gust of wind forcing in through the crannies, and shaking the jingling old windows in their sockets. The cradle was an empty one. The girl fell back with a look of horror on her pale face that I shall never forget, then, flinging her arms above her head, she dashed from the room.

I followed her as fast as I was able, but the wild white figure was too swift for me. I had lost her before I reached the bottom of the staircase. I searched for her, first in one room, then in another, neither could I see her foe (as I already believed to be), the lady of the silver train. At length I found myself in a small ante-room, where a lamp was expiring on the table. A window was open, close by it the golden-haired girl was lying sobbing in a chair, while the magnificent lady was bending over her as if soothingly, and offering her something to drink in a goblet. The moon was rising behind the two figures. The shuddering light of the lamp was flickering over the girl's bright head, the rich embossing of the golden cup, the lady's silver robes, and, I thought, the jewelled eyes of the serpent looked out from her bending head.

As I watched, the girl raised her face and drank, then suddenly dashed the goblet away; while a cry such as I never heard but once, and shiver to remember, rose to the very roof of the old house, and the clear sharp word "*Poisoned!*" rang and reverberated from hall and chamber in a thousand echoes, like the clash of a peal of bells. The girl dashed herself from the open window, leaving the cry clamouring behind her. I heard the violent opening of doors and running of feet, but I waited for nothing more. Maddened by what I had witnessed, I would have felled the murderess, but she glided unhurt from under my vain blow. I sprang from the window after the wretched white figure. I saw it flying on before me with a speed I could not overtake. I ran till I was dizzy. I called like a madman, and heard the owls croaking back to me.

The moon grew huge and bright, the trees grew out before it like the bushy heads of giants, the river lay keen and shining like a long, unsheathed sword, couching for deadly work among the rushes. The white figure shimmered and vanished, glittered brightly on before me, shimmered and vanished again, shimmered, staggered, fell, and disappeared in the river. Of what she was, phantom or reality, I thought not at the moment; she had the semblance of a human being going to destruction, and I had the frenzied impulse to save her. I rushed forward with one last effort, struck my foot against the root of a tree, and was dashed to the ground. I remember a crash, momentary pain and confusion; then nothing more.

When my senses returned, the red clouds of the dawn were shining in the river beside me. I arose to my feet, and found that, though much bruised, I was otherwise unhurt. I busied my mind in recalling the strange circumstances which had brought me to that place in the dead of the night. The recollection of all I had witnessed was vividly present to my mind. I took my way slowly to the house, almost expecting to see the marks of wheels and other indications of last night's revel, but the rank grass that covered the gravel was uncrushed, not a blade disturbed, not a stone displaced. I shook one of the drawing-room windows till I shook off the old rusty hasp inside, flung up the creaking sash, and entered. Where were the brilliant draperies and carpets, the soft gilding, the vases teeming with flowers, the thousand sweet odours of the night before? Not a trace of them; no, nor even a ragged cobweb swept away, nor a stiff chair moved an inch from its melancholy place, nor the face of a mirror relieved from one speck of its obscuring dust!

Coming back into the open air, I met the old man from the gate walking up one of the weedy paths. He eyed me meaningly from head to foot, but I gave him good-morrow cheerfully.

"You see I am poking about early," I said.

"I' faith, sir," said he, "an' ye look like a man that had been pokin' about *all night*."

"How so?" said I.

"Why, ye see, sir," said he, "I'm used to 't, an' I can read it in yer face like prent. Some sees one thing an' some another, an' some only feels an' hears. The poor jintleman inside, *he* says nothin', but he has beautyful dhrames. An' for the Lord's sake, sir, take him out o' this, for I've seen him wandherin' about like a ghost himself in the heart of the night, an' him that sound sleepin' that I couldn't wake him!"

★★★★★★★★★★★★★★★★★

At breakfast I said nothing to Frank of my strange adventures. He had rested well, he said, and boasted of his enchanting dreams. I asked him to describe them, when he grew perplexed and annoyed. He remembered nothing, but that his spirit had been delightfully entertained whilst his body reposed. I now felt a curiosity to go through the old house, and was not surprised, on pushing open a door at the end of a remote mouldy passage, to enter the identical chamber into which I had followed the pale-faced girl when she beckoned me out of the drawing-room.

There were the low brooding roof and slanting walls, the short wide latticed windows to which the noonday sun was trying to pierce through a forest of leaves. The hangings rotting with age shook like dreary banners at the opening of the door, and there in the middle of the room was the cradle; only the curtains that had been white were blackened with dirt, and laced and overlaced with cobwebs. I parted the curtains, bringing down a shower of dust upon the floor, and saw lying upon the pillow, within, a child's tiny shoe, and a toy. I need not describe the rest of the house. It was vast and rambling, and, as far as furniture and decorations were concerned, the wreck of grandeur.

Having strange subject for meditation, I walked alone in the orchard that evening. This orchard sloped towards the river I have mentioned before. The trees were old and stunted, and the branches tangled overhead. The ripe apples were rolling in the long, bleached grass. A row of taller trees, sycamores and chestnuts, straggled along by the river's edge, ferns and tall weeds grew round and amongst them, and between their trunks, and behind the rifts in the foliage, the water was seen to flow. Walking up and down one of the paths I alternately faced these trees and turned my back upon them. Once when coming towards them I chanced to lift my glance, started, drew my hands across my eyes, looked again, and finally stood still gazing in much astonishment. I saw distinctly the figure of a lady standing by one of the trees, bending low towards the grass.

Her face was a little turned away, her dress a bluish-white, her mantle a dun-brown colour. She held a spade in her hand, and her foot was upon it, as if she were in the act of digging. I gazed at her for some time, vainly trying to guess at whom she might be, then I advanced towards her. As I approached, the outlines of her figure broke up and disappeared, and I found that she was only an illusion presented to me by the curious accidental grouping of the lines of two trees which had shaped the space between them into the semblance of the form I have described. A patch of the flowing water had been her robe, a piece of russet moorland her cloak. The spade was an awkward young shoot slanting up from the root of one of the trees. I stepped back and tried to piece her out again bit by bit, but could not succeed.

★★★★★★★★★★★★★★★★★

That night I did not feel at all inclined to return to my dismal chamber, and lie awaiting such another summons as I had once received. When Frank bade me goodnight, I heaped fresh coals on the fire, took down from the shelves a book, from which I lifted the dust in layers with my penknife, and, dragging an armchair close to the hearth, tried to make myself as comfortable as might be. I am a strong, robust man, very unimaginative, and little troubled with affections of the nerves, but I confess that my feelings were not enviable, sitting thus alone in that queer old house, with last night's strange pantomime still vividly present to my memory. In spite of my efforts at coolness, I was excited by the prospect of what yet might be in store for me before morning. But these feelings passed away as the night wore on, and I nodded asleep over my book.

I was startled by the sound of a brisk light step walking overhead. Wide awake at once, I sat up and listened. The ceiling was low, but I could not call to mind what room it was that lay above the library in which I sat. Presently I heard the same step upon the stairs, and the loud sharp rustling of a silk dress sweeping against the banisters. The step paused at the library door, and then there was silence. I got up, and with all the courage I could summon seized a light, and opened the door; but there was nothing in the hall but the usual heavy darkness and damp mouldy air. I confess I felt more uncomfortable at that moment than I had done at any time during the preceding night. All the visions that had then appeared to me had produced nothing like the horror of thus feeling a supernatural presence which my eyes were not permitted to behold.

I returned to the library, and passed the night there. Next day I sought for the room above it in which I had heard the footsteps, but could discover no entrance to any such room. Its windows, indeed, I counted from the outside, though they were so overgrown with ivy I could hardly discern them, but in the interior of the house I could find no door to the chamber. I asked Frank about it, but he knew and cared nothing on the subject; I asked the old man at the lodge, and he shook his head.

"Och!" he said, "don't ask about that room. The door's built up, and flesh and blood have no consarn wid it. It was *her* own room."

"Whose own?" I asked.

"Ould Lady Thunder's. An' whist, sir! *that's her grave!*"

"What do you mean?" I said. "Are you out of your mind?"

He laughed queerly, drew nearer, and lowered his voice. "Nobody has asked about the room these years but yourself," he said. "Nobody misses it goin' over the house. My grandfather was an old retainer o' the Thunder family, my father was in the service too, an' I was born myself before the ould lady died. Yon was her room, an' she left her eternal curse on her family if so, be they didn't lave her coffin there. She wasn't goin' undher the ground to the worms. S'there it was left, an' they built up the door. God love ye, sir, an' don't go near it. I wouldn't have told you, only I know ye've seen plenty about already, an' ye have the look o' one that'd be ferretin' things out, savin' yer presence."

He looked at me knowingly, but I gave him no information, only thanked him for putting me on my guard. I could scarcely credit what he told me about the room; but my curiosity was excited regarding it. I made up my mind that day to try and induce Frank to quit the place on the morrow. I felt more and more convinced that the atmosphere was not healthful for his mind, whatever it might be for his body. The sooner we left the spot the better for us both; but the remaining night which I had to pass there I resolved on devoting to the exploring of the walled-up chamber. What impelled me to this resolve I do not know. The undertaking was not a pleasant one, and I should hardly have ventured on it had I been forced to remain much longer at the Rath.

But I knew there was little chance of sleep for me in that house, and I thought I might as well go and seek for my adventures as sit waiting for them to come for me, as I had done the night before. I felt a relish for my enterprise, and expected the night with satisfaction. I did not say anything of my intention either to Frank or the old man at the lodge. I did not want to make a fuss, and have my doings talked of all over the country. I may as well mention here that again, on this evening, when walking in the orchard, I saw the figure of the lady digging between the trees. And again, I saw that this figure was an elusive appearance; that the water was her gown, and the moorland her cloak, and a willow in the distance her tresses.

As soon as the night was pretty far advanced, I placed a ladder against the window which was least covered over with the ivy, and mounted it, having provided myself with a dark lantern. The moon rose full behind some trees that stood like a black bank against the horizon, and glimmered on the panes as I ripped away branches and leaves with a knife, and shook the old crazy casement open. The sashes were rotten, and the fastenings easily gave way. I placed my lantern on a bench within, and was soon standing beside it in the chamber. The air was insufferably close and mouldy, and I flung the window open to the widest, and beat the bowering ivy still further back from about it, so as to let the fresh air of heaven blow into the place. I then took my lantern in hand, and began to look about me.

The room was vast and double; a velvet curtain hung between me and an inner chamber. The darkness was thick and irksome, and the scanty light of my lantern only tantalised me. My eyes fell on some tall spectral-looking candelabra furnished with wax candles, which, though black with age, still bore the marks of having been guttered by a draught that had blown on them fifty years ago. I lighted these; they burned up with a ghastly flickering, and the apartment, with its fittings, was revealed to me. These latter had been splendid in the days of their freshness: the appointments of the rest of the house were mean in comparison. The ceiling was painted with fine allegorical figures, also spaces of the walls between the dim mirrors and the sumptuous hangings of crimson velvet, with their tarnished golden tassels and fringes.

The carpet still felt luxurious to the tread, and the dust could not altogether obliterate the elaborate fancy of its flowery design. There were gorgeous cabinets laden with curiosities, wonderfully carved chairs, rare vases, and antique glasses of every description, under some of which lay little heaps of dust which had once no doubt been blooming flowers. There was a table laden with books of poetry and science, drawings and drawing materials, which showed that the occupant of the room had been a person of mind. There was also a writing-table scattered over with yellow papers, and a work-table at a window, on which lay reels, a thimble, and a piece of what had once been white muslin, but was now saffron colour, sewn with gold thread, a rusty needle sticking in it.

This and the pen lying on the inkstand, the paper-knife between the leaves of a book, the loose sketches shaken out by the side of a portfolio, and the ashes of a fire on the wide mildewed hearth-place, all suggested that the owner of this retreat had been snatched from it without warning, and that whoever had thought proper to build up the doors, had also thought proper to touch nothing that had belonged to her.

Having surveyed all these things, I entered the inner room, which was a bedroom. The furniture of this was in keeping with that of the other chamber. I saw dimly a bed enveloped in lace, and a dressing-table fancifully garnished and draped. Here I espied more candelabra, and going forward to set the lights burning, I stumbled against something. I turned the blaze of my lantern on this something, and started with a sudden thrill of horror. It was a large stone coffin.

I own that I felt very strangely for the next few minutes. When I had recovered the shock, I set the wax-candles burning, and took a better survey of this odd burial-place. A wardrobe stood open, and I saw dresses hanging within. A gown lay upon a chair, as if just thrown off, and a pair of dainty slippers were beside it. The toilet-table looked as if only used yesterday, judging by the litter that covered it; hair-brushes lying this way and that way, essence-bottles with the stoppers out, paint pots uncovered, a ring here, a wreath of artificial flowers there, and in front of all that coffin, the tarnished Cupids that bore the mirror between their hands smirking down at it with a grim complacency.

On the. corner of this table was a small golden salver, holding a plate of some black mouldered food, an antique decanter filled with wine, a glass, and a phial with some thick black liquid, uncorked. I felt weak and sick with the atmosphere of the place, and I seized the decanter, wiped the dust from it with my handkerchief, tasted, found that the wine was good, and drank a moderate draught. Immediately it was swallowed I felt a horrid giddiness, and sank upon the coffin. A raging pain was in my head and a sense of suffocation in my chest. After a few intolerable moments I felt better, but the heavy air pressed on me stiflingly, and I rushed from this inner room into the larger and outer chamber. Here a blast of cool air revived me, and I saw that the place was changed.

A dozen other candelabra besides those I had lighted were flaming round the walls, the hearth was all ruddy with a blazing fire, everything that had been dim was bright, the lustre had returned to the gilding, the flowers bloomed in the vases. A lady was sitting before the hearth in a low armchair. Her light loose gown swept about her on the carpet, her black hair fell round her to her knees, and into it her hands were thrust as she leaned her forehead upon them, and stared between them into the fire. I had scarcely time to observe her attitude when she turned her head quickly towards me, and I recognised the handsome face of the magnificent lady who had played such a sinister part in the strange scenes that had been enacted before me two nights ago. I saw something dark looming behind her chair, but I thought it was only her shadow thrown backward by the firelight.

She arose and came to meet me, and I recoiled from her. There was something horridly fixed and hollow in her gaze, and filmy in the stirring of her garments. The shadow, as she moved, grew more firm and distinct in outline, and followed her like a servant where she went.

She crossed half of the room, then beckoned me, and sat down at the writing-table. The shadow waited beside her, adjusted her paper, placed the ink-bottle near her and the pen between her fingers. I felt impelled to approach her, and to take my place at her left shoulder, so as to be able to see what she might write. The shadow stood motionless at her other hand. As I became accustomed to the shadow's presence he grew more visibly loathsome and hideous. He was quite distinct from the lady, and moved independently of her with long ugly limbs. She hesitated about beginning to write, and he made a wild gesture with his arm, which brought her hand quickly to the paper, and her pen began to move at once. I needed not to bend and scrutinise in order to read. Every word as it was formed flashed before me like a meteor.

"I am the spirit of Madeline, Lady Thunder, who lived and died in this house, and whose coffin stands in yonder room among the vanities in which I delighted. I am constrained to make my confession to you, John Thunder, who are the present owner of the estates of your family."

Here the hand trembled and stopped writing. But the shadow made a threatening gesture, and the hand fluttered on.

"I was beautiful, poor, and ambitious, and when I entered this house first on the night of a ball given by Sir Luke Thunder, I determined to become its mistress. His daughter, Mary Thunder, was the only obstacle in my way. She divined my intention, and stood between me and her father. She was a gentle, delicate girl, and no match for me. I pushed her aside, and became Lady Thunder. After that I hated her, and made her dread me. I had gained the object of my ambition, but I was jealous of the influence possessed by her over her father, and I revenged myself by crushing the joy out of her young life. In this I defeated my own purpose. She eloped with a young man who was devoted to her, though poor, and beneath her in station. Her father was indignant at first, and my malice was satisfied; but as time passed on, I had no children, and she had a son, soon after whose birth her husband died. Then her father took her back to his heart, and the boy was his idol and heir."

Again, the hand stopped writing, the ghostly head drooped, and the whole figure was convulsed. But the shadow gesticulated fiercely, and, cowering under its menace, the wretched spirit went on:

"I caused the child to be stolen away. I thought I had done it cunningly, but she tracked the crime home to me. She came and accused me of it, and in the desperation of my terror at discovery, I gave her poison to drink. She rushed from me and from the house in frenzy, and in her mortal anguish fell in the river. People thought she had gone mad from grief for her child, and committed suicide. I only knew the horrible truth. Sorrow brought an illness upon her father, of which he died. Up to the day of his death he had search made for the child. Believing that it was alive, and must be found, he willed all his property to it, his rightful heir, and to its heirs for ever. I buried the deeds under a tree in the orchard, and forged a will, in which all was bequeathed to me during my lifetime.

I enjoyed my state and grandeur till the day of my death, which came upon me miserably, and, after that, my husband's possessions went to a distant relation of his family. Nothing more was heard of the fate of the child who was stolen; but he lived and married, and his daughter now toils for her bread—his daughter, who is the rightful owner of all that is said to belong to you, John Thunder. I tell you this that you may devote yourself to the task of discovering this wronged girl, and giving up to her that which you are unlawfully possessed of. Under the thirteenth tree standing on the brink of the river at the foot of the orchard you will find buried the genuine will of Sir Luke Thunder. When you have found and read it, do justice, as you value your soul. In order that you may know the grandchild of Mary Thunder when you find her, you shall behold her in a vision——"

The last words grew dim before me; the lights faded away, and all the place was in darkness, except one spot on the opposite wall. On this spot the light glimmered softly, and against the brightness the outlines of a figure appeared, faintly at first, but, growing firm and distinct, became filled in and rounded at last to the perfect semblance of life. The figure was that of a young girl in a plain black dress, with a bright, happy face, and pale gold hair softly banded on her fair forehead. She might have been the twin-sister of the pale-faced girl whom I had seen bending over the cradle two nights ago; but her healthier, gladder, and prettier sister.

When I had gazed on her some moments, the vision faded away as it had come; the last vestige of the brightness died out upon the wall, and I found myself once more in total darkness. Stunned for a time by the sudden changes, I stood watching for the return of the lights and figures; but in vain. By-and-by my eyes grew accustomed to the obscurity, and I saw the sky glimmering behind the little window which I had left open. I could soon discern the writing-table beside me, and possessed myself of the slips of loose paper which lay upon it. I then made my way to the window. The first streaks of dawn were in the sky as I descended my ladder, and I thanked God that I breathed the fresh morning air once more, and heard the cheering sound of the cocks crowing.

★★★★★★★★★★★★★★★★

All thought of acting immediately upon last night's strange revelations, almost all memory of them, was for the time banished from my mind by the unexpected trouble of the next few days. That morning, I found an alarming change in Frank. Feeling sure that he was going to be ill, I engaged a lodging in a cottage in the neighbourhood, whither we removed before nightfall, leaving the accursed Rath behind us.

Before midnight he was in the delirium of a raging fever.

I thought it right to let his poor little *fiancée* know his state, and wrote to her, trying to alarm her no more than was necessary. On the evening of the third day after my letter went I was sitting by Frank's bedside, when an unusual bustle outside aroused my curiosity, and going into the cottage kitchen I saw a figure standing in the firelight which seemed a third appearance of that vision of the pale-faced golden-haired girl which was now thoroughly imprinted on my memory,—a third, with all the woe of the first and all the beauty of the second. But this was a living, breathing apparition. She was throwing off her bonnet and shawl, and stood there at home in a moment in her plain black dress. I drew my hand across my eyes to make sure that they did not deceive me. I had beheld so many supernatural visions lately that it seemed as though I could scarcely believe in the reality of anything till I had touched it.

"Oh, sir," said the visitor, "I am Mary Leonard, and are you poor Frank's friend? Oh, sir, we are all the world to one another, and I could not let him die without coming to see him!"

And here the poor little traveller burst into tears.

I cheered her as well as I could, telling her that Frank would soon, I trusted, be out of all danger. She told me that she had thrown up her situation in order to come and nurse him. I said we had got a more experienced nurse than she could be, and then I gave her to the care of our landlady, a motherly country-woman. After that I went back to Frank's bedside, nor left it for long till he was convalescent. The fever had swept away all that strangeness in his manner which had afflicted me, and he was quite himself again.

There was a joyful meeting of the lovers. The more I saw of Mary Leonard's bright face the more thoroughly was I convinced that she was the living counterpart of the vision I had seen in the burial chamber. I made inquiries as to her birth, and her father's history, and found that she was indeed the grandchild of that Mary Thunder whose history had been so strangely related to me, and the rightful heiress of all those properties which for a few months only had been mine. Under the tree in the orchard, the thirteenth, and that by which I had seen the lady digging, were found the buried deeds which had been described to me.

I made an immediate transfer of property, whereupon some others who thought they had a chance of being my heirs disputed the matter with me, and went to law. Thus, the affair has gained publicity, and become a nine days' wonder. Many things have been in my favour, however: the proving of Mary's birth and of Sir Luke's will, the identification of Lady Thunder's handwriting on the slips of paper which I had brought from the burial chamber; also, other matters which a search in that chamber brought to light. I triumphed, and I now go abroad, leaving Frank and his Mary made happy by the possession of what could only have been a burden to me.

★★★★★★★★★★★★★★★★

So, the MS. ends. Major Thunder fell in battle a few years after the adventure it relates. Frank O'Brien's grandchildren hear of him with gratitude and awe. The Rath has been long since totally dismantled and left to go to ruin.

The Ghost at Wildwood Chase

It happened only five summers ago. I had had a hard winter and spring of unfitness for work, which, following close on my first successes in Art, had been rather impatiently borne, seeming as they did to destroy my hope while it was budding. Furthermore, I was assured by a doctor that I was threatened with consumption, and I acknowledged that he was probably right, as the disease was in my family. In the beginning of a hot June, I sat in my studio in London, weary in body and mind, when a letter came to my hand like a freshening breeze. It was from Lord Wylder, who had bought a picture of mine a few months before, and who now asked me to come down to Wildwood Chase to paint his portrait.

Though not particularly fond of portrait painting, I liked the invitation. I knew the country round Wildwood Chase was beautiful, famous for its roses and nightingales. In a few weeks the latter would have left off singing; I should be in time to hear their richest notes. There was also a good gallery of pictures at Wildwood. In a short time, my arrangements were made, and I was in the train, spinning through fields and woods in their freshest verdure, and among hedges white and fragrant with the hawthorn in full bloom.

I found the great house full of people. Lord Wylder was a genial old man, who had a large family of children and grandchildren whom he loved to gather round him, and the portrait I was to paint was intended for one of his daughters, who had lately been married. His kind flattery of my works gave me a sort of distinction in the eyes of the company, and nothing could be pleasanter than the position in which I found myself. I had a charming studio overhanging a green retreat, through leafy rifts in which a teeming rose-garden was discernible, against a distance blotted with mingled greens and purples. Here I worked, solitary as long as I pleased, and always returning to my seclusion happier for the courtesy with which the struggling artist was treated by enthusiastic admirers of his art.

The state of my health at the moment disinclining me for the society of strangers, I lived chiefly a dreamlike life of my own among the delicious summer haunts which surrounded me at Wildwood Chase.

At such a time of the year, and in such delightful relations with nature, if one has not actually a close sympathetic companionship with some other living creature, one is apt to create something of the kind out of one's own imagination, and with this reflection I accounted to myself for my extraordinary attraction towards a certain picture in the gallery, the head and shoulders of a girl set against a background of the woven boughs of trees. The face had a mysterious charm impossible to describe, and was slightly leaned forward, looking straight at the gazer with an expression which seemed to me as though the creature were longing to whisper a secret.

The wide overshadowed grey eyes had a spiritual intensity such as I had never seen in any woman's face, while the sweet parted lips promised that, strong as imagination and mind might be in the character, the heart would always have the casting-vote if ever intellect and feeling should come in conflict. The hair was light, like new-mown hay, and lay in soft drifts across the delicate forehead. The peculiarity of the picture was that, wherever you moved in the gallery within sight of it, the eyes followed you with wonderful changes of expression. Sometimes they were sad and wistful, sometimes smiling, as if in mischievous amusement, and again they had a high strange outlook that tantalised you with a desire to follow it.

I ascertained that this was the portrait of a young girl of Lord Wylder's family, who had lived and died about a hundred years ago. Somehow, I felt pleased that she had died early. There were portraits of beautiful women all round, who had been the grandmothers and great-grandmothers of the Wylders, caught here in their lovely girlhood, and perpetuated in youth for the eyes of posterity; but they did not interest me, and I smiled at my own satisfaction in the knowledge that my leaf-embowered goddess had never been promoted while on earth to wifehood, motherhood, and great-grandmotherhood. She had come up like a flower, appeared like the leaves on the boughs from among which her face looked forth, and even as flower and leaf she had vanished, after a short sweet summer of life, with the dews still fresh on the roses of her tender lips and cheeks.

She was a fitting companion and friend, I thought, for one like me, living a saddened ideal life, threatened with disease, overshadowed by death, uncertain of more than a very short duration of mortal existence. Smiling at this conceit, I visited her every evening at twilight, vowing vows to her, and making believe to be her lover. She had been dust already for nearly a century, and I should be dust perhaps before another year. Therefore, I said we should be lovers.

Though always in love with love, I had never loved any woman in my life before, so that the June romance, sprung among roses and nightingales, and woven round the dream-maiden in the gallery nook whose eyes were dust, and whose voice (what a low sweet voice it must have been!) would never more be heard on earth, was perfectly satisfactory, inexpressibly consoling and delightful to me.

A man can hardly confess all the weak things he sees when, being in low health, and tired of pretending to be strong, the child in his nature, never quite lost in any of us, rises irresistibly and asserts itself. In such a mood he will cry like a girl over a lock of his dead mother's hair, or babble to himself words of tenderness heard long ago, and only grown precious to memory in the hour of desolation. In such mood I raved softly in the dusk and solitude to my little love, with the hair like new-mown hay and the eyes that seemed to listen to me and answer me. One evening, when I was in a particularly fantastic humour, I began to wonder if the spirit that had lived in the creature knew anything of this wayward devotion of mine, and whether, in case she did, she would be pleased or displeased at it.

Upon this, the idea that my dream-love was after all no dream, but a living being in another world, which might be only separated from us by the veils upon our eyes, struck me with a force which was a very new and strange experience. It was as if she had indeed been spiritually present, and had made her presence felt by me. I thought, how strange that, were she to make herself visibly known to me, it might be only anticipating matters, seeing that in a short time I should be thoroughly qualified to join her where she abode, and I formed a distinct wish that Mayflower (so she was named), with the eyes of spiritual meaning and the brow like that of a child-angel, would come and confer with me here in the shadows, and tell me that secret, perhaps the secret of immortality, which it had seemed to me when I first saw her that she was longing to unfold.

I had turned away and walked the length of the gallery, charmed with and half smiling at my fancy, and I was within a few yards of the door, when it opened noiselessly and quickly; there was a grey flutter of drapery, shone through by the early-risen moon, which looked towards me from beyond the window in the passage on which the end of the gallery gave. I saw a young light-tinted head set against the glistening moon, which formed a golden disc behind it. I saw the spiritual gleam of eyes clear like water; I saw shoulders of a peculiar outline, and a light gossamer swathing them; and then the door shut, leaving me nothing but the living glance that had been flung towards me from the very face which I had adored and apostrophised on the canvas, now hidden by twilight at the more distant extremity of the gallery.

I remained standing where I was for several minutes. Fantastic as my humour had been, it had not been insane, but now I asked myself whether I had suddenly passed the boundary of sanity. That I had seen a vision of the girl Mayflower, who had bloomed a hundred years ago, there could be no doubt, but whether the vision was conjured up by my own disordered mind was a question which troubled me impertinently. I had not been led to expect that my mind was bound to decay sooner than my body, yet I had seen the spirit of Mayflower whom I had adjured to come to me. I believed that I had positively adjured her. And she had come.

Insomnia was part of the ailment from which I suffered, but at Wildwood I had found it scarcely irksome to lie awake and hear all the rich full sounds of the life of the summer night—the occasional rapture of the nightingale, the urgent cry of the landrail in the grass, the distant lowing of cattle, the rustling of the woods. On this night the marvel of Mayflower's spiritual apparition absorbed me; she seemed to float through the air of the midsummer night and dawn, drawing me towards her. During the next week I was feverish, impatient, altogether the worse instead of the better for my absence from London. In my calmer moments I thought of breaking my engagements, pretending inability to work on the portrait, packing up, and returning to London. The reason was that I made up my mind that the vision I had seen was a real vision, and that I was hungering to see it again. Therefore, I would escape while I had a remnant of sanity.

I did not go, however, for the insanity kept me rooted to the spot. A week passed, and the weird impression I had received was becoming a little weakened. Occasionally I admitted to myself that my imagination had played me a trick. One night, in a more than ordinarily rational frame of mind, and tired of lying awake, I rose, and letting myself out by a garden door, went for a long ramble through the park and out on the open downs, where the first faint breaking of dawn overtook me.

It was just during that spell of visible darkness which is the forerunner of the return of light, and while I stood on the verge of a small ragged-edged lake, skirted by trees and bushes—stood smoking calmly, and expectant of nothing but the sunrise, that I had my second vision of the spirit of Mayflower. I dropped my cigar, and stood breathless, as the first flutter of the slim robe came out of the tall rushes, and I beheld her floating towards me, clad in long light garments, her small head set backwards, her sweet eyes wide open, and full of that expression which in the picture most fascinated me—the high, strange, far-looking gaze which had so followed me at times that I felt utterly unable to escape from it.

Her hands gathered the folds of her dress on her breast, as in the picture, and she went by with a gliding movement, like a mist-wreath. I looked her in the face, advanced towards her, involuntarily stepped aside as she took no notice of me, and finally let her pass, daunted by her unconsciousness or indifference. No sooner had she passed than I sprang to follow her. I would speak to her at any cost. I made a spring to reach a mound in front of her, where I might again wait and watch her approach, but missed my footing and fell. When I had got upon my feet again, she was gone.

The next day I laid down my brushes, and told my sitter and host that I felt I was going to be ill, and had better be at home. I went back to London, and had my illness—typhoid fever, the doctor said; and I was extremely shaken when convalescent. To my great surprise the doctor informed me that this illness had been of much service to me, and that, though weak and needing care, I was no longer in danger of consumption. If cautious I might live to be a vigorous man.

Extremely cheered by the news, I began to look back upon my experiences of Wildwood Chase as part of the hallucinations of the fever that had long been creeping over me, and with a smile and a sigh for Mayflower and her mysterious dream-sympathy, I dismissed the little romance from my reinvigorated mind. By Christmas-time I was completely recovered, and was gratified by receiving a note from Lord Wylder regretting my illness, and hoping that I would run down to Wildwood during the holidays for change of air. He wrote from Florence, saying the Chase was deserted this winter, but the housekeeper had received orders to make me comfortable. My first impulse was to decline the invitation, but on second thoughts I decided to seize the opportunity of laying in a store of strength for coming work, and of looking on the picture of Mayflower once more, this time with the eyes of bodily and mental sanity.

After the day of my arrival had been arranged, something occurred to detain me in London, and I wrote to the housekeeper naming a later date. Within two days of the later period, I found myself free, and telegraphed that I was coming twenty-four hours sooner than had been my latest intention. Owing to the snow, which had fallen in the country before it appeared in London, it happened that my telegram was not received, but of that I knew nothing as I made my way along roads just cleared for travellers, and arrived at my destination, unexpected.

The avenue had not been cleared, and leaving the trap which had brought me from the station at the lower gates, I walked by the shortest way to the house, went in by the open back way, ascended to the great hall without meeting anyone, deposited my wrappings and rugs, and proceeded to make myself at home, awaiting the appearance of the housekeeper. Seeing firelight under the not quite closed door of the library, I turned in there, and glancing round the brown-panelled room, book-lined and irradiated with firelight, I saw a figure rise from the hearthrug, and stand in a wavering attitude, like a wild bird poising for flight.

The form of the head and shoulders was weirdly familiar, the shine of the eyes fell on me, like a blinding revelation of things inconceivable. This was Mayflower, seen actually as if in the flesh, not by the ghost-seeing eyes of disease, but by the eyes of healthy manhood. So real was she, that after a long pause of surprise, incredulity, ending in complete assurance, I uttered some words of apology for disturbing a lady, and then remained gazing at her to see what she would do.

A few murmured words in Mayflower's true voice—the voice I had endowed her with, but had never heard before—came towards me. What they were I did not catch, but the sound acted on me like a spell, and I stood silently gazing at her as she went past me, and disappeared out of the library.

When she was gone, I wakened up and rang the bell, and in a few minutes the housekeeper appeared, bearing lights, and full of apologies. She had not expected; she must have misunderstood.

I made my explanations, and then asked her as unconcernedly as I could who the lady was whom I feared my unlooked-for arrival had disturbed.

"Oh, that is Miss Mayflower," she said. "She loves this library, and lives in it mostly when she gets the house to herself. If you had come tomorrow, sir, as we expected, you would not have caught sight of

Miss Mayflower."

"Do you mean the lady whose portrait is in the gallery?"

"Well, it is her portrait; everybody says so. It proves her to be a true Wylder, orphan though she may be. These likenesses do turn up after a hundred years or more. There's Lady Gwendolen is the very image of her grandmother in the powdered hair in the left-hand corner as you go out at the drawing-room end."

"I thought I had seen all Lord Wylder's granddaughters," I said, with an unaccountable sinking of the heart.

"Oh, she's none of them, poor child; only the daughter of a far-off branch of the family, and was left in care of Lord Wylder as a charity, and has been educated to be a governess. When her health is a little stronger the ladies will get her a good appointment; meantime she's here in my charge, and enjoys herself well when the family are all away from home. She's too shy to appear when there's company about the place."

I reflected, and drew rapid conclusions.

"She was here during my visit last summer!" I said.

"She was here and not very well, and I was greatly concerned about her. Her delicacy took an awkward turn; she walked in her sleep, and only that I watched her something would have happened to her. Once I found she had been out of the house at night, and might have walked into the lake, or killed herself by falling down a bank. It was a serious anxiety to me, and I did not like to tell the family. She's cured of it now, I am glad to say, and will very soon be able to go out into the world for herself. Not that I shall be pleased to lose her, for I am really fond of Miss Mayflower."

The rest is too sacred to be told; but Mayflower is the name of my wife. As I look at her this moment, she is less mysterious, less dream-like than my first love in the gallery; her cheeks have a warmer tint, her eyes a happier light than the eyes like grey water, which still look stirlessly out from the newly leaved boughs of a hundred springs ago, among the shadows of the old walls of Wildwood Chase. But the likeness of feature is wonderful; and there, now, as the little head, thatched with new-mown hay, is lifted under my scrutiny, the very eager whispering look of the picture comes out on the face, and while the smile on her lips fades in wistful wonder, I remember, with a sort of awe mixed with delight, how I twice looked on this living and blooming creature of the flesh, and was fantastic enough to mistake her for a disembodied spirit.

The Haunted Organist of Hurly Burly

There had been a thunderstorm in the village of Hurly Burly. Every door was shut, every dog in his kennel, every rut and gutter a flowing river after the deluge of rain that had fallen. Up at the great house, a mile from the town, the rooks were calling to one another about the fright they had been in, the fawns in the deer-park were venturing their timid heads from behind the trunks of trees, and the old woman at the gate-lodge had risen from her knees, and was putting back her prayer-book on the shelf.

In the garden, July roses, unwieldy with their full-blown richness, and saturated with rain, hung their heads heavily to the earth; others, already fallen, lay flat upon their blooming faces on the path, where Bess, Mistress Hurly's maid, would find them, when going on her morning quest of rose-leaves for her lady's potpourri. Ranks of white lilies, just brought to perfection by today's sun, lay dabbled in the mire of flooded mould. Tears ran down the amber cheeks of the plums on the south wall, and not a bee had ventured out of the hives, though the scent of the air was sweet enough to tempt the laziest drone. The sky was still lurid behind the boles of the upland oaks, but the birds had begun to dive in and out of the ivy that wrapped up the home of the Hurlys of Hurly Burly.

This thunderstorm took place more than half a century ago, and we must remember that Mistress Hurly was dressed in the fashion of that time as she crept out from behind the squire's chair, now that the lightning was over, and, with many nervous glances towards the window, sat down before her husband, the tea-urn, and the muffins. We can picture her fine lace cap, with its peachy ribbons, the frill on the hem of her cambric gown just touching her ankles, the embroidered clocks on her stockings, the rosettes on her shoes, but not so easily the lilac shade of her mild eyes, the satin skin, which still kept its delicate bloom, though wrinkled with advancing age, and the pale, sweet, puckered mouth, that time and sorrow had made angelic while trying vainly to deface its beauty.

The squire was as rugged as his wife was gentle, his skin as brown as hers was white, his grey hair as bristling as hers was glossed; the years had ploughed his face into ruts and channels; a bluff, choleric, noisy man he had been; but of late a dimness had come on his eyes, a hush on his loud voice, and a check on the spring of his hale step. He looked at his wife often, and very often she looked at him. She was not a tall woman, and he was only a head higher. They were a quaintly well-matched couple, despite their differences. She turned to you with nervous sharpness and revealed her tender voice and eye; he spoke and glanced roughly, but the turn of his head was courteous.

Of late they fitted one another better than they had ever done in the heyday of their youthful love. A common sorrow had developed a singular likeness between them. In former years the cry from the wife had been, "Don't curb my son too much!" and from the husband, "You ruin the lad with softness." But now the idol that had stood between them was removed, and they saw each other better.

The room in which they sat was a pleasant old-fashioned drawing-room, with a general spider-legged character about the fittings; spinet and guitar in their places, with a great deal of copied music beside them; carpet, tawny wreaths on pale blue; blue flutings on the walls, and faint gilding on the furniture. A huge urn, crammed with roses, in the open bay-window, through which came delicious airs from the garden, the twittering of birds settling to sleep in the ivy close by, and occasionally the pattering of a flight of raindrops, swept to the ground as a bough bent in the breeze. The urn on the table was ancient silver, and the china rare. There was nothing in the room for luxurious ease of the body, but everything of delicate refinement for the eye.

There was a great hush all over Hurly Burly, except in the neighbourhood of the rooks. Every living thing had suffered from heat for the past month, and now, in common with all Nature, was receiving the boon of refreshed air in silent peace. The mistress and master of Hurly Burly shared the general spirit that was abroad, and were not talkative over their tea.

"Do you know?" said Mistress Hurly, at last, "when I heard the first of the thunder beginning, I thought it was—it was——"

The lady broke down, her lips trembling, and the peachy ribbons of her cap stirring with great agitation.

"Pshaw!" cried the old squire, making his cup suddenly ring upon the saucer, "we ought to have forgotten that. Nothing has been heard for three months."

At this moment a rolling sound struck upon the ears of both. The lady rose from her seat trembling, and folded her hands together, while the tea-urn flooded the tray.

"Nonsense, my love," said the squire; "that is the noise of wheels. Who can be arriving?"

"Who, indeed?" murmured the lady, reseating herself in agitation.

Presently pretty Bess of the rose-leaves appeared at the door in a flutter of blue ribbons.

"Please, madam, a lady has arrived, and says she is expected. She asked for her apartment, and I put her into the room that was got ready for Miss Calderwood. And she sends her respects to you, madam, and she'll be down with you presently."

The squire looked at his wife, and his wife looked at the squire.

"It is some mistake," murmured madam. "Some visitor for Calderwood or the Grange. It is very singular."

Hardly had she spoken when the door again opened, and the stranger appeared—a small creature, whether girl or woman it would be hard to say—dressed in a scanty black silk dress, her narrow shoulders covered with a white muslin pelerine. Her hair was swept up to the crown of her head, all but a little fringe hanging over her low forehead within an inch of her brows. Her face was brown and thin, eyes black and long, with blacker settings, mouth large, sweet, and melancholy. She was all head, mouth, and eyes; her nose and chin were nothing.

This visitor crossed the floor hastily, dropped a courtesy in the middle of the room, and approached the table, saying abruptly, with a soft Italian accent:

"Sir and madam, I am here. I am come to play your organ."

"The organ!" gasped Mistress Hurly.

"The organ!" stammered the squire.

"Yes, the organ," said the little stranger lady, playing on the back of a chair with her fingers, as if she felt notes under them. "It was but last week that the handsome *signor*, your son, came to my little house, where I have lived teaching music since my English father and my Italian mother and brothers and sisters died and left me so lonely."

Here the fingers left off drumming, and two great tears were brushed off, one from each eye with each hand, child's fashion. But the next moment the fingers were at work again, as if only whilst they were moving the tongue could speak.

"The noble *signor*, your son," said the little woman, looking trust-

115

fully from one to the other of the old couple, while a bright blush shone through her brown skin, "he often came to see me before that, always in the evening, when the sun was warm and yellow all through my little studio, and the music was swelling my heart, and I could play out grand with all my soul; then he used to come and say,' Hurry, little Lisa, and play better, better still. I have work for you to do by-and-by.' Sometimes he said, '*Brava!*' and sometimes he said '*Eccellentissima!*' but one night last week he came to me and said, 'It is enough. Will you swear to do my bidding, whatever it may be?' Here the black eyes fell. And I said, 'Yes.' And he said, 'Now you are my betrothed.' And I said, 'Yes.' And he said, 'Pack up your music, little Lisa, and go off to England to my English father and mother, who have an organ in their house which must be played upon. If they refuse to let you play, tell them I sent you, and they will give you leave. You must play all day, and you must get up in the night and play. You must never tire. You are my betrothed, and you have sworn to do my work.' I said, 'Shall I see you there, *signor?*' And he said, 'Yes, you shall see me there.' I said, 'I will keep my vow, *signor.*' And so, sir and madam, I am come."

The soft foreign voice left off talking, the fingers left off thrumming on the chair, and the little stranger gazed in dismay at her auditors, both pale with agitation.

"You are deceived. You make a mistake," said they in one breath.

"Our son——" began Mistress Hurly, but her mouth twitched, her voice broke, and she looked piteously towards her husband.

"Our son," said the squire, making an effort to conquer the quavering in his voice, "our son is long dead."

"Nay, nay," said the little foreigner. "If you have thought him dead have good cheer, dear sir and madam. He is alive; he is well, and strong, and handsome. But one, two, three, four, five" (on the fingers) "days ago he stood by my side."

"It is some strange mistake, some wonderful coincidence " said the mistress and master of Hurly Burly.

"Let us take her to the gallery," murmured the mother of this son who was thus dead and alive. "There is yet light to see the pictures. She will not know his portrait."

The bewildered wife and husband led their strange visitor away to a long gloomy room at the west side of the house, where the faint gleams from the darkening sky still lingered on the portraits of the Hurly family.

"Doubtless he is like this," said the squire, pointing to a fair-haired young man with a mild face, a brother of his own who had been lost at sea.

But Lisa shook her head, and went softly on tiptoe from one picture to another, peering into the canvas, and still turning away troubled. But at last, a shriek of delight startled the shadowy chamber.

"Ah, here he is! See, here he is, the noble *signor*, the beautiful *signor*, not half so handsome as he looked five days ago, when talking to poor little Lisa! Dear sir and madam, you are now content. Now take me to the organ, that I may commence to do his bidding at once."

The mistress of Hurly Burly clung fast by her husband's arm.

"How old are you, girl?" she said faintly.

"Eighteen," said the visitor impatiently, moving towards the door.

"And my son has been dead for twenty years!" said his mother, and swooned on her husband's breast.

"Order the carriage at once," said Mistress Hurly; recovering from her swoon; "I will take her to Margaret Calderwood. Margaret will tell her the story. Margaret will bring her to reason. No, not tomorrow; I cannot bear tomorrow, it is so far away. We must go tonight."

The little *signora* thought the old lady mad, but she put on her cloak again obediently, and took her seat beside Mistress Hurly in the Hurly family coach. The moon that looked in at them through the pane as they lumbered along was not whiter than the aged face of the squire's wife, whose dim faded eyes were fixed upon it in doubt and awe too great for tears or words. Lisa, too, from her corner gloated upon the moon, her black eyes shining with passionate dreams.

A carriage rolled away from the Calderwood door as the Hurly coach drew up at the steps. Margaret Calderwood had just returned from a dinner-party, and at the open door a splendid figure was standing, a tall woman dressed in brown velvet, the diamonds on her bosom glistening in the moonlight that revealed her, pouring, as it did, over the house from eaves to basement. Mistress Hurly fell into her outstretched arms with a groan, and the strong woman carried her aged friend, like a baby, into the house. Little Lisa was overlooked, and sat down contentedly on the threshold to gloat awhile longer on the moon, and to thrum imaginary *sonatas* on the doorstep.

There were tears and sobs in the dusk, moonlit room into which Margaret Calderwood carried her friend. There was a long consultation, and then Margaret, having hushed away the grieving woman into some quiet corner, came forth to look for the little dark-faced stranger, who had arrived, so unwelcome, from beyond the seas, with

117

such wild communication from the dead.

Up the grand staircase of handsome Calderwood, the little woman followed the tall one into a large chamber where a lamp burned, showing Lisa, if she cared to see it, that this mansion of Calderwood was fitted with much greater luxury and richness than was that of Hurly Burly. The appointments of this room announced it the sanctum of a woman who depended for the interest of her life upon resources of intellect and taste. Lisa noticed nothing but a morsel of biscuit that was lying on a plate.

"May I have it?" said she eagerly. "It is so long since I have eaten. I am hungry."

Margaret Calderwood gazed at her with a sorrowful, motherly look, and, parting the fringing hair on her forehead, kissed her. Lisa, staring at her in wonder, returned the caress with ardour. Margaret's large fair shoulders, Madonna face, and yellow braided hair, excited a rapture within her. But when food was brought her, she flew to it and ate.

"It is better than I have ever eaten at home!" she said gratefully. And Margaret Calderwood murmured, "She is physically healthy, at least."

"And now, Lisa," said Margaret Calderwood, "come and tell me the whole history of the grand *signor* who sent you to England to play the organ."

Then Lisa crept in behind a chair, and her eyes began to burn and her fingers to thrum, and she repeated word for word her story as she had told it at Hurly Burly.

When she had finished, Margaret Calderwood began to pace up and down the floor with a very troubled face. Lisa watched her, fascinated, and, when she bade her listen to a story which she would relate to her, folded her restless hands together meekly, and listened.

"Twenty years ago, Lisa, Mr. and Mrs. Hurly had a son. He was handsome, like that portrait you saw in the gallery, and he had brilliant talents. He was idolised by his father and mother, and all who knew him felt obliged to love him. I was then a happy girl of twenty. I was an orphan, and Mrs. Hurly, who had been my mother's friend, was like a mother to me. I, too, was petted and caressed by all my friends, and I was very wealthy; but I only valued admiration, riches—every good gift that fell to my share—just in proportion as they seemed of worth in the eyes of Lewis Hurly. I was his affianced wife, and I loved him well.

"All the fondness and pride that were lavished on him could not keep him from falling into evil ways, nor from becoming rapidly more and more abandoned to wickedness, till even those who loved him best despaired of seeing his reformation. I prayed him with tears, for my sake, if not for that of his grieving mother, to save himself before it was too late. But to my horror I found that my power was gone, my words did not even move him; he loved me no more. I tried to think that this was some fit of madness that would pass, and still clung to hope. At last, his own mother forbade me to see him."

Here Margaret Calderwood paused, seemingly in bitter thought, but resumed:

"He and a party of his boon companions, named by themselves the 'Devil's Club,' were in the habit of practising all kinds of unholy pranks in the country. They had midnight carousings on the tomb-stones in the village graveyard; they carried away helpless old men and children, whom they tortured by making believe to bury them alive; they raised the dead and placed them sitting round the tombstones at a mock feast. On one occasion there was a very sad funeral from the village. The corpse was carried into the church, and prayers were read over the coffin, the chief mourner, the aged father of the dead man, standing weeping by. In the midst of this solemn scene the organ sud-denly pealed forth a profane tune, and a number of voices shouted a drinking chorus.

"A groan of execration burst from the crowd, the clergyman turned pale and closed his book, and the old man, the father of the dead, climbed the altar steps, and, raising his arms above his head, uttered a terrible curse. He cursed Lewis Hurly to all eternity, he cursed the organ he played, that it might be dumb henceforth, except under the fingers that had now profaned it, which, he prayed, might be forced to labour upon it till they stiffened in death. And the curse seemed to work, for the organ stood dumb in the church from that day, except when touched by Lewis Hurly.

"For a bravado he had the organ taken down and conveyed to his father's house, where he had it put up in the chamber where it now stands. It was also for a bravado that he played on it every day. But, by-and-by, the amount of time which he spent at it daily began to increase rapidly. We wondered long at this whim, as we called it, and his poor mother thanked God that he had set his heart upon an occupation which would keep him out of harm's way. I was the first to suspect that it was not his own will that kept him hammering at the organ so many laborious hours, while his boon companions tried vainly to draw him away. He used to lock himself up in the room with the organ, but one day I hid myself among the curtains, and saw him writhing on his seat, and heard him groaning as he strove to wrench his hands from the keys, to which they flew back like a needle to a magnet.

"It was soon plainly to be seen that he was an involuntary slave to the organ; but whether through a madness that had grown within himself, or by some supernatural doom, having its cause in the old man's curse, we did not dare to say. By-and-by there came a time when we were wakened out of our sleep at nights by the rolling of the organ. He wrought now night and day. Food and rest were denied him. His face got haggard, his beard grew long, his eyes started from their sockets. His body became wasted, and his cramped fingers like the claws of a bird. He groaned piteously as he stooped over his cruel toil. All save his mother and I were afraid to go near him. She, poor, tender woman, tried to put wine and food between his lips, while the tortured fingers crawled over the keys; but he only gnashed his teeth at her with curses, and she retreated from him in terror, to pray. At last, one dreadful hour, we found him a ghastly corpse on the ground before the organ.

"From that hour the organ was dumb to the touch of all human fingers. Many, unwilling to believe the story, made persevering endeavours to draw sound from it, in vain. But when the darkened empty room was locked up and left, we heard as loud as ever the well-known sounds humming and rolling through the walls. Night and day the tones of the organ boomed on as before. It seemed that the doom of the wretched man was not yet fulfilled, although his tortured body had been worn out in the terrible struggle to accomplish it. Even his own mother was afraid to go near the room then. So, the time went on, and the curse of this perpetual music was not removed from the house. Servants refused to stay about the place. Visitors shunned it.

"The squire and his wife left their home for years, and returned; left it, and returned again, to find their ears still tortured and their hearts wrung by the unceasing persecution of terrible sounds. At last, but a few months ago, a holy man was found, who locked himself up in the cursed chamber for many days, praying and wrestling with the demon. After he came forth and went away the sounds ceased, and the organ was heard no more. Since then, there has been peace in the house. And now, Lisa, your strange appearance and your strange story convince us that you are a victim of a ruse of the Evil One. Be warned in time, and place yourself under the protection of God, that you may be saved from the fearful influences that are at work upon you. Come——"

Margaret Calderwood turned to the corner where the stranger sat, as she had supposed, listening intently. Little Lisa was fast asleep, her hands spread before her as if she played an organ in her dreams.

Margaret took the soft brown face to her motherly breast, and kissed the swelling temples, too big with wonder and fancy.

"We will save you from a horrible fate!" she murmured, and carried the girl to bed.

In the morning Lisa was gone. Margaret Calderwood, coming early from her own chamber, went into the girl's room and found the bed empty.

"She is just such a wild thing," thought Margaret, "as would rush out at sunrise to hear the larks!" and she went forth to look for her in the meadows, behind the beech hedges, and in the home park. Mistress Hurly, from the breakfast-room window, saw Margaret Calderwood, large and fair in her white morning gown, coming down the garden-path between the rose bushes, with her fresh draperies dabbled by the dew, and a look of trouble on her calm face. Her quest had been unsuccessful. The little foreigner had vanished.

A second search after breakfast proved also fruitless, and towards evening the two women drove back to Hurly Burly together. There all was panic and distress. The squire sat in his study with the doors shut, and his hands over his ears. The servants, with pale faces, were huddled together in whispering groups. The haunted organ was pealing through the house as of old.

Margaret Calderwood hastened to the fatal chamber, and there, sure enough, was Lisa, perched upon the high seat before the organ, beating the keys with her small hands, her slight figure swaying, and the evening sunshine playing about her weird head. Sweet unearthly music she wrung from the groaning heart of the organ—wild melodies, mounting to rapturous heights and falling to mournful depths. She wandered from Mendelssohn to Mozart, and from Mozart to Beethoven. Margaret stood fascinated awhile by the ravishing beauty of the sounds she heard, but, rousing herself quickly, put her arms round the musician and forced her away from the chamber. Lisa returned next day, however, and was not so easily coaxed from her post again. Day after day she laboured at the organ, growing paler and thinner and more weird-looking as time went on.

"I work so hard," she said to Mrs. Hurly. "The *signor*, your son, is he pleased? Ask him to come and tell me himself if he is pleased."

Mistress Hurly got ill and took to her bed. The squire swore at the young foreign baggage, and roamed abroad. Margaret Calderwood was the only one who stood by to watch the fate of the little organist. The curse of the organ was upon Lisa; it spoke under her hand, and her hand was its slave.

At last, she announced rapturously that she had had a visit from the brave *signor*, who had commended her industry, and urged her to work yet harder. After that she ceased to hold any communication with the living. Time after time Margaret Calderwood wrapped her arms about the frail thing, and carried her away by force, locking the door of the fatal chamber. But locking the chamber and burying the key were of no avail. The door stood open again, and Lisa was labouring on her perch.

One night, wakened from her sleep by the well-known humming and moaning of the organ, Margaret dressed hurriedly and hastened to the unholy room. Moonlight was pouring down the staircase and passages of Hurly Burly. It shone on the marble bust of the dead Lewis Hurly, that stood in the niche above his mother's sitting-room door. The organ room was full of it when Margaret pushed open the door and entered—full of the pale green moonlight from the window, mingled with another light, a dull lurid glare which seemed to centre round a dark shadow, like the figure of a man standing by the organ, and throwing out in fantastic relief the slight form of Lisa writhing, rather than swaying, back and forward, as if in agony. The sounds that came from the organ were broken and meaningless, as if the hands of the player lagged and stumbled on the keys.

Between the intermittent chords low moaning cries broke from Lisa, and the dark figure bent towards her with menacing gestures. Trembling with the sickness of supernatural fear, yet strong of will, Margaret Calderwood crept forward within the lurid light, and was drawn into its influence. It grew and intensified upon her, it dazzled and blinded her at first; but presently, by a daring effort of will, she raised her eyes, and beheld Lisa's face convulsed with torture in the burning glare, and bending over her the figure and the features of Lewis Hurly! Smitten with horror, Margaret did not even then lose her presence of mind.

She wound her strong arms around the wretched girl and dragged her from her seat and out of the influence of the lurid light, which immediately paled away and vanished. She carried her to her own bed, where Lisa lay, a wasted wreck, raving about the cruelty of the pitiless *signor* who would not see that she was labouring her best. Her poor cramped hands kept beating the coverlet, as though she were still at her agonising task.

Margaret Calderwood bathed her burning temples, and placed fresh flowers upon her pillow. She opened the blinds and windows, and let in the sweet morning air and sunshine, and then, looking up at the newly awakened sky with its fair promise of hope for the day, and down at the dewy fields, and afar off at the dark green woods with the purple mists still hovering about them, she prayed that a way might be shown her by which to put an end to this curse. She prayed for Lisa, and then, thinking that the girl rested somewhat, stole from the room. She thought that she had locked the door behind her.

She went downstairs with a pale, resolved face, and, without consulting any one, sent to the village for a bricklayer. Afterwards she sat by Mistress Hurly's bedside, and explained to her what was to be done. Presently she went to the door of Lisa's room, and hearing no sound, thought the girl slept, and stole away. By-and-by she went downstairs, and found that the bricklayer had arrived and already begun his task of building up the organ-room door. He was a swift workman, and the chamber was soon sealed safely with stone and mortar.

Having seen this work finished, Margaret Calderwood went and listened again at Lisa's door; and still hearing no sound, she returned, and took her seat at Mrs. Hurly's bedside once more. It was towards evening that she at last entered her room to assure herself of the comfort of Lisa's sleep. But the bed and room were empty. Lisa had disappeared.

Then the search began, upstairs and downstairs, in the garden, in the grounds, in the fields and meadows. No Lisa. Margaret Calderwood ordered the carriage and drove to Calderwood to see if the strange little Will-o'-the-wisp might have made her way there; then to the village, and to many other places in the neighbourhood which it was not possible she could have reached. She made inquiries everywhere; she pondered and puzzled over the matter. In the weak, suffering state that the girl was in, how far could she have crawled?

After two days' search, Margaret returned to Hurly Burly. She was sad and tired, and the evening was chill. She sat over the fire wrapped in her shawl when little Bess came to her, weeping behind her muslin apron.

"If you'd speak to Mistress Hurly about it, please, ma'am," she said. "I love her dearly, and it breaks my heart to go away, but the organ haven't done yet, ma'am, and I'm frightened out of my life, so I can't stay."

"Who has heard the organ, and when?" asked Margaret Calderwood, rising to her feet.

"Please, ma'am, I heard it the night you went away—the night after the door was built up!"

"And not since?"

"No, ma'am," hesitatingly, "not since. Hist! hark, ma'am! Is not that like the sound of it now?"

"No," said Margaret Calderwood; "it is only the wind." But pale as death she flew down the stairs and laid her ear to the yet damp mortar of the newly-built wall. All was silent. There was no sound but the monotonous sough of the wind in the trees outside. Then Margaret began to dash her soft shoulder against the strong wall, and to pick the mortar away with her white fingers, and to cry out for the bricklayer who had built up the door.

It was midnight, but the bricklayer left his bed in the village, and obeyed the summons to Hurly Burly. The pale woman stood by and watched him undo all his work of three days ago, and the servants gathered about in trembling groups, wondering what was to happen next.

What happened next was this: When an opening was made the man entered the room with a light, Margaret Calderwood and others following. A heap of something dark was lying on the ground at the foot of the organ. Many groans arose in the fatal chamber. Here was little Lisa dead!

When Mistress Hurly was able to move, the squire and his wife went to live in France, where they remained till their death. Hurly Burly was shut up and deserted for many years. Lately it has passed into new hands. The organ has been taken down and banished, and the room is a bedchamber, more luxuriously furnished than any in the house. But no one sleeps in it twice.

Margaret Calderwood was carried to her grave the other day a very aged woman.

The Hungry Death

It has been a wild night in Innisbofin, an Irish island perched far out among Atlantic breakers, as the bird flies to Newfoundland. Whoever has weathered an ocean hurricane will have some idea of the fury with which the tempest assaults and afflicts such lonely rocks. The creatures who live upon them, at the mercy of the winds and waves, build their cabins low, and put stones on the roof to keep the thatch from flying off on the trail of Mother Carey's chickens; and having made the sign of the cross over their threshold at night, they sleep soundly, undisturbed by the weird and appalling voices which have sung alike the lullaby and death-keen of all their race. In winter, rain and storm are welcome to rage round them, even though fish be frightened away, and food be scarce; but when wild weather encroaches too far upon the spring, then threats of the "hungry death" are heard with fear in its mutterings.

Is anyone to blame for this state of things? The greater part of the island is barren bog and rock. No shrub will grow upon it, and so fiercely is it swept by storm that the land by the northern and eastern coasts is only a picturesque wilderness, all life sheltering itself in three little thatched villages to the south. The sea is the treasury of the inhabitants, and no more daring hearts exist than those that fight these waves, often finding death in their jaws; but a want of even the rudest piers as defence against the Atlantic makes the seeking of bread upon the waters a perilous, and often an entirely impossible, exploit.

Bofin is of no mean size, and has a large population. Light-hearted and frugal, the people feel themselves a little nation, and will point out to you with pride the storied interest of their island. In early ages it was a seat of learning, witness the ruins of St. Coleman's school and church; in Elizabeth's day the queen, Grace O'Malley, built herself a fort on a knoll facing the glories of the western sky; and on the straggling rocks which form the harbour Cromwell raised those blackened walls, still welded into the rock and fronting the foam. The island has a church, a school, a store where meal, oil, soap, ropes, etc., can be had, except when contrary winds detain the *hooker* which plies to and from Galway with such necessaries.

Foreign sailors, weather-bound in Bofin, are welcomed, and invited to make merry. Pipers and fiddlers come and go, and, when times are pretty good, are kept busy making music for dancing feet. Even when the wolf is within a pace of the door laughter and song will ring about his ears, so long as the monster can be beaten back by one neighbour from another neighbour's threshold. But there comes a day when he enters where he will, and the bones of the people are his prey.

Last night's was a spring storm, and many a "Lord, have mercy on us!" went up in the silent hours, as the flooding rain that unearths the seedlings was heard seething on the wind; yet Bohn wakened out of its nightmare of terror green and gay, birds carolling in a blue sky, and the ring of the boat-maker's hammer suggesting peace and prosperity.

Through the dazzling sunshine a girl came rowing herself in a small boat that darted rapidly along the water. The oars made a quick pleasant thud on the air, the larks sang in the clouds, and the girl poured out snatches of a song of her own in a plaintive and mellow voice. The tune was wild and mournful; the words Irish.

Thud, thud, went the oars, the girl's kerchief fell back from her head as the firm elastic figure swayed with the wholesome exercise. Never was a fairer picture of health, strength, and beauty. Her thick, dark red hair filled with the sunshine as a sponge fills with water; her red-brown eyes seemed to emit sparks of fire as the shadows deepened round them in the strong light. Two little round dimples fixed at the corners of the proud curved mouth whispered a tale of unusual determination lying at the bottom of a passionate nature. There was nothing to account for her curious choice of a song this brilliant morning, except the love of dramatic contrasts that exists in some eager souls.

Suddenly she shipped her oars, and sat listening to the waves lapping the edges of the seaweed-fringed cliffs. u I thought I heard someone calling me," she muttered, looking up and down with a slight shudder, but a bold gaze—"Brigid, Brigid, Brigid!" then, with a little laugh, she dipped her oars again, burst into a lively song, so reeling with merriment that it was wonderful how she found breath for it, and her boat flew along the glittering waves like a gull.

Above the broad, shelving, shingly beach within the harbour stood the school, the store, and some of the best dwellings on the island, and high and dry on the gleaming shingle the boat-maker was at work with a knot of gossips around him. The sky over their heads was a vivid blue; the brown-fringed rocks loomed against a sea almost too dazzling to look upon; the dewy green fields lay like scattered emeralds among the rocks and hollows.

"Lord look to us!" said a man in a sou'-wester hat, "if the spring doesn't mend. Half my pratees was washed clane out o' the ground last night."

"Whisht, man, whisht," said the boat-maker cheerfully. "Pick them up an' put them in again."

"Bedad," said an old fisherman, "the fish has got down to the bottom of all etarnity. Ye might as well go fishin' for mermaids."

"Aren't yez ashamed to grumble," cried a hearty voice, joining the group, "an' sich a mornin' as this? I tell ye last night was the last o' the rain."

"Ye have the hopes o' youth about ye, Coll Prendergast," said the old fisherman, looking at the strong frame and smiling bronzed face of the young man before him. "If yer words is not truth it's the sayweed we'll be atin' afore next winther's out."

"Some of it doesn't taste so bad," said Coll, laughing, "an' a little of it dried makes capital tabaccy. But whisht! If here isn't Brigid Lavelle, come all the way from West Quarter in her pretty canoe."

The sound of oars had been heard coming steadily nearer, and suddenly Brigid's boat shot out from behind a mass of rock, making, with its occupant, such a picture on the glittering sea that the men involuntarily smiled as they shaded their eyes with their hands to look. Resting on her oars she smiled at them in return, while the sunshine gilded her oval face, as brown as a berry, burnished the copper-hued hair rippling above her black curved brows, and deepened the determined expression of her full red mouth. Her dress, the costume of the island, was only remarkable for the freshness and newness of its material—a deep crimson skirt of wool, with a light print bodice and short tunic, and a white kerchief thrown over the back of her head.

As she neared the shore Coll sprang into the water, drew her canoe close to the rocks, and, making it fast, helped her to land.

"That's a han'some pair," said the old fisherman to the boat-maker. "I hear their match is as good as made."

"Coll's in luck," said the other. "A rich beauty is not for ivery man."

"She's too proud, I'm thinking. Look at the airs of her now, an' him wet up to the knees in her sarvice."

"Ye'r' ould, man, an' ye forget yer coortin.' Let the crature toss her head while she can."

Brigid had proceeded to the store, where her purchases were soon made: a sack of meal, a can of oil, a little tea and sugar, and some white flour. The girl had a frown on her handsome brows as she did her business, and took but little notice of Coll, who busied himself gallantly with her packages. When all were stored in the boat, he handed her in, and stood looking at her, wondering if she would give him a smile in return for his attentions.

"Let me take the oars, Brigid. Ye'll be home in half the time."

"No, thank ye," she answered shortly. "I'll row my own boat as long as I can."

Coll smiled broadly, half amused and half admiring, and again sought for a friendly glance at parting, but in vain. The face that vanished out of his sight behind the cliff was as cold and proud as though he had been her enemy. After he had turned and was striding up the beach the look that he had wanted to see followed him, shot through a rift in the rocks, where Brigid paused and peered with a tenderness in her eyes that altered her whole face. If Coll had seen that look this story might never have been written.

As the girl's boat sped past the cliffs towards home she frowned, thinking how awkward it was that she should have met Coll Prendergast on the beach. He must have known the errand that brought her to the store, and how dare he smile at her like that before he knew what answer she would give him? Coll's uncle and Brigid's father had planned a match between the young people, and the match-making was to be held that night at Brigid's father's house. Therefore, had she come early in the morning in her boat to the store, to buy provisions for the evening's entertainment. Obedience to her father had obliged her to do this, but her own strong will revolted from the proceeding. She was proud, handsome, and an heiress, and did not like to be so easily won.

Brigid's father was sitting at the fire—a consumptive-looking man, with a wistful and restless eye.

"Father, I have brought very little flour. The *hooker* hasn't got in."

"Sorra wondher, an' sich storms. 'Tis late in the year for things to be this ways."

Brigid arranged her little purchases on the dresser and sat down at the table, but her breakfast, a few roasted potatoes and a tin mug of butter-milk, remained untasted before her.

"Father, isn't you an' me happy as we are? Why need I marry in sich a hurry?"

"Because a lone woman's betther with a husband, my girl."

"I'm not a lone woman. Haven't I got you?"

"Nor for long, avourneen machree. I'm readyin' to go this good while."

"But I will hold you back," cried Brigid passionately, throwing her strong arms around his neck.

"You can't, asthoreen. I'm wanted yonder, and it's time I was gettin' on with my purgatory. An' there's bad times comin', an' I will not let you face them alone."

"I could pack up my bundles and be off to America," said Brigid stoutly, dashing away tears.

"I will not have you wanderin' over the world like a stray bird," said the father emphatically; and Brigid knew there was nothing more to be said.

Lavelle's prosperity appeared before the world in a great deal of clean whitewash outside the house, and an interior more comfortable than is usual on the island. The cabin consisted of two rooms: the kitchen, with earthen floor and heather-lined roof, roosting-place for cocks and hens, and with its dresser, old and worm-eaten, showing a fair display of crockery; and the best room, containing a bed, a few pictures of sacred subjects, some sea-shells on the chimney-piece, an ornamental tray, an old gun, and an ancient time-blackened crucifix against the wall, this last having been washed ashore one morning after the wreck of a Spanish ship.

This was the finest house in Bofin, and Tim Lavelle, having returned from seeing the world and married late in life, had settled down in it, and on the most fertile bit of land on the island. It was thought he had a stockingful of money in the thatch, which would of course be the property of his daughter; so, no wonder if the handsome Brigid had grown up a little spoiled with the knowledge of her own happy importance.

As she went about her affairs this morning, she owned to herself that she would not be sorry to be forced to be Coll's wife in spite of her pride. True he had paid her less court hitherto than any other young man on the island, and she longed to punish him for that; but what would become of her if she saw him married to another? Oh, if they had only left the matter to herself, she could have managed it so much better—could have plagued him to her heart's content, and made him anxious to win her by means of the difficulties she would have thrown in his way.

Had Coll been as poor as he seemed to be, with nothing but his boat and fishing-tackle, she would have been easier to woo, for then eagerness to bestow on him the contents of that stocking in the thatch would have swept away the stumbling-block of her pride. But his uncle had saved some money, which was to be given to Prendergast on the day of his marriage with her. It was a made-up match like Judy O'Flaherty's, while Brigid's proud head was crazed on the subject of being loved for her love's sake alone.

"I'll have to give him my hand tonight," she said, folding her brown arms, and standing straight in the middle of the room she had been dusting and decorating. "I be to obey father, an' I'll shame nobody afore the neighbours. But match-makin' isn't marryin'; and if it was to break my heart an' do my death I'll find means to plague him into lovin' me yet."

Having made this resolve she let down her long hair, that looked dark bronze while she sat in the corner putting on her shoes, and turned to gold as she walked through a sunbeam crossing the floor, and having brushed it out and twisted it up again in a coil round her head, she finished her simple toilet and went out to the kitchen to receive her visitors.

The first that arrived was Judy O'Flaherty, an old woman with a smoke-dried face, who sat down in the chimney corner and lit her pipe. Judy was arrayed in a large patchwork quilt folded like a shawl, being too poor to indulge in the luxury of a cloak. But the quilt, made of red-and-white calico patches, was clean, and the cap on her head was fresh and neat.

"I give ye joy of Coll Prendergast," said Judy heartily. "Ye ought to be the glad girl to get sich a match."

"Why ought I be glad?" asked Brigid angrily. "It's all as one may think."

"Holy Mother, girl! don't be sendin' them red sparks out o' yer eyes at me! Where d'ye see the likes o' Coll, I'm askin', with his six feet if he's an inch, an' his eyes like the blue on the Reek afore nightfall?"

Brigid's heart leaped to hear him praised, and she turned away her face to hide the smile that curled her lips.

"An' yer match so aisy made for ye, without trouble to either o' ye. Not like some poor cratures, that have to round the world afore they can get one to put a roof over their heads or a bit in their mouths. It's me that knows. Sure, wasn't I a wanderin' bein', doin' day's works in the mountains, and as purty a girl as you, Miss Brigid, on'y I hadn't the stockin' in the thatch, nor the good father to be settlin' for me. An' sore an' tired an' spent I was when one night I heard a knock at the door o' the house I was workin' in, and a voice called out: 'Get up, Judy; here's a man come to marry you!' Maybe I didn't dress quick; an' who was there but a woman that knew my mother long ago, an' she had met a widow-man that wanted somebody to look after his childer.

"An' she brought him to me, an' wakened me out o' my sleep for fear he'd take the rue. An' we all sat o'er the fire for the rest o' the night to make the match, and in the first morning light we went down to Father Daly and got married. There's my marriage for ye, an' the rounds I had to get it, an' many a wan is like me. An' yet ye'r' tossing yer head at Coll, you that hasn't as much as the trouble o' bein' axed."

The smile had gone off Brigid's face. This freedom from trouble was the very thing that troubled her. She would rather have had the excitement of being "axed" a hundred questions. As they talked the sunshine vanished, and the rain again fell in torrents. Brigid looked out of the door with a mischievous hope that the guests might be kept at home and the matchmaking postponed. Judy rocked herself and groaned:

"Oh, musha, the piatees, the piatees! O Lord, look down with mercy on the poor!" then suddenly became silent, and began telling her beads.

A slight lull in the storm brought the company in a rush to the door, with bursts of laughter, groans for the rain and the potatoes, shaking and drying of cloaks and coats, and squealing and tuning up of pipes. Among the rest came Coll, smiling and confident as ever, with an arch look in his eyes when they met Brigid's, and not the least symptom of fear or anxiety in his face. Soon the door was barred against the storm, the fish-oil lamp lighted, laughter, song, and dancing filled the little house, and the rotting potatoes and the ruinous rains were forgotten as completely as though the Bofin population had been goddesses and gods, with whose nectar and ambrosia no such thing as weather could dare to interfere.

"Faith, ye must dance with me, Brigid," said Coll, after she had refused him half-a-dozen times.

"Why must I dance with you?"

"Oh, now, don't ye know what's goin' on in there?" said Coll roguishly, signing towards the room where father and uncle were arguing over money and land.

"I do," said Brigid, with all the red fire of her eyes blazing out upon him. "But, mind ye, this matchmakin' is none o' my doin'."

"Why then, avourneen?"

"I'm not goin' to marry a man that on'y wants a wife, an' doesn't care a pin whether it's me or another."

"Bedad, I do care," said Coll awkwardly. "I'm a bad hand at the speakin', but I care entirely."

But Brigid went off, and danced with another man. Coll was puzzled. He did not understand her in the least. He was a simple, straightforward fellow, and had truly been in love with Brigid—a fact which his confident manner had never allowed her to believe. Latterly he had begun to feel afraid of her; whenever he tried to say a tender word, that red light in her eyes would flash and strike him dumb. He had hoped that when their "match was made" she would have grown a little kinder; but it seemed she was only getting harsher instead. Well, he would try and hit on some way to please her; and, as he walked home that night, he pondered on all sorts of plans for softening her proud temper and satisfying her exacting mind.

On her side, Brigid saw that she had startled him out of his ordinary easy humour, and, congratulating herself on the spirit she had shown, resolved to continue her present style of proceeding. Not one smile would she give him till she had, as she told herself, nearly tormented him to death. How close she was to keep to the letter of her resolution could not at this time be foreseen.

Every evening after this Coll travelled across half the island to read some old treasured newspaper to the sickly Lavelle, and bringing various little offerings to his betrothed. Everything that Bofin could supply in the way of a love-gift was sought by him, and presented to her. Now it was a few handsome shells purchased from a foreign sailor in the harbour, or it was the model of a boat he had carved for her himself; and all this attention was not without its lasting effect. Unfortunately, however, while Brigid's heart grew more soft, her tongue only waxed more sharp, and her eyes more scornful.

The more clearly, she perceived that she would soon have to yield, the more haughty and capricious did she become. Had the young man been able to see behind outward appearances he would have been thoroughly satisfied, and a good deal startled at the vehemence of the devotion that had grown up and strengthened for him in that proud and wayward heart. As it was, he felt more and more chilled by her continued coldness, and began to weary of a pursuit which seemed unlikely to be either for his dignity or his happiness.

Meanwhile the rain went on falling. The spring was bad, the summer was bad, potatoes were few and unwholesome, the turf lay undried, and rotting on the bog. Distress began to pinch the cheerful faces of the islanders, and laughter and song were half drowned in murmurs of fear. At the sight of so much sorrow and anxiety around her Brigid's heart began to ache, and to smite and reproach her for her selfish and unruly humours. One night, softened by the sufferings of others, she astonished herself by falling on her knees and giving humble thanks to Heaven for the undeserved happiness that was awaiting her.

She vowed that the next time Coll appeared she would put her hand in his, and let the love of her heart shine out in the smiles of her eyes. Had she kept this vow it might have been well with her, but her habit of vexing had grown all too strong to be cured in an hour. At the first sight of her lover's anxious face in the doorway all her passion for tormenting him returned.

It was an evening in the end of May; the day had been cold and wet, and as dark as January, but the rain had ceased, the clouds had parted, and one of those fiery sunsets burst upon the world that sometimes appear unexpectedly in the midst of stormy weather. In Bofin, where the sun drops down the heavens from burning cloud to cloud, and sinks in the ocean, the whole island was wrapped in a crimson flame.

Brigid stood at her door, gazing at the wonderful spectacle of the heavens and sea, looking herself strangely handsome, with her bronze hair glittering in the ruddy sunlight, and that dark shadow about her eyes and brows which, except when she smiled, always gave a look of tragedy to her face. She was waiting for Coll, with softened lips and downcast eyes, and was so lost in her own thoughts that she did not see when he stood beside her.

He remained silently watching her for a few moments, thinking that if she would begin to look like that, he would be ready to love her as well as he had ever loved her, and to forget that he had ever wearied of her harassing scorn. At this very moment Brigid was rehearsing within her mind a kind little speech which was to establish a good understanding between them.

"I'm sorry I vexed you so often, for I love you true," were the words she had meant to speak; but suddenly seeing Coll by her side the habitual taunt flew involuntarily to her lips.

"You here again!" she said disdainfully. "Then no one can say but you're the perseverin'est man in the island!"

"Maybe I'm too perseverin'," said Coll quietly, and, as Brigid looked at him with covert remorse, she saw something in his face that frightened her. His expression was a mixture of weariness and contempt. He was not hurt, or angry, or amused, as she had been accustomed to see him, but tired of her insolence, which was ceasing to give him pain. A sudden consciousness of this made Brigid turn sick at heart, and she felt that she had at last gone a little too far, that she had been losing him all this time while triumphantly thinking to win him. Oh, why could she not speak and say the word that she wanted to say?

While this anguish came into her thoughts her brows grew darker than ever, and the warmth ebbed gradually out of her cheek. They went silently into the house, where Brigid took up her knitting, and Coll dropped into his seat beside Lavelle. The bad times, the rotting crops, the scant expectations of a harvest, were discussed by the two men while Brigid sat fighting with her pride, and trying to decide on what she ought to say or do. Before she had made up her mind Coll had said good-evening abruptly, and gone out of the house.

The young fisherman's home was in Middle Quarter Village, a cluster of grey stone cabins close to the sea, and, to reach it, Coll had to cross almost the whole breadth of the island. He set out on his homeward walk with a weary and angry heart. Brigid's dark, unyielding face followed him, and he was overwhelmed by a fit of unusual depression. He whistled as he went, trying to shake it off. Why should he fret about a woman who disliked him, and who probably loved another whom her father disapproved? Let her do what she liked with herself and her purse. Coll would persecute her no more.

The red light had slowly vanished off the island, and the dark cliffs on the oceanward coast loomed large and black against the still lurid sky. Deep drifts of brown and purple flecked with amber swept across the bogs, and filled up the dreary horrors of the barren and irreclaimable land, which Coll had to traverse on his way to the foam-drenched village where the fishermen lived. The heavens cooled to paler tints, a ring of yellow light encircled the island with its creeping shadows and ghost-like rocks. Twilight was descending when Coll heard a faint cry from the distance, like the call of a belated bird or the wail of a child in distress.

At first, he thought it was the wind or a plover, but straining his eyes in the direction whence it came he saw a small form standing solitary in the middle of a distant hollow, a piece of treacherous bog, dangerous in the crossing except to knowing feet. Hurrying to the spot, he found himself just in time to succour a fellow-creature in distress.

Approaching as near as he could with ease to the person who had summoned him, he saw a very young girl standing gazing towards him with piteous looks. She was small, slight, poorly and scantily clad, and carried a creel full of sea-wrack on her slight and bending shoulders. A pale after-gleam from the sky fell where she stood, young and forlorn, in the shadowy solitude, and lit up a face round and delicately pale, reminding one of a daisy; a wreath of wind-tossed yellow hair and eyes as blue as forget-me-nots.

Terror had taken possession of her, and she stretched out her hands appealingly to the strong man, who stood looking at her from the op-posite side of the bog. Coll observed her in silence for a few moments. It seemed as if he had known her long ago, and that she belonged to him; yet if so, it was in another state of existence, for he assured himself that she was no one with whom he had any acquaintance. However that might be, he was determined to know more of her now, for, with her childlike appealing eyes and outstretched hands, she went straight into Coll's heart, to nestle there like a dove for evermore.

"Aisy, asthoreen," cried Coll across the bog, "I'm goin' to look after ye. Niver ye fear."

He crossed the morass with a few rapid springs, and stood by her side.

"Give me the creel, avourneen, till I land it for ye safe."

A few minutes, and the burden was deposited on the safe side of the bog, and then Coll came back and took the young girl in his arms.

"Keep a good hoult round my neck, machree."

It was a nice feat for a man to pick his way through the bog with even so small a woman as this in his arms. The girl clung to him in fear, as he swayed and balanced himself on one sure stone after an-other, slipping here and stumbling there, but always recovering himself before mischief could be done. At last, the deed was accomplished, the goal was won.

"Ye were frightened, acushla," said Coll tenderly.

"I was feared of dhrownin' ye," said the girl, looking wistfully in his face with her great blue eyes.

"Sorra matther if ye had," said Coll laughingly, "except that maybe ye'd ha' been dhrowned too. Now which ways are ye goin'? And maybe ye'd be afther tellin' me who ye are."

"I'm Moya Maillie," said the girl; "an' I live in Middle Quarter Village."

"Why, ye'r' niver little Moya that I used to see playing round poor Maillie's door that's dead an' gone? And how did ye grow up that ways in a night?"

"Mother says I'll niver grow up," laughed Moya; "but I'm sixteen on May mornin', and I'll be contint to be as I am."

"Many a fine lady would give her fortune to be contint with that same," said Coll, striding along with the creel on his shoulders, and glancing down every minute at the sweet white-flower-like face that flitted through the twilight at his side. Thus, Brigid's repentance would now come all too late, for Coll had fallen in love with little Moya.

How he brought her home that night to a bare and poverty-stricken cabin in the sea-washed fishing village, and restored her like a stray lamb to her mother, need not be told. Her mother was a widow and the mother of seven, and Moya's willing labour was a great part of the family support. She mended nets for the fishermen, and carried wrack for the neighbours' land, knitted stockings to be sent out to the great world and sold, and did any other task which her slender and eager hands could find to do. Coll asked himself in amazement how it was that having known her as a baby he had never observed her existence since then. Now an angel, he believed, had led her out into the dreary bog to stand waiting for his sore heart on that blessed day of days. And he would never marry anyone but little Moya.

It was impossible they could marry while times were so bad, but, every evening after this, Moya might be seen perched on an old boat upon the shingle, busy with her knitting—her tiny feet, bare and so brown, crossed under the folds of her old worn red petticoat, with a faint rose-pink in her pale cheeks, and a light of extraordinary happiness in her childlike blue eyes. Coll lay on the shingle at her feet, and these two found an Elysium in each other's company. There was much idleness perforce for the men of Bofin at this time, and Coll filled up his hours looking after the concerns of the Widow Maillie, carrying Moya's burdens, and making the hard times as easy for her as he could. When people would look surprised at him and ask, "Arrah, thin, what about Brigid Lavelle?" Coll would answer, "Oh, she turned me off long ago. Everybody knows that she could not bear the sight of me."

In the meantime, Brigid, at the other end of the island, was watching daily and hourly for Coll's reappearance. As evening after evening passed without bringing him, her heart misgave her more and more, and she mourned bitterly over her own harshness and pride. Oh, if he would only come once again with that wistful, questioning look in his brave face, how kindly she would greet him, how eagerly put her hand in his grasp! As the rain rained on through the early summer evenings there would often come before sunset a lightening and brightening all over the sky, and this was the hour at which Brigid used to look for her now ever-absent lover.

Climbing to the top of the hill, she would peer over the sea-bound landscape, with its dark stretches of bog, and strips and flecks of green, towards the grey irregular line of the fishing village, the smoke of which she could see hanging against the horizon. Her face grew paler and her eyes dull, but to no one, not even to her father, would she admit that she was pining for Coll's return. She had always lived much by herself, and had few gossiping friends to bring her news. At last, unable to bear the suspense any longer, she made an excuse of business at the store on the beach; and before she had gone far among the houses of that metropolis of the island, she was enlightened as to the cause of her lover's defection.

"So ye cast him off? So ye giv' him to little Moya Maillie?" were the words that greeted her wherever she turned. She smiled and nodded her head, as if heartily assenting to what was said, and content with the existing state of things; but as she walked away out of the reach of observing eyes, her face grew dark, and her heart throbbed like to burst in her bosom. Almost mechanically she took her way home through the Middle Quarter Village, with a vague desire to see what was to be seen, and to hear whatever was to be heard.

She passed among the houses without observing anything that interested her, but, as she left the village, by the sea-shore she came upon Coll and Moya sitting on a rock in the yellow light of a watery sunset, with a mist of sea-foam around them, and a net over their knees which they were mending between them. Their heads were close together, and Coll was looking in her face with the very look which, all these tedious days and nights, Brigid had been wearying to meet. She walked up beside them, and stood looking at them silently with a light in her eyes that was not good to behold.

"Brigid," said Coll, when he could bear it no longer, "For Heaven's sake, are ye not satisfied yet?"

She turned from him and fixed her strange glance on Moya.

"It was me before, an' it's you now," she said shortly. "He's a constant lover, isn't he?"

"I loved ye true, and ye scoffed and scorned me," said Coll gently, as the gleam of anguish and despair in her eyes startled him. "I wasn't good enough for Brigid, but I'm good enough for Moya. We're neither of us as rich nor as clever as you, but we'll do for one another well enough."

Brigid laughed a sharp sudden laugh, and still looked at Moya.

"For Heaven's sake take that wicked look off her face!" cried Coll hastily. "Whatsomdever way it is betune us three is yer own doin'; an', whether ye like it or not, it cannot now be helped."

"I will never forgive either of you," said Brigid in a low hard voice; and then, turning abruptly away, she set out on her homeward walk through the gathering shadows.

CHAPTER 2

All through that summer the rain fell, and, when autumn came in Bofin, there was no harvest either of fuel or of food. The potato-seed had been, for the most part, washed out of the earth without putting forth a shoot, while those that remained in the ground were nearly all rotted by a loathsome disease. The smiling little fields that grew the food were turned into blackened pits, giving forth a horrid stench. Winter was beginning again, the year having been but one long winter, with seas too wild to be often braved by even the sturdiest of the fishermen, and the fish seeming to have deserted the island. Accustomed to exist on what would satisfy no other race, and to trust cheerfully to Providence to send them that little out of the earth and out of the sea, the people bore up cheerfully for a long time, living on a mess of Indian meal once a day, mingled with such edible seaweed as they could gather off the rocks.

So long as shopkeepers in Galway and other towns could afford to give credit to the island, the *hooker* kept bringing such scanty supplies as were now the sole sustenance of the impoverished population. But credit began to fail, and universal distress on the mainland gave back an answering wail to the hunger-cry of the Bofiners. It is hard for anyone who has never witnessed such a state of things to imagine the condition of ten or twelve hundred living creatures, on a barren island girdled round with angry breakers; the strong arms among them paralyzed, first by the storms that dash their boats to pieces, and rend and destroy their fishing gear, and the devastation of the earth that makes labour useless, and later by the faintness and sickness which come from hunger long endured, and the cold from which they have no longer a defence.

Accustomed as they are to the hardships of recurring years of trial, the Bofiners became gradually aware that a visitation was at hand for which there had seldom been a parallel. Earth and sea alike barren and pitiless to their needs, whence could deliverance come unless the heavens rained down manna into their mouths? Alas! no miracle was wrought, and after a term of brave struggle, hope in Providence, cheerful pushing off the terrible fears for the worst—after this, laughter, music, song, faded out of the island; feet that had danced as long as it was possible now might hardly walk, and the weakest among the people began to die.

Troops of children that a few months ago were rosy and sturdy, sporting on the sea-shore, now stretched their emaciated limbs by the fireless hearths, and wasted to death before their maddened mothers' eyes. The old and ailing vanished like flax before a flame. Digging of graves was soon the chief labour of the island, and a day seemed near at hand when the survivors would no longer have strength to perform even this last service for the dead.

Lavelle and his daughter were among the last to suffer from the hard times, and they shared what they had with their poor neighbours; but in course of time the father caught the fever which famine had brought in its train, and was quickly swept into his grave, while the girl was left alone in possession of their little property, with her stocking in the thatch and her small flock of "beasts" in the field. Her first independent act was to despatch all the money she had left by a trusty hand to Galway to buy meal, in one of those pauses in the bad weather which sometimes allowed a boat to put off from the island.

The meal arrived after long, unavoidable delay, and Brigid became a benefactor to numbers of her fellow-creatures. Late and early, she trudged from village to village and from house to house, doling out her meal to make it go as far as possible, till her own face grew pale and her step slow, for she stinted her own food to have the more to give away. Her "beasts" grew lean and dejected. Why should she feed them at the expense of human life? They were killed, and the meat given to her famishing friends. The little property of the few other well-to-do families in like manner melted away, and it seemed likely that "rich" and poor would soon all be buried in one grave.

In the Widow Maillie's house, the famine had been early at work. Five of Moya's little sisters and brothers had one by one sickened and dropped upon the cabin floor. The two elder boys still walked about looking like galvanised skeletons, and the mother crept from wall to wall of her house trying to pretend that she did not suffer, and to cook the mess of rank-looking sea-weed, which was all they could procure in the shape of food. Coll risked his life day after day trying to catch fish to relieve their hunger, but scant and few were the meals that all his efforts could procure from the sea.

White and gaunt he followed little Moya's steps, as with the spirit of a giant she kept on toiling among the rocks for such weeds or shell-fish as could be supposed to be edible. When she fell Coll bore her up, but the once powerful man was not able to carry her now. Her lovely little face was hollow and pinched, the cheek bones cutting through the skin. Her sweet blue eyes were sunken and dim, her pretty mouth purple and strained. Her beauty and his strength were alike gone.

Three of the boys died in one night, and it took Coll, wasted as he was, two days to dig a grave deep enough to bury them. Before that week was over all the children were dead of starvation, and the mother scarcely alive. One evening Coll made his way slowly across the island from the beach carrying a small bag of meal which he had unexpectedly obtained. Now and again his limbs failed, and he had to lie down and rest upon the ground; but with long perseverance and unconquerable energy he reached the little fishing village at last. As he passed the first house Brigid Lavelle, pallid and worn, the spectre of herself, came out of the door with an empty basket.

Coll and she stared at each other in melancholy amazement. It was the first time they had met since the memorable scene on the rocks many months ago, for Coll's entire time had been devoted to the Maillies, and Brigid had persistently kept out of his way, striving, by charity to others, to quench the fire of angry despair in her heart. Coll would scarcely have recognised her in her present deathlike guise, had it not been for the still living glory of her hair.

The sight of Coll's great frame, once so stalwart and erect, now stooping and attenuated, his lustreless eyes, and blue cold lips, struck horror into Brigid's heart. She uttered a faint sharp cry and disappeared. Coll scarcely noticed her, his thoughts were so filled with another; and a little further on he met Moya coming to meet him, walking with a slow uneven step, that told of the whirling of the exhausted brain. Half blind with weakness she stretched her hands before her as she walked.

"The hungry death is on my mother at last. Oh, Coll, come in and see the last o' her!"

"Whisht, machree! Look at the beautiful taste o' male I am bringin' her. Hard work I had to carry it from the beach, for the eyes o' the cratures is like wolves' eyes, an' I thought the longin' o' them would have dragged it out o' my hands. An', Moya, there's help comin' from God to us. There's kind people out in the world that's thinkin' o' our need. The man that has just landed with a sack, an' giv' me this, says there's a *hooker* full o' male on its road to us this day. May the great Lord send us weather to bring it here."

"I'm feared—I'm feared it's too late for her," sobbed Moya, clinging to him.

They entered the cabin where the woman lay, a mere skeleton covered with skin, with the life still flickering in her glassy eyes. Coll put a little of the meal, as it was, between her lips, while Moya hastened to cook the rest on a fire made of the dried roots of heather. The mother turned loving looks from one to the other, tried to swallow a little of the food to please them, gasped, shuddered a little, and was dead.

It was a long, hard task for Coll and Moya to bury her, and when this was done, they sat on the heather clasping each other's wasted hands. The sky was dark; the storm was coming on again. As night approached a tempest was let loose upon the island, and many famishing hearts that had throbbed with a little hope at the news of the relief that was on its way to them, now groaned, sickened, and broke in despair. Louder howled the wind, and the sea raged around the dangerous rocks towards which no vessel could dare to approach. It was the doing of the Most High, said the perishing creatures. His scourge was in His hand. Might His ever-blessed will be done.

That evening Moya became delirious, and Coll watched all night by her side. At morning light, he fled out and went round the village, crying out desperately to God and man to send him a morsel of food to save the life of his young love. The suffering neighbours turned pitying eyes upon him.

"I'm feared it's all over with her when she can't taste the sayweed any more," said one.

"Why don't ye go to Brigid Lavelle?" said another. "She hasn't much left, poor girl; but maybe she'd have a mouthful for you."

Till this moment Coll had felt that he could not go begging of

Brigid; but, now that Moya's precious life was slipping rapidly out of his hands, he would suffer the deepest humiliation she could heap upon him, if only she would give him so much food as would keep breath in Moya's body till such time as by Heaven's mercy the storm might abate, and the *hooker* with the relief-meal arrive.

Brigid was alone in her house. A little porridge for some poor creature simmered on a scanty fire, and the girl stood in the middle of the floor, her hands wrung together above her head, and her brain distracted with the remembrance of Coll as she had seen him stricken by the scourge. All these months she had told her jealous heart that the Maillies were safe enough since they had Coll to take care of them. So long as there was a fish in the sea, he would not let them starve, neither need be in any danger himself. And so, she had never asked a question about him or them. Now the horror of his altered face haunted her. She had walked through the direst scenes with courageous calm, but this one unexpected sight of woe had maddened her.

A knock came to the door which at first, she could not hear for the howling of the wind; but when she heard and opened there was Coll standing before her.

"Meal," he said faintly—"a little meal, for the love of Christ! Moya is dying."

A spasm of anguish and tenderness had crossed Brigid's face at the first words; but at the mention of Moya her face darkened.

"Why should I give to you or Moya?" she said coldly. "There's them that needs the help as much as ye."

"But not more," pleaded Coll. "Oh, Brigid, I'm not askin' for myself. I fear I vexed ye, though I did not mean it. But Moya niver did anyone any harm. Will you give me a morsel to save her from the hungry death?"

"I said I niver would forgive either o' ye, an' I niver will," said Brigid slowly. "Ye broke my heart, an' why wouldn't I break yours?"

"Brigid, perhaps neither you nor me has much longer to live. Will ye go before yer Judge with sich black words on yer lips?"

"That's my affair," she answered in the same hard voice; and then, suddenly turning from him, shut the door in his face.

She stood listening within, expecting to hear him returning to implore her, but no further sound was heard; and, when she found he was gone, she dropped upon the floor with a shriek, and rocked herself in a frenzy of remorse for her wickedness.

"But I cannot help everyone," she moaned; "I'm starving myself, an' there's nothin' but a han'ful o' male at the bottom o' the bag."

After a while she got up, and carried the mess of porridge to the house for which she had intended it, and all that day she went about, doing what charity she could, and not tasting anything herself. Returning, she lay down on the heather, overcome with weakness, fell asleep, and had a terrible dream. She saw herself dead and judged; a black-winged angel put the mark of Cain on her forehead, and at the same moment Coll and Moya went, glorified and happy, hand in hand, into heaven before her eyes. "Depart from me, you accursed!" thundered in her ears; and she started wide awake to hear the winds and waves roaring unabated round her head.

Wet and shivering she struggled to regain her feet, and stood irresolute where to go. Dreading to return to her desolate home, she mechanically set her face towards the little church on the cliffs above the beach. On her way to it she passed prostrate forms, dying or dead, on the heather, on the roadside, and against the cabin walls. A few weakly creatures, digging graves, begged from her as she went past, but she took no notice of anything, living or dead, making straight for the church. No one was there, and the storm howled dismally through the empty, barn-like building. Four bare, whitewashed walls, and a rude wooden altar with a painted tabernacle and cross—this was the church.

On one long wall was hung a large crucifix, a white, thorn-crowned Figure upon stakes of black-painted wood, which had been placed there in memory of a "mission" lately preached on the island; and on this Brigid's burning eyes fixed themselves with an agony of meaning. Slowly approaching it she knelt and stretched out her arms, uttering no prayer, but swaying herself monotonously to and fro. After a while the frenzied pain of remorse was dulled by physical exhaustion, and a stupor was stealing over her senses, when a step entering the church startled her back to consciousness. Looking round, she saw that the priest of the island had come in, and was wearily dragging himself towards the altar.

Father John was suffering and dying with his people. He had just now returned from a round of visits among the sick, during which he had sped some departing souls on their journey, and given the last consolation of religion to the dying. His own gaunt face and form bore witness to the unselfishness which had made all his little worldly goods the common property of the famishing. Before he had reached the rails of the altar Brigid had thrown herself on her face at his feet.

"Save me, father, save me!" she wailed. "The sin of murther is on my soul!"

"Nonsense, child! No such thing. It is too much that you have been doing, my poor Brigid! I fear the fever has crazed your brain."

"Listen to me, father. Moya is dying, an' there is still a couple o' han'fuls of male in the bag. Coll came an' asked me for her, an' I hated her because he left me, an' I would not give it to him, an' maybe she is dead."

"You refused her because you hated her?" said the priest. "God help you, my poor Brigid. 'Tis true you can't save every life; but you must try and save this one."

Brigid glanced at him, brightly at first, as if an angel had spoken, and then the dark shadow fell again into her eyes.

The priest saw it.

"Look there, my poor soul," he said, extending a thin hand towards the Figure on the cross. "Did *He* forgive His enemies, or did He not?"

Brigid turned her fascinated gaze to the crucifix, fixed them on the thorn-crowned face, and, uttering a wild cry, got up and tottered out of the church.

Spurred by terror lest her amend should come too late, and Moya be dead before she could reach her, she toiled across the heather once more, over the dreary bogs, and through the howling storm. Dews of suffering and exhaustion were on her brow as she carefully emptied all the meal that was left of her store into a vessel, and stood for a moment looking at it in her hand.

"There isn't enough for all of us," she said, "an' some of us be to die. It was always her or me, her or me; an' now it'll be me. May Christ receive me, Moya, as I forgive you." And then she kissed the vessel, and put it under her cloak.

Leaving the house, she was careless to close the door behind her, feeling certain that she should never cross the threshold again, and, straining all her remaining strength to the task, she urged her lagging feet by the shortest way to the Middle Quarter Village. Dire were the sights she had to pass upon her way. Many a skeleton hand was out-stretched for the food she carried; but Brigid was now deaf and blind to all appeals. She saw only Coll's accusing face and Moya's glazing eyes staring terribly at her out of the rain-clouds. Reaching the Mail-lies' cabin, she found the door fastened against the storm.

Coll was kneeling in despair by Moya, when a knocking at the door aroused him. The poor fellow had prayed so passionately, and was in so exalted a state, that he almost expected to see an angel of light upon the threshold, bringing the food he had so urgently asked for. The priest had been there and was gone, and the neighbours were sunk in their own misery; why should anyone come knocking like that unless it were an angel bringing help? Trembling he opened the door; and there was Brigid, or her ghost.

"Am I in time?" gasped she, as she put the vessel of food in his hand.

"Ay," said Coll, seizing it. In his transport of delight he would have gone on his knees and kissed her feet; but before he could speak, she was gone.

Whither should she go now? was Brigid's thought. No use returning to the desolate and lonesome home, where neither food nor fire was any longer to be found. She dreaded dying on her own hearthstone alone, and faint as she was, she knew what was now before her. Gaining the path to the beach, she made a last pull on her energies to reach the whitewashed walls, above which her fading eyes just dimly discerned the cross. The only face she now wanted to look upon again was that thorn-crowned face, which was waiting for her in the loneliness of the empty and wind-swept church.

Falling, fainting, dragging herself on again, she crept within the shelter of the walls. A little more effort, and she would be at His feet. The struggle was made, blindly, slowly, desperately, with a last rally of all the passion of a most impassioned nature; and at last, she lay her length on the earthen floor beneath the cross. Darkness, silence, peace, settled down upon her. The storm raved around, the night, came on, and when the morning broke Brigid was dead.

★★★★★★★★★★★★★★★★★

Mildly and serenely that day had dawned, a pitiful sky looked down on the calamities of Bofin, and the vessel with the relief-meal sailed into the harbour. For many even then alive the food came all too late, but to numbers it brought assuagement and salvation. The charity of the world was at work, and though much had yet to be suffered, yet the hungry death had been mercifully stayed. Thanks to the timely help, Moya lived for better times, and when her health was somewhat restored, she emigrated with Coll to America. Every night in their distant backwoods hut they pray together for the soul of Brigid Lavelle, who, when in this world, had loved one of them too well, and died to save the life of the other.

The Lady Tantivy

Had I been napping? My head had fallen back, and my cap was awry. I had been in the garden all the afternoon gathering roses for *pot-pourri*, hoping that the absent might one day return to enjoy it, and thankful for occupation, as the summer days were long and lonesome in this remote spot, this great unpeopled house. When one is tired one easily falls asleep. But, then, how could I have been awakened by the horn of a coach?

Yet there it came again. Even in these days of extraordinary enterprise, who would run a coach through our out-of-the-world bit of country—a solitude leading, as one might say, from nowhere to nowhere else.

I put my cap straight and stood at the window, while again, louder and clearer, sounded the unusual music on the summer evening air. I left my sitting-room and stood at the open door of the great hall and looked out. Between mountainous walls of dark trees poured an avenue of sunshine across that bend in the hills where the sun was setting. Not from that side was the sound coming; but there again—*tantivy—tantivy—tantivy!* From the winding road that skirts the long miles of downs lying between us and ——shire. My ears strained to catch the cheerful echo, and I wished I were a passenger by that coach out into the lively world. But another blast of the bugle and the roll of quick coming wheels, startlingly near, assured me that the coach in question had turned in at our gates, and was posting towards me.

I stepped forward and strained my neck to see the first appearance of the vehicle as it rounded the corner of the broad drive; and here it came, speeding towards the house, as fine a specimen of a four-in-hand as ever was turned out in style by a coaching club. It was covered with passengers on the outside, and faces were looking laughingly out of the windows. They had all the air of gay ladies and gentlemen out for amusement.

As they drove up with a long flourishing blast of the horn, I was struck by the eccentricity of the dress of this coaching company: the men in peculiarly shaped hats, high-collared coats and tight waists, the ladies with immense bonnets and scanty skirts. The horses were foaming, and I thought of the stables without grooms, nobody about but an old gardener and myself, and one woman-servant. I advanced a step, but nobody seemed looking at me, or even to perceive me.

When the coach stopped a gentleman descended from the box-seat, opened the door of the coach, and handed out a lady, closed the door again, conducted her to the hall-door steps, left her there, and immediately remounted to his own seat. The driver gathered up the reins, the horn was blown, and the horses started. In a few moments the coach was out of sight, the sound of the retreating bugle grew fainter and fainter, and the lady remained standing on the doorsteps, alone and with her back to me.

When the horn was no longer audible, she turned round, and came tripping up the steps, a charming young figure, her white muslin gown crisp and fresh with little frills and furbelows such as I had only seen in pictures of my grandmother's days. Her blue sash and the little silk bag of the colour of forget-me-nots that hung from her waist had a coquettish grace, matching the curve of her long slender neck, round which golden ringlets clung, and the arch smile on her rose-mouth and in the eyes that were looking up at me. Her headdress, a peculiar basket-like object, hung from her arm, as did a long, slim, white scarf of some silken fabric.

"I am coming to spend a night with you," she said, so sweetly that I was captivated at once. "I have travelled from what would seem to you a distance——"

"Pray come in, though I cannot promise you much in the way of entertainment," I said. "I am only caretaker in the home of my relative, who is abroad—unfortunately." My sigh, and the word "unfortunately" would, I hoped, remind her of the misfortunes of our house, of which she had probably heard.

"I know all about it," she answered. "I am a member of the family. As I said, I have come a long way, according to your ideas, to spend a night with you. Will you take me all over the old house, and talk to me about the family? I am more interested than I can tell you in the fortunes of my kindred."

"But, my dear child," I said, "where have you come from, if I may ask, and—pardon me—but how am I to know——?"

"That I am not a robber? Sit up, and watch all night—you and your servant and the old gardener. I am only one girl against the three of you. But, cousin, give me better treatment than this. You need have no doubt of me."

I felt ashamed of what she had seen in my eyes, and, wondering still at her reticence, I ran over in my mind an outline of the various far-out branches of the family tree, trying to guess which of them had dropped me this blossom. I could not recall that any of my distant cousins owned a daughter of her age.

"No," she said, seeming, as before, to answer my thought, "you cannot place me among our relatives, and I do not intend to enlighten you tonight. Tomorrow you shall know more about me. In the meantime, take me round the old garden before the daylight goes, and tell me everything you can about the present-day family."

I thought "present-day" a curious term to use, but noticing that she replied to my questions without informing me as to the point, I put on my cloak and gathered up my skirts, and led the way through the dewy alleys of green to the great old garden, which had of late become almost a wilderness. As she went, she put her arm through mine, and with a curious thrill I noticed that I did not feel her do so, but only saw the action.

"You know, I dare say, that the present owner of the house is in trouble and in exile?" I explained.

"About a will," she remarked.

"An ancient will and title-deed. The documents were lost a hundred years ago."

"A hundred and nine years to the day," she replied smiling at me.

"You are singularly accurate," I said; "but the chief thing that matters is the loss."

"How have they got on without it for a hundred years?"

"There was no one to dispute their right; but within the last few years a distant relative has sprung up and laid claim to what he declares was the inheritance of his grandfather. He pretends that the lost will was made in favour of this ancestor. He has succeeded in so far that he has got the estate into Chancery, and my cousin, having first been impoverished by years of law expenditure, has had to quit his old home with his wife and children, and is living almost in poverty in an obscure part of France."

I spoke with tears, and the bright eyes of my companion flashed sunshine into my face.

"You are tenderly attached to your cousin?"

"You may say so. My own story is an unhappy one, and when I became a widow, I should have been homeless had not Geoffry Wetherwilder taken me in. I have lived in the family for years, and even now, when they have had to give up everything, he has contrived to secure me a shelter as caretaker of the Hall."

"Worthy Wetherwilders, both of you," said the girl, who also claimed to be a Wetherwilder, and she stooped to gather a splendid rose of the old, almost obsolete oriflamme, which was just in flower all over the Maiden's Bower, close to the French rosery. "How well I remember this rose!" and she kissed it.

"You have been here before!" I exclaimed in astonishment.

"Have I not! The happiest hours of my short life were spent in this garden."

"Really!"

"'Twas this rose that Geoffrey Wetherwilder gave me, the evening—just such a June evening as this—when he told me he loved me; just a hundred and eight years ago."

I stared at her, and laughed. "What are you saying?" I asked impatiently.

"Perhaps I am talking poetry," she said, "may not one do so in such a spot, on such an evening, and after?"

Her eyes roved over the garden, taking in all its beauties, and with a look behind their youthful brightness, of age and memory, which amazed and perplexed me.

"Talk as you please," I said, but I began to feel her uncanny.

"I have only a short time to be with you," she said quickly. "Let us enjoy it. I have been very happy in this place, though not so happy as we are now—I and my beloved. But love never forgets, and the things and places associated with it are eternally sweet. I shall take him these roses, and even in the place where we are now——"

I was truing to believe that here, in the days before I came to Wetherwilder Hall, this creature's romance had been enacted, though her apparent youth made folly of the idea. But I was growing quite bewildered by her looks and words, and was glad when she consented to leave the fading glories and the fragrance of the garden and to return with me indoors.

My handmaiden had provided a hasty supper—one or two light dishes, a sweetmeat, and grapes, coffee and shortbread. A great silver candelabra, with wax candles alight, stood in the middle of the round table in my sitting-room, which overlooked the garden, beyond which the great mounds of the trees were black against a golden stretch of sky. The flames of the candle hung like flowers in the air, for the gold sky-gleam was still at least equal with them in power of light within the room, and both together filled the place with a kind of mystic glamour.

We sat down to table, but I was too much excited to eat, and my guest, though plates were placed before her, seemed to behave as if they contained nothing but air. However, I had become afraid of observing her too closely, so quickly did she apprehend my thought, and I allowed myself to drift with her humour.

After supper she protested that she must see the old house, and so we proceeded upstairs just as the newly burnished moon-silver began to struggle in the sky with the sun-gold which was rusting away into darkness down west among wildernesses of grotesque-seeming ink-black oak woods. The white glory poured down the wide way of the great staircase as we went up; corridors, passages, and unused chambers lay beyond and above. I felt that I would rather have remained downstairs, but my companion hurried on, looking round here, and peeping in there, as if truly revisiting places that were dear and familiar to her.

She lingered only abut a minute in each spot until we came to a small music-room, all brown with polished wood, without curtains or carpet, and hung round with musical instruments, some of them very old, an accumulation of years. Violin, guitar, *mandolina*, tambourine, cymbals, all were there, and an old-fashioned spinet and a harp held place of honour in the middle of the floor.

With an air of rapture she stepped a-tiptoe across the floor, stretched her long delicate arm to take down the guitar from its hanging place, and slipping a faded blue ribbon that dangled from it over her head, she perched herself on a carved wooden stool, and sung with the most exquisite grace a soft, cooing love-song, the like of which for sweetness I had never listened to. When the piercing melody ceased, she looked up at me, and never shall I forget the beauty of her as she did so, with the moonlight that struck through the narrow window just touching her face and shoulder. Her song sung, she replaced the guitar on the wall, and turning to me with a little laugh signed to me that she desired to quit the chamber.

Proceeding with our visitation we made little pause till we reached another small room, one which had been for generations a kind of schoolroom or study for the young people of the family. It was lined with books, and a table with drawers stood in the middle of the floor. Here had many a lesson been learned, and many a lecture listened to, Again, as in the music-room, the stranger's look of recognition became rapturous, as she walked round the rows of books with her eyes close to them, though I could scarcely imagine that the twilight from the window enabled her to read the titles of them.

Suddenly she drew forth from a corner, where it had evidently lain hid behind others, a small velum-covered volume, and with a laugh of delight turned its pages over with a rapid hand, then placed it in mine with an eager movement saying—

"Take it, cousin, and tomorrow look into it. It will explain away your perplexity."

I was growing weary of following her, of my ignorance of who she was and why she was here; and my wits were oppressed by the consciousness of something about her which I found quite unintelligible. I longed to be alone, that away from the fascination of her presence I might think the matter over, and arrive at some conclusion regarding her. I was therefore, much relieved when she suddenly announced that she would retire for the night.

"Give me the yellow chamber," she said with her charming imperiousness.

I knew that my maiden had prepared for her a smaller room and nearer to my own, and remarked that she might perhaps feel lonesome in the greater apartment, which was situated at the other end of the house. But she reiterated her request, which was rather, indeed, a demand. In a short time, the statelier chamber was made ready for her, and I accompanied her there. The yellow hangings on the bed and windows were let down and shaken out, but she would not allow the blinds to be drawn or the windows closed.

It is a splendid old room, the walls completely panelled in oak, the darkness of which is relieved by the gold-colour of the furniture. She bade me goodnight, bending to kiss me, but I did not feel her lips, and experienced again that uncanny thrill at finding my sense of touch unaffected by her nearness. I last saw her standing there with her graceful arms extended dismissing me. Two candles were burning in the tall silver candlesticks on the dressing-table; the moon, full-orbed and glorious, shone out of the lovely green-greyness of the sky of a midsummer midnight, filling the framework of one window, while the other window showed the startling black fretwork formed by the huge boughs of a hundred-year old chestnut tree against the silvery cloud-light.

Between these and the flames of the candles the young slight figure stood, aerial in its lightness and grace, the face radiant with intelligence, the eyes of a brightness which seemed strange by such light as there was, the moon's soft ray making a luminous ring round her hair. She kissed her hand to me with a smile that is still in my heart; and then I retreated to my own quarters, glad to escape, and feeling indescribably limp and overdone.

I did not find my brain cleared by solitude as immediately and effectively as I had hoped, and felt unable to do anything but huddle myself up in bed with a sense of the most utter prostration. After half an hour's rest I sat up and lit my candle, polished my spectacles, and opened the vellum-covered book which the stranger had handed to me. But whether from fatigue or for some other reason, I could not read a word of the contents, and soon consigned myself once more to repose and darkness.

Sleep took me by surprise, and I knew no more till I wakened with a thin clear sound in my ears, curiously familiar as the repetition of something I had been aware of lately. It was the lively sound of a coach-horn blown from a distance. Again, it came lightly, and again and again more faintly on the air—*tantivy, tantivy, tantivy!* The great cedar outside flung its boughs about in the breeze, and their rustling drowned the retreating music. I sat up, and saw that the light of the midsummer dawn was gilding the edges of the window-blinds.

I dressed hurriedly, and feeling a strange reluctance to visiting the yellow chamber, I wakened my maid-servant and directed her to make me a strong cup of tea, which I swallowed nervously. The maid was a sturdy country wench, devoid of imagination, and she smiled at my discomfiture.

"It's my belief you won't find her, ma'am," she said. "They gay friends of hers called for her and took her off, early. I heard the coachin'-horn an hour ago, comin' an' comin', and goin' an' goin'. I put my head out of the winda, and I saw the coach, and the waft of her white gownd gettin' into it; and the whole caravan went clatterin' down the drive and out of sight, among the trees just as the sun was risin'. And I wouldn't be frettin' for her, if I ere you ma'am, for she's a queer kind of a visitor, takin' people short and givin' them trouble, and then goin' off without as much as saying good morning to them!"

"Come upstairs with me, Jenny, that I may assure myself she is gone," I said.

We entered the room. The windows still stood wide open, but their dark woodwork was framed the brilliant sunshine and blue sky of a June morning. Rooks were cawing in the huge chestnut, which threw half the room into transparent shadow. The room was empty of its occupant of the night before. The bed had not been lain in, and everything stood undisturbed, as I had left it with her in it. And yet there was a change, for one of the panels in the wooden wall stood open as a door, showing a deep recess like a cupboard, about five feet above the level of the floor.

Thrilling with expectation of I knew not what, I looked into the open recess, and putting in my hand drew forth an Indian box containing some old yellow papers, the miniature of a girl, which was a faithful portrait of my late guest, and a few jewels in old-fashioned settings. Having read the papers, I telegraphed at once to Geoffry Wetherwilder, and to his solicitor, and both arrived as quickly as steam could carry them. The papers soon proved to be the long-lost will, so urgently needed for the welfare of our family.

It was long before I ventured to relate to my cousin, or his man of business, the story of the finding of the document as I have set it down here. When I did so each received my communication characteristically. The solicitor laughed and tapped his forehead with an amused glance at me. "Don't tell that monstrous tale again, my dear lady," he said, "for I can't undertake to defend you from the consequences."

He accepted as quite natural the finding of the papers behind a sliding panel, but the rest he put down to a dream.

Geoffry, on the contrary, heard my story with the most serious attention, and received it as truth in all its details. He had the Celtic strain in him which rapidly responds to a message from the unknown. The spiritual side of his nature was deeply stirred, and having been made suddenly very happy just when his fortunes looked darkest, the heart in him turned gratefully, like my own, to the lovely visitant from another state of being, who had taken thought of him and his, and restored them to their own.

"Don't say a word of it to Vanda, however," he said, speaking of his wife, who was already on her joyful way home, with her little children. "The thought of such an occurrence in the house would be an everlasting terror to her." And the mistress of Wetherwilder remains in ignorance of the story to this day.

The vellum-covered book proved to be a diary kept in disjointed, schoolgirl fashion. Inside the cover was written:

Elsinore Wetherwilder, aged seventeen today. Called by some impertinent cousins 'the Lady Tantivy,' because she loves riding to hunt, and in a four-in-hand coach.

And after this was added in a masculine youthful hand:

And sometimes even insists on blowing the horn!

The first entry was of an earlier date than the inscription on the cover:

This week I have arrived at Wetherwilder Hall. It is a change indeed for an orphan girl leaving her convent school with no family or relatives to receive her. What should I have done, where should I have gone, had not dear old squire arrived at Avignon, and put me in his portmanteau and carried me home? Really, and really home. And such a home!
I am wild with delight. I have a readymade mother, and the big-boy cousins are brothers to me. And the best of it is they are all as happy as I am, for the Wetherwilders had no daughter until I came.

Various girlish and pretty writings followed, filling up a year. In the first winter, this:

The snow is deep, yet the ball came off. The squire gave me a wonder of a white satin dress. My head is turned with flatteries. The duke proposed to me, but I should have refused him had he been king of the world, and that though he is a very goodly gentleman. It is Geoffry that I love, and never another man than Geoffry. If Geoffry does not love me, then will I back to my convent at Avignon and cover up this golden hair with a nun's veil——

The next summer:

This evening Geoffry told me that he loved me. It was in the garden among the oriflamme roses. I knew it before, but it was sweet to hear it——"

In the following autumn:

I have been trying to plague Geoffry. He is so sweet-tempered one can hardly do it. I have hidden the will and documents he was showing me yesterday. I have put them behind the sliding panel in the yellow chamber, where I am now installed. As all his inheritance depends on them, he will be rather in a fright. I will tease him for a while, and then make amends by being ever so kind to him.

No more. Each time I close the little book, which I always keep by me with the miniature, I think I hear the faint horn blowing that announced the coming and going of my Lady Tantivy. She will never come again. When we meet, it must be that I shall go to her. Time and place are delusions. I am very old now, and as I gaze over the trees into the great space out of which she came in her ever-young delightfulness, my heart grows young and is glad.

The Mystery of Ora

There is something inexplicable in the story, but I tell it you exactly as it happened.

Born to the expectation of wealth, certain casualties of fortune swept away my possessions at a blow. I was young enough to relish the thought of work, and for three years worked unremittently, till my health began to feel the strain, and I resolved to take an open-air holiday. A friend who was to have accompanied me changed his mind at the last moment, and I set out alone.

I chose to visit the wildest parts of the west coast of Ireland, and was rewarded by the sight of some of the finest scenes I had ever beheld. Keeping the Atlantic on my right, losing sight of it for a time, and again finding it when some heathery ascent was gained, I walked for two or three days among lonely mountains, accepting hospitality from the poor occupants of the cabins I occasionally met with. It was fine August weather. All day the hill-peaks lay round me in blue ether; every evening the sun dyed them first purple, then blood-red, while the solitary slopes and vales became transfigured with a glory of colour quite indescribable. At night the solemn splendour that hung over this wilderness kept me awake, enchanted by the spells of a more mysterious moon than I had ever known elsewhere,

One morning I started to cross a ridge of mountain that separated me from the seashore, and was warned by the peasant whose breakfast of potatoes I had shared that I must travel a considerable distance before I could meet with shelter or food again.

"Ye'll see no roof till ye meet with the glasshouse of ould Collum, the stargazer," he said. "An' ye needn't call there, for he spakes to no one, an' allows no man to darken his door. Keep away to yer left, an' ye'll get to the village of Gurteen by nightfall."

"Who is this Collum, who allows no man to darken his door?" I asked.

"Nobody rightly knows what he is by this time, sir; but he was wanst a dacent man, only his head was light with always lookin' up at the stars. He built himself this glasshouse, for all the world like a light-house; an; so far so good, for it did the turn of a lighthouse on them Eriff rocks, that'll tear a man. An' there he did be porin' into books an' pryin' up at the heavens with his lamp burnin' at night; and' drawin' what he called horry-scopes, thinkin' he could tell a man's future an' know the saycrets of the Almighty.

"His wife was a nice poor thing, an' very good to travellers passing the way, an' his little girl was as gay and free as any other man's child; but somehow there's no good to be got of spyin' on the Creator; an after his wife died, he got queerer an' queerer, an' fairly shut himself up from his fellow-creatures; an' there he bes, an' there he remains. An' the daughter seems to have grown up as queer as himself, for she niver spakes to nobody, not these last three or four years, though she used to be so friendly."

"Well," I said, "I shall keep out of old Collum's way;" and I started for my long day's walk.

I had walked a good many hours, and had crossed the steep ridge that separated me from the seaboard; had lain and rested at full length in the heather, and gazed in delight at the magnificent view of the Atlantic with its fringe of white low-lying serrated rocks interrupt-ed here and there by a group of black fortress-like cliffs, looking as though on their hither side they might show "*casements opening on the foam of perilous seas*" in these "*faëry worlds forlorn.*"

I had begun to descend the face of the mountain by a winding path, when I became conscious of something moving at a little dis-tance from me, and sheltering my eyes from the sun, saw the figure of a woman against the strong light—a figure which came towards me with such a vehement movement that it seemed almost as if she had been shot from the blazing sky across my path. She put both her hands on my arm with a grasp of terror, and then stammering some inco-herent words, extended one arm and pointed wildly to the sea—that serene ocean which a moment ago had looked to me like the very image of majestic peace, with its happy islets sparkling on its breast.

What was there in that smiling, storm-forgetting ocean to ex-cite the fear of any reasonable being? My first thought was that she was some poor maniac, whose all had gone down out there on some stormy night, and who had ever since haunted the scene of her ship-wreck, calling for help. I could not see her features at first, so dark was she against the strong light that dazzled my eyes.

"What is the matter?" I asked. "What can I do for you?"

As I spoke, I shifted my position so that I was in the shade, while the light fell upon her; and then I saw that she was no madwoman, but a very beautiful girl, with a face full of strong character and vivid intelligence. The look in her eyes was the sane appeal of one human creature to another for protection; the white fear on her lips was a rational fear. The firm gracious lines of her young countenance suggested that no mere cowardly impulse had caused her to seize my arm with that agonised grasp.

As she stood gazing at me, with that transfixed look of terror and appeal, I saw how very beautiful she was, with the sunlight pouring round her and almost through her. Her glowing hair, which I had thought black, had flashed into the warmest auburn, and lay in sunny masses on her shoulders; her eyes, deep grey and heavily fringed, glowed from her pale face with a splendour I had never seen before. She was poorly and singularly dressed in a faded calico gown, and an old straw hat, tied down with a scarlet handkerchief; but even as she stood, nothing could be more perfect than the artistic beauty of colour and form which she presented to my astonished eyes.

Almost unconsciously I noticed this, for all my mind was engaged with the expectation of what she had to tell me, with the awe of that look of living imploring anguish, and the wonder as to what that message could be which she seemed to be bringing me from the ocean.

As she did not speak, I repeated my question: "What is the matter? Tell me, I beg, what can I do to help you?"

Her eyes slowly loosened their gaze from my face, her arm fell to her side, a slight shudder passed over her, and she turned away.

"Nothing." She almost whispered the word, and moved a step from me.

"That is nonsense," I said, placing myself in her path. "Pardon me; but you are in some trouble—in some danger, and you thought I could save you from it, or at least, help you. Let met try. Let me know how I can serve you."

"I cannot tell you," she murmured, and then raised her eyes again to mine with another wild look full of unutterable meaning. Behind her gaze there seemed to lie a lonely trouble, which peered out from its prison-house and asked for human sympathy, but was crossed and driven back by a cloud of unearthly fear. I thought so weird a look had never passed from one living creature to another.

I felt puzzled. So sure, was I of the reality of her forlorn anguish, that I could not think of passing on and leaving her to be the victim of whatever calamity threatened her under the shadow of this lonely mountain. And I felt, by an instinct, that the womanly weakness within her was clinging to me for protection in spite of the steadfast denial of her words.

"I am a stranger," I said, "and you are afraid to trust me; but I give you my word I am an honourable man—I will not take advantage of anything you may tell me."

Her lips quivered, and she glanced at me wistfully. She looked so young—so piteous! I took her passive hand firmly in mine, and said again: "Trust me."

"I do. I could," she faltered; "but oh! It is not that. It must never be told. I dare not speak."

She turned slowly round, and her eyes went fearfully out to the sea, wavered towards the cliffs, and lit on a glittering point among them; then she snatched her fingers from mine with a wail of terror, and, dropping on her knees before me, hid her face in her hands and wept.

I waited till her agony had spent itself, and then I raised her up gently and tried to reason with her. But it was all in vain. No confidence would pass her lips. She became every moment firmer, colder, more controlled. All her weakness seemed to have been washed away by her tears; and yet the calm despair on her soft face, bringing out its strongest lines of character, somehow touched me more than any complaint could have done.

"I thank you deeply," she said. "You would have helped me if you could. Go your way now, and I will go mine."

"I will at least bring you to your home," I said. "Where do you live?"

"There," she said, pointing to the glittering point on the rocks.

I shaded my eyes and looked keenly through the sunlight, and suddenly it flashed upon me that yon glitter came from "old Collum's glass-house", and that this was his daughter.

"Is your father's name Collum?" I asked.

A sudden change passed over her—I knew not what—like an electric thrill.

"That is his name."

"And he lives at yonder observatory?"

"It is our home," she replied after a pause.

"Let me accompany you," I said.

"No one comes there; he—he does not make anyone welcome.

I beg you will not mind me; I am accustomed to roam about alone."

"I have walked a long way," I said, after a few moments' reflection, "and I am tired and hungry. I hope you will not forbid my throwing myself on your father's hospitality for a few hours. I cannot reach the nearest village before nightfall."

This clever appeal of mine had its effect. She no longer urged me to leave her, though a painful embarrassment hung upon her. Under other circumstances delicacy would have forced me to relieve her from this, but I had made up my mind to leave no means untried to help her. I had a strong suspicion that old Collum was cruel to his child, and that she feared to let a stranger witness his ill-conduct. I determined to discover for myself, if I could, what sort of life he forced her to lead. We descended the mountain silently together, and, crossing a difficult passage of rocks, arrived at old Collum's house.

It was a curious old grey weather-beaten building, wedged into and sheltered by the cliffs, and looking as if in some early age it might have been carved out of their grim masses. The observatory was a much newer erection—a round tower with a glass chamber at the top, looking like a lighthouse to warn mariners from these dangerous rocks. The house was of two storeys—three rooms below and three above, and we ascended a narrow spiral stair to the higher chambers. My companion led the way to an apartment in the front—a dimly-lighted gloomy place, with two small windows set high in the wall, from which nothing could be seen but two square spaces of ocean.

The interior of this room showed how very ancient the building must be, and it had, in fact, been built as a hermitage by monks in an early century. The stone walls, made without mortar, had never been plastered, and the rough dark edges of the stones had been polished and smoothed by time. Upon them hung a map of the world, one or two sea-charts, a compass, a great old-fashioned watch of foreign workmanship, ticking the time loudly, and a few pieces of ancient Irish armour and ornament dug out of a neighbouring bog. The floor was paved with stones, worn into hollows here and there, and skins of animals were strewn over it.

The fireplace was a smoke-blackened alcove, and across it, sheltering its wide nakedness, the skin of a seal was hung, fixed in its place by an ancient skein, or knife, of curious workmanship. On the rude hearthstone lay the red embers of a peat fire; and though an August sun was glowing in the heavens, yet fire did not seem out of place in the chill of this vault-like dwelling.

As we entered my companion cast a hurried glance into the room, and seemed relieved to find it unoccupied. She threw off her hat, and opening a cupboard began to prepare the table for the meal which I had begged of her. All her movements were graceful and ladylike, and her beauty seemed to take a new character as she made her simple housewifely arrangements. Excitement and exaltation were gone from her manner, wildness and brilliance from her looks. No longer glorified by the sunlight, her hair had ceased o flash with gold, and had darkened to blackness in the shadow of the room. Her downcast eyes expressed only a gentle care for my comfort, and as I watched her with increasing interest, a faint colour came and went in her face.

I took up a curious old drinking cup of gold which she had placed on the table. On it was engraved "Ora," and I asked her what it meant.

"It is my name," she said. "The cup was found not far from here, and my father put my name upon it."

Now when she said this there was wonder in my mind, not that she bore so strange and original a name, but because the words "my father" were pronounced in a tone of such mournful and compassionate lovingness as to startle all my preconceived notions as to the reason of her unhappiness.

"Perhaps, if not wicked, he is mad," I thought, "and she is afraid of having him taken away from her."

As I wondered this thought with my eyes fixed on the door, it opened, and a sallow withered face appeared, set with two dull black eyes, which fastened in blank astonishment on my face. "Collum, the madman!" was my mental exclamation on beholding this vision; but as the door opened farther, and a figure was added to the face, I saw that the intruder was a woman.

Ora turned to her, and raising her hands, talked to her on her fingers; then, as the old creature began to make up the fire, said to me, "She is deaf and dumb, but a faithful soul, and all the servant we have. She goes our messages, fetches our provisions, and does little things which I cannot do myself."

"A strange household," I reflected: "an aged madman, a deaf and dumb crone, and this beautiful, living, vigorous creature! Outside the wilderness of mountain and ocean. What a place—what company for Ora on winter nights!"

I said aloud: "And you, and she, and your father, are really the only dwellers in this lonely spot?"

She glanced u quickly, and a shudder of agitation passed over her, such as I had seen before. She did not reply for a few seconds, and then she said in a low pained voice—

"There are only three of us."

A most distressing feeling came over me—a conviction that the girl was answering me with a wary reserve, veiling her meaning so that, while she did not speak absolute untruth, she resolutely kept something hidden from me. Everything about her persuaded me that this was done against her will. Her eyes expressed a candid nature; her manner trusted me, except at moments when my words jarred on the secret chord of anguish. Some terrible dread made her treat me at such moments as an enemy.

I sat at table, and she waited upon me, serving me with an anxious care which made me feel ashamed of the pretence which had thrown me on her hospitality as a hungry man. I had little appetite, but, like Geraint, felt longing in me ever more "to stoop and kiss the tender little thumb that crossed the platter as she laid it down." My meal over I felt that she would expect me to depart and as I ate, I pondered as to how I could contrive to remain in old Collum's dwelling.

I was resolved not to go without making his acquaintance—yet how was I to force myself into the old man's presence? Even as the thought passed through my mind my question was answered. The door opened, and the master of this strange domicile appeared.

My first thought was that I found him much younger, keener, more vigorous and wide-awake than I had expected. Despite his long white hair, beard, and eyebrows, I saw at once that he was not a very old man; even his manner of opening the door, and the step with which he entered the room, gave one the idea of physical strength in its prime. There was no droop of the dotard about his features or figure—no dreamy absent look of the stargazer in his fierce black eyes—no lines of abstracted thought upon his cunning brow. As he entered the room, not expecting to see me, I saw him just as he was—in all his reality; and I felt at once that had he known I was there he would have presented a different appearance. I seemed to know this by instinct, as one does sometimes divine certain things, by a sudden flash of intelligence, in the first moment of meeting with a fellow-creature.

As he stood in the doorway, looking at me with rage in his eyes, I saw his soul unveiled; the next moment—how or why I knew not—I beheld (my gaze having never been withdrawn from his face) a different being. The tension of his figure had slackened; the lines of his face lengthened and weakened the shaggy grey brows veiled the languid eyes; the forehead had assumed the look of the forehead of a visionary. He flung himself on a seat, and said feebly—

"Excuse me, sir; but I did not know that our poor dwelling was honoured by the presence of a guest. Ora, my dear, you ought to have told me."

Ora was behind me, and so intent was I upon watching the strange being before me that I did not look to see how she had taken this address. Besides something warned me that it would be better to notice her as little as possible in her father's presence. Striving to overcome the extreme repugnance I felt to my host, I said—

"It is I who ought to apologise for my intrusion, but"—here it seemed to me that I felt the thrill that quivered through Ora standing behind me—"but finding myself a complete stranger in need of rest and food in this lonely region, I ventured to throw myself on your daughter's hospitality. I am afraid; indeed, I forced myself upon her kindness."

"You are welcome, sir," he said, "welcome to all we have to give. We live out of the world, and have little to offer to those who are accustomed to better things."

His civil speech seemed to clear the difficulties from my path, only to put greeter ones in my way. That this wily man, had, as well as his daughter, a secret to guard, was an established fact in my mind. That cruelty to her was not the whole of it I felt sure. Whether his civility was a proof that he feared, or did not fear detection by me, I could not at the moment decide, but put the question away for after consideration, along with another fact which I had noted without weighing what its value might be. The man spoke with a foreign accent, and with a manner which suggested that English was not familiar to him, and had been learnt late in life. He was of foreign workmanship, as surely as was the quaint old watch that ticked so loudly over the rugged fireplace.

As I talked to my host I studied the name on my drinking-cup more frequently than his countenance. Something warned me that he would not endure anything like scrutiny; at the same time, I felt that I was undergoing a searching examination from the keen cruel eyes half hidden under their drooping eyelids.

"You are an Englishman, I suppose?" he said

"Yes."

"And have never been in this country before?"

"Never."

"And in all probability what you see of it in this holiday will be enough for you. You will hardly come back."

This was said with an affectation of carelessness which would have imposed upon me had suspicion not been aroused within me.

"Nothing is more unlikely than my return."

As I said this my conscience smote me, for I already felt that I could never more be entirely indifferent to the country which held Ora. The answer pleased him, however. There was a certain relief in his voice which I felt, and this encouraged me to make a bold stroke towards attaining my own purpose.

"I am going to make a request," I said, "which I hope you will not think impertinent. This bit of coast scenery is so beautiful that I feel a great longing to explore it further. I could not do so unless you will be so very good as to allow me to return here in the evening, and give me shelter for the night. I am well aware there is no dwelling in the direction I would take, and my health is not good enough for sleeping out of doors."

I prolonged my speech after my request was made to give him time to prepare his answer; and I forbore to raise my eyes to his so that he might have a moment to quench whatever light of ire my audacity might happen to call into them. There was a slight pause, which told me my precaution had not been an unnecessary one, but when I looked up his face was placid and blend.

"You are welcome," he said, "to what poor accommodation we can offer. Ora let a room be prepared for this gentleman."

I thanked him, and took up my hat to go upon the excursion I had so newly designed. My host also rose and prepared to leave the room with me.

"The old owl must go back to his nest," he said, with an attempt at pleasantry. "I am a dabbler in astronomy, an observer of the stars, and my days pass in making calculations. My observatory is my home. When I entered the room some time ago, I was irritated beyond measure by a problem., the solution of which still eludes me. A little society has soothed me, and I shall return to my labours refreshed."

This speech convinced me more than ever that he was an imposter. Not only had his words of information about himself a false ring in them, but his apology for his appearance in the moment when he had stood unveiled before me revealed a depth of consciousness which was betrayed by the effort to hide it. If anything had been wanting to complete the impression made by him upon me, it would have been supplied by the evil look which he turned upon Ora as he left the room. This look he, of course, intended to be unseen by me, and I was thankful my interception of it was unperceived. It was a significant look of warning, and contained a threat. He went down to his observatory, and I took my way over the jagged rocks along the seashore, thinking deeply over all I had seen and heard.

It seemed to me that I had to sum up a number of contradictory evidences. That old Collum was not the visionary nor the stargazer which public report and his own representations declared him to be, was to me past doubting. That he had some heavy stake in this lower world, and was playing a part to win it, I believed, upon the strength of my own observations. Yet what object was to be gained by a life of such entire seclusion as his? The wildest ideas occurred to my imagination as to the possibilities of leading a criminal life in this wilderness; and were rejected almost as quickly as they took shape in my mind.

His well-known inhospitality forbade the supposition that he could be a waylayer of travellers; and besides had he been a murderer, Ora would not have stayed by him. She was free to roam where she pleased, and could as easily have escaped to the nearest town as she could have climbed the mountain upon which she had met me. It was more likely that he might be a forger, and an undertaker of secret journeys into the world and back again to his den. Could her knowledge of his evil life account for her conduct? I thought it might, and yet, having granted this, I still felt that there was a mystery behind which I could not unravel.

One moment I felt convinced that Ora hated and feared him, and that it was from him she would have appealed to me for protection; the next I remembered the accent of love with which she dwelt on the words "my father," uttering them in a tone that was crossed by neither shame nor terror. And another point remained in my thoughts, though I knew not what conclusion I could draw from it. The man was of foreign nation. I believed that he was not a European.

True, my informant might have overlooked this fact when giving me his slight sketch of the unloved recluse, but from his name I had concluded he was an Irishman. "Collum" I had supposed must be a namesake of St. Columb; but, of course, it might as easily be a corruption of some difficult Eastern word. From an Irish mother Ora might have inherited her wonderful grey eyes and tender bloom, together with a mind and heart as beautiful as her exquisite face.

The only result my cogitations produced was a feeling of satisfaction that I was going to pass one night at least under old Collum's roof. I acknowledged to myself that there seemed very little likelihood of my being thus enabled to make any discovery; but the vague hope, that during the next twenty-four hours I might find some faint clue to Ora's mystery, cheered me in spite of reasonable probability. I felt no pang of conscience at the thought of playing the spy upon my host.

The one fact that remained clear on my mind regarding him was that he was a criminal who ought to be detected, whose existence blighted the life of the innocent girl who had the misfortune to be his child. And then my thoughts wandered from him and rested exclusively on Ora.

As I lay upon the rocks with my hands clasped behind my head, gazing out to sea, my eyes roamed over the numerous islands that lay scattered on its bosom for miles towards the horizon. Some looked large enough to support life, others were clusters of rocks; yonder one was gleaming like an emerald in the sun and seeming to invite the tired traveller to a seagirt paradise, while over there another lowered, making a spot of sinister gloom on the smiling ocean.

One that bore this latter character had a peculiar fascination for me. Its jagged rocks were like cruel teeth; it showed no cheerful fleck of green even when the sun touched it for a moment and fled away. It seemed always in shadow, and had a fierce gloom in its aspect that made one shiver. "All that enter here leave hope behind," I murmured, looking at it, and fancying it might well be the home of despairing spirits. Birds were wheeling above it, and as I watched them, now black in the shadow and now white in the sun, I fell into a sort of dream—slumbering lightly, yet never losing the consciousness of where I was. I thought I heard the birds talking loudly to each other, and they talked of Ora.

"Pluck her out of yonder dungeon," said one, "and carry her far over the sea!"

"I cannot," said the other; "she is chained to the rock. Her father has chained her, and she will not tell."

I started out of this dream to find that the sun had set, and I resolved to return at once to the observatory. When I arrived the door of the house lay open, and I went in without seeing anyone, and ascended the winding stone stair, which did not creak under the foot.

In the room where I had left her Ora was sitting alone. Outside it was still daylight, but in this gloomy chamber with its small high windows dusk had long set in, and a small lamp burned on the table, throwing a heavier darkness into the corners around. The young girl sat by the lamp, poring intently over a book. The lamplight fell full on her face; and on that beautiful face was such a look of horror as it froze blood to see. So absorbed was she that she did not perceive my approach, and I paused involuntarily, pained at seeing her suffering soul thus laid bare before me once more.

Surprise derived me for some moments of the power of speech. To find Ora a student was about the last thing I should have expected. To see her buried in a study which, from the expression of her face, I could not but fancy in some way connected with the woe of her life, was a still greater cause for amazement. Could she be conning some task which had been set her; or striving to forget in the pages of a book moments of terror which were only just past? But no; as she read, all her mind, all her being, were engaged with what the book conveyed to her; and as the moments passed, that fearful indescribable look grew and grew on her face, till at last she raised her eyes and fixed them on vacancy with a gaze which seemed to threaten madness.

I could not bear it any longer.

"Ora!" I cried, touching her shoulder, "for Heaven's sake tell me what horrible thing you are looking at!"

She started violently, and let the book fall, put out her arm to bar my taking it up, and then sank back in her chair exhausted by conflicting feeling. As before, I seemed to feel her passionate desire to confide in me—a desire struggling in the chains of her deadly fear. I gently put away her hand and took up the book.

"Let me look at it?" I said. "What harm can it do? You shall not tell me anything but what you please. The book can surely betray no secrets."

She bent her head, and I opened the book. It was old and worn, the cover worm-eaten, the pages yellow and brown with time. The type was so strange, that at first sight it seemed to be written in a foreign language; but as my eyes became accustomed to it, I was able to read.

It was a book on necromancy, treating of the power of the Evil One, and of the mighty and terrible things he enabled those to do who leagued themselves with him and played into his hands. It was written with a certain force of imagination and diction, and, apparently, a thoroughness of faith in what it set forth, which was calculated to exercise an almost fiendish influence over a sensitive and delicate mind, and of which even the strongest and most sceptical reader must for a moment feel the spell.

As I turned page after page, and gradually mastered the entire drift of the book, I asked myself could it be that all the terrors of the supernatural had been brought to bear upon Ora's imagination, and that the fears which bound her were of this extraordinary nature.

"You do not believe a word of all this terrible nonsense?" I said smiling, as I closed the uncanny volume, which seemed almost to smell of brimstone.

She gazed at me with a look of amazement, in which there was for a second a gleam of something like relief.

"Ah," she said, "you talk like that because you are ignorant. You are not so well educated as I am. See here!"

She drew back a curtain that covered some rows of rude bookshelves, all filled with volumes looking like fit companions of the book on the table.

"Look over these," said Ora, "and you will see that my instruction has not been neglected."

I did look through them, and found the most extraordinary assemblage of compositions that ever were brought together for the bewilderment of human creatures. There were several long treatises on astrology, dream-like mystical books full of fascination; then came augury, the knowledge of signs and omens; necromancy, witchcraft, and vividly detailed information regarding leagues with the person of Satan which powerfully underlay all the movements of the world.

"If these and these only have been your schoolbooks," I reflected, "Heaven help you, poor Ora!"

I thought of a lonely childhood and youth passed in this wilderness of rock and ocean, of winters which were probably all one long howling storm, and asked myself how the poor girl had preserved her senses, fed upon such teaching as this.

"Are these books your father's?" I asked, hardly able to contain my indignation against the wretch who had so poisoned her mind.

"Some of them," she answered, with a quiver of the lip; "those on astrology."

"And who gave you the others?"

She trembled, cast at me the wild look she had given me on the mountain, and threw her hands in a defensive attitude.

"Don't!" she said hoarsely. "Don't ask me questions. If I answer them, I shall have to hate you for evermore."

She then turned quickly towards the wall, and leaning against it, hid her face between her hands.

The words, the movement, gave me a thrill of gladness.

"Ora," I said, "you must never hate me. Nay, listen to me. If you can love me instead, I will take you away out of this miserable life, with its secret dread of—Heaven only knows what! As my wife you shall have every happiness that a loving heart can procure for you. And I shall ask you no questions. If ever a moment comes when you feel that you can confide in me, dear, I shall trust that then you will speak."

I drew her hands from her face, and she looked at me with a bewildered blush of surprise.

"You?" she said. "You would marry me?"

"Is that so very unreasonable?"

Her face became gradually glorified by a look which showed me for an instant what happiness might make of her; but it quickly faded away: the joy went out like a light in a gust of wind; the blush was replaced by an ashen pallor.

"Oh, why has this come to me," she murmured with quivering lips, "only to be found impossible, only to deepen my misery?"

"Why impossible, Ora?"

"That I cannot tell you. If I were to tell you it would bring such ruin as you could not bear to hurl upon me."

Having said this, her reticent calm descended upon her like armour; she withdrew herself from me, went over to the table, and taking up the book she had been reading, replaced it on the shelf with its companions, drawing the curtain across, as if to prevent any return to the discussion of the subject of her studies. Then she stood silently waiting, as if expecting me to leave her.

"You had better go to your room," she said gently. "He—he will be displeased if he finds you here with me."

I obeyed her desire at once, fearing to bring down a tyrant's wrath upon that tender head.

The room assigned to me was small, but its window was well-placed, being in the gable of the house, and thus commanding a noble view both of the inland, with its mountains, and the island-strewn sea. True, it was rather out of reach, and at an inconvenient height—so that an effort must be made if one wanted to enjoy the outer world through its medium. It would seem, indeed, as if the windows of this house had been planned with a view to shutting out the perpetual sight of the ocean which was so near. Had the builder foreseen that future dwellers within the walls might find the companionship of the great ocean monotonously intolerable? Whether or not, the blindness, so to speak, of the house, and the bold and peering inquisitiveness of the observatory close by, struck me as contrasting with each other curiously.

I extinguished my light and threw myself on the bed, but felt that I was not likely to sleep. My mind flew back over all the events of the day, and I could scarcely believe that I was the same person who had parted from his peasant-entertainer in the morning, saying, "I will take care to avoid old Collum's dwelling." I felt as if years must have elapsed since the time when I had never seen Ora, since the moment when I saw her darting to meet me upon the mountain, as if the sun had cast her upon my path.

Since I had beheld that light of joy in her face, I resolved that nothing would induce me to give up the hope of making her my wife—no impenetrable mystery should daunt me; no terror, natural or supernatural, should be allowed to wretch her away from me. At the same time, I must be careful not to persecute her. Ignorant as I was of the cause of her sorrow and fear, I must be content to wait patiently; if necessary, to watch over her from a distance. Time, which unveils wonders, would be certain to unravel the mystery in which Ora was entangled.

As the night advanced, I became more and more fevered with tantalising thoughts and vain speculations, and at last, just as the first faint indications of approaching dawn appeared, I left my bed, and with some difficulty established myself in such a position at the window as enabled me to have a view of all the landscape beauties below. I looked sheer down into a bed of rocks, which went like jagged steps to the sea; and beyond this foreground lay the ocean, with its islands dimly discernible in the misty daybreak. One by one the darkness gave up its hidden treasures, and allowed them to creep under the mysterious grey veil of the morning.

"The sun will come," I said to myself. "The sun will come; and presently how beautiful all this will be!"

I was trying to persuade myself that so would the clouds and mysteries of Ora's life dissolve away, when a slight sound immediately below startled me, a sound no greater than the flutter of a bird's wing, but sufficient in the intense stillness to make me look to see whence it proceeded. And I did look, and beheld a sight which surprised me: Ora gliding over the rocks like a spirit, stopping to look about anxiously as if afraid of being observed, and then hurrying on towards the sea. A shawl was round about her head and shoulders, and she carried a basket on her arm. She was clearly going a journey, and was making towards the verge of the cliffs. Was it possible her household duties could take her away to a distance at this extraordinary hour? And whither could she be going by water?

I lost sight of her for a few moments as she disappeared among the rocks, but soon a little boat shot out from beyond them, and Ora was in it, rowing away from the land with all her might.

Outward, still outward, I saw her darting like an impatient bird over the calm sea in the still grey dawn. The wildest thoughts came into my mind. Was she fleeing away frantically, trying to escape from all her troubles at once; from the mystery of her home, from my love and the discoveries it might impel me to make, from every difficulty that beset her? And whither? Had she any plan; or did she in her ignorance hope vaguely that she might reach by chance some goal of safety, touch with her little hunted feet some shore of peace, where unknown and unquestioned, she might loosen the cords of misery by forgetting her own identity?

Suddenly my crazy thoughts were rebuked, and I saw that she had a simple and definite purpose in her voyage. She was making for one of the islands yonder that were creeping one by one out of the shadows of the night. It was that particular islet of gloomy and fantastic shape and expression on which yesterday the sun had refused to shine, and over which the birds had talked and wheeled in my dream. She neared it, touched it; I saw her moor the boat, and vanish among the rocks of the island shore.

After an interval of half an hour she reappeared, and presently I saw her coming, small and scarcely visible as she and her skiff were in the distance, and looking, as she plied her oars, like some dark seabird on the wing. Landing where she had embarked, she returned along the rocks, with swift glances of alarm cast on all sides, and sped like a frightened dove into the shadows of the house.

I mused long over this secret expedition of Ora's. Her evident fear of being seen, and the fact that she bore with her a well-filled basket, which she carried carefully, bringing back the same basket empty, forbade me to suppose that she could have gone to fetch any simple produce of the island for household purposes. Whose observation had she feared? Not mine, for she never once glanced towards my window. Had she waited till her father had left his observatory, and might be supposed to be asleep, before she stole forth on her solitary adventure? And if not, what was the purpose of her visit to the island? I felt assured that some human creature's need had drawn her to the secret expedition; she was supplying sustenance to that creature unknown to and in defiance of her father. I did not guess these facts; I divined them at once; and the knowledge gave an added pang to my mind.

Who was the person lingering in retreat upon the gloomy island? Why did he stay there? If it were a man who had thus secured the devotion of a woman like Ora, why did he not free himself and her? Why did he not step into her boat, and escape with her into the safety of the vastness of the world? I wearied myself with asking questions, with indulging my indignation against this cowardly *protégé* of Ora's, who was content to lie by and let her suffer, till my reasoning powers returned, and I remembered that I knew nothing of the facts of the case.

On leaving my tiny apartment I found breakfast ready for me in the sitting-room, and Ora waited upon me as she had done the day before. She looked unnaturally pale, and there were dark circles round her eyes that told a tale of suffering. She was in her most impenetrable mood, and I scarcely ventured to speak to her.

Whilst I was at breakfast old Collum came into the room, and though he kept up an appearance of civility in his manner towards me, yet I felt that my hour had come and that I must go. He had bestowed his society upon me in order that he might see me out of the house. There, in his presence, I was obliged to say goodbye to Ora, and left the place accompanied by the man, who walked with me a mile along the shore.

I arrived at Gurteen in the evening, but found it impossible either to stay there or go farther away from old Collum's observatory. The knowledge of Ora's lonely trouble held me like a cord, and the thought of that gloomy island, with Ora's little boat speeding towards it, haunted me wherever I turned. The overwhelming desire to know more of the mystery I had left behind me so deprived me of the power of pursuing any other idea, so I ignored all difficulties in the way of discovery, that I gave up battling with it, and resolved to spend the remaining time at my disposal in hovering near the spot which I had quitted in the morning.

Having rested a few hours at the village inn, I set out again in the twilight to walk back again the way I had come, without having any positive purpose in so doing, and drawn only by the craving to see whether Ora's little boat would again be on the water in the still grey hour that lies between the night and the dawn.

At a certain distance from Ora's home, I found a cave in the rocks in which I could rest, with my eyes on that line across the sea from the house by the observatory to the gloomy island. A faint moonlight illuminated the track as I began my watch; but it soon vanished with its shadows, and in the pale obscurity that followed I saw the thing I had expected to see—Ora's small bark on its solitary voyage. She went and came as on the preceding night, and in the sunrise, there shone a vivid light across my mind.

I remembered that when Ora met me on the mountain she had pointed towards the sea: she had indicated the very island which she now visited by night. I had felt that she was bringing me some message from the ocean, but afterwards had forgotten this striking impression made by her gesture in the first moment of her appearance. Now the first and the last seemed to join and close the circle of my speculations: the beginning and the end of Ora's mystery was centred in the island.

I passed the succeeding hours in making up my mind to a certain course, as a man does who finds he must steer between two inevitable dangers. I felt that I must run the risk of incurring Ora's hate—of overwhelming her with that ruin of which she had spoken. I must dare even that in the effort to save her. And yet what ruin could overtake her innocent youth? There was no shadow of guilt on her face, and I would never allow her to involve herself in the well-deserved ruin of others. With all this reasoning I came to my conclusion, and made my arrangements with a sense of the deepest pain. I was going to win Ora, or to lose her. At all events I would set her free.

Retracing my steps to the village, I hired a boat and set out to row myself to the mysterious island. Rowing through the red sunset on my strange quest, like a man in a dream, I touched the lonely shores of my desire, and mooring my boat in a creek on the seaward side of the isle, I slowly went my way to discover what it might support or contain. Nothing did I find but rocks and heather and a sprinkling of grass. There was no sign of any human habitation, no evidence of life except the occasional cries of the gulls and curlews. What brought Ora here night after night, in the silent hours? Did she come to feed the birds, or did some supernatural power compel her to a rendezvous with unquiet spirts?

I smiled as this latter thought passed through my mind; but there was something witchlike in the shapes and expressions of the surrounding rocks as twilight came on—something uncanny and eerie in the sough of the breeze through the heather, and the lapping and murmuring of the great calm ocean that girdled me. All through the hours of the night I walked the island, listening, watching, straining every faculty in the intensity of my vigil; sometimes starting in pursuit of an imaginary figure which seemed to climb the rocks on before me or to dart across the streaks of the moonlight, but always finding that fancy had taken advantage of some accidental form of an inanimate thing to deceive me.

At last, the moon set, and that scared wakening look came over the sea which means the dawn; and the pale hours brought Ora. When I saw her coming my heart misgave me as to the wisdom of my adventure. I was going to spy on her, hunt her down, to possess myself by stratagem of her secret. The fear of her hate unmanned me; but with a strong effort I thrust aside such weakness. I had come there, not to injure, but to save her. She landed close to where I lay hidden. She moored her boat and climbed the cliffs, and I followed her. So safe from observation did she consider herself, that she never once thought of turning her head, and I kept near her easily till I saw her suddenly stoop, and apparently vanish into the rock.

Coming to the spot where she has disappeared, I found an opening in the stone, and, stooping as she had stooped, followed her down an irregular winding passage, which led to a subterranean cave. I had completely lost her, and groped my way in the dark; but after some minutes I heard the murmur of voice, and presently saw the glimmer of a light. Approaching this light, I came to an opening into a wider cave, on the floor of which a lamp burned, throwing a dreary light on two figures that clung together in the gloom of the subterranean solitude. One of them was Ora, who had flung herself on the neck of the man, who was evidently a prisoner in this natural dungeon.

A dizziness seized me, and for some moments made me forget myself and my purpose in coming to the place. I stood as if stunned. I had no idea of listening; but across the cloud that had descended on my mind I heard the low tones of Ora's voice murmuring with infinite tenderness—"Oh father! Oh Father! Oh poor, poor father!" The soft words, with their despairing, caressing monotony, flowed into my ear and into my brain like a river of light. Her father was here. The other was an imposter. Foul work had been done, I thought no more of displeasing Ora, but stepped into the cave.

At sight of me Ora uttered a low cry of anguish that I can never forget, and wound her arms round the old man (who looked to me like an aged, etherealised likeness of the knave in the observatory), as if she would protect him from some deadly harm. The man's eyes were turned in the direction where I stood with a look of ghastly expectancy rather than fear, while Ora's were fixed on his face with that sort of gaze we turn on the dying when the parting soul is hovering upon their lips. So, they remained, locked in each other's arms, waiting as if for a sword to pierce them.

"Ora," I said, "what does this mean? I am come to save, not to hurt you."

She answered not a word—she did not seem to hear me; but the old man spoke to me at last, slowly and awfully, as if from the verge of another world.

"Sir," he said, "you mean well; but unknown to yourself, you have brought ruin to me. This is the hour of death."

His head sank on his breast, and again I endured a long silence, which seemed hardly broken by our breathing. I bore it as long as I could, and then I spoke again.

"Let me beg you to listen to me," I said. There is no one on this island, save ourselves. I am a friend; I can help. Why do you associate me with death?"

With a long sigh the strange old man raised his head, and said—

"I know not why I am still here to answer you; but I believe that I do not blame you. You are but the voice of fate. Yes, Ora; I read it long ago in the stars, and it was folly of me to think to escape my doom. Stranger, the blow that I expect will not fall from any human hand, but none the less will it fall. You are innocent of all purpose against my life, yet your discovery of me here is the signal for my death. Suffer me to pass my last moments in peace with my child."

Hearing this speech, I made up my mind that the poor old man was mad; and resolving to humour him, I retreated to some distance, and gave no sign of my existence for a considerable time. After an interval which seemed to me an age, I at last spoke again.

"Pardon me," I said; "but you perceive that from some cause or other the event you expect has been delayed. Will you not make use of the time thus given you to think of your daughter? The doom you speak of does not include her."

"I have no fear for her. I have read her happy fate in the stars. Freed from me, the last of her troubles will be over. Friend, I feel a desire to tell you, my story. If time be granted to me, I will do it."

I hailed the words with joy, and prepared to listen.

"I am an astrologer. For long years I lived among the stars, and they revealed to me secrets not known to men who walk the earth looking downward. I knew early that misfortune would cloud the latter days of my life; but the nature of the misfortune was not made clear to me. When I lost my dear wife, I thought for a time that the trouble I was forewarned of had come; but my child grew up loving me, and happiness returned to my heart. I kept a close sharp watch for the shadow that was sure to descend upon me, and yet it took me unawares.

"The winters on this coast are terrible, and on wild nights I used to place a light in my observatory as an assistance to mariners. More than once, I was thanked by sailors who had seen 'Collum's light' in time. Yet through this charity to others came my doom.

"One terrible night I became convinced that a ship was wrecking somewhere among these dangerous islands, and I got out my boat, and pushed my way to sea as well as I could, hoping to be the means of saving life. I heard cries, but could not reach the spot, nor discover the direction whence they came. I was driven on this island a little before dawn, and then the voices had ceased, and I felt that all was over without my having been able to afford any help.

"Pacing along the shore, my foot struck against something unusual, and by the first glimmer of daybreak I perceived that it was a chest which had evidently been washed up from the wreck. Examining it carefully, I found that it was locked and sealed. 'Something valuable, no doubt,' I thought, and wondered what I should do with it. As I bent over it, I suddenly became aware that someone was near, and looking up, saw a young man standing beside me. I stared at him in amazement, for he was neither wet nor ill, nor did he bear any trace of having lately striven with death on the sea. he had a gentlemanly, thoughtful air, and returned my gaze with a half anxious, half confiding look.

"'What can I do for you?' I asked as soon as surprise would allow me to speak.

"'Guard this,' he said, pointing to what lay at our feet. 'It is all I possess. Save it from my enemy. Keep it for me till I come for it.'

"'Where shall I put it?' I asked, and stopped to try if I could lift it.

"When I looked again the young man had disappeared. A second ago my eyes had been fixed on his; now I was alone. I gazed up and down the lonely shore, and climbed the rocks and called. Nothing human met my eyes. No one replied to me. Then I remembered something strange about the young man's manner—the sudden way he had come upon me, the unsuitableness of his dress, the impossibility of his having found his way to the island without a boat, and I knew I had seen an apparition.

"The peculiar, anxious, confiding expression of his eyes remained upon my memory, and I vowed I would be true to his trust. I buried the chest where no man save myself can ever find it, and then I went to look for my boat.

"As I went, I met with another startling object. Right across my path lay what seemed the corpse of a man, cold and blue—a drowned waif from the wreck. He bore no likeness to the young man who had so strangely appeared and disappeared, but was extremely dark, with sallow skin and Egyptian features. Why did I touch him? But had I left him lying there, the stars had been untrue in their reckoning.

"I knelt beside him, restored him to life, and brought him home. Ora and I nursed him. He was ill some time, and I amused his sickbed with stories of my way of life, and told him many of the wonderful things the stars had revealed to me. He listened with great interest, and seemed grateful and friendly. I gave him all my confidence, and in an unlucky moment related to him the strange occurrence of my vision on the island, and of the burying of the coffer I had found. He told me he was the master of the merchant vessel that had been lost, and was concerned about all the details of the wreck.

"As soon as he was able to move, he asked me to accompany him to this island, that he might search for such scraps of his property as the winds and waves might cast upon its shore. He picked up several things which he claimed as his own; and after he had ceased to find anything from day to day, he still kept urging me to visit this place with him. I soon perceived that he was trying to discover whereabouts I had buried the coffer.

"Finding that I would not betray myself, he at last spoke to me plainly—told me that the coffer was his, that my pretence of having seen an apparition was a trick to deprive him of his property, and that he meant to have it, whether I would or not. Now I knew that the thing I had hidden was neither his nor mine, and so I resisted him.

"We were here, in this cave, where he had beguiled me on pretence of looking for waifs from the wreck. Suddenly he struck me on the head, and I fell senseless. When I recovered consciousness, I was here as you see me, chained by the ankles in this miserable hole.

"My enemy then returned to my house, took advantage of a certain likeness to myself in his features to personate me, and established himself in my place. From time to time, he visits me here, trying to persuade me to give up the coffer; but that I will never do till the owner comes for it."

Here the poor creature paused, and I said quickly—

"All this I fully understand. You have been treated most foully. But why, in Heaven's name, did you not suffer your daughter to make known your state? Why do you shrink from me and talk of death in the very moment when I have come to deliver you?"

Now up to this time the old man had told his story with the air of an intelligent person; but the moment I asked the latter question a gleam of insanity seemed to dart across his brain.

"Why?" he asked excitedly. "Because my enemy is a wizard, a magician; he is in league with the Evil One, who holds me in his claw, ready to strike death into my veins the instant my case is made known to any creature. Have I not seen Satan in the long black hours pacing up and down yonder passage, and stopping to look and gloat over his prey? But he could not touch me so long as we—as Ora and I kept the secret to ourselves. I would not speak, and I would not suffer her to betray me. And so, I baffled them."

There was a ring of triumph in the poor old creature's voice as he said this, and he patted Ora's head almost gleefully, where she leaned with her face buried in his breast. I said to myself that he was mad—driven quite mad by this solitary confinement, and his unhappy daughter had never discovered it.

"How could you believe," I said, "that your enemy had this supernatural power over your life?"

"How can I believe that the sun shines?" he asked gravely. "He comes here and sits beside me, and tells me of his dealings with Satan. He has lived, and will live, hundreds of years, though Lucifer, who does his will now, is bound to get him at last. You might not have believed him, but I knew better. The secrets of the stars had taught me many things."

"But tell me," I said: "If this terrible person has Satan for his servant, why does he not find him the coffer without your assistance?"

"It is a fault in the plan," answered the old man dreamily. "When Satan tried to see, he was baffled by an angel's wing. I cannot explain it to you, but I know it well enough myself."

"The angel was your daughter, then. Through her I have come here. Now listen to me, old man. Why were you not brave enough to die, and let your child go free?"

He hung his head on his breast, and fondled Ora's hair.

"You are right, sir," he said. "I will die, and she shall go free. Let the blow fall; it is due ere this."

"Then, if you are ready, I will strike off your chain, and let Satan do his worst."

Ora started up as I drew near, and seized my arm.

"Ora," I whispered, "poor child! Do you not see that affliction has crazed your father's brain? Do not you also be mad, but let me deal with him."

I examined the chain, and found, as I expected, that it was eaten with rust. It was probably something belonging to the shipwrecked vessel which had come ashore. I laid a rusty link upon a large sharp stone, and lifting another stone, as heavy a one as I could raise, to a considerable height, let it fall upon the iron. As I raised my arms to do this, the lamplight fell full on my face, and I glanced at the poor old maniac, who, with folded arms, awaited his imaginary doom. In the instant, as the stone dropped, and he fell back with a groan, just as his chain split sunder.

"He is dead. We have murdered him!" moaned Ora, falling on her knees beside him.

"No, he is not dead!" I exclaimed joyfully; for I had feared that the shock of expectation might have really deprived him of life. I poured brandy down his throat, and after a time he revived.

"The apparition," he muttered; "he has the face of the apparition. Ora, where is the young man who met me that morning on the shore?"

"He is wandering," I said to Ora. "Do not be afraid."

"I am not wandering," said the old man. "What I saw I saw. Reach me to the lamp."

He raised the light to my face, and looked at me with a solemn, awful look.

"It was you who met me on the shore," he said; "you who gave the coffer in charge to me."

★★★★★★★★★★★★★★★★

When the wretch whom I had known as "old Collum" saw us coming in our boat from the island, he escaped on the instant, and we saw him no more. The police made efforts to track him, but in vain.

I told you that there was a strange point about this story, and so, when the haze of folly and madness has been cleared away, there still remains something in it that is inexplicable. Urged by the poor old dotard whom I had rescued, I went with him to unearth the coffer which it had cost him so much to guard. It proved to be my own property, and its contents restored to me the fortune I had lost.

Its loss in a ship that went down at sea had been the cause of the reverses which I mentioned in the beginning of my tale. A comparison of dates proved, if proof were necessary, that the vessel wrecked off the island was the same that had borne my heritage across the sea. The incident of the apparition I do not attempt to account for. That, on the morning after the wreck, I had spoken with him on the shore, and committed my property to his care, was firmly believed by old Collum up to the moment of his death—a moment not far distant from that which saw his rescue from the cave.

Wrought upon so long by a knave on the one side, and a visionary and madman on the other, it was long ere Ora's tender imagination recovered from the morbid state into which it had been thrown by her terrible experiences. But time and change cleared away all clouds from her mind; while the energy and devotion that characterised the wild mountain girl remain to my beautiful wife.

The Signor John

1

It seems but this morning that I got up before the sun, in our little wooden house, to cook, bake, wash in the river, help to mow the grass, coax my father, serve my brother Niccolo, and be as happy as the grasshoppers that sing both night and day. We lived upon a very high Alp, and we were poor, though we did not suffer hardship. In winter we had plenty of pine logs to keep the fire alive, and at night we were very gay, singing songs and playing the zither. In summer we breakfasted on the grass in the faint dawn, dined under the long roof at the sheltered side of the house, and supped by the starlight; after which I danced for my father, while Niccolo played the pipes. The chance passing of travellers was an excitement to us.

A wood-carver from the Tyrol sprained his foot near our place, and taught Niccolo to carve whilst we nursed him. This was something to be grateful for, as travellers would buy the work, and, besides, it gave our boy something to do. He was a cripple from his birth; one foot did not come to the ground somehow, and his back was a good deal bent. He had a little square face, with bright eyes and brown hair, and was said to be quite a Swiss, as our mother had been.

The first figure he carved was my patron saint, Christopher, wading through the torrent with the Child-God on his shoulders, and it was given me after he had bitten one of my fingers because I had stayed out alone in the moonlight, forgetting to fetch him. He never was so vexed, however, that I could not offer him comfort, asking him to plait my long hair, which came to my ankles.

I would sit down on the ground with my back against his knees, when he would dress the hair beautifully. If I were restless, he would hurt me; if I were patient he would kiss me; and if his work pleased him fully, he was blithe the rest of the day. Once I went with my father to a feast at a lower village, the *festa* of St. Florian. This was the first occasion on which I wore my mother's costume.

On the night before the feast, I was holding out my foot to note how my shabby skirt had crept up my leg. My father came and measured me with his alpenstock. "You are now as tall as your mother," he said; "you may henceforth wear her clothes." He shed tears in the morning when he saw me in her dress, but was so well pleased afterwards that I ran to the nearest tarn to see what I might be like. The tarn was nearly filled with rosy clouds, besides a gigantic pine tree, which tapered up and broke them. I seized the sombre draperies of the pine tree, and, gazing into the water, saw a maiden like the women whose fathers are wealthy vine-dressers. Her petticoat was of orange cloth, her long, narrow apron of a rich shade of blue, her black velvet bodice was laced with gold over white, and a deep red sash was folded well about her waist.

The only part of the picture that I knew was a pale, dark countenance with red lips, and the wide black eyes that seemed to take up half the face. I marked Niccolo's plaits and the silver arrows he had fastened in them, and the bunch of scarlet ash-berries which he had fixed behind my ear. I saw that this was myself, and I ran merrily to the chalet to hug my little Niccolo, and tell him not to pinch our neighbour Teresa, who was kindly coming to keep house for him whilst my father and I were away.

Placido with his mule came to meet us: a young man of the village, who had sometimes business on our Alp. He brought us to see his house, in which he had just put pretty furniture, and asked us to praise the *fresco* of St. Florian upon the gable, which he had lately got retouched for the *festa*. He had also made a new staircase up to his balcony, and the people joked Placido, saying he meant to take a wife.

It was a very pleasant *festa*. People treated me as a woman, now that I was grown enough to wear my mother's clothes. I was often asked to dance, and listened to with attention when I sang and played the zither. The next day Placido brought us a long way upon our road towards home; we could not get him to leave us till the worst of the journey was past. Thanks to his stout mule, we got over all our difficulties, and were going along merrily, when we heard a voice above us shouting through the pines.

Right above our heads there was a desert of lonely crags, a wild and dreaded place, where death lies in wait for men. My father left me sitting upon a pine-stump, and went shouting up the crags, seeking the stranger who had called. He returned with him by-and-by, and we hurried along on our journey; for though the air was flushed with colour, yet the darkness was close at hand. We hastened along in silence, dragging each other up steeps, and going hand in hand, step by step, slowly along narrow shifty places. The traveller had a fair foreign look, which is to us most perfect beauty. His locks shone in the twilight after my father's dusky head had got lost in the gloom of the pines.

Arrived at our Alp at last, we found Teresa preparing supper, and Niccolo sitting in the doorway piping shrilly up to the moon. The stranger gave me his hand up the last ascent, then raised it to his lips.

"My pretty little girl," he said, "you have certainly saved my life."

When Niccolo saw us coming he limped to meet us.

"Who is this that has come with you, Netta, who smiles and kisses your hand?"

"Hush! Niccolo; he is English, but he understands our talk."

The stranger threw down his hat and knapsack before the door. The firelight shone over the threshold, and our neighbour Teresa appeared carrying out the supper-table, which she placed upon the grass.

The next morning when I wakened, I peeped down between the rafters of my bedroom in the loft, and saw the stranger talking to my father in the doorway.

I crept down the ladder, and found nobody in the place. Niccolo had lit the fire for me, and gone away to his work, and I heard my father's voice shouting in the distance. The *signor* was then gone. I heaved a sigh between regret and relief, and seized hold of a pitcher and prepared to go to the tarn. I made a step across the threshold and started back; the *signor* was leaning smoking against our chalet.

I sprang back so quickly that I broke the pitcher, and had to press my hands on my eyes to keep the tears from falling.

"Child!" said the *signor*, smiling in at me, "why do you take such pains to hide your face? One does not see so pretty a thing every day."

"I am not pretty this morning," I said. "It was only my mother's clothes. And I was hiding my face in trouble because I have broken my jug."

"And you were going to fetch water?" he said, "and yonder pail is too heavy for you? And it was all owing to me that you broke the pitcher?"

He lifted the pail on his shoulders. "Come, let us fetch the water," he said; "I shall want you to show the way."

We fetched the water together, and the stranger taught me to call him Signor John. He had an air grand and gentle, and a pleasant light in his eyes. He laughed gaily when amused, and that encouraged me. At breakfast we saw no Niccolo, and I invited the Signor John to look at his carvings: at St. Barnaba with her tower, St. Dorothy and her roses, St. Vincent among his orphans, St. Elizabeth, whose royal mantle was filled with bread. Niccolo had carved them all, and they stood in a row in his workshop. They were far the finest things we had got in our chalet; yet when I brought the *signor* to look at them Niccolo shut the door in his face.

"Never mind!" said the Signor John, "we can amuse ourselves; I wish to make a sketch of you if you don't object to sit."

"I ought to be at my work," I said; but ran to tell my father, who was chopping wood in the pine-brake.

"It is an honour not to be refused," he said. "You must ask the good Teresa to stay and prepare our dinner."

The *signor* spread out his pictures for me to see, saying he was an artist only by love, and not by profession. I thought that love must have the best of it, so beautiful was his work; much finer than Placido's *fresco*, which was considered something fine. There were pictures of lovely ladies who were of his own country, and their beauty seemed to laugh at me, and my heart began to sink.

"*Signor*," I said, almost tearfully, "shall I not return to the chalet, and put on my mother's clothes?"

"Your mother's clothes!" he cried, amazed.

"Those I had on yesterday. The colours are gay and bright. Else I shall make such an ugly picture—you will throw it away."

"You make far the prettiest picture I have ever seen," he said, "and I shall hang it up where I can look at it every day."

I blushed with surprised delight. "Thank you, Signor John," I muttered, and crossed my hands as he had arranged them, and gazed over into the pine-forest in a way which he had already approved.

The *signor* remained at our chalet for a whole week. Every morning, we started on some new excursion; he and I together, for my father had not time to attend to him, and Niccolo could not walk.

One evening we were all at supper when Placido appeared with his mule coming up our Alp. My father welcomed him kindly, and bade him sit down and eat. He looked strangely at the Signor John, and then at me; but our new friend spoke to him pleasantly, and they were soon conversing together. Placido was a large man, with a calm face. He had dark thoughtful eyes, and brows well bent above them, and a heap of coal-black locks that left his temples broad and bare. He had a slow gentle smile, but was quick and firm in speech. "As steady as Placido Lorez," was a by-word in his village.

After supper was over Placido seized on the supper-table and carried it back to the chalet, I following on his steps with a dish and ewer. As I washed the platters and restored them to their shelves Placido put logs on the fire, and blew them into flames.

I finished my task and put off my apron, chattering gaily to him all the time. I could see his figure looming out against the firelight, and at the same time my father and the Signor John standing talking out in the moonlight.

Placido had given me very absent answers; but at last made a sudden move, and with two long strides stood right before me.

"Netta," he said, "I came to ask if you would marry me."

I was utterly amazed and a good deal frightened; he looked so very determined, as if I must come off that moment, whether I would or not. My knees knocked together, and I clung to the table.

"You don't really mean it, Placido; you cannot want a wife!"

"Not any wife," he said; "I only ask for you."

"Oh, Placido, don't!" I said.

"Look you, my little dearest one," he urged, "you may think me a rough lover. But never was a wife more loved and prized than you will be, if you come to me!"

"Thank you, Placido," I said, "you mean to be very kind to me; but I do not think about marrying; and please be so very good as not to ask me again."

My father and the Signor John here put in their heads at the door.

"What is this that is going on?" said my father. "Netta, are you scolding our neighbour?"

"Oh no, no!" cried Placido, "it is only that my suit displeases her. I asked her just now to marry me, and she does not wish to consent."

"What!" cried my father, turning to me. "You don't mean to say that you would refuse so kind an offer? Do not think about me, my daughter. I would rather see you provided for than to keep you for my comfort."

"I do not like to marry," I said, weeping. "I do not love Placido, and it would be dreadful to have to marry him."

Placido's face flushed and then turned pale again. "I did not come here to make you weep," he said sadly. "The pain of my disappointment is not worth one of your tears."

He turned to go away, but my father seized him by the arm. "Wait, my dear friend," he said, "and do not be offended at a girl who is still a child."

Then turning to the *signor*, who had looked on gravely at this scene:

"*Signor*, come to my assistance," he cried. "Netta will heed your counsel."

The *signor* looked at me tenderly, with an uneasy look in his face.

"As you say, she is only a child," he said. "I beg you will give her a little longer time to play."

"So be it then," said my father.

I drew a long breath of relief, and looked gratefully at the friend who had saved me. Placido gazed from me to the *signor*, and from the *signor* back to me; then suddenly laid hold of his alpenstock and bade us a quick goodnight.

After this we had some more pleasant days, till at last there arrived a sad one when the *signor* prepared to leave us. I felt an odd pain in my heart which I could not drive away. The night before his departure I was standing at the fire alone; the logs were almost burnt, and lay in a red heap on the hearth. The *signor* came and stood by me.

"Netta, when I am gone you must often think of me."

I strove with a sensation of choking.

"What! have you not a word for me?"

"I do not want to weep," I cried, and my tears came down in a storm.

"I will certainly come back next year," said the *signor*, "and then you will be a woman grown."

I wrung my hand away from him, and fled to my loft. The next morning at breakfast he scarcely looked at me. My father was going a journey with him, and they talked about the roads. Niccolo, who had now become merry, made faces behind the *signor's* back, while I stood miserably in the doorway, rubbing my chilly hands together. The travellers bade us goodbye, and Niccolo went off to his workshop; but I stood gazing drearily down the Alp.

The *signor* turned and came back to me.

"Buy yourself a ribbon, pretty one," he said, "when you go to the next *festa*."

In another moment he was gone, and I had a piece of gold in my hand. I uttered a moan of indignation, and went flying down the Alp. "Signor John! Signor John!" I cried, in a voice that must have been shrill enough to frighten the eagles.

I crushed the money into his hand, but it fell to the ground between us; and he hurried off, laughing and looking over his shoulder. I dug the earth with my nails, and buried the gold where it lay; then fled away into the pine-brake, to weep long and fiercely. That evening Placido came back and repeated his question. I gave him a sullen "No!" and he went away more sadly than he had done before. And then I began to get happy again, for Niccolo did not pinch me, and talked to me all about his carvings, just as before the *signor* came.

But my father came back from his journey with a troubled face.

"Placido has left his village," he said, "and gone to push his way in the world!"

2

Three years passed, and I was a staid maiden, who did not care much for *festas* nor gay clothes. I was not of so merry a temper as I had promised to be, and people thought I was haughty, and some of the girls disliked me. This was partly owing to Niccolo, who would say, "You need not speak to Netta, she is grown so proud; she thinks herself quite a princess since the Englishman kissed her hand!" A little thing gets one a character when gossips are by to talk. Then I did not choose to marry, and that was the worst; for, though suitors might not plead like Placido Lorez, yet no one likes to be refused, and their friends resented my coldness. So, I was a lonely kind of creature, and lived in my own way, clinging fast to my father, and only vexed when he would say, "When I am dead and gone, who will take care of you and our peevish Niccolo?"

So, things went on till the avalanche came down upon us, killing my poor father, and burying him in the ruins of our house. The goats and kids were killed, and Niccolo was sorely hurt; only I, as if by miracle, escaped.

We sat for many hours on the fallen rocks, till the people from the village reached us, when they brought us down to their houses, and treated us like their own.

I tried to give little trouble, for I had nothing to give them in return; nothing at all had we saved but the clothes we wore; Niccolo's arm was hurt, so that he could not carve, and a woman's work is not much when she has not got a home to work in. The housewives in the village had got daughters of their own, and nobody seemed in need of a girl to help them. The worst was that nobody would love Niccolo, for, besides being utterly helpless, the lad had a biting tongue.

Placido's aged mother came out to look at me; when she saw my saddened face the tears came down her cheek.

"My girl," she said, "I have hated you, for you sent my son away, but the Lord has sent you trouble, and I must forgive you."

She brought me into her house, and I told her my bitter thoughts, and that I wanted to go down to the world where wages are given to labour.

"At Como," she said, "are the silk factories; and there is many a way of earning when one gets down to the level world. You used to play the zither, and sing a song."

"That is long ago," I said, "and the zither is buried with my father. I fear that all my music is buried with it."

"At your age the music is not hushed so quickly," she said kindly, and pulled an old zither down from a shelf. "It used to be sweet enough," she added; "take it with my blessing. At least it may cheer your way if it puts no money in your purse. And the village shall see to your Niccolo; though it must be owned he is an imp."

So, I resolved to go down to the level world, to work at the silks of Como, or at anything I could find to do. The zither was to go with me, and Niccolo was to stay at the village till such time as I should have money to come back and fetch him.

I took my zither on my shoulder, and a wallet in my hand, and, committing myself to God, I set out on my lonely way. Niccolo limped along with me half a mile; and when we found he could go no further we stopped on the lonely road for a last embrace. The poor lad had always loved me dearly, and his spirit was quite broken now, and he clung to me with cries. It was a moment of the cruellest anguish when I had to push him at last from me, and to hurry away. I heard his sobs behind me for a long way as I went, and later fancied I could hear them still, in the rush of the falling river and the faint wail of the pines.

I had passed two pretty villages along my way, and the sun had already set when I reached the third. There was a glare behind the mountains, and a warm golden haze floated in the vale. The houses came down a hill and the streets were flights of steps. Far above the roofs, and out of the chestnut trees, rose the burning brazen cap of the campanile, and the bell was sounding lazily, as if ringing itself to sleep. The pines I had left behind me, in fringe of olive and purple, on the dusky heights; and here there were only the heavily laden fruit trees, chestnuts drooping over my shoulder, cherries dropping into my mouth, walnuts lining the roadside, and fig-bushes thrust in my path.

Vines ran over the walls and upon the crimsoned roofs, and clusters of ripened grapes hung in at the doors and windows. A cloud of silvery smoke had blent with the haze of the sunset, and there was a smell as of burning logs and fragrant wood.

The next day I passed through still more villages, and got down to the flush and bloom of the Lombard plains. The mountains here became walls of a gigantic garden, vines wrapped their terraces, and melons ripened in the meadows in the midst of the corn. Plums were as lumps of gold, and the peaches glowed in the fruit-gatherer's basket, while nectarines and apricots added perfume to the coloured air. Great rows of mulberry trees reminded me now of the silk works, and the grasshoppers sang so loud that I took them for birds.

I got on board a small sailing vessel that plied upon the lake, earning my fare by a little music, and went singing down to Como, weary, travel-soiled, and with blisters on my feet. I fell asleep in the middle of my songs, and was gently shaken awake again by the captain's merry wife. She wore a white-and-scarlet head-dress, and a large cross of gold, and crushed grapes out of a basket into her baby's laughing mouth. The gaiety here on the lake was a thing to make one stare: boats with scarlet cushions, ladies in lace mantillas, boatmen with dazzling shirts and brilliant sashes. The lake glowed with the most exquisite bluish-green, and out of it rose the palaces, with terraces climbing the heights. We passed towns like straggling castles, whose streets were ladders of stone creeping up from the water; and all these wonderful novelties were to me a fantastic dream.

Giulia, the captain's wife, found me a lodging in the town of Como, a closet under a chimney, beside the room where she and her husband had their home. In order to reach this nest, I had to climb a hundred steps, which wound in and out of the houses up to the roofs. Noises roused me by three o'clock in the morning, wheels rolling, voices shouting, tambourines ringing, besides the sound of many novel kinds of music. I brushed up my dusty clothes, and went out to look at the town. The people were holding their market in the piazza of the Duomo, and tables were there set out with provisions piled on them lavishly.

The shops under the loggie were already all alive, and deep amber curtains fluttered gaily out of the arches. Flowers teemed from the dark and crooked balconies overhead, which hung like crazy cages from the upper windows. Colours were flashing everywhere: from brilliant oleander blossoms like living flames in the air; from the gay dresses of the people, the piles of monster melons, the red marbles of the Broletto, and the Duomo's deeper hues.

I lifted the heavy curtain, and went into the Duomo; Mass was over, and most of the people were gone; but others kept pouring in, and the place was full. Somebody touched me on the shoulder, and I looked up with a start. Here was Placido in the dress of a boatman!

"Netta!" he whispered excitedly. His face was flushed, and there were tears in his eyes.

"Oh, Placido Lorez!" I cried, and gave him both my hands.

We sat on a bench and whispered in a shady corner of the church. Each had a story to tell, and each had a ready listener.

"My father is dead, Placido," I said, "and Niccolo is hurt in the Alps. I have come down here to Como to try and earn money at the silk. This is my whole story; so, life is sad enough."

"I guessed it was so," said Placido. "I knew how it must be with you when I saw you crying at the Mass. As for me, I have travelled far. I have stored crops and driven oxen, and helped with the vines in the South. For some months I have been a boatman here on the lake; and yesterday I had it in mind to return to the Alps. But now I believe I'll wait a bit. There's never good in haste."

"There is a captain's wife who is good to me," I said, it being now my turn again; "and she says I shall earn money by singing, for the people here in the plains are as fond of music as ourselves. I sing better than I used to do, and your mother has given me her zither."

"Little Netta!" he said, "I have made a good bit of money, and I don't like to think that you must work. I can't forget the day when you declared you could not love me, but maybe if you were to try you might change your mind. It's not that I am much to care for, but the love in my heart is strong. Who knows but that, after all, I could make you happy!"

"Placido," I said, "you are a kind man, but as I refused to marry you before, when I had got a home, so I will not accept you now, because I am in need of one."

"I would not bribe you with anything but just my love," he answered mournfully. "So, if it cannot be, it can't, and I will not vex you. You must at least let me be your friend, however."

"My best friend," I said; and after that we walked hand in hand about the church, Placido showing me the pictures, and explaining what they meant, and telling me the touching stories that are painted in the jewelled windows.

The captain's wife befriended me, and people liked my music, and I could earn more money with my zither than in the factories. The people would gather round me, asking each for his favourite song, and my story got whispered among them, and they were kinder than I could tell. "She sings for a helpless brother," they said, and fees were therefore doubled as they dropped in my lap. Great people also would send for me now from their villas; and I began to save a little money.

I had to sing one evening at a palace on the lake, and it was dark when I took my seat in the verandah. The lake glittered with moonlight, and all along the terraces hung dimly coloured lamps. A crowd of gay figures had gathered on the marble steps that led into the water. When I sang every one listened; when I ceased, I was forgotten; save that somebody went to a table and fetched me wine.

I looked up to thank this somebody, and saw the Signor John.

"Little Netta!" he exclaimed amazed. "Can it be possible that this is you?"

"Yes, *signor*," I said.

"Tell me how it has happened," he asked. "What can have fetched you down out of the snows to Como?"

"My father is killed by the avalanche," I said, "and I am earning money for Niccolo, who is hurt in the Alps. It is now time for me to go, *signor*; goodbye!"

"Stay, I am going with you!" he said, and followed me out on the hill, carrying my zither.

"Sit down here and rest," he said, when we had gone a little way.

"But I have still to get to Como," I said, "and I want to rest in my bed."

"That is true," said the *signor*, smiling. "Let us then take a boat at once."

I looked up the water, and assured myself that Placido was nowhere waiting for me. I stepped into the *signor's* boat, and went floating with him down the moonlit lake.

"How beautiful you have grown, Netta!" said the *signor* as we went. "Did I not tell you that you would be a woman when we should meet again?"

I gravely shook my head. I remembered that he had not come back, even to see if I were alive.

"You have also grown prim and cold," he added presently. "Indeed, you are so changed that I wonder how I knew you."

"It is only that one cannot always be a child," I said sadly; and he lifted me out of the boat, and brought me to the foot of the staircase which led up to my nest in the roof. When I peered down from the top, I saw him looking up. I looked then into the glass at the face which the Signor John had called so beautiful.

"Placido never told me that I was beautiful," I reflected.

3

After that I saw the *signor* every day. I had long walks on the hills with him, and many a pleasanter hour on the moonlit lake. He used to meet me at the Duomo, so that I could not think of my prayers; and Giulia began to tease me, calling me a noble English dame.

"You'll not forget me and baby?" she said. "You'll send us a present from England?" and I had already considered in secret about what I should send her.

I thought I should be extremely happy were it not for Placido Lorez; but his face was always before me, and his eyes had got grave and sad.

His sadness troubled me so much that I tried to keep out of his way, and he soon saw that I avoided him, and was careful not to annoy me. Once when I went out on the lake with the Signor John, it happened that Placido's boat was the boat he hired. Not till I was fairly seated did I see the boatman.

Placido picked up his oars, and took his seat so that he could not see me; and never spoke a word nor moved his head. His oars dipped in the lake and scattered the shining water to right and left; but except for this sign of life he might have been a man of stone. He did not even glance at me as I passed him out of the boat, but his downcast face haunted me all that night.

The next day I was tripping along by the boats on the verge of the lake; my zither perched on my shoulder, and flowers blooming in my breast; rare bright flowers, sent me that morning by the Signor John. It was far in the afternoon, when there is a glitter about the place, such a burning of colour and flashing of water, such a glow and dazzle overhead and underfoot, that sometimes one can hardly see one's way. The boats look all the same, with their crimson cushions, and with the dash, as of ink, in the water under the side that is against the sun. The boatmen's white shirts make them also one like another, though none were so tall as Placido, nor so quiet, nor yet so strong. This time I did not see him, however, till he put himself right in the way.

"Netta, I want to speak to you."

"Make haste then!" I said gaily.

Placido took my hand and made me sit on the side of his boat. Before this I had rather believed in his strength than known it.

He looked at me, straight in the face, with a long wistful gaze. "You are going to meet the *signor?*" he said.

"Yes."

"Netta, has he asked you to be his wife?"

I said, "Not yet, Placido;" and I began to get angry.

"Netta, do you think you love him?"

I hung my head and blushed, which might mean anything.

"Dear," he said, "you need not be angry, but you must listen to me. Gentlemen seldom marry peasant girls, though it may charm them to walk and sail with one like you. And you have yourself to look to. Don't think me selfish, for I have no wish on earth, if it be not to see you happy. If *I* could have made you happy, I would have done it; but as that is not to be—by Heaven, I'll see that no one shall make you wretched!"

"I am not so easily made wretched," I said haughtily.

Placido looked at me tenderly for a moment, and then turned away his face.

"Wicked tongues can break the purest heart," he said softly.

I looked at him in great amazement, and then I blushed; my face blushed, and my ears, my throat, and my naked arms; and then the blood seemed to freeze within me, and my pulses got cold and still. I did not speak for a minute, but gazed on the ground and thought.

"Placido, you may look at me now," I said presently, "for I am only going to thank you."

Then I turned and left him, and went my way. I did not flaunt so gaily, nor trip so lightly as usual. The pain in Placido's face had given me a shock.

The *signor* was already waiting for me up in the hills; it being now a matter of course that I should meet him there in the evenings, when we would watch the sun set redly behind the vineyards; while he talked to me all about England, and of his home where my pretty portrait now hung on the wall. I had believed that he always thought of me as future mistress of this honoured home, never thinking at all of the gulf between us. Now I sat by him silently looking down on the shining lake.

"Netta," he said, "what ails you?"

"I have been thinking of how I can tell you that I must not come here again," I said.

"Must not come here again!" he echoed. "Who has the right to prevent you?"

"Only my own will," I answered.

"Then that must bend to mine," he said, smiling, "for I cannot live without you."

A lump rose up in my throat, but I choked it down.

"*Signor*," I said sadly, "I am an ignorant girl from the mountains, while you—you know the world. You might have been kinder."

He glanced quickly at my face; his brow suddenly reddened, and he turned his head away from me. So had Placido looked when he feared to pain me; only Placido had nothing to blush for; the blush had been left for me.

"There is no need to be vexed," I said, "and I did not mean to hurt you. I am going back to the town now. I shall always be proud of your friendship, Signor John."

I waited a minute patiently, but he did not move his head. I did not see any reason why I should wait or speak to him again, so I turned away, and began walking towards the town.

I heard his steps coming behind me.

"Netta!" he called.

"Well?" I said.

"Netta, will you be my wife?"

I felt a great shock of triumph. He had really said the words, and I could tell Placido; and yet somehow all the gladness had gone out of my heart. In an hour my life was changed; yet I did not know it.

I said "Yes," slowly, for I thought I loved him, and I remembered that he was a noble *signor*, and that in this he was very good. Placido had said truly that lords do not marry peasants; and the *signor* had made a sacrifice in order to win my hand. I knew that I ought to be proud of it, and yet somehow, I felt ashamed. I could not forget his face when he had turned it away from me, nor the struggle which I had then witnessed, nor the wound that had been given to my pride. Surely, I might be content, I thought, yet I wept that whole night through; I thought I had been a great deal happier when alone on the Alpine paths.

The *signor* brought me gifts; a chain for my neck, and trinkets for my ears, and a ring for my fingers, as pledge of troth. Never was a more generous lover than the Signor John. The evening after I received them, I decked myself in the jewels, and ran out into the twilight to bring my news to Placido. This friend had been away at Colico since early dawn, and I watched for his coming back from my little window up in the roof. His boat pulled into the harbour just after sunset.

"Oh, Netta! is it you?" he cried, and sprang eagerly to the beach.

I shook my head at him laughingly, and the dying flare of the sun blazed on my jewels.

"Placido, I have come to tell you about it; I am to be married this day week!"

Placido bent his head: "I thank God for your welfare," he said.

I bit my lips cruelly, and the tears sprang to my eyes. I had thought that he might have been just a little grieved.

"It is wonderful," I said, "how friends can be glad to lose one."

Placido looked at me in wonder. His face was deadly pale, and he appeared to be very tired, or to have lately suffered. Somehow, I could not be satisfied, though I had come out here to triumph over him. He had thought I could be treated lightly, and I had shown him his fears were vain. He had thanked God for my happiness, and that was all.

He began now to speak cheerfully, seeing that clouds had gathered on my face.

"So you are going to be a noble lady," he said, "in some splendid place beyond the seas. Maybe in the course of years you will come back to Como."

I did not believe a word of it; it seemed all a lying tale. It was like the stories told out of the curling smoke when the logs are burning in the Alps. I stood upon a heap of sails, with my foot on the edge of the boat, my jewels flashing as the boat swayed, and my eyes on the west where the light was fading. Yes, yes, I was to be a noble lady, and to live in a foreign country with the Signor John, and there would be a very vast difference, in the days that were still to come, between me up in my high place and Placido plying his boat on the lake.

The light faded away, and the water lapped darkly at the side of the boat. My jewels ceased to flash, and there was a long, long silence, which Placido broke.

"And Niccolo?" he asked abruptly, as if following out some train of thought.

I gave a sudden, violent start, and stared at him blankly. In the midst of my excitement, I had forgotten Niccolo. In arranging for my own welfare, I had let my poor helpless brother slip out of my thoughts.

"The *signor* will take care of him," I muttered; "I will take him with me to England."

"Your *signor* is a generous man," returned Placido; and then I bade him goodnight, and went up to my nest to think.

I sat on my bed in the dark, tossing my twinkling jewels about in my lap. The *signor* had gone to a ball at one of the palaces on the lake; he was dancing even at this moment with the ladies who were quite his equals, yet whom he had not found so lovable as simple me. Ah, for the sake of my love, would he be good to Niccolo? It seemed to me, as I sat there in the depths of my sore remorse, that there was no one half so dear to me as that lone, helpless creature whom people disliked and called the imp: I had promised to come back for my brother, and I vowed I would keep my word.

Next day I was earlier than I need have been at the familiar seat on the hill.

"*Signor*," I said, as soon as he was seated beside me.

"You must not call me '*signor*,' Netta."

"Ah, I always forget. You remember my brother Niccolo?"

The *signor's* face clouded. "I do remember him well," he said.

"He is waiting till I return for him, up in the Alps."

"He must wait a long time then, Netta, if you are coming with me."

"*Signor!*" I said, "can we not bring Niccolo with us?"

He laughed a low laugh. He did not mean to be unkind, I think; it was only that he felt amused.

"No, Netta; indeed, we could not take him."

"He has no one at all but me," I said, speaking low, holding my breath.

"He must learn to do without you, then. Once for all, my pretty one, you must leave your friends behind you; though you can still provide for your brother—getting someone to take good care of him up in the mountains."

"No one loves Niccolo," I muttered reflectively.

"Therefore, you need not think me cruel," said the *signor*.

"Therefore, I cannot leave him," I whispered.

The *signor* began to look angry.

"Netta!" he said, "you talk like a spoiled child. You must try to forget Italy, and that is the plain truth. It will be quite hard enough upon me——"

Here he stopped.

"Yes," I said, looking at him. "Tell me what will be hard."

"Nothing," he said, smiling again; "nothing that will not be set right when you have been a year in England."

"And have quite forgotten Italy?"

"And have almost forgotten Italy. And now, since that is settled, my Netta, tell me what you will have for a wedding gift?"

"*Signor*," I said, "you have already given me too much. You have, indeed, been very good to me—that I cannot forget."

"Tush, Netta! what is the matter with you?" he said. "I will give you anything you like."

I sat silent again, looking out over the water. In the distance some elegant ladies were embarking from their marble staircase. Away at the bottom of the lake towered the azure walls of the Alps, and away, farther still, folded up somewhere in their royal purple, sat my sad, crippled brother, my poor, peevish lad, whom nobody, save myself, would ever love. Yonder, with the dainty ladies, was the place for the Signor John; mine was in the Alps, with Niccolo.

"*Signor*," I said at last, "I am an ignorant girl, but I have been lately thinking more than you would believe. I acknowledge that it was generous of you to ask me to be your wife, and that my love would not be worth to you all the trouble it must cost. Like should mate with like, and you and I are unlike; yet I should hardly have dared to speak had it not been for Niccolo?"

The *signor* looked at me in amazement.

"You mean that you want to be free again, Netta?"

"Yes," I said, "if you please."

"You mean to give up everything for Niccolo?"

"Tomorrow I shall be on the Alps, going back for him," I said.

"Netta, you shall not jilt me!"

"No, Signor John, that would, indeed, be too saucy. You shall jilt me, if you like it better."

"This is very fine," he said, "but I shall alter your way of thinking!"

"In the meantime, say goodbye, *signor*, for I shall not see you tomorrow."

"Goodbye, Netta, for the present."

"Goodbye, Signor John, and may God be with you!"

He had caught both my hands, as if he would not let me go; but I twisted them from him suddenly, and went running down the hill and out of his sight.

I packed up my jewels and sent them back to their owner, who had been generous enough to give them, as though I had been fit to be his wife. My good Giulia carried them, after mourning over them for an hour, and early on the following day I went out to look for Placido.

"I've come to say goodbye, Placido. I'm off now to the Alps."

"The Alps!" cried Placido wonderingly.

"For Niccolo," I said brightly. "We are not going to England though. The *signor* is going alone."

Placido sprang from his boat with a radiant face.

"Ah, Netta! is it true? But you shall not travel alone."

"Of course I shall travel alone. I did it before with a sadder heart."

"I am going to see my mother," said Placido. "I hope you will not object."

"Why should I object?" I said. "Your mother will be glad to see you."

"As glad as your Niccolo to see you."

"I'll take care to tell her you are coming," I said.

"You think, then, that you are likely to outwalk me?"

"What! do you mean to say that you are coming with me now?"

"I mean to be your fellow-traveller," he said, "unless you tell me truly that you would rather go alone."

I could not say that I would rather go alone, so we made our journey together back to the Alps. As we went along Placido told me much of his former journeys, and what grief he had suffered, and what dreary things he had said to himself; and I knew well that his misery had been because I could not love him. As for me, I confessed my carelessness with regard to Niccolo, and my feelings towards the English *signor*, which had been all made up of pride; and Placido tried to excuse me a little, and promised not to think ill of me. It was much happier travelling with him than wandering quite alone, and by the time we got near his village I was grieved that the journey was past.

We sat upon two large pine-stumps then, and looked at each other gravely. Another wind of the road would bring us within sight of friends. I had felt a strange joy in being alone in the world with Placido, and I knew by Placido's face that he liked taking care of me.

"Netta," said Placido simply, "will you be my wife at last?"

"I wonder you ask me again," I said; "but it would cost me far too dear to refuse you now."

So it happened that we were married in his village church, with his mother and my Niccolo, besides many friends, around us. And now we are again at Como. Niccolo, who has got stronger, is carving figures under our trees, while grandmother teaches our child to touch the zither. And Placido is not a boatman now; we live in our own vineyard, where the Signor John has been to see us, bringing his charming English bride.

A Will o' the Wisp

"*Ring, ding! tinkle, tinkle, ting!*" rang the chimes in the cathedral tower, beginning to play their airy tune in the clouds, as a bewitched old lady came into the town of Dindans one evening, following a Will o' the wisp.

Dindans is a dreamy old Flemish town, with canals full of yellow-green water, and brown boats with little scarlet flags; with strange old beetle-browed houses overshadowing the streets; with a market-place and fountain, a multitude of pointed gables, a cathedral covered with saints and angels, little children in muslin caps, and bells that make delicate music aloft in the air. A real traveller stopping at Dindans is a rare apparition, and people came out of their houses that evening to gaze at the little old Englishwoman who trotted behind the truck which jolted her luggage along the pavement.

When the tired little woman stopped before the wide entrance of the queer old inn, La Grue, there was no one about, and she walked into the sanded hall and glanced through the opening at the other end down the long, ancient courtyard, with its vines and gallery and rows of little windows, and on to where apple-trees and scarlet geraniums were blushing through the sunlight from the garden. A curious stone staircase wound out of the hall, and there were doors on each side of her. She hesitated, and glanced all round the unpeopled interior, until the sound of a voice came out of the nearest door.

"With her hands on her knees, and the knitting lying in her lap," said the shrewish voice of a woman in clumsy Flemish French, "though I told her yesterday that the stocking must be done immediately."

"Thou hearest," said a man's voice; "thou must be more industrious."

"And with a look on her face that would sour the wine," continued the woman, "enough to make people think one was unkind to her."

"Thou must be more cheerful," grumbled the man.

"And see! There are travellers at our door, and here she is gossiping, so that we do not even perceive them!"

A door, which had been ajar, was quickly opened, and a young girl came out with a pale face, and eyes heavily encircled with the redness of suppressed tears. The young figure looked so much more refined than anything one could have expected in the place, that the traveller forgot her own business in the surprise. At the same moment a waiter came running to take the luggage, a little man, with a keen and perturbed face, and something like a hump on his shoulders. This was the oldest inn in Dindans, explained the girl. There were not many chambers ready, for travellers did not often stop to pass a night in the town. There was a suite of small rooms running round the courtyard, but they were at present used as fruit-lofts or lumber-closets.

Over the archway into the garden was a little apartment, like a glass case, which was occupied by a gentleman who had been long established here, and must not be moved. But *madame* should have the best chamber, occupied by *monsieur* and his wife when nobody came. It should be made ready for the Dame Anglaise at a moment's notice.

The stranger had had an intention of trying to escape, but something in the girl's manner mysteriously vanquished her. She took possession of an ancient-looking room, with heavy, dark wainscots and one window, in which the only things noticeable were two well-painted portraits on the walls. They were Monsieur and Madame Van Melckebecke, explained Jacques, the waiter, painted by Monsieur Lawrence, the English artist, who lived in the little glass chamber, and studied all his evenings in the painting-room of the *Cercle des Beaux* Arts, above in the tower; a very respectable club, which reflected credit on the house. Their meeting-room for social purposes was behind the *salle-à-manger*.

Madame, the stranger, got rid of her dust, and made herself at home in her chair by the window, feeling herself to be a disappointed old woman, who had been flitting about the world for years, seeking an object which it now seemed folly to think of finding.

In the pleasant courtyard the evening sunlight was gilding the peaks of the little windows, and the grapes that hung from the vines, but leaving a cool well of shadow about the old archway, through which flamed softly the illuminated garden, brilliant with scarlet and green, and bristling with gold-tipped apple-trees. As *madame* looked, a man's head was thrust from one of the queer little windows in the glass chamber, an English head, brown-haired and thoughtfully intelligent. It leaned out of the golden background, glanced at a deserted ironing-table, which stood under the vines below, withdrew itself quickly, and disappeared. This was Monsieur Lawrence, no doubt.

Our little old woman had returned to her own perplexities, when the maiden who had received her again appeared at her door, a ray from the window touching the girl as she announced that *madame* was served. Her face shone upon the traveller out of the shadows under the doorway—a pale, delicate-featured face, with a distinct beauty of its own, which was partly owing to its subdued intensity of expression. The eyes had still that look of suffering from unshed tears; the mouth had a look of heroic patience. She hovered on the threshold, while *madame* fixed a sudden stare upon her, and made a sharp ejaculation in English.

"*Madame's* dinner!" said the girl, thinking that she had not been understood in French. But the stare was not removed from her face till she fell back abashed across the threshold, and closed the door.

"What is it?" cried the little Englishwoman to herself, with piteous energy. "A likeness? No, not a likeness! Yes—no—yes. Certainly not! With brooding over this matter, I am becoming silly!"

Madame reflected, and made up her mind that she was too hungry and tired, to think to any purpose. She dined, and Jacques brought her some coffee in her chamber.

Madame could not refrain from questioning Jacques. For many long years it had been the business of her life to question. Stine was the girl's name. She was the niece of *monsieur*, and her fate was sad.

"Why do they treat her badly?"

"It seems to come by nature," said Jacques. "At present she is in great disgrace because she refuses to marry me; although I have declared to *monsieur* that I will not have her."

"But is she not good and nice?" cried *madame*.

"*Cependant*," persisted Jacques, "I will not have her. She likes me as it is; she would hate me if I pressed her to marry me. *Mon Dieu!* Heaven must do something better for her than that."

Our traveller was on her way to England, and had broken her journey to rest but a night; yet she had already become curiously interested in the inhabitants of La Grue. She decided that she would make an indefinite stay at Dindans. That night she wrote some letters, and looked over papers, in her chamber. She was very much excited, and did not settle to rest until it was another day.

She was only in her first sleep when Stine got up to begin her daily work. No one in the house was awake but herself as she went into the garden, fetched vegetables, and prepared them for use, placed saucepans on the stove, and then went into the courtyard to make ready her laundry table for an hour's ironing. As she trotted about the dewy garden and the cool, grey courtyard, she held up her head and moved lightly, delighting in the taste of fresh air, space, and peace. Her crisp, white bodice rustled with freshness, and smelt of lavender; her little apron fluttered as if enjoying itself.

She went to her ironing under the vines, but had hardly plaited a frill when she remembered that she had not put the things straight in the painting-room of the club. In a minute she was busy folding up the tangled drapery that had been used in costuming a model the night before. The next moment someone came into the room, and Stine seemed all at once in a great hurry as she said,—

"Good-day, Monsieur Lawrence; you are up early;" turning away as she spoke, and making haste with her work.

"Stine, will you not put that away for a moment, and speak to me?"

"I have spoken, *monsieur.* I have said good-day."

The young man looked half sad and half angry, as she opened the door, curtseyed, and disappeared. The painter sat down, and began to work at his picture.

"This place is not good for me," he reflected; "I shall leave it as soon as possible. Elsewhere I shall have greater advantages, and be rid of heartache. Ah! why do I love her, when she does not care for me? Yet what a life I see before her in this place! Worked to death, or wedded to Jacques, or to the owner of the nearest *estaminet.* I have not much to offer her, but in time I shall succeed; we could be frugal. She need not work for two of us as they work her here."

Lawrence was alone in the world. His art was his delight, and he had left England for the purpose of studying in one of the best Continental schools. Passing through Dindans he had been attracted, first by the quaintness of the old inn, and afterwards by Stine's sad face; and here he had been content to follow his art studies, without pushing on further to the higher point of his ambition. He had been able on occasions to save the girl from harsh treatment, and he recalled now her amazement at being so shielded, her gratitude so simply shown, and the frank, warm friendship that had sprung up between them.

He had watched her at her daily work in the kitchen, in the courtyard, everywhere, and had made sketches of her by stealth under every aspect. Later there had come upon him dreams in which he fancied her flitting about in a home which should be her own, and also his; and one day, when she had been in trouble, he had spoken to her, and then he had found his mistake. His love had appeared to vex her, and their friendship was at an end. She was now as sad and reserved as when he had first set eyes on her. "It must be that I am quite unlovable," thought Lawrence, "since she will rather endure unkindness than share my lot."

Meanwhile, Stine was working with nimble fingers at her ironing-table; linens were folded, and muslins crimped, while now and again a few tears flashed out of her eyes like sparks of fire, and burnt her cheeks. She remembered one day when a kind face had come into the inn, and somebody had saved her from a beating; she being then considered young enough to be so punished. She remembered how light had become her tasks after what wonderful day, how the consciousness of being protected had grown habitual to her, while the wonder swelled within her at finding herself a person to be so deeply respected.

She began to think that even a life like hers might come to have a beautiful side to it, till that first dreadful night, when she had told herself it would be better if she should never see Monsieur Lawrence again. The next day had brought the trouble of her disobedience about Jacques, as well as that strange, supreme moment when Lawrence, having heard of it, had asked her to be his wife, and had been refused. Yes, and she would refuse him tomorrow again, if put to it! *Flash!* came a tear on the frill she was ironing, so that she was obliged to crimp one inch of it over again; and Madame Van Melckebecke came scolding into the courtyard.

The little Dame Anglaise dined at the *table d'hôte* that day. *Monsieur* sat at the top of his board, and his wife and stepdaughter, a giggling girl with sharp features, sat beside him. After dinner, *monsieur*, his wife, and daughter went out to take coffee in the garden, sitting under an apple-tree, with a tiny table between them: *monsieur* in his white linen coat and scarlet skull-cap, the girl in a gay muslin with flaming bows, *madame* in brilliant gown and enormous gold earrings. The ladies chatter, *monsieur* smokes and drinks his coffee, and Jacques comes into the garden and announces that the Dame Anglaise wishes to join their circle. She comes, she is agreeable, she gossips familiarly over their concerns, and tells them a great deal about her travels.

So agreeable did she make herself, that next afternoon the stranger was invited once more to join the circle in the garden. Never had been known so pleasant an Englishwoman.

"*Monsieur and madame*," said the stranger, by-and-by, "I am going to tell you a story. Yesterday I spoke of my travels, and you were good enough to be amused; today I will try to relate to you some of the most important events of my life. I have lived under the shadow of a great trouble for many years. For sixteen years I have been following a Will o' the wisp."

"A Will o' the wisp?" cried all the listeners.

"It has led me from country to country, and from town to town. I arrived here the other night utterly disheartened, when, lo! it sprang up again; here—under this roof—as soon as I entered."

"Here!" cried the Van Melckebeckes.

Madame shifted her chair so that she sat facing *monsieur*, who had taken his cigar from his mouth, and sat gazing at her in amazement, with his scarlet skull-cap a little on one side, and a slight look of apprehension on his stolid countenance.

"Let *madame* proceed!"

The strange old lady paused before she began her tale, and a tragic look swept across her dim blue eyes.

"My friends," she said, with a quiver in her voice, "sixteen years ago there lived in a pleasant part of England an English gentleman and his wife, who had very great wealth and a beautiful home, and up to the time of the beginning of my story they had scarcely known what it is to grieve. They had one child, a little girl of three years old, the idol of both parents. They were fond of travelling abroad, and it happened once that they were in Paris on their way home; with them the child and three servants, including the nurse, a strange and wild-tempered woman. The lady was half afraid of this nurse, yet shrank from sending her away. The nurse was savagely fond of the child, and jealous of its mother. One day there was a quarrel, springing from this jealousy, and that evening the woman walked out of the hotel carrying the child in her arms, as if to give it an airing. She did not return, and the father and mother never heard of their child again."

Monsieur had turned on his seat and looked askance at the stranger. *Madame*, his wife, sat with open mouth gazing at her husband.

"Think of it, good people," went on the little old trembling lady. "I was the friend of that young mother, and I came to her in Paris in her affliction. We spent months traversing Paris, and we advertised, offering large rewards; but no tidings of woman or child were to be had. We gave up the search in Paris, and went moving from place to place, lingering so sadly, and making such frantic inquiries, that people began to point to my friend as the 'poor crazed mother who was looking for her child.' Ah, my friends, if you had seen her as I did—her eyes dim, her cheeks wasted, weeping herself to death over a toy, a tiny garment, a little shoe! Search was useless, and by the time we could prevail on her to give it up the poor thing was so broken in heart and body that we only brought her home to die.

"She died in my arms, and I promised to keep up the search so long as I lived. She had a firm belief that her child was not dead, and the horror of its growing up among bad people haunted her perpetually. Her husband lived ten years after her death, and though he never kept up such a constant search as I did, yet he could not forget that there was a chance of his lost daughter's being alive somewhere. I think his heart was broken too—more by the loss of his wife, perhaps, than by that of his child. Both parents had been rich, and when the father died, he willed all their possessions to their child, who might yet be discovered living in ignorance of her parentage.

"After a certain time, if nothing has been heard of the girl or her descendants, the property will be broken up and divided in charity. Since the father's death I have never for one moment relaxed my efforts to discover some trace of the child of my friends. I now begin to grow old, and I fear I shall not be able to keep it up much longer. I have cheered my heart many a time, telling myself that the girl would be a daughter to me in my advancing age, and would repay me with her love for all the labour I have had for her. She would now be nineteen years of age. When a child, her hair was dark; it would now be darker still. Her eyes, I think, would be grey, the colour of her mother's. I have often fancied I saw a face like what I had pictured her to myself, and spent feverish days in finding out my mistake. Now you know what I meant by a Will o' the wisp."

The faces of the innkeeper and his wife had changed so that they did not seem to be the same persons who had sat there half an hour ago. They now nodded their heads, while neither spoke.

"But why say that the Will o' the wisp had appeared under our roof?" asked Rosalie sharply.

The old lady trembled wildly, and looked round on the three faces. At this moment Stine appeared coming down the courtyard with a fresh supply of coffee.

"My friends! my friends!" cried the little old lady, stretching out her hands to them, "I believe that there"—pointing to Stine— "comes the child I have been seeking for these many years!"

Monsieur Van Melckebecke sprang to his feet, while his wife pushed back her chair, and stared furiously at the stranger.

"*Madame* has lost her mind!" cried *monsieur*, eyeing the lady with terror.

"Ah no, *monsieur*! Tell me that I am right, or help me to the proof of it. My child has in some strange way been thrown upon your charity. Some feeling of honour makes you wish to keep a secret."

"*Madame* is all wrong," said the man, a little mollified. "The girl is my niece. I will bring you face to face with her mother. She lives at some distance, but she shall be brought here to satisfy you."

"Bring her at once," said the old lady.

Next morning a coarse, loud-voiced woman came into the inn, and *Madame* the Stranger was summoned to meet her in the garden under the apple-tree. All the family were present at the interview—*monsieur*, *madame*, Rosalie, Stine, and Jacques.

"She is my daughter," said the coarse woman; "but I gave her up to my brother for the good of the family. Speak out, Stine, and say if I am not your mother."

"I have always known you as my mother," said Stine, shrinking from her. "Dear *madame*," to the Englishwoman, "give up this fancy. I am grieved to be such a trouble to you."

"Help me, good Jacques, to get back to my chamber," said the poor old lady faintly.

That night, very late, when Stine was wearily toiling up her tower staircase, a door opened, and the English *madame* came out, wrapped in her shawl.

"My dear," she said, "take me up to your tower room to see the view from your window. It must be fine this starry night. Besides, I want to talk to you."

Stine's little room seemed situated in a star, so high was it above the peaks of the Flemish houses away down in the town below. The cathedral tower looked over at her in ghostly magnificence. Her small lattice lay open, and the music of the chimes came floating dreamily in as they played their melody through in honour of the midnight hour. The room was cool, dark, and quiet. *Madame* sat down on Stine's little bed, and the cathedral clock struck twelve.

"My dear," she said to Stine, "I am not going to afflict you with my trouble. I am used to disappointment, yet there is something in this case which is different from all my former experiences. I cannot shake off the interest I feel in you. Granted that I am a crazed old woman, still I would like to leave my mark, a good mark, upon your fate. Do not be afraid to speak freely to me, my child. They are harsh to you in this house?"

"They are not very kind."

"You would wish to get out of their power, and yet not marry Jacques?"

"I will not marry Jacques—Heaven bless him!"

"Yet a husband could protect you."

"They are not going to kill me; and I am able to bear my life."

The little old English *madame* was silent, reflected a minute, and then began again.

"I went out this evening to calm my heart in the cathedral. I found it almost deserted, and full of a solemn peace. I prayed, and became resigned. Having finished, I was resting myself, when I found the painter, Monsieur Lawrence, standing beside me. He addressed me as your friend, and we had some whispered conversation. He talked about you. He loves you. You have repulsed him. Is it possible that you are so hard?"

"*Madame*, I am not hard," gasped Stine, after a pause.

"I can believe it."

"*Madame*, before I knew Monsieur Lawrence, I had never loved anything; now it seems as if I could love the whole world for his sake. He is to me all that one lives for, lives by. He is absolutely as my life. I speak extravagantly, *madame*; but remember, at least, that I did not wish to speak at all."

"Go on," urged the little lady.

"There was a time," said Stine, leaning on the sill, and gazing over clasped hands into the starry outer dimness, "a time when I never thought of checking my love, seeing nothing in it that was not beautiful and good. But I was forced to change my mind. *Madame*, I will tell you about it. I was sitting one evening in the courtyard at 'my knitting, and the students were supping in their club-room; the blind was down, the window open. I heard the men's voices talking, but I was not minding what they said. I was thinking of Monsieur Lawrence, of some words that he had said to me, and of the beautiful look that always came into his eyes when he saw me. He was away that day, and I always allowed myself to think of him most when he was at a distance; it seemed less bold, somehow, than when he was near.

"Suddenly I heard his name mentioned in the club-room, and he became the subject of conversation among the students. They spoke of his noble character, and of his genius, and someone said, 'If he only keeps out of harm's way he has a fine career before him.' Then there was confusion of voices, and by-and-by I learned that the chief thing he had to fear was marriage with a woman as poor as himself. Then my own name was brought into the conversation, and there was more confusion, till a voice said severely, 'That, indeed, would be his total ruin.' *Madame*, the words came out through the window to me, and buzzed about my head like fiery gnats, and then made their way inward, and settled and burned their way down to my heart.

"When I came up here that night I sat down here, and thought about it. At first, I said to myself, 'It is untrue; I should help, and not hinder him; I should work so hard, and privation would be nothing to me.' But soon my mind came round to see the truth. The poorest bread costs money, and a woman is often in the way. A man of genius must not be fettered. If he drudges to boil the pot, how shall he soar to his just ambition? After that I used to go about saying to myself, to keep up my courage, 'I will not be his ruin. I will not spoil his life.' And then, when one day he found me in trouble, and asked me to marry him, I had strength to refuse him. This is the whole of my secret, *madame*. I love him, and will protect him from the harm that I could do him."

"My dear," said the Englishwoman, "I believe you are indeed the stuff to make a good wife; and I warn you not to let your honourable scruples carry you out of reach of a well-earned happiness that may be yours. You and Monsieur Lawrence are young, and can wait. Meantime, you need not give the lie to your hearts. Take the word of an old woman; there is nothing so precious in this world as love, when it is wise; and especially if it has been made holy by passing through pain."

Next evening Stine went to the convent, a mile out of the town, to fetch eggs and melons for the inn housekeeping. Coming back again, along the canal under the poplars, she sat down to rest a minute, with her basket by her side. The sun had set, the brown sails in the canal had still a red tinge on their folds, and the spires and peaks of the town loomed faint and far through an atmosphere as of gold-dust. Stine's heart bounded with a painful delight, as she saw Monsieur Lawrence coming towards her, under the shadow of the poplars. She would have liked to run away, but that was not to be thought of.

She rose, however, to her feet, and he came beside her, and they stood looking at each other.

"I did not mean to frighten you," he said; "and I am not going to annoy you. I have come to bid you goodbye, as I leave the town to-morrow. After all that has come and gone, Stine, you will not deny me a kind word at parting."

"It is better for you to go, Monsieur Lawrence. I hope you will succeed, wherever you are."

"I shall do pretty well, I suppose. I should have done better, I think, if your love had blessed my life. But I will not vex you about that any more. One thing I ask, that you will let that good old English lady have a care over you."

"Do not be uneasy about me. Goodbye, Monsieur Lawrence. I suppose you are now going further up the road? I am already late; I must get home."

"Hard to the last!" said Lawrence bitterly.

The reproach was too much for Stine; it broke the ice about her heart, and the waters of desolation poured in upon her. She turned her face, white and quivering, on Monsieur Lawrence.

"I am not hard——" she began pitifully.

"Stine!" he cried, reading her face aright at last, and stretching out his arms to her.

"Oh, Monsieur Lawrence!" she cried, and fell upon his breast, weeping. "I have been hard," she said, defending herself; "only because I dared not be otherwise. I have hurt myself more than you. Even now I am wrong. Do not let me ruin you."

"You have been very near ruining me," he answered; "but that is past."

When Stine came into the inn with the eggs and melons she was scolded for being late; but Madame Van Melckebecke's abusive words fell about her ears like so many rose-leaves.

That night, when Stine and the Dame Anglaise were conversing up in the tower, a tap came at the door, and Monsieur Lawrence joined the conference. The three sat whispering together, barely able to see one another, by the light of the stars. Here it was arranged that Lawrence should go to Paris and seek his fortune, while Stine, as his betrothed, should remain at her work in the inn. They were to love and trust each other till Lawrence should find himself ready to come and take his wife. The chimes rang, the stars blinked, the old lady sat between the lovers, like the good godmother in the fairy tale. *Madame* was to watch over Stine till Lawrence should come for her, while no one else in the inn was to know the secret but Jacques.

Early one morning, while the inn was asleep, Stine came into the cathedral when the doors were just open, and even the earliest wor-shippers were not arrived. She laid a bunch of white flowers upon the step of the altar, and then Lawrence came beside her, and they vowed their vow of betrothal, and said goodbye.

After this the days went on as usual at La Grue. The painters paint-ed in their studio, and supped in their club-room, and regretted the absent Lawrence, but yet commended him for running away from danger. The English lady had taken up her residence regularly at the inn. The landlord was hardly pleased to have her. He always eyed her suspiciously, having a fear that that craze about Stine had not been altogether banished from her mind. In this, however, he was wrong. The poor little wearied-out lonely lady had given in to fate at last, telling herself that her faithful search had been in vain, that the child she had sought must be long since dead, that she needed repose, and might venture to indulge her fancy for employing herself in a kindly care of Stine.

She came and went about the inn, sitting in her little lofty chamber looking over at the chimes, exchanging civilities in the garden with *monsieur* and *madame*, wandering about the quaint old town, poking among ancient churches, or trying to talk a little Flemish to the poor. She did not dare show much sympathy for Stine, lest the powers that ruled the inn should take it in their heads to turn her out of doors. She had to listen to many a bitter scolding, and witness many an unkind action, and dared not interfere, lest worse might come of it. Only at night, when Stine came to the room of her little friend, did they ven-ture on any intercourse.

Then Lawrence's latest news was discussed, and his prospects talked over; and Stine went to bed as happy as though there were not a scold-ing tongue in the world. Harshness did not hurt her now as it used to do. She had lost her fragile and woebegone air; she grew plump and rosy, and her eyes began to shine. She sang over her work, and often smiled to herself with happiness, when no one was by.

The elders perceived this change, and pointed it out to Jacques.

"Thou seest," said *monsieur*, "she is getting quite pretty. Thou canst not be so stupid as still to refuse to marry her?"

"Pretty!" cried Jacques; "I do not see it. To my thinking, the Dame Anglaise is prettier."

"At least, she would make a thrifty wife."

"*Cependant*" said Jacques, "she is better as a fellow-servant."

"Thou art too hard to please," said *monsieur* angrily, surveying the crooked figure of the little man.

"Every man has a right to choose his wife," said Jacques, "and I mean to do better than to marry that Stine."

The innkeeper was baffled.

"Our affairs stand still," he grumbled to his wife. "The law will not allow you to marry a man against his will. I do not see what we can do."

"Wait a bit," said *madame*; "is it not possible that Jacques dislikes her?"

"And thou—dost thou also like her?" sneered *monsieur*.

"But that is a different thing," declared *madame*; "I cannot like a creature who keeps me in fear and stands in my way."

"It is true," groaned *monsieur*, "she is a bright-eyed marmot, but she keeps us in deadly fear."

Whatever the fear was, it preyed upon the master of La Grue. From being merely a brutishly sulky man, he became irritable and violent; even *madame*, his wife, began to moderate her temper, lest, being both in a flame together, they should burn their establishment to death. He began to vow often to his wife that he would not have that *Anglaise* in the house a week longer; that he would have Jacques popped into the canal, and Stine shipped off to the antipodes. He would wait on his guests himself for the future; his wife should do the cooking, and let Rosalie work at the ironing and keep the books. His wife soothed him as well as she was able, but *monsieur* was hard to soothe, and when quiet he was timorous and moody. He left off eating much, and his flesh began to fall away.

"I feel that I shall have a fever," he complained, "and when I am raving, I shall be sure to tell the story."

"Nobody shall come near you but me," said his wife; and, when his fears came to be verified, and she put him to bed in a state of delirium, she suffered no one to help her in the task of nursing him. The little *Anglaise* came once on tip-toe to the chamber door to ask how *monsieur* fared, but *madame* greeted her with a face so dark that she never cared to venture on this mission again. The crisis of the fever passed, and *monsieur* was restored to his senses, without having betrayed in his ravings any secret that might be rankling in his mind. The inn became more lively, and *madame* the landlady was persuaded by her daughter to take a drive out of the town for change of air. *Monsieur* was not able to speak much, and Jacques was allowed to sit by him till his wife returned.

"Jacques," said the sick man faintly, "they think I am getting better, but I know I am going to die."

"No, *monsieur*, no," said Jacques.

"I have not long to live, my friend, and you must go for the *curé* and the *maire*. Bring them to me quickly, before my wife comes back."

"But, *monsieur*——"

"Go, or I shall die on the instant, and my death will be on your head."

Stine had quiet times just now, and she was in the garden leaning against a tree, with her knitting-needles clinking in her fingers. The *Anglaise* sat opposite to her, and they were talking of Monsieur Lawrence. While thus engaged, they saw Jacques, the *curé*, and the *maire* coming down the courtyard. *Monsieur* desired to make his will and prepare for death, they said to one another; and both were shocked.

Sometime afterwards Jacques came running through the archway into the garden, his face and manner so excited that the women stood amazed.

"Come, *madame*," he said to the *Anglaise*, "you are wanted immediately in *monsieur's* chamber." The Englishwoman followed him wondering, and Stine went back to her kitchen to prepare for supper.

Half an hour passed. Stine was standing at the window straining the soup, when she saw the little *Anglaise* coming hurrying down the courtyard, white-faced, her head hanging as if with weakness, missing a step now and then, striking her foot against the stones of the pavement, and feeling, as if blindly, for the door as she entered the kitchen. She snatched the ladle out of Stine's hand and flung it on the floor, seized the girl by the shoulders, laughed in her face, gave a sob, and fell back swooning into the arms of Jacques; all of which meant that the Will o' the wisp had turned out a veritable hearth-light at last.

"Ah, *monsieur le maire, monsieur le curé!*" she cried, recovering; "let them come here and tell the story, for my head is still astray, and I want to hear it again. Come out of this place, girl! thou art not Stine, thou art Bertha, daughter of Sir Sydney Errington and Millicent his wife, both of broken-hearted memory, in Devonshire, in England. It is all written down. Jacques, we saw it written down. Will the gentlemen come and read it to us, or will they not?"

The *curé* and *maire* came in with solemn faces. *Madame* sat on a bench, and drank from a glass of water, while Jacques stood on guard by her side. Stine retreated, and leaned with her back against the wall, looking doubtfully at these people who had come to change her life.

There was no mistake at all about the innkeeper's dying statement. The nurse who had stolen the child had been his first wife, from whom he had separated for a time that they might earn some money. When she came home to him with the child, he, being afraid of her, had helped her to conceal it. He was then a waiter in Paris, and they took up house together, and prospered. She assured him that her motive for stealing the child had been revenge, and that one day, after the parents had suffered enough, a large reward should be obtained for restoring her to them. With this he had been obliged to be satisfied.

His wife set up business as a clear-starcher, and made money enough for the child's support and her own. She used to smudge the child's face with brown, and dress it in boy's clothing; but she died suddenly when it was five years of age. Then had *monsieur* thought of ridding himself of the burden, but had been frightened out of his senses by someone whom he had consulted on the subject. He became afraid for his very life of any one discovering the identity of the girl. Heaviest punishment, he feared, must be the reward of his daring to restore her to her sorrowing friends. When he came to Dindans as owner of the inn, he brought with him Stine as his niece, and a strange woman came to live in a cottage outside the town who pretended to be his sister-in-law, and the mother of the girl.

He had trained Stine to be useful, and, by marrying her to Jacques, had thought to turn her to still further account in his service. No one but his second wife and the pretended mother had ever shared the secret which had sat for years on this cowardly soul. Now that he was going to die, he would shuffle it off. He had always, he declared, meant to tell the truth before he died. If the Dame Anglaise had not arrived then, he would have left the story and its proofs with the *curé* of the town.

"Gentlemen," said Stine, coming out of her corner, "let us not disturb the house of death. Madame Van Melckebecke returns, and these things will not please her."

The landlady's voice was here heard, and the *maire* and the *curé* disappeared very willingly, while Stine brought the *Anglaise* away to her chamber. The poor little lady was beside herself, and kept caressing Stine, and telling what fine things were waiting for her. "My child, my little queen!" she said, "my lady of the manor! Ah, wait, my love, till you see your English home!"

Stine was quite confounded by the news; sat silently leaning her face on her hand, and gazing at her friend.

217

"I do not understand it," she said. She was not willing to follow the idea of any change so complete. It seemed to break up her expectation of that striving and hopeful life with Lawrence in Paris. She did not as yet perceive how good it would be for him.

Suddenly the *Anglaise* gave a shriek. "*Mon Dieu!* child, you are plighted to a humble artist. Ah! how fate has been cheating us! Why was I such a fool as to counsel such a step? But it is not yet too late. Monsieur Lawrence must give you up. You shall marry in your own rank———"

"*Madame!*" cried Stine, springing to her feet; "I know not anything of your England, and I will have nothing to do with it. If my husband is not fit to be a nobleman there, why, we will be noble after our own fashion in our *grenier* in Paris." Then, suddenly perceiving the prosperity which her transformation would bestow upon Lawrence, she burst into a passion of delight, and knelt, laughing and sobbing, by the side of the bed.

"Forgive me, my dear," said the old lady, half terrified; "my senses are coming back to me, and I love you for that speech. Lawrence is now in London; let us set out at once, and take him by surprise."

Lawrence had finished his business in London, and was on the eve of starting for Paris when, returning one night to his lodgings, he found a note, in a lady's handwriting, waiting for him on the table. The writing was not Stine's, and it was not a foreign letter. It announced that Miss Errington begged him to visit her at her manor-house in Devonshire. Now, who was Miss Errington? for Lawrence had no acquaintance with Erringtons, nor yet with manor-houses. He considered the matter gravely, and finally wrote to Stine, at Dindans, telling her of the occurrence; also, that he had accepted the invitation, hoping to find that some wealthy connoisseur had taken a fancy to his pictures. Between his paragraphs was inserted a comical sketch of this possible patron; a lady of venerable aspect, with nut-cracker features, and leaning on a long staff.

It was evening when he arrived at the manor-house, just so light that he could see the rich country through which he was travelling— could discern, with his artist-eyes, the beautiful wooded lands, which he was told had belonged to the Erringtons for numberless generations. He dressed for dinner in a handsome, old-fashioned chamber, and was conducted to the drawing-room. The door closed behind him, and he was in a room softly lighted, in which everything was rich, antique, tasteful, beautiful. A lady sat by the fire alone—a young and graceful figure, clothed in soft white draperies.

She rose as he approached, but kept her face averted. He saw the lovely and familiar outline of a cheek, a head with a crown of braided hair, yet for one moment more he did not know that upon this home-hearth burned for him, now and evermore, that life-light which had once been called a Will o' the wisp. The lady turned her face, and Lawrence, bowing, advanced a step. Then, suddenly, there arose a sort of cry from two voices, rent by passionate surprise, and joy took eternal possession of the lives of these happy lovers.

Krescenz

An Idyl on the Moselle.

It was evening in the ancient town of Trier; the Angelus was ring-ing down from the great fortress-like Dom; the little carts and stalls had vanished out of the market-place; and the carved saints, clustered on the fountain, smiled benignly in the setting sun. Old women in strange head-dresses, beads and books in hand, passed in and out of St. Gondolphus's curious gates; young girls, with long, fair, plaited hair, moved in groups across the open place; brilliant uniforms shone up on the balconies of the Rothe Haus; the shopkeepers in the queer little peaked houses stood at their doors and amused themselves; while the awful black arches of the Porta Nigra frowned more grimly than ever in the glowing light, and the gay and quaint little frescoes at the street corners seemed to blaze out with new colour at its touch.

One particularly high-peaked roof was suddenly covered with a flock of white pigeons alighting to rest, and at the same moment a face appeared at a little open window among the birds, looked up and down the streets, and was withdrawn again. The face belonged to a young girl, and the room into which she withdrew was pleasant and neat, if a little bare. A work-table at the window showed that it was the home of a seamstress; a little shrine hung in a corner, with a tiny lamp burning; a few rude pictures decorated the walls. The girl was clothed in a holiday dress of dark green stuff, with white sleeves and apron, and wore a scarlet flower in her breast. She had a soft, sweet, innocent face, and her fair hair hung behind in two long golden braids from her neck to her knees.

As she turned from the window, a curly-haired boy burst into the room.

"I have a message for you, Krescenz. I met Karl, and he told me to tell you he could not see you tonight. He is suddenly sent on busi-ness."

A look of disappointment clouded the girl's face; but, after a few

221

moments of silence, she said:

"How good it is that they find him so useful! But come, Max, you shall not be disappointed of your excursion. You and I will go for our walk, and I will take you for a peep at our cottage."

Max snatched his hat, which he had flung off in disgust, and, locking the door behind them, the sister and brother descended many stairs, and took their way through the streets, and out by the Porta Nigra, into the country.

"Look here, Max, did you ever see anything so gloriously blue as the Moselle this evening? Could you bear to live away from it? How glad I am that our new home will be near it! And look, how magnificent the red light is upon the vine-covered banks, with the crimson earth glowing between! How the tall dark poplars and the golden acacias seem to thrill as they bask in this wonderful light! If I had been a man, Max, I should certainly have tried to be an artist. Karl laughs at me when I say so; he does not care for such things, and gets annoyed when I talk about them; and yet I never saw half the beauty of things till he loved me."

"How many people are out walking tonight, Krescenz. I never saw the road so gay. Oh, there is that Gretchen kissing her hands to me, and I will not look at her. Why? Because she was impertinent this morning, telling me that Karl had left off loving you, and was going to marry Luise."

"It was a silly joke, Max. I hope you did not get angry. What did you say?"

"Something that ought to have stopped her kissing hands to me," said Max.

"It was too foolish to be angry about, little brother. Someone said it to myself the other day, and I only laughed. I knew so well it was because I sent Karl a message by Luise the other evening. But Gretchen ought not to have said it to you, Max. When I go to my new home I don't think I shall ask her to come and see me. I do not want to hate anybody, and———"

"I will do the hating for you, Krescenz, and I hate everyone who says that Karl does not love you."

"Everyone! Don't give such a big name to two people, Max. If Karl did not love me, should not I be the first to know of it? Ah! do you see our little house peeping above the acacias up in the fields over there? How delightful it will be to live there, Max, with all the flowers growing in at one's windows. And Karl is providing this home for me! Ah, little Max, this looks rather like loving one, doesn't it?"

Max was silent, and kept his face turned away, with a slight frown on the brows.

"I wish I could suddenly grow big, Krescenz," he said abruptly.

The sister laughed. "My dear, you must wait," she said gaily. "By-and-by you shall copy your brother Karl, and if you can manage to grow like him you will do very well. In the meantime, you are not quite so small as you were, my boy, when I first took you in my arms, and carried you about our poor garret, trying to put you to sleep. Mother had died the day before I was ten years old, and you had only just been born. I was a very little nurse, wasn't I? But it seemed to me that my heart was a hundred years old. How proud I was of you, and how I loved you!"

"And you worked for me, Krescenz?"

"Ah, didn't I! We were alone in the world, only you and me. I paid a poor old woman, a very, very old woman, who could not do anything else, a penny a day for taking care of you, and I worked for us two. I was a strong little girl, and as industrious as a bee. People gave me work to do: it was very hard until I was about fourteen, and then I learned to sew, and things began to be better. At sixteen I was able to rent a little room for myself, and so bring home my little brother. Ah, Max, how often we have been hungry together! and yet you are a brave boy for your age. I have pulled you through the worst, and now God has taken us both into happiness and safety. No more scanty crusts for you. No more sitting up all night, sewing by a candle, for me. No more pinching at the heart when rent-day is coming round.

"Who could have thought of it; that Karl, whom every one admires, should have sought out me! I did not accept him hastily, Max, for I was afraid he might change his mind; afraid that he had not known what he was saying, or that he did not know perfectly how much people thought of him. But he would persist in loving me, he would, indeed; and that is why I laugh so much when the people tell idle tales. 'If you only knew, my good people,' I think; 'if you only knew how well I know.' And, Max—you see I do not mind saying anything to you—I must confess that the greatest trouble I have had lately has been the fear that so much sitting up at night was taking away all my good looks. I look so sickly sometimes when the morning light comes in. Stare me well in the face, Max, and tell me if I am getting ugly."

"You are the prettiest and loveliest girl in the town, sister Krescenz."

"But I am not rosy, like Gretchen, nor are my eyes so big and bright as Luise's, nor——"

"No matter," persisted Max. "Not one of them can smile the way you do."

"After that I must say something nice to you, Max. Sit down here on the grass, and let me tell you the kind of life we shall have over in our little house yonder. We shall have four rooms of our own, and there are vines growing round all the windows. We shall have a pretty garden with bees and flowers, and a field with a cow in it. I shall do my sewing sitting under a tree, looking down on the Moselle. You will go to work with Karl, and in the evening you will both come home, and we shall have supper in the garden."

"I wish we had some now, Krescenz."

"I wish we had, my boy; and I think it is time to go and look for some coffee and bread."

The sister and brother turned their steps towards a pleasant summer-house of refreshment, built among trees, upon the high overhanging bank of the river, where the people of Trier love to drink coffee in the cool of the evening. As the girl and child took their simple meal in the nook of the projecting terrace, the blue Moselle rushed under their feet, and Trier lay bathed in ruddy glory in the distance before their eyes, with its strange contrasting outlines softened into magnificent harmony, and the fierce black Roman gates making a frown on the very front of the sunny landscape.

"How splendid it looks, the dear old town!" cried Krescenz. "Do you know, Max, I cannot understand why people ever leave their own homes to go out into the world."

"I should like to go out and see the world," said Max. "You mustn't say so, Max. Nothing would ever induce me to leave Trier."

They were rambling among the trees on the hill-side, stopping now and then to lean forward and take a fresh peep at the beauty of the river and the exquisite gleams of the distance on either side.

★★★★★★★★★★★★★★★★

"Oh, Krescenz, Krescenz! I have found a pair of lovers."

"No! Have you, Max?" said Krescenz with interest.

"Behind that large tree, in such a pretty nook. Just peep round and you can see."

"Hide, then, while I peep, so carefully."

Max retired while Krescenz leaned forward with a smile of mischievous delight, and peered from behind a screen of leaves, herself unseen by the objects of her interest. When the boy thought he had waited long enough, he came forth again, and plucked her by the skirt.

She turned to him slowly, and put her finger on her lip.

"Krescenz! Krescenz!" whispered the child, "what makes your face so dreadful? Are they ghosts?"

"Hush, Max! I cannot see, take me by the hand, and get me into some quiet place, where nobody will find us."

"Oh, Krescenz, you are ill! Are you going to die?"

"No, dear, I shall not die. Fetch me some water, and tell nobody."

Max obeyed, and while the red light paled on the Moselle, and purple mingled with the crimson and olive of its banks, the girl's white face lay on the moss, gazing blankly upward with fixed eyes. The tears trickled over Max's innocent cheeks as he nestled at her side and kissed her lips, her hands, and her hair.

"Oh, Krescenz! may I not call someone to come and help you home?"

"No, dear, no," said the young girl, starting up. "We are not going home any more. We are going away somewhere else, you and I together."

"What, away from Trier?"

"Yes, I am tired of Trier."

"I thought you said you could never leave Trier; and what will Karl say to you?"

"Oh, Max! oh, Max!"

"Where shall we sleep tonight, if we keep walking on at this rate?"

"We shall rest on the road, and tomorrow we will travel farther. There are other towns besides Trier, where industrious people can get work to do."

"Oh, Krescenz! I am afraid you have gone mad. Those people behind the trees must have been the wicked spirits we read about, and they have harmed you."

"Do you know who they were, Max? Karl and Luise. Gretchen was right, after all."

"But did they say they were going to be married?" said the boy. "Oh, don't groan, Krescenz, and I will try and ask no more questions."

"Dear Max, there is nothing more for me at Trier. That is why we are going together out into the world."

"Oh that I could grow big and go back and kill him!"

"Hush! you must not talk such nonsense. You must take care of me now, as I have nobody else."

"That I will, indeed; but oh, Krescenz, my canary!"

"Somebody will take care of it, dear. We can get another."

"And your pretty little shrine?"

"Somebody else will kneel at it. I can pray to God anywhere, you know."

Deepening shadows dropped on the Moselle, and the two young figures hurried on through the purple twilight away from Trier.

Not to be Taken at Bedtime

This is the legend of a house called the Devil's Inn, standing in the heather on the top of the Connemara mountains, in a shallow valley hollowed between five peaks. Tourists sometimes come in sight of it on September evenings; a crazy and weather-stained apparition, with the sun glaring at it angrily between the hills, and striking its shattered window-panes. Guides are known to shun it, however.

The house was built by a stranger, who came no one knew whence, and whom the people nicknamed Coll Dhu (Black Coll), because of his sullen bearing and solitary habits. His dwelling they called the Devil's Inn, because no tired traveller had ever been asked to rest under its roof, nor friend known to cross its threshold. No one bore him company in his retreat but a wizen-faced old man, who shunned the good-morrow of the trudging peasant when he made occasional excursions to the nearest village for provisions for himself and master, and who was as secret as a stone concerning all the antecedents of both.

For the first year of their residency in the country, there had been much speculation as to who they were, and what they did with themselves up there among the clouds and eagles. Some said that Coll Dhu was a scion of the old family from whose hands the surrounding lands had passed; and that, embittered by poverty and pride, he had come to bury himself in solitude, and brood over his misfortunes. Others hinted of crime, and flight from another country; others again whispered of those who were cursed from birth, and could never smile, nor yet make friends with a fellow creature till the day of their death.

But when two years had passed, the wonder had somewhat died out, and Coll Dhu was little thought of, except when a shepherd looking for sheep crossed the track of a big dark man walking the mountains, gun in hand, to whom he did not dare say "Lord save you!" when a housewife rocking her cradle of a winter's night, crossed herself as gust of storm thundered over her cabin roof, with the excla-

227

mation, "Oh, it's Coll Dhu that has enough o' the fresh air about his head up there this night, the crature!"

Coll Dhu had lived thus in his solitude for some years, when it became known that Colonel Blake, the new lord of the soil, was coming to visit the country. By climbing one of the peaks encircling his eyrie, Coll could look sheer down a mountain-side, and see in miniature beneath him, a grey old dwelling with ivied chimneys and weather-slated walls, standing amongst straggling trees and grim warlike rocks, that gave it the look of a fortress, gazing out to the Atlantic forever with the eager eyes of all its windows, as if demanding perpetually, "What tidings from the New World?"

He could see now masons and carpenters crawling about below, like ants in the sun, over-running the old house from base to chimney, daubing here and knocking there, tumbling down walls that looked to Coll, up among the clouds, like a handful of jack-stones, and building up others that looked like the toy fences in a child's farm. Throughout several months he must have watched the busy ants at their task of breaking and mending again, disfiguring and beautifying; but when all was done, he had not the curiosity to stride down and admire the handsome panelling of the new billiard-room, nor yet the fine view which the enlarged bay-window in the drawing-room commanded over the watery highway to Newfoundland.

Deep summer was melting into autumn, and the amber streaks of decay were beginning to creep out and trail over the ripe purple of moor and mountain, when Colonel Blake, his only daughter, and a party of friends, arrived in the country. The grey house below was alive with gaiety, but Coll Dhu no longer found an interest in observing it from his eyrie. When he watched the sun rise or set, he chose to ascend some crag that looked on no human habitation. When he sallied forth on his excursion, gun in hand, he set his face towards the most isolated wastes, dipping into the loneliest valleys, and scaling the nakedest ridges. When he came by chance within call of other excursionists, gun in hand he plunged into the shade of some hollow, and avoided an encounter. Yet it was fated, for all that, that he and Colonel Blake should meet.

Toward the evening of one bright September day, the wind changed, and in half an hour the mountains were wrapped in a thick blinding mist. Coll Dhu was far from his den, but so well had he searched these mountains, and inured himself to their climate, that neither storm, rain, nor fog, had power to disturb him. But while he stalked on his way, a faint and agonised cry from a human voice reached him through the smothering mist. He quickly tracked the sound, and gained the side of a man who was stumbling along in danger of death at every step.

"Follow me!" said Coll Dhu to this man, and, in an hour's time, brought him safely to the lowlands, and up to the walls of the eager-eyed mansion.

"I am Colonel Blake," said the frank soldier, when, having left the fog behind him, they stood under the lighted windows. "Pray tell me quickly to whom I owe my life."

As he spoke, he glanced up at his benefactor, a large man with a sombre sunburned face.

"Colonel Blake," said Coll Dhu, after a strange pause, "your father suggested to my father to stake his estates at the gaming table. They were staked, and the tempter won. Both are dead; but you and I live, and I have sworn to injure you."

The colonel laughed good humouredly at the uneasy face above him.

"And you began to keep your oath tonight by saving my life?"

Said he. "Come! I am a soldier, and you know how to meet an enemy; but I had far rather meet a friend. I shall not be happy till you have eaten my salt. We have merrymaking tonight in honour of my daughter's birthday. Come in and join us?"

Coll Dhu looked at the earth doggedly.

"I have told you," he said, "who and what I am, and I will not cross your threshold."

But at this moment (so runs my story) a French window opened among the flowerbeds by which they were standing, and a vision appeared which stayed the words on Coll's tongue. A stately girl, clad in white satin, stood framed in the ivied window, with the warm light from within streaming around her richly-moulded figure into the night. Her face was as pale as her gown, her eyes were swimming in tears, but a firm smile sat on her lips as she held out both hands to her father.

The lights behind her, touched the glistening folds of her dress—the lustrous pearls round her throat—the coronet of blood-red roses which encircled the knotted braids at the back of her head. Satin, pearls, and roses—had Coll Dhu, of the Devil's Inn, never set eyes upon such things before?

Evleen Blake was no nervous tearful miss. A few quick words—

"Thank God! You're safe; the rest have been home an hour"—and a tight pressure of her father's fingers between her own jewelled hands, were all that betrayed the uneasiness she had suffered.

"Faith, my love, I owe my life to this brave gentleman!" said the blithe colonel. "Press him to come in and be our guest, Evleen. He wants to retreat to his mountains, and lose himself again in the fog where I found him; or, rather where he found me! Come sir" (to Coll), "you must surrender to this fair besieger."

An introduction followed. "Coll Dhu!" murmured Evleen Blake, for she had heard the common tales of him; but with a frank welcome she invited her father's preserver to taste the hospitality of that father's house.

"I beg you to come in, sir," she said; "but for you our gaiety must have been turned into mourning. A shadow will be upon our mirth if our benefactor disdains to join in it."

With a sweet grace, mingled with a certain hauteur from which she was never free, she extended her white hand to the tall looming figure outside the window; to have it grasped and rung in a way that made the proud girl's eyes flash their amazement, and the same little hand clench itself in displeasure, when it had hid itself like an outraged thing among the shining folds of her gown. Was this Coll Dhu mad, or rude?

The guest no longer refused to enter, but followed the white figure into a little study where a lamp burned; and the gloomy stranger, the bluff colonel, and the young mistress of the house were fully discovered to each other's eyes. Evleen glanced at the newcomer's dark face, and shuddered with a feeling of indescribable dread and dislike; then, to her father, accounted for the shudder after a popular fashion, saying lightly: "There is someone walking over my grave."

So, Coll Dhu was present at Evleen Blake's birthday ball. Here he was, under a roof which ought to have been his own, a stranger, known only by a nickname, shunned and solitary. Here he was, who had lived among the eagles and foxes, lying in wait with a fell purpose, to be revenged on the son of his father's foe for poverty and disgrace, for the broken heart of a dead mother, for the loss of a self-slaughtered father, for the dreary scattering of brothers and sisters.

Here he stood, a Samson shorn of his strength; and all because a haughty girl had melting eyes, a winning mouth, and looked radiant in satin and roses.

Peerless where many were lovely, she moved among her friends, trying to be unconscious of the gloomy fire of those strange eyes which followed her unweariedly wherever she went. And when her father begged her to be gracious to the unsocial guest whom he would fain conciliate, she courteously conducted him to see the new picture-gallery adjoining the drawing-rooms; explained under what odd circumstances the colonel had picked up this little painting or that; using every delicate art her pride would allow to achieve her father's purpose, whilst maintaining at the same time her own personal reserve; trying to divert the guest's oppressive attention from herself to the objects for which she claimed her notice.

Coll Dhu followed his conductress and listened to her voce, but what she said mattered nothing; nor did she wring many words of comment or reply from his lips, until they paused in a retired corner where the light was dim, before a window from which the curtain was withdrawn. The sashes were open, and nothing was visible but water; the night Atlantic, with the full moon riding high above a bank of clouds, making silvery tracks outward towards the distance of infinite mystery dividing two worlds. Here the following little scene is said to have been enacted.

"This window of my father's own planning, is it not creditable to his taste?" said the young hostess, as she stood, herself glittering like a dream of beauty, looking on the moonlight.

Coll Dhu made no answer; but suddenly, it is said, asked her for a rose from a cluster of flowers that nestled in the lace on her bosom.

For the second time that night Evleen Blake's eyes flashed with no gentle light. But this man was the saviour of her father. She broke off a blossom, and with such good grace, and also with such queen-like dignity as she might assume, presented it to him. Whereupon, not only was the rose seized, but also the hand that gave it, which was hastily covered with kisses.

Then her anger burst upon him.

"Sir," she cried, "if you are a gentleman, you must be mad! If you are not mad, then you are not a gentleman!"

"Be merciful," said Coll Dhu; "I love you. My God, I never loved a woman before! Ah!" he cried, as a look of disgust crept over her face. "You hate me. You shuddered the first time your eyes met mine. I love you, and you hate me!"

"I do," cried Evleen, vehemently, forgetting everything but her indignation. "Your presence is like something evil to me. Love me?—your looks poison me. Pray, sir, talk no more to me in this strain."

"I will trouble you no longer," said Coll Dhu. And, stalking to the window, he placed one powerful hand upon the sash, and vaulted from her sight.

Bare-headed as he was, Coll Dhu strode off to the mountains, but not towards his home.

All the remaining dark hours of that night he is believed to have walked the labyrinths of the hills, until dawn began to scatter the clouds with a high wind. Fasting, and on foot from sunrise the morning before, he was then glad enough to see a cabin right in his way. Walking in, he asked for water to drink, and a corner where he might throw himself to rest.

There was a wake in the house, and the kitchen was full of people, all wearing out with the night's watch; old men were dozing over their pipes in the chimney-corner, and here and there a woman was fast asleep with her head on a neighbour's knee. All who were wake crossed themselves when Coll Dhu's figure darkened the door, because of his evil name; but an old man of the house invited him in, and offering him milk, and promising him a roasted potato by-and-by, conducted hm to a small room off the kitchen, one end of which was strewed with heather, and where there were only two women sitting gossiping over a fire.

"A traveller," said the old man, nodding his head at the women, who nodded back, as if to say "he has the traveller's right." And Coll Dhu flung himself on the heather, in the farthest corner of the room.

The women suspended their talk for a while; but presently, guessing the intruder to be asleep, resumed it in voices above a whisper. There was but a patch of window with the grey dawn behind it, but Coll could see the figures by the firelight over which they bent: an old woman sitting forward with her withered hands extended to the embers, and a girl reclining against the hearth wall, with her healthy face, bright eyes, and crimson draperies, glowing by turns in the flickering blaze.

"I do know," said the girl, "but it's the quarest marriage iver I h'ard of. Sure it's not three weeks since he tould right an' left that he hated her like poison!"

"Whist, asthoreen!" said the colliagh, bending forward confidentially: "throth an' we all known that o' him. But what could he do the creature! When she put the burragh-bos on him!"

"The *what?*"

"Then the burragh-bos machree-o? That's the spanchel o' death, avoureen; an' well she has him tethered to her now, bad luck to her!"

The old woman rocked herself and stilled the Irish cry breaking from her wrinkled lips by burying her face in her cloak.

"But what is it?" asked the girl eagerly. "What's the burragh-bos, anyways, an' where did she get it?"

"Och, och! It's not for comm' over to young ears, but cuggir (whisper), acushla! It's a sthrip o' the skin o' a corose, peeled from the crown o' the head to the heel, without crack or split, or the charm's broke an' that, rowled up, an' put on a shtring roun' the neck o' the wan that's cowled by the wan that wants to be loved. An' surre enough it puts the fire in their hearts, hot an' strong, afore twinty-four hours is gone."

The girl started from her lazy attitude, and gazed at her companion with eyes dilated by horror.

"Merciful Saviour!" she cried. "Not a sowl on airth would bring the curse out o' heaven by sich a black doin'!"

"Aisy, Biddeen alannal! An' there's wan that does it, an' isn't the divil. Arrah, asthoreen, did ye niver hear tell o' Pexie na Pishrogie, that lives betune two hills o' Madame Turk?"

"I h'ard o' her," said the girl, breathlessly.

"Well, sorra bit lie, but t's hersel' that does it. She'll do it for money any day. Sure, they hunted her from the graveyard o' Salruck, where she had the dead raised; an' glory be to God! They would ha' murthered her, only they missed her thracks, an' couldn't bring it home to her afther."

"Whist, a-wauher" (my mother), said the girl; "here's the thraveller getting' up to set off on his road again! Och, then, it's the shortest rest he tuk, the sowl!"

It was enough for Coll, however. He had got up, and now went back to the kitchen, where the old man had caused a dish of potatoes to be roasted, and earnestly pressed his visitor to sit down and eat of them. This Coll did readily; having recruited his strength by a meal, he betook himself to the mountains again, just as he rising sun was flashing among the waterfalls, and sending the night mists drifting down the gleans. By sundown the same evening he was striding over the hills of Madame Turk, asking of herds his way to the cabin of one Pexie na Pishrogie.

In a hotel on a brown desolate heath, with scared-looking hills flying off into the distance on every side, he found Pexie: a yellow-faced hag, dressed in a dark-red blanket, with elf-locks of coarse black hair protruding from under an orange kerchief swathed round her wrinkled jaws.

She was bending over a pot upon her fire, where herbs were simmering, and she looked up with an evil glance when Coll Dhu darkened her door.

"The burragh-bos is it her honour wants?" she asked, when he had made known his errand.

"Ay, ay; but the arighad, the arighad (money) for Pexoiex. The burragh-bos is ill to get."

"I will pay," said Coll Dhu, laying a sovereign on the bench before her.

The witch sprang upon it, and chuckling, bestowed on her visitor a glance which made even Coll Dhu shudder.

"Her honour is a fine king," she said, "an' her is fit to get the burragh-bos. Ha! Ha! Her sall get the burragh-bos from Pexie. But the arighad is not enough. More, more!"

She stretched out her claw-like hand, and Coll dropped another sovereign into it. Whereupon she fell into more horrible convulsions of delight.

"Hark ye!" cried Coll. "I have paid you well, but if your infernal charm does not work, I will have you hunted for a witch!"

"Work!" cried Pexie, rolling up her eyes. "If Pexie's charm not work, then her honour come back here an' carry these bits o' mountain away on her back. Ay, her will work. If the colleen hate her honour like the old diaoul hersel', still an' withal her love will love her honour like her own white sowl afore the sun sets or rises. That (with a furtive leer,) or the colleen dhas go wild mad afore wan hour."

"Hag!" returned Coll Dhu; "the last part is a hellish invention of your own. I heard nothing of madness. If you want more money, speak out, but play none of your hideous tricks on me."

The witch fixed her cunning eyes on him, and took her cue at once from his passion.

"Her honour guess thrue," she simpered; "it is only the little bit more arighad poor Pexie want."

Again, the skinny hand was extended. Coll Dhu shrank from touching it, and threw his gold upon the table.

"King, king!" chuckled Pexie. "Her honour is a grand king. Her honour is fit to get the burragh-bos. The colleen dhas sall love her like her own white sowl. Ha, ha!"

"When shall I get it?" asked Coll Dhu, impatiently.

"Her honour sall come back to Pexie in so many days, do-deag (twelve), so many days, fur the burragh-bos is hard to get. The lonely graveyard is far away, an' dead man is hard to raise——"

"Silence!" cried Coll Dhu; "not a word more. I will have your hideous charm, but what it is, or where you get it, I will not know."

Then, promising to come back in twelve days, he took his departure. Turning to look back when a little way across the heath, he saw Pexie gazing after him, standing on her black hill in relief against the lurid flames of the dawn, seeming to his dark imagination like a fury with all hell at her back.

★★★★★★★★★★★★★★★★★

At the appointed time Coll Dhu got the promised charm. He sewed it with perfumes into a cover of cloth of gold, and slung it to a fine wrought chain. Lying in a casket which had once held the jewels of Coll's broken-hearted mother, it looked a glittering bauble enough. Meantime the people of the mountains were cursing over their cabin fires, because there had been another unholy raid upon their graveyard, and were banding themselves to hunt the criminal down.

A fortnight passed. How or where could Coll Dhu find an opportunity to put the charm round the neck of the colonel's daughter? More gold was dropped into Pexie's greedy claw, and then she promised to assist him in his dilemma.

Net morning the witch dressed herself in decent garb, smoothed her elf-locks under a snowy cap, smoothed the evil wrinkles out of her face, and with a basket on her arm locked the door of the hovel, and took her way to the lowlands. Pexie seemed to have given up her disreputable calling for that of a simple mushroom-gatherer. The housekeeper at the grey house bought poor Muireade's mushrooms of her every morning. Every morning, she left unfailingly a nosegay of wild flowers for Miss Evleen Blake. "God bless her! She had never seen the darling young lady with her own two longing eyes, but sure hadn't she heard tell of her sweet purty face, miles away!"

And at last, one morning, whom should she meet but Miss Evleen herself returning alone from a ramble. Whereupon poor Muireade "made bold" to present her flowers in person.

"Ah," said Evleen, "it is you who leave me the flowers every morning? They are very sweet."

Muireade had sought her only for a look at her beautiful face. And now that she had seen it, as bright as the sun, and as fair as the lily, she would take up her basket and go away contented.

Yet she lingered a little longer.

"My lady never walk up big mountain?" said Pexie.

"No," said Evleen, laughing; she feared she could not walk up a mountain.

"Ah yes; my lady ought to go, with more gran' ladies an' gentlemen, ridin' on purty little donkeys, up the big mountains. Oh, gran' things up big mountains for my lady to see!"

Thus, she set to work, and kept her listener enchanted for an hour, while she related wonderful stories of those upper regions. And as Evleen looked up to the burly crowns of the hills, perhaps she thought there might be sense in this wild old woman's suggestion. It ought to be a grand world up yonder.

Be that as it may, it was not long after this when Coll Dhu got notice that a part from the grey house would explore the mountains next day; that Evleen Blake would be on of the number; and that he, Coll, must prepare to house and refresh a crowd of weary people, who in the evening should be brought, hungry and faint, to his door. The simple mushroom gatherer should be discovered laying in her humble stock among the green places between the hills, should volunteer to act as guide to the party, she should lead them far out of their way through the mountains and up and down the most toilsome ascents and across dangerous places; to escape safely from which, the servants should be told to throw away the baskets of provision which they carried.

Coll Dhu was not idle. Such a feats was set forth, as had never been spread so near the clouds before. We are told of wonderful dishes furnished by unwholesome agency, and from a place believed much hotter than is necessary for purposes of cookery.

We are told also how Coll Dhu's barren chambers were suddenly hung with curtains of velvet, and with fringes of gold; how the blank white walls glowed with delicate colours and gilding; how gems of pictures sprang into sight between the panels; how the tables blazed with pate and gold, and glittered; with the rarest glass; how such wines flowed, as the guests had never tasted; how servants in the richest livery, amongst whom the wizen-faced old man was a mere nonentity, appeared, and stood ready to carry in the wonderful dishes, at whose extraordinary fragrance the eagles came pecking to the windows, and the foxes drew near the walls, snuffing.

Sure enough, in all good time, the weary party came within sight of the Devil's Inn, and Coll Dhu sallied forth to invite them across his lonely threshold. Colonel Blake (to whom Evleen, in her delicacy, had said no word of the solitary's behaviour to herself) hailed his appearance with delight, and the whole party sat down to Coll's banquet in high good humour. Also, it is said, in much amazement at the magnificence of the mountain recluse.

All went in to Coll's feast, save Evleen Blake, who remained standing on the threshold of the outer door; weary, but unwilling to rest there; hungry, but unwilling to eat there. Her white cambric dress was gathered on her arms, crushed and sullied with the toils of the day; her bright cheek was a little sunburned; her small dark head with its braids a little tossed, was bared to the mountain air and the glory of the sinking sun; her hands were loosely tangled in the strings of her hat; and her foot sometimes tapped the threshold-stone. So she had been seen.

The peasants tell that Coll Dhu and her father came praying her to enter, and that the magnificent servants brought viands to the threshold; but no step would she move inward, no morsel would she taste.

"Poison, poison!" she murmured, and threw the food in handfuls to the foxes, who were snuffing on the hearth.

But it was different when Muireade, the kindly old woman, the simple mushroom gatherer, with all the wicked wrinkles smoothed out of her face, came to the side of the hungry girl, and coaxingly presented a savoury mess of her own sweet mushrooms, served on a common earthen platter.

"An' darlin', my lady, poor Muireade her cook them hersel', an' no thing o' this house touch them or look at poor Muireade's mushrooms."

Then Evleen took the platter and ate a delicious meal. Scarcely was it finished when a heavy drowsiness fell upon her, unable to sustain herself on her feet, she presently sat down upon the door-stone. Leaning her head against the framework of the door, she was soon in a deep sleep, or trance. So, she was found.

"Whimsical, obstinate little girl!" said the colonel, putting his hand on the beautiful slumbering head. And taking her in his arms, he carried her into a chamber which had been (say the story-tellers) nothing but a bare and sorry closet in the morning but which was now fitted up with oriental splendour. And ere on a luxurious couch she was laid, with a crimson coverlet wrapping her feet. And here in the tempered light coming through jewelled glass, where yesterday had been a coarse rough-hung window, her father looked his last upon her lovely face.

The colonel returned to his host and friends, and by-and-by the whole party sailed forth to see the after-glare of a fierce sunset swath-ing the hills in flames. It was not until they had gone some distance that Coll Dhu remembered to go back and fetch his telescope. He was not long absent. But he was absent long enough to enter that glowing chamber with a stealthy step, to throw a light chain around the neck of the sleeping girl, and to slip among the folds of her dress the hideous glittering burragh-bos.

After he had gone away again, Pexie came stealing to the door, and. Opening it a little, sat down on the mat outside, with her cloak wrapped round her. An hour passed, and Evleen Blake still slept, her breathing scarcely stirring the deadly bauble on her breast. After that, she began to murmur and moan, and Pexie pricked up her ears. Pres-ently a sound in the room told that the victim was awake and had risen. Then Pexie put her face to the aperture of the door and looked in, gave a howl of dismay, and fled from the house, to be seen in that country no more.

The light was fading among the hills, and the ramblers were re-turning towards the Devil's Inn, when a group of ladies who were considerably in advance of the rest, met Evleen Blake advancing to-wards them on the heath, with her hair disordered as by sleep, and no covering on her head. They noticed something bright, like gold, shifting and glancing with the motion of her figure. There had been some jesting among them about Evleen's fancy for falling asleep on the doorstep instead of coming in to dinner, and they advanced laugh-ing, to rally her on the subject.

But she stared at them in a strange way, as if she did not know them, and passed on. Her friends were rather offended, and com-mented on her fantastic humour; only one looked after her, and got laughed at by her companions for expressing uneasiness on the wilful young lady's account.

So, they kept their way, and the solitary figure went fluttering on, the white robe blushing, and the fatal burragh-bos glittering in the reflexion from the sky. A hare crossed her path, and she laughed out loudly, and clapping her hands, sprang after it. Then she stopped and asked questions of the stones, striking them with her open palm be-cause they would not answer. (An amaze little herd sitting behind a rock, witnessed these strange proceedings.) By-and-by she began to call after the birds, in a wild shrill way startling the echoes of the hills as she went long. A party of gentleman returning by a dangerous path, heard the unusual sound and stopped to listen.

"What is that?" asked one.

"A young eagle," said Coll Dhu, whose face had become livid; "they often give such cries."

"It was uncommonly like a woman's voice!" was the reply; and immediately another wild note rang towards them from the rocks above: a bare saw-like ridge, shelving away to some distance ahead, and projecting one hungry tooth over an abyss. A few more moments and they saw Evleen Blake's light figure fluttering out towards this dizzy point.

"My Evleen!" cried the colonel, recognising his daughter, "she is mad to venture on such a spot!"

"Mad!" repeated Coll Dhu. And then dashed off to rescue with all his might and swiftness of his powerful limbs.

When he drew near her, Evleen had almost reached the verge of the terrible rock. Very cautiously he approached her, his object being to seize her in his strong arms before she was aware of his presence, and carry her many yards away from the spot of danger. But in a fatal moment Evleen turned her head and saw him. One wild ringing cry of hate and horror, which started the very eagles and scattered a flight of curlews above her head, broke from her lips. A step backward brought her within a foot of death.

One desperate though wary stride, and she was struggling in Coll's embrace. One glance in her eyes, and he saw that he was striving with a mad woman. Back, back, she dragged him, and he had nothing to grasp by. The rock was slippery and his shod feet would not cling to it. Back, back! A hoarse panting, a dire swinging to and fro; and then the rock was standing naked against the sky, no one was there, and Coll Dhu and Evleen Blake lay shattered far below.

LEONAUR

ALSO FROM LEONAUR
AVAILABLE IN SOFTCOVER OR HARDCOVER WITH DUST JACKET

MR MUKERJI'S GHOSTS *by S. Mukerji*—Supernatural tales from the British Raj period by India's Ghost story collector.

KIPLINGS GHOSTS *by Rudyard Kipling*—Twelve stories of Ghosts, Hauntings, Curses, Werewolves & Magic.

THE COLLECTED SUPERNATURAL AND WEIRD FICTION OF WASHINGTON IRVING: VOLUME 1 *by Washington Irving*—Including one novel 'A History of New York', and nine short stories of the Strange and Unusual.

THE COLLECTED SUPERNATURAL AND WEIRD FICTION OF WASHINGTON IRVING: VOLUME 2 *by Washington Irving*—Including three novelettes 'The Legend of the Sleepy Hollow', 'Dolph Heyliger', 'The Adventure of the Black Fisherman' and thirty-two short stories of the Strange and Unusual.

THE COLLECTED SUPERNATURAL AND WEIRD FICTION OF JOHN KENDRICK BANGS: VOLUME 1 *by John Kendrick Bangs*—Including one novel 'Toppleton's Client or A Spirit in Exile', and ten short stories of the Strange and Unusual.

THE COLLECTED SUPERNATURAL AND WEIRD FICTION OF JOHN KENDRICK BANGS: VOLUME 2 *by John Kendrick Bangs*—Including four novellas 'A House-Boat on the Styx', 'The Pursuit of the House-Boat', 'The Enchanted Typewriter' and 'Mr. Munchausen' of the Strange and Unusual.

THE COLLECTED SUPERNATURAL AND WEIRD FICTION OF JOHN KENDRICK BANGS: VOLUME 3 *by John Kendrick Bangs*—Including twor novellas 'Olympian Nights', 'Roger Camerden: A Strange Story', and ten short stories of the Strange and Unusual.

THE COLLECTED SUPERNATURAL AND WEIRD FICTION OF MARY SHELLEY: VOLUME 1 *by Mary Shelley*—Including one novel 'Frankenstein or the Modern Prometheus', and fourteen short stories of the Strange and Unusual.

THE COLLECTED SUPERNATURAL AND WEIRD FICTION OF MARY SHELLEY: VOLUME 2 *by Mary Shelley*—Including one novel 'The Last Man', and three short stories of the Strange and Unusual.

THE COLLECTED SUPERNATURAL AND WEIRD FICTION OF AMELIA B. EDWARDS *by Amelia B. Edwards*—Contains two novelettes 'Monsieur Maurice', and 'The Discovery of the Treasure Isles', one ballad 'A Legend of Boisguilbert' and seventeen short stories to cill the blood.

LEONAUR

ALSO FROM LEONAUR
AVAILABLE IN SOFTCOVER OR HARDCOVER WITH DUST JACKET

THE COMPLETE FOUR JUST MEN: VOLUME 2 *by Edgar Wallace—The Law of the Four Just Men & The Three Just Men*—disillusioned with a world where the wicked and the abusers of power perpetually go unpunished, the Just Men set about to rectify matters according to their own standards, and retribution is dispensed on swift and deadly wings.

THE COMPLETE RAFFLES: 1 *by E. W. Hornung—The Amateur Cracksman & The Black Mask*—By turns urbane gentleman about town and accomplished cricketer, life is just too ordinary for Raffles and that sets him on a series of adventures that have long been treasured as a real antidote to the 'white knights' who are the usual heroes of the crime fiction of this period.

THE COMPLETE RAFFLES: 2 *by E. W. Hornung—A Thief in the Night & Mr Justice Raffles*—By turns urbane gentleman about town and accomplished cricketer, life is just too ordinary for Raffles and that sets him on a series of adventures that have long been treasured as a real antidote to the 'white knights' who are the usual heroes of the crime fiction of this period.

THE COLLECTED SUPERNATURAL AND WEIRD FICTION OF WILKIE COLLINS: VOLUME 1 *by Wilkie Collins*—Contains one novel 'The Haunted Hotel', one novella 'Mad Monkton', three novelettes 'Mr Percy and the Prophet', 'The Biter Bit' and 'The Dead Alive' and eight short stories to chill the blood.

THE COLLECTED SUPERNATURAL AND WEIRD FICTION OF WILKIE COLLINS: VOLUME 2 *by Wilkie Collins*—Contains one novel 'The Two Destinies', three novellas 'The Frozen deep', 'Sister Rose' and 'The Yellow Mask' and two short stories to chill the blood.

THE COLLECTED SUPERNATURAL AND WEIRD FICTION OF WILKIE COLLINS: VOLUME 3 *by Wilkie Collins*—Contains one novel 'Dead Secret,' two novelettes 'Mrs Zant and the Ghost' and 'The Nun's Story of Gabriel's Marriage' and five short stories to chill the blood.

FUNNY BONES *selected by Dorothy Scarborough*—An Anthology of Humorous Ghost Stories.

MONTEZUMA'S CASTLE AND OTHER WEIRD TALES *by Charles B. Cory*—Cory has written a superb collection of eighteen ghostly and weird stories to chill and thrill the avid enthusiast of supernatural fiction.

SUPERNATURAL BUCHAN *by John Buchan*—Stories of Ancient Spirits, Uncanny Places & Strange Creatures.

LEONAUR

ALSO FROM LEONAUR
AVAILABLE IN SOFTCOVER OR HARDCOVER WITH DUST JACKET

THE COLLECTED SCIENCE FICTION AND FANTASY OF STANLEY G. WEINBAUM 1—INTERPLANETARY ODYSSEYS *by Stanley G. Weinbaum*—Classic Tales of Interplanetary Adventure Including: A Martian Odyssey, its Sequel Valley of Dreams, the Complete 'Ham' Hammond Stories and Others.

THE COLLECTED SCIENCE FICTION AND FANTASY OF STANLEY G. WEINBAUM 2—OTHER EARTHS *by Stanley G. Weinbaum*—Classic Futuristic Tales Including: *Dawn of Flame* & its Sequel The Black Flame, plus The Revolution of 1960 & Others.

THE COLLECTED SCIENCE FICTION AND FANTASY OF STANLEY G. WEINBAUM 3—STRANGE GENIUS *by Stanley G. Weinbaum*—Classic Tales of the Human Mind at Work Including the Complete Novel The New Adam, the 'van Manderpootz' Stories and Others.

THE COLLECTED SCIENCE FICTION AND FANTASY OF STANLEY G. WEINBAUM 4—THE BLACK HEART *by Stanley G. Weinbaum*—Classic Strange Tales Including: the Complete Novel The Dark Other, Plus Proteus Island and Others.

THE COLLECTED SCIENCE FICTION & FANTASY OF JACK LONDON 1—BEFORE ADAM & OTHER STORIES *by Jack London*—included in this Volume Before Adam The Scarlet Plague A Relic of the Pliocene When the World Was Young The Red One Planchette A Thousand Deaths Goliah A Curious Fragment The Rejuvenation of Major Rathbone.

THE COLLECTED SCIENCE FICTION & FANTASY OF JACK LONDON 2—THE IRON HEEL & OTHER STORIES *by Jack London*—included in this Volume The Iron Heel The Enemy of All the World The Shadow and the Flash The Strength of the Strong The Unparalleled Invasion The Dream of Debs.

THE COLLECTED SCIENCE FICTION & FANTASY OF JACK LONDON 3—THE STAR ROVER & OTHER STORIES *by Jack London*—included in this Volume The Star Rover The Minions of Midas The Eternity of Forms The Man With the Gash.

THE CRETAN TEAT *by Brian Aldiss*—The Cretan Teat is a wry and comic novel that interweaves its own fiction with an inner fiction about the discovery of a Byzantine painting of the Mother of the Blessed Virgin Mary suckling the infant Jesus and a fake ikon that becomes an instrument of Nemesis.